REVERBERATIONS

REVERBERATIONS

MANABOUND BOOK 2

TRAVIS ALBRECHT

Podium

For Bri
What a wild ride it's been.

Copyright © 2024 by Travis Albrecht

Cover design by Antti Hakosaari

ISBN: 978-1-0394-5060-8

Published in 2024 by Podium Publishing
www.podiumaudio.com

REVERBERATIONS

EXPANDING OPPORTUNITIES

UNIFIED KINGDOM OF YORUBA AND DAHOMEY
THE FLASH

Adaega Merbaker glanced over at the clock on the mantle in her office and noticed it was already nearly time to leave for the evening. She took a deep breath and splayed her fingers, working out the soreness from using the typewriter for the last several hours to draft a new university policy.

As the distinguished director of operations, Adaega held a position of prominence within the vibrant nexus of Lokoja University. Her ability to navigate the complexities of the academic behemoth bespoke years of experience and dedicated service.

Under her administration, the university had grown not just as a beacon of education, but also as a vital institution supporting research aimed at keeping the nation one step ahead in the ongoing Cold War against the specter of communism. This commitment was woven into her daily tasks, be they large policy decisions or small administrative matters.

This particular day, bathed in the benign glow of sunlight filtering through the rustling leaves of ancient trees, appeared no different. After tackling a morning inundated with meetings and paperwork, she emerged from her office, ready to navigate the familiar trails etched into the university's landscape.

Her path wound through the academic labyrinth, leading her toward the parking lot, where countless vehicles were neatly parked. Among them was her car, with its elegant curves and gleaming chrome accents basking under the dappled shade of a grand baobab tree.

As she reached out to the car door, her world transformed. The serene expanse of azure overhead erupted into a spectacle of shifting colors—blues, greens, and purples that seemed to breathe with life. Enthralled, Adaega froze, her hand resting on the cold metal of the door handle, her eyes captivated by the cosmic dance above.

This visual symphony was interrupted by a blinding flash, which rendered the world momentarily sightless and was closely followed by an earsplitting sonic boom. The ground beneath her trembled as her car, reflecting the otherworldly kaleidoscope in its chrome trim, rattled slightly.

A sudden gust-like force washed over her, a chilling sensation that surged through her body, causing an involuntary shudder.

Then, as quickly as the spectacle had begun, Adaega was devoured by an abyss of darkness.

When she next opened her eyes, Adaega found herself somewhere else.

BODING STAR SYSTEM — TERRAN INTERSTELLAR UNION

The TMS *Idryss*, a reconnaissance frigate belonging to the Terran Interstellar Union, tore through the inky vastness of space, its engines laboring at their maximum capacity.

Lieutenant Aedan Solla felt panic creeping into his veins. They had been summoned by a beacon to investigate an unexplained anomaly, an unidentified substance that seemed to be originating from some sort of void. Now, it was advancing toward them—and everywhere else—with alarming speed.

The captain's voice reverberated throughout the bridge. "Communications, transmit the emergency sensor data to Command. Now!"

Transmitting data packets via faster-than-light channels was a power-hungry task—hence, smaller vessels like the *Idryss* were equipped with such capabilities only for dire emergencies. Aedan flipped open a protective cover and turned a key that would unavoidably overload their relays as the demanding emergency communication system guzzled power from their already strained reactor.

Inhaling deeply, Aedan slammed his palm down on the transmission switch. Instantaneously, all sensor readings and internal communications were amalgamated and dispatched to Command Headquarters.

Suddenly, the sensor operator's face contorted with increased alarm. "Whatever that anomaly is, it's closing in rapidly! We can't outpace it while our FTL drive is recuperating. Captain, it's almost on us!"

The captain responded immediately, hitting the shipwide intercom.

"All hands! Initiate anti-radiation protocols! Brace for impact!"

Aedan reached out for his helmet, but before his fingers could curl around it, the wave was upon them.

He stared at the forward viewscreen, the image of a massive glittering nebula-like bubble hurtling toward them seared into his retinas. He drew a sharp breath, holding it as the ship convulsed violently. The twinkling mass penetrated their shields in a heartbeat, surging through the hull and crew.

Then, all was darkness.

Four weeks had passed since Aedan had found himself in this primitive world.

He strolled through the vast underground passages, tunnels, and spaces that made up the dwarven city of Dheg Malduhr and soon arrived at a structure carved into the wall of the cavern. He walked in, smiling and waving at the young dwarf receptionist who sat at the counter, and made his way through to the office in the back.

He smiled as he walked in. Standing there was Norie, the dwarven woman with whom he had become acquainted and worked closely since his arrival.

The shorter woman was hunched over something but turned to him as he entered. "Aedan! I'm glad you're here. I think I've cracked it!" she exclaimed.

His eyes widened in surprise and curiosity. He strode forward, recognizing the object of her scrutiny: his conduit probe from the ship that had somehow arrived with him.

At the workbench, Norie animatedly pointed at a series of glowing symbols that had somehow been added to the probe's surface during his arcane transit to this world.

"I've been analyzing these, and I am positive that they're exuding the arcane energy. Now, with that in mind, I am inclined to suspect that these are words of power, or akin to it," she theorized, her voice brimming with conviction.

Puzzled, Aedan leaned closer, studying the symbols. "You're suggesting the arcane energy has an intrinsic language? That implies—"

"Exactly!" Norie interrupted. "It means it's not random, it's being directed! These changes we've seen, they're guided by something!"

Taken aback, Aedan lifted his gaze, lost in thought. After a few moments of silence, he felt Norie's comforting grip on his hand. "Consider the potential of this, Aedan. The council is becoming anxious about the mounting tension between the Empire and the Sovereign Cities. Let's delve into this discovery, and perhaps we can contribute to preserving the safety of my—*our* people."

Looking down at Norie, her eyes ablaze with hope and wonder, he couldn't help but smile. If he could never return to his home, maybe he would be okay here.

Aedan was fortunate. Despite the disparity in their knowledge, Norie's intellectual prowess was unmatched. He had no doubt she would soon bridge the gap.

And for that, he was eagerly waiting. "Let's see what we can do with this revelation."

She smiled and nodded.

* * *

DUCAL RESIDENCES, STRATHMORE

Roslyn Tiloral, future heiress to the Duchy of Tiloral, sat at her vanity in the soft light of a new day. Her role in her grandfather's dominion had been carefully etched in her daily lessons and rigid etiquette training. Her mother was the designated heiress, yet, after her ascension, the mantle would fall upon Roslyn.

While the servants meticulously prepared her hair, Roslyn contemplated the day's schedule. The foremost item was a meeting with her mother, the purpose of which she could only surmise. Now that she was in her eleventh year, it was customary that her family discuss her impending duties and responsibilities.

Perhaps it is about my future path.

This very notion made Roslyn scoff, causing an involuntary tug on her hair from the surprised servant. Roslyn winced at the sudden pain.

Ouch. Focus, Roslyn.

"My apologies, my lady," the telv woman hastily said, regret reflecting in her eyes through the mirror.

"It was no fault of your own," Roslyn reassured her. *Just mine, but an heiress never directly apologizes to the staff, and she deflects blame away from them.*

She resisted the urge to rub the area, as she knew that would just require her to sit there longer to correct her hair.

After giving Roslyn a moment to recuperate, the servant resumed her task, and Roslyn returned to her thoughts. The upcoming meeting, if it was indeed about her path, would be purely ceremonial. Her future was predestined, inscribed in the annals of Tiloral tradition.

She was bound for the prestigious Royal Academy of Avira, to walk the path paved by previous dukes and duchesses of Tiloral. As the next in line after her mother, her obligations extended beyond mere attendance; she was expected to excel.

Such was the weight of her heritage, and she was ready to shoulder it.

After her appointment with her mother, Roslyn was certain the remainder of her morning would be claimed by some other duty. An empty space in her schedule was like a canvas for her mother's whims. Fortunately, her afternoon was earmarked for a walk through the bustling market, a brief respite, where she intended to procure attire for the upcoming court her grandfather was hosting in the near future. The event was in honor of a newly arrived house in the city—a tedious affair, in her opinion.

And one that I do not want to attend but am being forced to.

However, the singular focus on this new house hinted at its importance.

Likely a marquess. What do I care about some marquess?

It seemed characteristic of her grandfather to establish ties with a new march; anything lesser wouldn't warrant such a ceremony.

Once she was primped and primed for the day, Roslyn stepped out of her suite to find Ser Roderick and Ser Janine, her loyal telv knights, awaiting her. The pair bowed slightly, and Ser Roderick greeted her. "Good morning, my lady. Trust all is well?"

Roslyn responded with a slight nod. "Indeed, it is. I took my breakfast in my suite and am prepared for the day ahead." Turning to Ser Janine, who managed her schedule, she confirmed, "We're scheduled to meet with Lady Tiloral, are we not?"

At her formal reference to her mother, Ser Roderick raised an eyebrow, a reaction she had grown accustomed to.

Practice makes perfect. Mother insists upon it.

Ser Janine, however, remained composed. "Yes, my lady. We will see what Lady Tiloral has for you at the meeting, I suspect. She should be leaving to return to Maireharbora soon. I believe Lady Tiloral has specific tasks for you to undertake during her absence."

Suppressing a scoff, Roslyn responded, "Naturally. Lady Tiloral never falls short of expectations. Whatever tasks she assigns, we shall ensure they are fulfilled."

Hopefully, she will at least give me time to myself. I'm tired of all the social events in particular.

Leading the way, Roslyn navigated the sprawling ducal palace toward the wing designated for the ducal heiress during her stay. Nestled beside a verdant courtyard, the heiress's wing lay adjacent to the opulent estate occupied by her mother's younger brother.

This lavish abode served not only as residence but also as the administrative center for the current count or countess of Strathmore; thus the roles of city governance fell to the duke's second child.

That will be my brother, one day. When Mother takes her seat as duchess, I will be required to move into the castle at Maireharbora.

Roslyn herself would inherit a courtesy title of viscountess on her fifteenth birthday. This title would serve her until she inherited the responsibilities and status of the marchioness of Maireharbora.

The Duchy of Tiloral, among the kingdom's wealthiest, showcased its affluence through the grandeur of the ducal palace. Its prominence was rivaled only by the Duchy of Avira, although Roslyn seldom considered this comparison, given that duchy's exclusive association with the royal family and the fact that the crown prince held the title of Duke of Avira.

Roslyn herself was firmly within the noble faction.

Or I will be when people do not see me as just a child.

She heard how often her grandfather and mother complained about the stranglehold the royals liked to put them in. The royal family seemed almost fearful of the influence and power of the Duchy of Tiloral and constantly established mandates that seemed to target only them. This perception bred frustration in her grandfather, a man who had always held unwavering loyalty to his kingdom.

Her mother had reprimanded her several times when Roslyn had expressed her feelings on the subject and her desire to support the noble faction. She remembered what her mother had said: *We must remain neutral, Roslyn. We cannot choose a side in the Polite War. Our status and the importance of our role in the kingdom necessitates it.*

Hmph. I don't see why we have to remain neutral when the royal family constantly pushes us and treats us as a threat to their power.

Tiloral was host to three important cities within the kingdom, and its only access to the sea. The responsibility of housing the kingdom's naval forces consequently fell on the duchy.

While the Royal Fleet was larger, the duchy's fleet was nothing to scoff at—it commanded respect with its modern, formidable vessels. Their role was to defend the limited coastal access of the kingdom, while the Royal Fleet was more expeditionary in function. *The roles should be reversed. It's an embarrassment for such old ships to be seen more than our own glorious vessels. That will change when I am duchess.*

Though Strathmore didn't match the size or economic vibrancy of Maireharbora, the duchy's largest city, it functioned as an essential trade hub, linking the dwarves of Dirn Loduhr and the Kingdom of Meris. As the primary port of the kingdom, Maireharbora stood second only in wealth and population to the capital, offering her mother a level of power and influence commensurate with most duchies. *As it should. It is only right that we are respected for all our family has accomplished, even with the pressures we withstand.*

Upon entering her mother's wing, Roslyn and her knights were greeted by Ser Primrose, one of her mother's advisors. "My lady, the marchioness is expecting you. Please, right this way." She gestured down the hall, leading them to the office where Roslyn anticipated her mother would be.

As they approached the door, a number of individuals filed out, recognized by Roslyn as representatives from various guilds. The last to exit, Lady Maeva Batteux, graced Roslyn with a smile. "Lady Roslyn, it's lovely to see you. How are you today?"

"I am well, Guildmistress Batteux," Roslyn replied, noting the woman's business with the marchioness.

Matching the reaction of many when Roslyn referred to her mother by her formal title, Lady Batteux lifted an eyebrow. "Indeed, some potential business matters to discuss with your mother. Nothing too serious," she shared, her expression light.

"I'm eager to hear more, Guildmistress. But if you'll excuse me, I don't want to keep Lady Tiloral waiting."

Lady Batteux's surprise was brief before her adept recovery—no less than Roslyn would expect from the head of the guilds in Strathmore. "In that case, I wish you a pleasant day," the guildmistress replied, offering a respectful nod before heading off to join her colleagues.

Roslyn observed their departure, recalling what she had been told about Lady Batteux. As the guildmistress of the Banking Guild in Strathmore, the woman was an anomaly, being a noble within an organization that typically eschewed nobility. Her title was the result of a favor owed by the kingdom to the guilds—a favor Batteux had earned through impressive deeds.

Guided by Ser Primrose, Roslyn entered her mother's office while Ser Roderick stayed outside. Ser Janine, on the other hand, allowed in to document the proceedings, settled quietly in a chair near the entrance.

Roslyn's mother stood at her desk, back turned, engrossed in a ledger. As the door closed behind Roslyn, her mother shut the ledger and turned around.

"Ah, Roslyn. Thank you for coming. How are you this morning?"

Roslyn drew in a deep breath. They were in private. It was an appropriate time. "I am well, Mother. Naturally, I would not miss our scheduled meeting. I see you've had a meeting with the guilds. Hopefully, it was productive."

Her mother dismissed it with a casual wave. "Yes, yes. They were keen to discuss these newcomers who have surfaced—the terrans. An entirely new people who supposedly appeared after the Flash."

Roslyn's brows furrowed. She *had* heard whispers, but nothing definitive. "I may have heard a passing mention, yes."

Her mother smiled and gestured to the two chairs in front of a fireplace. "Please, join me."

As mother and daughter took their seats, a servant entered quietly from a side door, bearing a tray laden with tea. Roslyn liked her tea sweetened with just a single sugar cube, while her mother preferred a touch of honey, stirred into her cup with a small silver spoon.

Roslyn leaned back, savoring the delectable aroma of her beverage. Her mother, thanks to her title and influence in Maireharbora, always managed to secure some of the finest teas brought in by ship. The tea before Roslyn now had journeyed from a small tropical kingdom in the south. Its bouquet was a captivating blend of floral notes, subtly punctuated by hints of herbs and spices.

Roslyn patiently waited for her tea to cool to a drinkable temperature, but her mother, evidently growing impatient, rolled her eyes.

"Drink the tea, Roslyn. It's going to get cold."

Roslyn winced at the reprimand and tentatively sipped her tea, which, despite being too hot for her liking, was still undeniably exquisite.

They spoke brief niceties while they sat, and Roslyn counted down the time until her mother would finally address the real reason she was there. Her mother did not invite her for tea without requiring something. She set her cup back on the saucer and placed them on the table next to her. It seemed to be the cue her mother needed.

"My dear, I wanted to discuss a few important topics with you today, which is why I called upon you," her mother said.

Roslyn simply nodded.

"It is time for you to start taking on responsibilities befitting your status. You will soon leave for the Royal Academy, as expected of you. Now, both your grandfather and I believe you should be given duties until that time."

That's strange. There is no back and forth. No questioning of a path. "Of course, Mother," she replied, the slight stumble in her words betraying her confusion.

Her mother narrowed her eyes slightly. "It is expected of you. Surely, you did not consider anything other than what is required of an heiress?"

Again, Roslyn was surprised. She knew she was in line for the duchy, but everyone else . . . *Ah, there's my mistake. I considered incomparable circumstances. That will not happen again.*

Roslyn tipped her head in acknowledgment of her fault. "I had a brief lapse in thought. My apologies, Mother."

Her mother stared at her for several heartbeats, taking the measure of her. Finally, she nodded. "Very well. See that such errors do not occur in the future. Your role was given to you at birth. There has never been but a single path for you to follow. Now, where were we? Ah, yes, the Academy. You will attend next year. Therefore, you will need to leave before the end of the season. This will give you ample time to winter in Drakensburg. The manor there will be prepared to accept you and your retainers."

Roslyn looked down in thought. Reaching that city did not give her terribly long before she had to leave. While the distance to the capital was only about four hundred kilometers, the travel would take her months. Winters in West Ikios were severe, and the roads became even more dangerous during the worst part of the season.

Usually, wintering just meant the time between the festivals of hearth and love, which was about forty days.

Roslyn considered the route and realized she may need more than just Roderick and Janine to join her. She had never been to the capital herself. It was exciting. Especially since she would be representing her house and the duchy.

She looked up at her mother. "I will be prepared. Will you be here when I leave, or are you departing for Maireharbora soon?"

"I will be departing within a fortnight. The ferry to Fen's Crossing has already been reserved."

Roslyn nodded. Fen's Crossing was a town that sat on the opposite side of Lake Gori from Strathmore, and it was the quickest way to travel there, since the southern end of the lake bordered the Kingdom of Meris and the northern land route added a week to the travel time.

Roslyn glanced at the window, trying to gauge the time. "Was that all you wished to discuss, Mother?"

Her mother chuckled ruefully. "Roslyn, do you desire to leave my company so soon?"

Roslyn felt her eye twitch. "No, of course not, Mother. I merely considered that you have many pressing needs upon your time and did not unduly wish to burden you with idle talk."

Her mother sighed. "Roslyn, I am your mother. Could you please speak to me as such?"

"My apologies, Mother. I simply wish to maintain proprieties, as you have instructed."

Her mother tilted her head backward and closed her eyes. Roslyn was not sure what the problem was. It had been made clear to her numerous times how she was to speak in her mother's presence when on official business.

The marchioness took a deep breath and refocused on Roslyn. "Moving on. You have an additional appointment today," she said, glancing at Ser Janine, who nodded and prepared to take notes. "You are to meet with the archpriestess, herself, one bell past midday at the Grand Temple of the Celestials. Father set up this appointment, so do not be tardy."

Roslyn's eyes widened. *The archpriestess? In what situation would I be stupid enough to be late to meet with the leader of the Church?*

Oblivious to her daughter's thoughts, her mother continued. "There will also be duties to perform within the capital after you arrive. However, Father wishes to speak of that himself before you leave. Now, be off. You do not want to waste time if you still wish to go to the market."

Roslyn stood and bowed her head. "Thank you for the tea, Mother. I hope to see you again before you depart."

Her mother embraced her, then kissed her on either cheek. "You will. Now, be off with you."

Roslyn sighed lightly as she left the room. First, the upcoming court where her grandfather would acknowledge a new house, and now a meeting with the Church.

This is going to be a lot of politics. I hate politics. Nothing interesting ever happens. Just a bunch of pomp and circumstance.

CHAPTER ONE

REVERBERATIONS

Post-Flash, initial manifestations of magic were revered as divine acts, believed to be the Family's empowerment of chosen individuals. This divine narrative was fortified by magic's appearance among the virtuous, prominent, or even the terrans—who surely had been brought by the gods, fitting neatly into Eona's spiritual and societal structures. However, as magic use expanded beyond a select few, touching every stratum of society, this perception underwent seismic reverberations.

The omnipresence of magic forced a reinterpretation of the Flash. Instead of selective divine intervention, it was surmised that the gods had inundated Eona with mana, leaving its inhabitants to navigate this newfound power autonomously. This cultural shift from divine gift to shared resource marked a new epoch of self-determination and exploration in Eona's history.

One of the first organizations to see through the veil was, of course, that of the city guards.

A History of Mana, 184 SA

Sloane and her knightly escorts reached Thirdghyll without attracting much attention. The rest of their journey had been peaceful, leaving Sloane with an abundance of free time. She spent five days engrossed in crafting various designs, most of which were whimsical. Still, a few seemed immediately beneficial, especially one vital for her travels.

She had even started working on a few. She had a couple of small hollowed-out spheres that could unscrew into two halves so she could put something inside. Sloane already had ideas of what to do with those.

Given her upcoming solitary travel, she took into consideration all her potential needs. That made her remember the wolves and how that pack attacked them on the road toward Valesbeck with the knights. She winced as she recalled the fear she felt when the wolf had fallen on top of her, not knowing she had already killed it. Or how scared she was when she saw that Ernald was hurt. Then Maud learning she could heal . . . It really helped put her need in focus.

I really need tools for self-defense.

Moreover, she needed a way to detect objects, or mana in general.

It's amazing how much you can get done when you don't have any modern distractions.

Her watch enabled mana sensing, but its range was limited. Surprisingly, mana seemed to exist everywhere, but could be sensed through her watch only when wielded—a fact contradicting her initial understanding. This, however, could be attributed to her fantasy-based knowledge, which real life evidently refuted.

Only a few hours prior—or bells, as the people here called them—Sloane and the knights had taken up lodging at an inn. This time, she had a room to herself. After all of the previously shared accommodations and the constant company of her escorts, she found the solitude of the inn room surprisingly unsettling.

The room was small but cozy, the kind of place a traveler would find a welcome respite after a long day. A single window offered a view of the quiet city, the sun setting behind the silhouette of buildings and casting a warm, red hue across the room. But the emptiness of the room seemed to magnify in the gathering dusk.

The quiet felt strange, an unwelcome departure from the comforting din of their company. Sloane realized how the journey, despite its purpose, had created a sense of unity among them—a fellowship borne of shared travels. Tonight, she felt the pangs of solitude more acutely. The loneliness was a sharp reminder of the solitary path she was soon to tread.

Frustration bubbled within Sloane stubbornly as she sat on her bed, her thoughts flitting through everything she'd gone through since the Flash.

Her journey thus far had been fraught with missteps and false hopes, each day passing with no sight of her daughter, Gwyn. The gnawing absence of her child was a constant thorn in her heart, a prickling reminder of the distance still to be covered, of the uncertainties still to be faced.

They had followed the lead she thought would help them find Gwyn, but instead, their pursuit for her daughter had led them down a winding path of darkness, revealing an underworld that shouldn't have existed—a large slave ring lurking in the shadows of civilization.

In the end, it wasn't Gwyn they found, but a telv girl, another innocent caught in the chains of a ruthless trade. After they rescued her from Lord Marweth, the noble girl was escorted by Ser Redding to her home near the Westaren capital.

Which made Sloane consider her own circumstances. She still didn't know the true story behind the knights, and Ismeld in particular, but through it all, Sloane had been bestowed a noble title. A baroness, although one without any land attached. The whole situation felt surreal, one that could only have happened in this crazy fantasy world she found herself in after the Flash.

I wonder if there are any nobles or knights like Gisele and the others around Gwyn.

It was all Sloane could do to motivate herself to continue—hope and pray to whatever gods ruled over this world that Gwyn was safe. Would they extend their hand in help, provide shelter, give a sense of security? Or was Gwyn having to navigate this world on her own? Perhaps some small family somewhere had given her help.

Now that they were in Thirdgyll, the search was going to be continued in a new direction. The focus was to engage the Westari Order of Secrets and probe for any traces of Gwyn's whereabouts. Ernald and Deryk had pledged to take the lead on this, which left Sloane to her own devices.

For her, the immediate task was to gain a foothold in this world, to exist beyond just a name and title. That meant doing things she had never even envisioned, like opening a bank account in a different world, and exploring ways to generate income.

The mundanity of these tasks was a stark contrast to the lofty ambitions she held—the recovery of her child, deciphering a new world's secrets, and forging a life for them in this post-Flash existence.

Yet, she understood that these were stepping stones in her journey, a path she had to tread meticulously if she wished to reunite with Gwyn. After all, potentially searching an entire world wouldn't be cheap.

Grabbing her journal, she forced herself to once more check over the current plan to reach the Kingdom of Avira and its academy, which would hopefully give her insight into finding Gwyn.

The travel would be long and hazardous, but Gisele had reassured her that going by sea would take months off the time required and be immeasurably safer. She wasn't sure of the conditions, but from what she was told, going by land would take at least half a year.

However, that didn't account for the fact that Sloane would have to hole up somewhere for the winter that would arrive in a couple of months.

Based on some quick math, she figured it would take her roughly two to three weeks to travel by boat to Maireharbora. Then she would travel north to a city named Anerval, and then on to another city, at which she would need to stay for the winter.

Sloane sighed.

Hopefully, Gwyn has somewhere safe to stay. I wonder what she's doing now?

Sloane placed her quill down as she tried to lock up the thoughts and emotions that threatened to rear their ugly faces. Every time she thought about Gwyn and finding her, she nearly had a panic attack. There was just so much space to cover and her daughter could be *anywhere*. She really didn't know what to expect from going to Avira, but it was the only potential lead she had.

The weight of all of the tasks before her made her feel heavy, but it was not just the burden of responsibility she carried. It was the longing for her daughter, the need to know she was safe, and the relentless desire to bridge the distance fate had placed between them.

That was what kept her going, the fuel for her determination. Even as the world around her changed, her goal remained constant: to find Gwyn and figure out a way to either get home or create one here.

She went to sleep and dreamed of exploring the world with Gwyn, and the magic she would teach her.

Sloane groggily walked down to the inn's dining area, not quite ready for the day. She entered and looked around at the tables, among all the various people, for the six she knew. She saw Ismeld and Gisele at a table along the wall and walked to them.

Ismeld looked up from her drink and gave her a nod.

The orkun knight at least addressed her. "Good morning, Sloane. Please, join us."

"Thank you, Gisele. Good morning, and to you, Ismeld," she said as she sat down.

"Yeah," Ismeld responded curtly.

"Ismeld didn't sleep well. There was a family in the room next to hers. The infant was awake, wailing all night."

Sloane nodded sympathetically. "Trust me, I understand that. Even though I've been there myself, I still find that I don't like it when babies can't be consoled. Especially on a plane."

Sloane leaned back so the barmaid could place a plate of food down for her, and asked her for a drink. She started to pick at her bread and cheese.

Ismeld scrutinized her. "So, what's a plane?"

Sloane squinted, trying to recall. "Didn't I already explain them?"

Gisele chuckled. "You've explained a lot, Sloane, but that one may have been to Maud or Ernald. Your wagon friends. The three of you definitely have a different relationship from the rest of us."

Sloane smirked at Gisele. "Hmm. Maybe. We three have to stick together. We can't all go gallivanting around on our horses with no care in the world. Some of us have to do the hard work.

"Buuuuuut . . ." She headed off any chance of retort. "A plane. It's a metal vehicle with wings that utilizes physics and technology to fly. I explained automobiles, right?"

The two knights nodded, so she continued. "Okay, so this is probably not one hundred percent accurate, but I explained how a car engine works. Fundamentals, at least.

"Now, imagine using a type of engine to pull in air and mix it with combustible fuel—like how your lamps use oil to maintain a fire. Burn this fuel to create a discharge of heated air and exhaust that pushes the plane forward. The wings it has do not flap like a bird, they are there to stabilize and provide lift, which allows them to stay in the air even though they are heavy. I can explain aerospace engineering and the physics that allows for it another time."

Ismeld squinted in thought. "So, the purpose of these planes is to travel, like a wagon?"

"Exactly! We use them to travel all over the world in hours—er, bells, I mean—rather than days, weeks, or months. Planes can be small and have only one person flying in them, or they may be large and have over eight hundred people."

Gisele's eyes opened in astonishment. "Eight hundred? That's incredible. Your people travel by these often?"

Sloane nodded. "All the time. I regularly traveled for my work, so there were times when I would have ten to twenty flights in a month. Sometimes flying over nine thousand kilometers for business."

Ismeld just shook her head. "I don't think I will ever get used to your stories from your world."

"I agree. They boggle the mind. But I admit that the idea of flying is appealing," Gisele chimed in.

They sat and ate their food, Ismeld looking like she would fall asleep at any moment. She mostly ignored Sloane and Gisele while they talked, joining in only when addressed directly.

Sloane finished her food last. She looked over at Ismeld, who was resting her head on her arms on the table.

"She's really tired, huh?"

"Yes," Gisele responded, and then nudged Ismeld, who groaned. "Ismeld, go back upstairs. I'll take Sloane to the others and you can join us later."

Ismeld just nodded as she dragged herself out of the chair and lethargically made her way back to her room.

"You have your waterskin?"

"Of course. I need to refill it, though."

"That's fine, there's a place to do it on the way. Let's go. The others should have barely started."

Sloane tilted her head. "Started what?"

"Training."

*　*　*

Sloane sat on a barrel and observed as Deryk and Cristole sparred. The two weren't going especially hard; they seemed to be practicing technique. Deryk had a more aggressive approach, while Cristole was slow and methodical.

They fought back and forth for two minutes before Deryk overextended and Cristole took advantage and tapped him on the shoulder with his blade. Sloane was impressed—it had been a long parry. She had fenced in college but had never been especially good at it. Those fights usually ended quickly; each round was until five touches or ended at three minutes.

This, however, was much different, with heavier weapons. She supposed that since it wasn't for sport but for *literal* life-and-death situations, they would need to have far more skill and knowledge.

Deryk saluted. "That was well-timed."

"You almost had me! I had nearly taken the momentum before you pressed harder. It was the only reason I was in a position to take advantage," Cristole explained.

"I need to rein in my aggressive tendencies as a fight progresses. Thank you for the spar."

Cristole looked over at Ernald. "Ernald! You're next. Let's go!"

Ernald groaned.

Sloane smiled. "Get over there! You've got this!"

Ernald glared at her. "You and I *both* know that I do *not* have this, Sloane."

"Psssh, Cristole's a big softie. You can do it with one arm behind your back!"

Cristole raised an eyebrow in her direction. "I'm not sure what you're joking around for, *Lady Reinhart*. You're after him."

"Oh."

Ernald laughed and Gisele joined in. "Come over here, Sloane. We'll do some stance work while they spar."

Sloane sighed but hopped down from the barrel and walked over.

Gisele got right to it. "Alright, so. Take your stance."

She looked over Sloane's foot placement. "Not bad, but it's the wrong type of stance for the type of sword you have. And you keep gravitating to it. I know you've been practicing a bit with Cristole here and there, but I can't remember if I've ever heard your answer. Have you used a sword before? In your world? I think I recall you saying you hadn't."

Sloane thought of how to explain. "Well, I don't know how to properly use a sword to *fight* and as a weapon of war. I was an amateur fencer years ago in . . . uh . . . an academy. It's a competitive sport."

Gisele nodded. "I understand. We need to break that habit. You've been busy doing a lot of other things during our travel here. Your mind has been over-whelmed. I think it's time for us to take your training seriously. You will need to know how to use a blade."

"You're right. I need to learn how to incorporate it with my magic as well."

"I agree. Now, stand like this."

Gisele proceeded to explain and show the correct fighting stance for her blade. They went over footwork and how to properly reposition for the most effective response or attack. Sloane enjoyed the knight's teaching style—Gisele was very involved in the process.

They continued that way for nearly forty-five minutes, doing various drills and exercises to get used to moving and holding a sword properly. Sloane was sweating profusely by the time they finished.

Gisele looked her over. "I think that's it for now. Also, I think we need to get you a different style of sword. We can talk later." She inclined her head and indicated to the side.

Sloane turned and saw Cristole simply standing and observing them. "Have you been watching long?"

"About ten minutes. You're doing well. Now, take a small break. Then it's our turn to fight."

Sloane was ready to go after taking a five-minute breather and drinking some water. She noticed that Gisele and Ernald were off to the side talking, and Deryk had disappeared.

Maybe he used stealth and is finally going full rogue. You never go full rogue, they prefer to do it from behind.

She quickly glanced behind herself and lazily swung an arm. *Just checking.* She laughed at herself and drew Cristole's attention.

"If you can laugh, you can fight. Let's go."

"Alright, already!"

She stepped out in the center of the courtyard they were in and raised the training blade Gisele had given her. It was blunted and wouldn't do damage other than bruising.

Sloane was about to let Cristole know she was ready when he launched forward. She hastily raised her blade and blocked his swing, then jumped back to avoid his follow-through.

"You should always be ready to fight," Cristole admonished.

"Well, you didn't get me yet. So, I'd say I'm doing okay so far," Sloane riposted.

She made a short thrust that he parried, and she followed it up with a cut toward his arm. Sloane thought she would get him, when she felt the painful slap of his blade on her opposite arm.

"Shit! Ouch. That hurt." She instinctively rubbed the area.

"You overextended and went for an attack when you didn't have the initiative or positioning. Be patient."

She nodded, and they restarted. She lasted fifteen seconds. The following time she made it to twenty-two.

They were at it again and she had just parried a thrust, then followed it up with a cut across his arm—her go-to strike due to the difference in reach.

Cristole hopped out of the way and swung his blade at her. She quickly brought up her blade to block and, without thinking about it, raised her left hand and pulsed a small orb of mana at him.

Her eyes went wide and so did his as he leaped backward trying to avoid it, cursing in surprise as he did. Sloane instinctively felt out to the mana and tried to will it to stop. Instead of just dissipating, she felt a *click* in her head as the orb detonated in a flash of light and sound, startling everyone around.

Sloane's eyes grew as she realized everyone around had their hands over their eyes.

Taking advantage of Cristole's disorientation, Sloane quickly rushed forward and tapped him in the chest with her blade. "Got ya!"

Cristole raised his hand for her to stop, using his other hand to rub at his eyes.

"Sloane, what the—" Cristole started.

She suddenly felt a bit sheepish. "Sorry . . . you okay?"

Cristole nodded as Gisele and Ernald approached. The orkun woman looked concerned. "What was that? Did you try to hurt him?"

Cristole spoke up before Sloane could. "I'm fine. Just momentarily made my vision go white. It's coming back. Like looking into the sun. My ears are still ringing, though."

Sloane was pretty sure she knew what had happened, even if it was unintentional.

"I accidentally cast [**Mana Bolt**] at him when I was surprised. I managed to gain control of the spell while it was flying toward him and caused it to detonate in what I had hoped wouldn't hurt him. I *think* I just accidentally cast a magical version of what my people know as a flashbang: a nonlethal disorienting device."

Ernald looked as if he were about to ask a question, but Gisele beat him to it. "Can you do it again?"

Ernald's eyes widened in surprise, and even Cristole raised an eyebrow while rubbing at his eyes.

Sloane looked between the two men. "Are you sure that's a good idea, Gisele?"

"Yes, it will be fine. Give it a try."

Sloane considered. "Please don't look directly at it, and cover your ears. Gisele, can you throw up a shield between you guys and the center area?"

Gisele nodded. "One moment."

Sloane observed Gisele as she focused on her mana and then cast a shield, exactly where specified. The shield looked just as it had the first time she'd done it. Sloane smiled. *She's getting better at that.*

She concentrated and launched another [**Mana Bolt**], then threw her intent into it. Sloane was able to feel the mana easier than before. She shaped it into the purpose she wanted before willing it to detonate.

The effect was much more refined and purposeful. The flash was quicker to dissipate, yet brighter, and the bang a bit louder as it reverberated throughout the area.

Sloane heard a scream from nearby and looked around. A few people who hadn't been there before stood covering their ears. She was just about to say something when a couple of guards rushed into the courtyard, following towns-people pointing at the knights.

The first guard who entered called out, "What's going on here?!"

Another guard, whose armor appeared to designate him as higher ranking, was right behind him. His gaze stopped on the shield, then regarded Sloane's outstretched hand. "All of you. Put any weapons you have down."

He pointed at Sloane. "And you, do not move."

The knights looked at the guards and Sloane.

Ser Gisele sighed. "Ah, shit."

CHAPTER TWO

EXCITING TIMES

Sloane sat off to the side with a guardswoman standing watch next to her. She watched Gisele and Ismeld gesticulate rapidly while speaking to the guard captain. They were showing the guards various scrolls and documents. *Likely the documents establishing my 'nobility.'* Interestingly, the deference the captain seemed to give Ismeld didn't match the way he was addressing Gisele.

Something to explore later.

The woman next to her hummed in amusement as Gisele threw her hands up when the guard captain pointed at Sloane.

Sloane turned her head and scrutinized the woman who was guarding her. She had to admit . . . she was too terrified to try and do anything to piss this woman off.

Probably why they told her to watch me.

Standing, Sloane was a hundred and eighty-six centimeters herself—or six-foot-one in freedom units. This woman looked as if a telv had mated with a giant who was at least a solid two meters tall and undoubtedly made of stone. It wasn't often people towered over Sloane, especially in Italy, where the average height of a woman was a good twenty centimeters shorter than her. The guard's tattooed arms were the size of Sloane's legs, and she was the very definition of a "muscle mommy," with her pretty face, striking golden eyes, and copper hair.

I wonder how many men she's crushed between those thighs. I just need to get on her good side. I don't want to be next.

"So, how's it goin'? I'm Sloane. What's your name?" she asked the female mountain.

The telv looked down at her blankly. "Nemura."

"It's a pleasure to meet you, Nemura. So . . . do you know what they're talking about over there?"

Nemura shrugged. "Whether you get fined or not, or if you're a *menace*." The last part she said with a small smile.

"And here I thought we were fast friends, Nemmy. But ya gotta go and call me a menace. Not nice, girlfriend. Not nice," Sloane schmoozed.

Sloane simply received a raised eyebrow at that, so she refocused on the knights defending her honor. Just thinking about it caused her to snort.

The woman next to her looked back down at her "What?"

Sloane shook her head. "Just thinking about how the knights are over there arguing on my behalf."

"Aren't you a baroness?"

Sloane shrugged. "Yeah, I guess I am. But it's all so different here. Where I'm from, knights in shining armor don't come and stand up for you. You have to do it yourself."

She could feel the woman's eyes boring into her. "Hmmm," Nemura hummed thoughtfully. "Perhaps the way your people do it is the proper way."

After that, Sloane tried to get Nemura to open up more while the others spoke, but it didn't go anywhere. The woman was a wall, and she barely spoke to Sloane.

It took a while, and Sloane was a bit peeved she couldn't be involved, but eventually, the exchange with captain of the guards ended. Gisele and the man started making their way over to Sloane, and she stood so as not to look rude. She wanted to make a good impression so the knights wouldn't get fined because of her.

Sloane looked over at the captain as he approached. He was a moon elf about her height, which meant he was at least fifteen centimeters shorter than the telv Amazon next to her. He was older, and if he were human, she would have guessed he was in his late forties. But she had learned that the Loreni—the sun, moon, and high elves—aged slower than other races. It wasn't that they lived longer, as she would have guessed. In the last five to ten years of their lives, what they called their "waning years," they aged rapidly until they passed on.

The Loreni life expectancy seemed similar to that of modern humans, based on what Sloane had been able to get out of Ismeld. Which, Sloane supposed, meant that they probably *did* live a bit longer than humans on average. With all of the changes to their world now, she had no idea how mana and magic would affect such things.

For her part, she felt physically healthier than ever before. Even more than when she was active in college in her early twenties. Sloane wasn't sure what mana was doing to her, but she was definitely seeing improvements. She would need to figure out a way to test and measure the effects.

Nemura nudged her and jolted her from her thoughts.

"Huh?"

The captain of the guards was looking at her with an unamused expression. "Baroness?"

Sloane tilted her head, which he took as acknowledgment, and started over. "So, as I was saying, I am Captain Jorin. Ser Gisele and Ser Ismeld explained what happened and that you're a bit of an eccentric . . . inventor?" He paused, then turned his head toward a raithe who was scanning the court. "Was there any damage, Quen?"

The guard raised his head. "None that I can see, Captain."

Captain Jorin nodded and faced her again. "Good. So, I'm not required to fine you, milady. Which is always a good thing. However, could we discuss what it was you were trying to test and why you did it in a courtyard filled with people?"

Sloane quirked her eyebrow. "To be fair, there wasn't anyone around when we were training. I didn't even see anyone come in until the end."

The captain closed his eyes for a moment and tried again, looking at the two of them. "Lady Reinhart, Ser Gisele, we have training halls or yards that can be rented out *specifically* for this purpose." He glared sternly at Ser Gisele. "*This* is a courtyard. *Anyone* can walk through at *any* time."

Gisele attempted to speak, but the captain held up his hand. "Ser Gisele, I *understand* what you intended. However, at the very *least*, this was a public disturbance situation that required guards to mobilize. That disruption itself is irresponsible."

Sloane took the chance to speak up. "Captain Jorin, I apologize for the disruption. I was not aware that my alchemical device would produce such a loud noise. It is a nonlethal tool to help scare away beasts or disorient bandits and the like. There isn't any damage because there isn't meant to be."

Captain Jorin rubbed his chin as he considered what she said. Gisele's face betrayed her confusion as she gave Sloane a questioning look, but Sloane was prepared.

She reached into her satchel and brought out one of her steel spheres. "This is one of the test devices. While this particular one isn't functional, it's a good way for you to see what it looks like." She handed the sphere to him, causing a raised eyebrow from Gisele, who luckily stayed mum.

The captain rolled the sphere in his hand as he examined it.

Yeah, okay, it's a grenade.

He looked up at her in disbelief. "This did that? How?"

She smiled, "My apologies, Captain. That's a trade secret. I'm still experimenting, and when it is complete, I will be selling them." She reached out for the orb and he handed it to her. "Again, I apologize for the disturbance. We will endeavor to utilize the appropriate venues for future tests."

Captain Jorin slowly nodded, still focused on the orb. "Thank you. If you start producing those in bulk, please come see me. I believe the guard would be interested in such a contraption."

Sloane smiled again. "Of course, Captain! I will keep you in mind. Thank you for your understanding."

The man squinted before gesturing to his other guards. "Guardsmen, let's go. They're cleared."

Nemura leaned closer to Sloane. "Your secret's safe with me . . . Baroness," she whispered, before nodding to Sloane and walking with the other guards out of the courtyard.

Captain Jorin looked at them all before addressing them one last time. "Please, remember your word. You will use the proper location next time."

"Certainly. We appreciate your discretion as well, Captain," Gisele responded.

The man nodded, turned, and left.

The others approached them.

"Well, that went better than I thought," Ernald said.

Ismeld shook her head. "No. It definitely did not. He now knows more about us than I wished to be known. He also didn't mention the shield he clearly saw before Gisele quickly ended it."

"He seemed a good man. I suspect that he will not use that knowledge for his own gain," Cristole reassured her.

Sloane's eyes flitted between Gisele and Ismeld. "So, did they not overly scrutinize my documents? He didn't catch that they were fake?"

Ismeld's eyes narrowed dangerously and her voice took on a steel edge. "Your documents are not fake," she said. "They *are* legitimate. Your past isn't entirely truthful, but nobles have been elevated on less."

Sloane tilted her head in confusion. "But . . . how?"

Before Ismeld could snap at her, Gisele placed a hand on the high elf's shoulder and gently pulled her back. "That isn't important for the time being," the orkun woman told Sloane before redirecting. "First, did you mean what you said? That sphere is going to be able to do what you did with your magic?"

Sloane narrowed her eyes at Ismeld, but let it go. "Yes, that is the goal. I am working on a way to do it. I have an idea. Testing that idea will come later, as we get more settled in."

"Good, because having the ability you demonstrated will be an edge we can utilize."

Cristole nodded with Gisele. "I agree," he said. "Having *experienced* the effect, we definitely need this capability. It is, as you've said before, a game-changer."

Sloane smiled. "Oh, if you think that's good . . . you should see some of the other ideas I have."

Ernald laughed. "Describe them to us over lunch. I think I speak for everyone when I say I'm hungry."

Sloane chuckled. "Ernald, you're always hungry, but yeah, let's go. I think I have a few things you guys will be interested in."

Sloane walked with Maud into the crowded tavern and was instantly taken aback by how busy it was. There didn't even appear to be any tables, but before she could suggest going somewhere else, Maud flagged down a passing barmaid and inquired about available seating.

The youthful raithe woman scanned the crowded space before shaking her head. "No, but there's two seats at the end of the bar. You're welcome to 'em."

Exchanging a glance with Sloane, who responded with an indifferent shrug, Maud accepted the offer. Taking the initiative, Sloane led the way to the stools and they promptly ordered their food from a burly raithe man with mutton chops and a jovial smile.

While waiting, Maud, the redheaded knight-medic, turned to Sloane with her green eyes and a warm smile. "So, how are you doing?"

Sloane exhaled deeply. "I'm alright. I think I've come to grips with everything that happened. I just . . ." A chuckle slipped past her lips. "How do we always end up in bars and taverns?"

Maud's lips twitched into an amused smile. "Because we're traveling? Where else would we go?"

Contemplating the question, Sloane's mind wandered. "Are there any restaurants? Stores? Spas?"

"There's all of that and more. Well, not spas, but there are the baths. Why don't we go tomorrow? We can take Gisele and Ismeld and make a ladies' day out of it."

Sloane's face lit up with a smile. "You know what, that sounds like fun."

Their drinks arrived, and Maud took a hearty swig of hers. "Then it's a plan."

Tasting her own drink, Sloane shrugged. It wasn't too bad.

"So," Maud said, "about your plans you talked about at lunch. Is that what you've been working on in your room?"

Sloane's mood brightened instantly. "Yes! I have so many ideas, Maud. I think we can do some good. Now, I know some of the more immediate ones are more uh . . . martial in design, but you guys *are* knights. So . . ."

Her words trailed off as Maud merely smiled, encouraging Sloane to share her thoughts. The sincere interest and insightful questions put Sloane at ease, letting her discuss her designs with someone who genuinely cared. It didn't matter if Maud's primary purpose was to evaluate her mental state.

That's what friends did, right?

She was beginning to view the knights as friends, which brought comfort to her. It was soothing to have a support network in a world that was still new and often overwhelming.

A bittersweet smile curled on Sloane's lips. *I don't know what I would do without that.*

"You know, I hope Gwyn has this too . . ." she said quietly.

Maud raised an eyebrow and placed a hand on Sloane's. "What's that?"

Sloane smiled. "Friends."

The telv gave her a genuine smile and nodded before the two returned to their drinks and started chatting about small things. It was nice, and Sloane found herself enjoying herself.

Finally.

Sloane and Maud were engaged in pleasant conversation when their food arrived.

And Sloane felt her mouth salivating as she took in the spread. It was an enticing platter laden with medley potatoes, something that looked like broccolini, and a pair of perfectly roasted quail.

Sloane and Maud shared a satisfied glance before digging in, the food fulfilling in taste and presentation. It was probably the best-tasting thing she'd had . . . ever.

Well, since being here, at least.

As they ate, Maud leaned over and murmured, "They can tell we're higher class. It's why we got the more expensive meal without asking."

Sloane merely nodded, unfazed.

She didn't care, and she sure as hell wasn't about to contest the wonderful food before her. After eating bland or poorly made food since arriving, this was like trying a high-end restaurant for the first time after a life of ramen.

The two of them dug into the meal with gusto, and the stress that had been knotting Sloane's shoulders gradually released as she finally just relaxed.

Which meant, of course, something had to happen.

In the midst of their feast, a sudden commotion stirred behind them.

Sloane and Maud turned in time to see a brawl unfolding between a burly raithe and an orkun. Food went flying, ale spilled, and as fists flew, the orkun man failed to block the fourth or fifth blow and received a nose-cracking punch that sent a spray of red over several onlookers as his head jerked to the side.

Oof. And that's why I would never get front row seats to a fight.

A gasp swept through the tavern that turned even more eyes to the spectacle.

Then, abruptly, the fighters were sent sprawling apart. Standing in their place was the towering telv guardswoman Sloane had met earlier.

She glanced sternly down at the battered men, her deep voice resonating through the tavern. "Enough. Unless you both want to spend the night in the stocks, you will clean up your mess and pay for the damages."

The orkun, his hand cradling his bleeding nose, pushed himself to stand, and winced.

Nemura stepped over to him and tugged his chin up roughly to examine his injury. "Let me see," she murmured, inspecting his broken nose. "Here, if I don't fix this, it won't set right."

As she reached toward him, Maud leaped to her feet.

"Wait!"

Nemura's and all other spectator's heads turned. The guardswoman's eyes narrowed slightly at the interruption. Hurrying forward, Maud clarified. "I'm a knight-medic. Let me help."

Nemura gave a nod of understanding, stepping back to let Maud take over.

As the redhead gently probed the man's face, she gave him a comforting smile. "Alright, this won't be too bad. You ready?"

With a hesitant nod from the orkun, Maud's eyes began to shimmer with a mystical green light. Her hands took on the same otherworldly glow, which soon enveloped the man's injured nose. A sharp snap echoed, followed by a gasp from the man. Yet, Maud held him steady, the glow subsiding as quickly as it had come, leaving no trace of the injury behind.

The tavern seemed to inhale in unison, silence blanketing the room as patrons stared wide-eyed at Maud. It felt as if time had momentarily paused, the only sound being the faint crackling of the hearth. Then, as if a pebble had been thrown into a still pond, murmurs began to ripple across the room, growing in volume and intensity.

"Praise Eona!" exclaimed a large man in the corner, breaking the spell of silence.

His cry seemed to open the floodgates, and the tavern was soon buzzing with excited chatter. "Did she just perform a miracle?" a woman gasped, her eyes wide with awe. The whispers echoed from table to table, gaining momentum and creating a chorus of speculation and wonder.

"Is she a priestess?" asked an elderly gentleman, fidgeting slightly as he squinted at Maud. His question was met with a shake of the head from his companion, a matron with graying hair. "No, she has to be a saint! Only they possess such divine powers." The notion was quickly picked up and spread like wildfire through the crowd.

"She's Eona's avatar! Eona protects!" someone else cried out. The reverence in the room was palpable, the awestruck faces of the patrons reflecting the divine reverence they associated with Maud's healing prowess.

As if driven by an unseen force, the crowd began to surge forward, their faces alight with reverence and curiosity. Each wanted a closer look at the miraculous knight-medic who had turned an ordinary evening into a spectacle of divine intervention. They pressed against one another, their eyes focused solely on Maud, the heroine of the hour.

Nemura intervened, her powerful voice cutting through the chatter. "That's enough! Everyone back up." Turning to Sloane and Maud, she suggested in a lowered voice, "We should get you two out of here."

As the commotion continued, Sloane reached out to Maud, placing a hand on her shoulder. "You good?"

Maud replied with an exuberant smile. "Yup!" She turned to address the orkun man, who was watching her in awe. "Are you?"

He nodded.

Nemura began to usher them out as the patrons of the tavern reached in an attempt to make contact with Maud. Each touch was filled with veneration, each face lit with respect for the knight-medic.

As they exited, Sloane caught the eye of a barmaid and hastily handed over two large silver coins, thanking her for the meal.

The barmaid's eyes widened. "That's too much!" she exclaimed, protesting the generous tip.

"No, it's fair," Sloane countered. "This was the best meal I've had in Westaren. Word will spread, and people will come in droves. Tell them it was a knight of Haven's Hope who healed that man."

There, now people will know the good they do.

Nodding, the barmaid accepted the coin, her face flushed with excitement. Turning on her heel, Sloane quickly caught up with Maud and Nemura, who had made their way outside.

Outside, Nemura became a physical barrier between the trailing patrons and Maud. Her stern voice echoing in the quiet night, she ordered, "Enough! Return to your meals and drinks. If you wish to praise Eona, visit the temple tomorrow."

Disappointed groans echoed after them, but each patron obeyed, returning to the warmth of the tavern.

Satisfied, Nemura turned back to them. "Well, that was certainly more excitement than I was prepared for on a drinking night."

A nervous chuckle escaped Maud, who appeared to be overwhelmed by the reaction of the patrons. "I . . . I just wanted to help."

Nemura shrugged, her gaze lingering on Maud. "And you did, thank you. That was . . . something. But . . . how?"

Maud looked at the ground, her shoulders hunching slightly.

Sloane filled the silence. "The Flash changed everything. Magic is every-where now; people are only beginning to discover it. You and your fellow guards will need to be careful."

The tall telv woman sighed, tilting her head in thought before responding. "Just what we needed. More to worry about. I'm off to find another place to drink after I report this to the garrison. By Thezmos's sagging sack . . ." Her voice trailed off as she shook her head. "Have a good night, you two."

Holding back a chuckle at Nemura's choice of words, Sloane bid her farewell.

Guiding Maud away from the tavern, Sloane finally addressed the elephant in the room. "Well, I think the cat's out of the bag now."

A sheepish look crossed Maud's face. "Sorry. I just . . . feel like I *have* to help."

Sloane nodded and gave the woman a small smile. She put an arm around her friend and squeezed. "I understand."

But a silent worry tugged at her heart.

I just hope no one tries to take advantage of you.

CHAPTER THREE

A NEW PEOPLE

Α nd it will just be the four of you, milady?"

Ismeld nodded. "Indeed."

The moon elf with teal hair and lavender skin scrutinized the four of them, and Sloane schooled her face not to react. Then, as if coming to a conclusion, the elf nodded.

"We are delighted by your patronage, Lady d'Argin," she said politely directed at Ismeld. "It will be fifteen small silver each for our more . . . restricted baths."

It was something that she had tried to ask Gisele about, the whole *lady* title for Ismeld, but Sloane was told to leave it be unless Ismeld spoke of it directly.

Maud winced, but Ismeld took it in stride and easily proffered the requested amount.

Their teal-haired escort glided through the ornate corridors of the bathhouse with an easy grace, leading the group through the maze-like interior. Sloane and the others followed her, passing a plethora of different rooms. The first one was an expansive bath area that housed both men and women, socializing and enjoying the warm waters together.

Intrigued by the sight, Sloane couldn't help but lean toward Gisele and whisper, "They have baths where men and women are together?"

The knight nodded. "That area is intended for the general public. The rest are separate."

"Gotcha," Sloane murmured, continuing to take in the unique atmosphere of the place. "And everyone is naked in the baths, right? That's what I see?"

At that, Ismeld turned her head with a quizzical raise of her eyebrow. "Of course. Is it not the same where you are from?"

Sloane shrugged nonchalantly. "In some places, maybe? Saunas and hot springs are popular, but public bathhouses aren't really mainstream anymore. Mostly they're seen as a recreational luxury, I think. I've never been to one, though. The closest I've come is using the communal showers back in college. I just didn't want to assume and cause a scene."

Gisele let out a soft, amused huff at her candidness. "You'll be fine, Sloane."

With a roll of her eyes, Sloane continued to follow their escort. They were led to a pair of adjoining changing rooms. Sloane and Ismeld were shown into one clearly meant for high-status patrons.

As Sloane was undressing, Ismeld called out that she would be with the others. Sloane acknowledged her without looking and continued taking off her dress and everything else.

Shrugging to herself, she neatly folded her clothes and placed them in a small cubby built into the wall, alongside the provided linen towel. She examined it, frowning slightly at the rough texture. It wasn't as plush or soft as what she was accustomed to.

Clad solely in her own skin and a pair of functional sandals, Sloane emerged from the changing room and stepped into the sprawling bath chamber reserved for noblewomen. The cool air danced across her bare skin and sent a shiver down her spine. The tantalizing promise of warm waters beckoned invitingly, casting an ethereal glow across the room.

The bathhouse had a tranquil elegance, with its gleaming marble and intricate mosaics. Yet, as Sloane moved farther into the space, she became aware of a shift in the atmosphere. A pair of women lounging at one side of the pool paused their conversation to cast appraising looks her way. Their unabashed scrutiny was something Sloane hadn't expected, and it unsettled her somewhat.

Then she realized.

They have towels on? Was I supposed to wear mine?

A few women sat along the wall with towels around their waist, but topless. But everyone had towels wrapped around their torso as they walked around.

Shit. Shit. Shit.

A strong sense of embarrassment filled her, but she did her best to push it down. *In for a penny, in for a pound. Own it, Sloane.*

Before she could fully dismiss the feeling, she noticed the moon elf attendant from before watching her. The teal-haired woman's eyes had widened slightly, and she, too, was looking at Sloane with scrutinous intensity. There was a hint of surprise in the elf's gaze, and perhaps even a touch of admiration.

Damn straight. I know I look good, but holy shit . . . maybe don't stare so openly?

Casting a look of mild defiance at the women, she maintained her stride and walked toward the inviting warmth of the bath waters. The contrast between the cool air and the steamy waters seemed to intensify the anticipation, making the bath seem all the more inviting.

Gisele, Ismeld, and Maud had been engaged in a quiet conversation at the edge of the bath. At the sight of Sloane's confident entrance, they turned around in unison. Gisele's and Ismeld's eyes widened in surprise, their cheeks slowly tinting a shade of pink. Maud promptly burst into a fit of laughter.

Gisele groaned and rounded on Ismeld. "Why didn't you explain it to her, Issy?"

"I thought she knew!" Ismeld defended herself, her face matching the bright red of her hair.

Gisele rolled her eyes, pressing her palm to her face in exasperation.

Ismeld hurriedly tried to explain to Sloane, her words tripping over each other. "It is customary to wear the towel while you are walking around and to take it off before entering the baths or sitting down, if that is what you desire, or leaving it on your waist if not."

Feeling her own blush intensify, Sloane took a deep breath, looking down at her naked form. Then, with a surge of determination, she plastered a smile on her face and spread her arms wide. "I'm proud of what I've got. You've all got the same parts, and now that you've all gotten an eyeful, let's do this."

A raucous cackle echoed behind her.

Turning around, Sloane saw an elderly raithe woman strolling toward her. "You tell them! When you have a body like that, you flaunt it!"

The woman's infectious laughter swept over Sloane, who couldn't help but join in. She gave the woman an awkward but grateful nod.

"You're one of those terrans I keep hearing about. Nice to see that your people also have those of more refined lineages. Keep at it, my dear," the old raithe commented.

As the woman passed by, she landed a swift smack on Sloane's rear, eliciting a surprised shriek from her. Her hands flew back to cover her ass.

At that, Ismeld's face turned an even darker shade of red, if that was even possible, and Gisele burst into a fit of laughter. Maud was beside herself, tears of laughter streaming down her face.

The room, which had been filled with quiet whispers and the gentle hum of relaxed conversation, was suddenly infused with an infectious energy. Even the women who had been openly appraising Sloane were now giggling, their attention deflected by the bold raithe woman.

Now with an overwhelming urge to be anywhere but on display, Sloane quickly strode toward the bath. Gisele and Maud teased her as they joined her. Even Ismeld's stoic persona finally cracked and she chuckled softly. Sloane's first bathhouse experience had been transformed from an awkward spectacle into a moment of friendship.

With a satisfied sigh, she sank into the warm water, allowing the heat to seep into her muscles and wash away the embarrassment, leaving only the light-hearted amusement of the moment behind.

In the calming warmth of the bath, the four women let their bodies relax. Maud broke the silence first, turning to Sloane with a curious expression. "How did you maintain your hair back on Earth?"

Sloane launched into an explanation of the myriad products she had to use—shampoos and conditioners, curl creams and frizz serums, and various treatments. She elaborated on the routines and procedures, the countless bottles crowding her bathroom, the time and patience needed to keep her curly locks looking fabulous and the struggle she had helping Gwyn get used to doing the same.

Maud listened, her eyes round with amazement. In turn, she started discussing what she used, mentioning a particular type of oil from the islands back home in Blightwych.

When Sloane heard the description, her eyes lit up. "Coconuts! Coconut oil is so good for your hair. I need to get some."

Maud told her the oil was expensive this far from the islands, but the benefits made the cost worthwhile. Sloane readily agreed.

Gisele and Ismeld watched their exchange with amusement in their eyes. Sloane rolled hers, playfully retorting, "You wouldn't understand. It's hard work keeping these curls looking on fleek."

Gisele snorted. "I have no idea what 'on fleek' means, but I've seen your hair since you arrived. I do not envy it. The slightest hint of rain and your hair turns into a frizzy mess."

Sloane gasped, feigning offense. "You take that back!"

Gisele playfully splashed her, laughing.

They settled back into the soothing embrace of the bath, and Sloane closed her eyes, choosing to simply enjoy the moment. Upon opening them again, she noticed Ismeld watching Gisele with a certain intensity. Sloane smiled softly, but when Ismeld caught her glance, the blonde's cheeks blossomed into a fiery blush, and she quickly averted her gaze.

Keeping her thoughts to herself, Sloane once again closed her eyes, letting the tranquil ambiance of the bathhouse wash over her.

Eventually, they rose from the water, each seeming rejuvenated. They dressed and bid their farewells to the moon elf woman, and stepped out into the afternoon sunlight as a relaxed, happy group.

As they began their walk back, Ismeld dropped back to walk beside Sloane. "Not. A. Word," she warned with a hiss.

With a teasing grin, Sloane replied, "Your secret's safe with me, my friend."

Ismeld paused for a moment, meeting Sloane's gaze. After a moment, she nodded gratefully. "Thank you."

"Have you—"

"No. Not a word to me either," Ismeld snapped.

Oh. It's like that.

Accepting the boundary, Sloane agreed. "Alright, Ismeld. Just know, that path is one filled with loneliness."

Ismeld sighed. "I've made it this far."

With a final nod, the high elf woman walked ahead to join Gisele, engaging her in light conversation.

Watching them, Sloane felt a sad smile curve on her face.

You poor woman.

Maud turned and waved Sloane forward, holding her arm out to hook hers into Sloane's. The shorter redhead looked up at her. "I'm glad we did this."

Sloane looked at each of her companions and realized that she was too. Relaxing, bonding, sharing laughs . . . it *had* been a good day. A good respite from all of life's struggles, and she knew those would keep her up in her nightmares later that night. But for now, she felt just a bit more . . . hopeful.

She smiled down at the woman holding her arm. "Me too."

Sloane and her companions returned to the inn, their bodies relaxed and their spirits lifted. Located in the heart of the bustling city, the inn was the perfect place to serve as their base for the time they'd be in Thirdghyll and to give them an opportunity to search the city while maintaining Sloane's assumed status.

As they walked into the inn's lobby, Sloane noticed two familiar figures waiting for them—Ernald and Deryk. Her brow furrowed as she took in their stern, tense expressions, decidedly out of place in the inn's warm, inviting atmosphere.

Her step slowed as she approached them. "What's wrong?" she asked, her voice taking on a hint of concern.

Deryk exchanged a glance with Ernald, whose frown deepened. "Nothing yet, but we're still looking. As of now, there have been some concerning rumors we've learned regarding terrans in the city, but none thus far have matched Gwyneth's description."

Sloane felt a tight knot forming in her stomach.

She glanced around the bustling inn, scanning over the patrons, none of whom seemed to be paying them any mind. In a low voice, she asked, "And the people you were searching for?"

Deryk shook his head. "Nothing yet, but we're still trying to . . . contact them. The two of us will continue. We'll be here for several weeks yet."

Sloane's eyes flicked to the stern expression on Ernald's face, but she found herself comforted by Deryk's reassuring words. She gave him a small nod, the knot in her stomach slowly beginning to unravel.

It's still early. It would have been nice to have a lead, but we haven't been here long. That was too much to hope for, I guess.

Feeling a hand on her shoulder, she turned to see Gisele, whose reassuring smile brought her more comfort. "He's right. We have time, and they've only just started," the woman said gently. "Come on, let's go change, and then we can relax. Tomorrow is a new day."

Ismeld stepped up beside her and nodded. "We will look around the market and get some lunch at a restaurant tomorrow. You're a traveling baroness. It will not be out of place for you to want to explore the central district, and even ask around for other terrans. We can use that to get a feel for how things are around here while Deryk and Ernald work. You have other things you need to accomplish too. Let them do what they're good at."

Sloane managed a small smile, feeling the stress of the situation slowly ebbing away.

"Got it." She turned back to Ernald. "Thanks, you two. Will you be here for dinner?"

Ernald and Deryk shared a look before nodding.

With her friends around her and the promise of a fresh start the next day, Sloane felt the energy return to her step. They went to their rooms, leaving the men to their work. Even as concerns clouded their return to the inn, Sloane found a silver lining in how committed they were in helping her.

Tomorrow is a new day.

Count Sylvain Kayser turned around as a knock resounded on the door of the chamber. He looked at one of the guards and nodded. The raithe hurried to see who would interrupt them. With a scrapping, creaking sound, he opened the heavy iron door to show one of the three leaders of the city guard, Captain Lars, who entered promptly.

The count of Thirdghyll prided himself on his strategic utilization of resources, especially those who pledged loyalty to him. Captain Lars, in his view, was a crucial asset to be deployed effectively. Above all, Lars's unwavering loyalty was a virtue Sylvain cherished.

In stark contrast to Sylvain's unblemished lineage and exquisite features, Lars bore the rough-hewn countenance of a warrior. However, Sylvain, never one to tolerate incompetence, recognized Lars's value. While the elf's dark purple skin was marred by scars and toned by muscle, a fitting testament to his occupation, his carefully cultivated intelligence enabled him to address complex situations without guidance.

A valuable trait indeed. Sylvain had nurtured it diligently throughout the man's life. He had been the patron that facilitated the young man's induction into the City Guard and his subsequent rise to the position of captain. This made him an irreplaceable asset to the shrewd count.

The captain walked forward and bowed deeply, with the appropriate amount of respect for his benefactor. Sylvain nodded his head, allowing the man to straighten.

"My Lord, I have received word that another one of those . . . *terrans* has arrived in the city. A woman."

A smile formed on Count Kayser's lips. "Intriguing. Do tell more."

"She is currently staying in an inn in the central district and is escorted by six knights from an order based in Blightwych," Lars reported.

"The terran travels with an *escort*?" Sylvain took no notice of the commotion stirring in the room behind him, keeping his gaze fixed on Lars.

"Yes, My Lord. That is what they reported at the gate. Also, she later provided Patents of Nobility to Captain Jorin, establishing her as a baroness. A House Reinhart."

The notion of a terran baroness so swiftly after her kind's arrival in the kingdom was intriguing, if somewhat puzzling. Sylvain thoughtfully drummed his fingers on the arm of his chair.

"Captain Jorin verified the authenticity, My Lord. You *could* contest them, of course, but they are not from Westaren. Evidently, one of the knights has the authority from the Crown of Blightwych to acknowledge nobility and establish a patent for a house that would be recognized within that nation," the captain explained.

A Blightwych *baroness* would be troublesome. But not insurmountable. "How did this information come to you?"

"From guards who were called to an incident near the inn. As it happens, the thoroughness of Captain Jorin's investigations yielded this gem."

"And what of this incident?"

"Apparently, it was a small mishap during their training. The terran alarmed a few townsfolk with an alchemical trick. No damage was noted, so they let her go. I do not know more as yet. The full report hasn't come through."

"This information could be of use. You said the terran's location is known?" Sylvain asked, undeterred by a sudden sound from an adjacent chamber.

"Yes, My Lord. There's more, though. One of your retainers extended an invitation to the knights when in Vilstaf for your upcoming ball. They seemed keen on attending."

Count Kayser contemplated this news, a cunning glint in his eyes. "Indeed, we can make use of this. It provides an opportunity for us to meet this terran baroness. I am curious about her and what she might know. There could be something advantageous in there."

"That was my thought as well, My Lord."

Count Kayser's appreciative nod acknowledged his subordinate's agreement. "Indeed. Stay vigilant and gather as much information as you can. This will certainly assist—"

A slam of hands on a table echoed through the chamber nestled deep within the bowels of his castle's dungeon, disrupting his instruction. Sylvain swung around in annoyance.

"My sincerest apologies, My Lord," a voice offered meekly.

Suppressing a sigh of exasperation, Sylvain retorted, "Patience, Kynthia, is the essence of cunning. Let's proceed regardless." He shifted his gaze back to Captain Lars. "You know what I require. Bring me the information I need before the ball."

Lars gave a curt nod. "Yes, My Lord. Wishing you a good day, My Lord." With that, he swiftly exited, and the raithe guard followed him to just outside the door, leaving Sylvain alone with his interrogator and the terran woman.

The room now quiet, Sylvain redirected his attention to the terran who was chained to the table and looking down. Sylvain's approach, while poised and calm, filled the chamber with an intimidating aura.

"We can make this easy," Sylvain started, his tone shrewd and firm. "Cooperate, and your lot will improve. You could be moved from the dungeons to more . . . sensible accommodations."

He looked down at the woman, noting how she held a similar complexion to the sun elves but possessed the proportions of a telv and the round ears of the terrans. Their people were curious in their similarities.

Another world, or worlds rather, filled with people so similar and yet so different. What are the gods playing at by bringing them here?

The woman's response was a blend of defiance and desperation. "I've told your people, I don't know anything about this . . . magic. I'm just a researcher. We came here seeking help after arriving. I don't know anything about what is going on. And then your people threw us into prison. We did nothing wrong!"

The count's laugh filled the chamber, a sound that combined amusement and skepticism. "Your feigned ignorance, my dear, does not convince me. Especially considering what the other terrans have already given us." His gaze momentarily fell on a collection of multicolored spheres resting on a nearby table.

His eyes, back on the terran, held a level of intensity that conveyed his determination. "These spheres—how are they connected to the terrans' abilities? Three of your people demonstrated magic. What are you hiding?"

"I swear, I don't know!" she cried, the panic clear in her voice. "My world—"

Suddenly, she broke into a fit of violent coughing. Sylvain gestured at Kynthia, signaling her to provide the woman with some water. The terran shot a defiant scowl at the interrogator but eventually accepted the water.

"When was the last time she had a meal?" Sylvain questioned Kynthia, whose indifferent shrug suggested it was some bells ago.

"Ensure she receives food," he ordered calmly.

His interrogator dipped her head respectfully.

He would need to be sure she followed the letter and spirit of what he ordered. It appeared she had too much freedom in how she interacted with the terrans. The first incident was telling in that regard.

"Jonathan," the terran's voice was tremulous, shaking him from his thoughts. "What did you do to him?"

Sylvain's response was nonchalant. "He has divulged all he could and has been relocated accordingly."

Fear flashed across the woman's face. Sylvain let out a rueful chuckle. "No, he has not been killed. We are merely utilizing his skills more productively."

As she began to raise her voice, Sylvain silenced her abruptly. "Oh, I perceive you are more perturbed about your friend than yourself," Sylvain conjectured, a thoughtful frown tracing his features. "A noble gesture, indeed. However, let me assure you, the man's return hinges upon your cooperation. If you persist in this obfuscation, the hospitality you've experienced so far will seem like luxury compared to what is to come."

At this, the woman's breath hitched as she tried desperately to conceal her escalating fear. Seeing this, Sylvain seized the moment to drive his point home.

"Understand this," he said, leaning closer, his voice icy. "I am determined to unravel the secrets of your terran magic, one way or another."

CHAPTER FOUR

TOURIST TRAPS

Sloane walked down the street with Maud and Ismeld. She took in the architecture and the various shops that lined the main boulevard of the central, or noble, district. The city reminded her of many of the old towns all over Europe.

She had been marveling at a particularly nice mansion through a gate when Maud called out to her. "Sloane! Over here! This is important!"

Sloane rolled her eyes. She was learning that Maud's definition of important was vastly skewed. She walked over to the redhead and looked at a monument of some type. It reminded her of Trajan's Column in Rome, except that there were three distinct parts broken up by a broad engraved flaming ring.

"Is this the monument that commemorates the three times the city has been rebuilt?" Sloane asked.

Maud nodded. "Yes! This is the Triumph of Ghyll. The images start with showing prominent people and locations that existed during that phase of the city and end each section with what was lost. That's why the top is empty, as a hope to never lose anything again, but always prepared to continue if it does happen."

"The cap has a statue of Relena and Tenera, the patron goddesses of the city. Relena watches over those who have been lost, and her sister provides the safety of night," Ismeld explained, referring to the two Moon Sisters.

"Safety of night?" Sloane questioned.

"Don't ask me. Moon elves and the raithe have a weird obsession with the night. We actually don't have many of either people in Blightwych. Our group is fairly indicative of our nation, as far as peoples go. The largest population of the islands belongs to high and sun elves, but we have a large group of orkun and telv," Ismeld added with a nod toward Maud.

Maud smiled. "Yup! We're one of the more . . . open nations in that our nobility isn't limited to one or two types of peoples, like Avira, for example. Gisele's family is actually one of the more powerful houses in the kingdom. One of the main Pillar Families, as we call them."

"Interesting. Is the rest of Westaren like this?"

Maud nodded as they continued on their tour. "Yes. Although Thirdghyll is not nearly as respected as a city. The area is more impoverished than the rest of the kingdom. Each noble is required to maintain their own demesne, and the count here is notorious for only caring about his own. It's why there's such a vast difference between the central district and the rest of the city."

Ismeld glanced over. "From what I have seen, the city would collapse into infighting and riots with the smallest spark."

"Sounds about right. The oppressed can only take so much before they rise and say enough. There have been many parallels in my own world's history."

The three of them continued to chat as Maud and Ismeld showed Sloane around the district. As they entered another plaza, Sloane noticed a building with tables outside. "Is that a restaurant?"

"Ah, yes. It's a new concept that started in the Sovereign Cities and is spreading through the noble districts of all the cities. It's quite popular, especially with visiting nobles," Ismeld responded.

Maud looked excited. "Let's check it out!"

They walked over to the outside seating area, where a finely dressed raithe woman was standing. Sloane noted how *she* was able to wear pants without being judged. *I chose to go along with this house business, but man . . . it would be nice to have the option again. Should have chosen the pants Ismeld suggested before having to move full-time to dresses.*

"Miladies, how may I assist you today?"

Sloane took the lead and smiled. "Do you have a table available for three?"

"We do, Ladies . . ."

"Lady Reinhart." She gestured to Ismeld, who continued.

"Lady d'Argin, and this is Ser Maud. We are here from the Kingdom of Blightwych."

The hostess curtsied smartly. "A pleasure, miladies. Right, this way."

The women sipped wine while talking about their homes and various trends across the numerous kingdoms of the area. It was a pleasant distraction, and Sloane enjoyed it. She thought it was fascinating how different the cultures here were from those back on Earth.

Socially, they had clearly entered their own Renaissance period, but looking at other facets of society, they were almost behind. Perhaps they simply lived in a time of transition. Maud and Ismeld talked about how they missed the Kingdom of Rosale and its obsession with the theater. Sloane told them about Shakespeare and Marlowe, and her descriptions of the two and their plays had the women enthralled. After a lull in the conversation, Ismeld broached a more difficult topic.

"Sloane, could you tell us about your daughter?"

Sloane froze. She hadn't expected Gwyn to come up today and had been trying to compartmentalize her feelings on the matter. In fact, she still cried herself to sleep most nights and had nightmares.

The only way she could reconcile having done the things she had and even enjoying herself was her fierce belief that Gwyn was okay somewhere on Eona. That didn't stop tears from welling up in her eyes. Ismeld caught on to her hesitation but jerked her head toward Maud, whom Sloane assumed had kicked her under the table.

"If it's too difficult, we can speak of something else."

Maud placed her hand on Sloane's. "Absolutely, Sloane. There's no need to talk about something that hurts so much. It's alright," she said reassuringly.

Sloane smiled and shook her head, wiping her eyes. "No, no. It's okay. I'd love to talk about Gwyn."

Ismeld glared at Maud, who glared back.

Sloane laughed lightly. "No, seriously, guys. It's okay. Gwyn is an amazing, intelligent, and sweet girl. She loves to draw and make crafts. She really enjoys board games and playing with friends." Sloane chuckled.

"She loves playing soccer. She's really good at it too. She enjoys playing against the boys and beating them." Sloane paused as she thought of everything she could say.

Thinking about the day of the Flash, she continued, "We would always go grab gelato, which is a sweetened, frozen, milk-and-cream-based dessert. There were little places called gelaterias all over where we lived, and we loved to walk to them and just sit and talk while eating. She loved getting the strawberry-flavored gelato. I'm a diehard chocolate fan. Dark chocolate is even better."

Maud smiled and almost said something, but Sloane continued.

"She does so well at school. It's not like when a parent says, 'Oh, my kid is so good' but actually isn't good at all. No, Gwyn genuinely excels at her education to a surprising degree and she loves doing science projects. Which makes me so happy."

Sloane felt a tear run down her cheek. She grabbed her napkin and dabbed at her eyes.

"I have wanted nothing but the best for her and have done so much to ensure she had access to anything she needed. It was just her and me, you know? It was so tough at times, but we got through it. Gwyn is resilient and strong."

Sloane ignored the two women as they glanced at each other before looking back at her.

She laughed. "And she's an amazing travel buddy. Just don't take her to a museum. You won't get time to look at anything before she wants to move along." Sloane smiled as she fell into her thoughts, remembering all the great things about her daughter.

"And your husband? He . . . was left behind?" Ismeld asked hesitantly.

Sloane froze. She hadn't thought about him in . . . *Oh, god. Katie. Momma. Papa . . .*

Tears started to roll down her face as her thoughts turned to her sister and parents. They probably thought she and Gwyn were dead or missing. She would probably never see them again . . .

"Sloane, it's okay. You don't have to talk about it if it's too much. I can't imagine being separated from everyone," Maud said, with a scowl at Ismeld.

Sloane shook her head. "No, it's alright. My husband died when Gwyn was just a baby. The circumstances regarding it are actually why I found a job and moved to the country my parents were from. I was just thinking about my sister and parents . . . How they likely believe Gwyn and I went missing. And . . . and now she's out there . . . alone."

She dabbed at her eyes again, trying to maintain composure.

Ismeld surprised her, reaching over and grabbing Sloane's hand and squeezing it. "You're going to find Gwyn. I do not doubt it. She sounds like an amazing young lady, and she's lucky to have you as a mother."

"Yeah. I will. It may take some time, but I'll find her. I just hope she's doing alright."

Maud smiled. "If she's anything like you, and as cute as you say, Gwyn's probably got people wrapped around her finger. You two seem very close, so I'm sure she's just as concerned about you. She's probably trying to find you, herself, as we speak."

Sloane smiled slightly at the thought. "Thanks, you two. I know I'm not the most rational at times, but I have to keep believing, yeah?"

"Of course. You need to keep hoping. Don't let go of it."

They continued with polite conversation, but the mood had become serious. Sloane's thoughts kept drifting back to her daughter.

After they finished, Ismeld settled the bill while Sloane and Maud waited for her outside the patio.

"What else do you want to do today, Sloane?"

"Well, Cristole said he would take me to the Banking Guild. I have to establish an acc—"

Someone bumped into her and she stumbled forward. Maud reached out and caught Sloane before she could fall. Sloane looked around, confused. "What the—?"

Maud 's eyes grew wide. "Your bag!"

Sloane instinctively shot her hands to where her bag was, finding it gone. She turned and saw a telv in an oversized coat walking away with it at a brisk pace. Not wanting to lose the important things she had inside, Sloane immediately started ran after him. "Hey! Thief!"

The man turned his head and his eyes went wide as he saw her advancing on him. He immediately began to run, knocking several people to the side as he hurried away. Sloane burst into a sprint after him. She heard Maud yell out to Ismeld but didn't spare the time to look back at them. The man was able to stay just ahead of her, constantly throwing things in her path, but she was slowly gaining on him. She'd reflect on it later, but her body had definitely improved.

"Someone stop that man! He's a thief!"

Numerous people turned their heads, but not a single person took a step toward the rushing man. She had seen no guards either, which was surprising. She pursued the thief down a side street, leaping over or dodging boxes and garbage the man flung at her. Sloane almost caught him, but he juked away, causing her to slam into a wall while he pivoted and darted down another street.

"Shit. This mother—" She exploded into a sprint, trying again to gain on him. He cut around a corner into an alley, and she followed into a dead end. He was panting heavily but didn't seem overly concerned. Sloane settled into a walk and strode toward the thief. "Just give me my bag back and we can go our separate ways. No harm done."

"You really got me running hard there, woman," the man said under his breath. He smiled as he gained control over his breathing, and Sloane got a good look at him for the first time. He was about her height and had a short scraggly beard that was brown like his curtain-style haircut. His brown eyes showed the confidence of someone who knew something she didn't.

"You want this?" he asked as he held up her satchel by the cut strap.

"Just give it back, man. There's nothing you'd want in there, anyway."

He surprised her when he tossed it aside. "You're right. It's not the bag we want."

She froze. *We?* Sloane instantly went on alert and quickly drew her sword from her hip. *Damn it. Why did I have to run off without Maud or Ismeld?*

The man laughed. "That little blade isn't going to save you."

Sloane heard steps behind her and shifted so she could still see the thief while looking back. Two raithe men were walking down the alley, and both were big. One was barely taller than her, but the other was at least a whole head taller, and both were solidly built. They were also armed with clubs.

The thief stepped forward. "You're coming with us. The boss wants to meet ya. We can do this gently or not."

She decided to delay. "Who's your boss and what does he want with me? I'm nobody."

The others laughed. "Lady Reinhart of Blightwych," the telv said wryly. "A terran. Brought here by the Flash, like so many others of your kind."

He knew about her, and she wasn't sure how. The man shook his head while she thought of her chances. "You're a long way from Blightwych, ain'tcha? But I think that's all just a scam. You're trying to hustle all those noble types. I can respect that. So, what do ya say? As one scammer to another. We won't touch ya. You come with us and you get to meet the boss."

"And what will the boss do after that?" she asked.

He spread his arms wide and splayed his fingers. "That's up to the boss. It's out of my hands from there."

"How magnanimous of you."

One of the two raithe stepped forward.

Of course, it's the bigger one.

"Look, you're coming with us. Your two friends won't find you here. There are no guards around, and no one else will help."

"You're crazy if you think I'm going to just come with you willingly."

The telv sighed. "Fine. Don't say I didn't try to be hospitable."

He jutted his chin forward and addressed the approaching raithe. "Grab her. Don't harm her too much. The boss wants her healthy."

Sloane turned toward the big man and lifted her blade. "Do not come near me. You will not like the result."

The big man laughed. "Lady, you talk too damn much."

She didn't give him another chance. She rushed toward him and swung her sword. He blocked the strike with his club and then punched her in the face with his other hand, causing her head to snap back as she fell. *Damn it. That was dumb.*

"Delon, I just said not to harm her too much."

Sloane rolled to her knees and spit blood from her split lip. She grabbed her sword and stood back up.

Delon smiled. "I got it, Ven. You have guts, lady. I'll give you that."

"Get fucked, Delon," Sloane snarled. She felt blood coating her teeth.

The man just laughed as he approached again. This time, Sloane knew she had no choice. She lifted her hand toward him, causing him to stop. "Last chance. Come closer and I'll fuck you up."

The other raithe stepped forward until he was behind the bigger man.

Sloane channeled mana into her hand and prepared to fire the **[Flashbang]** spell at the two thugs. The smaller raithe made up his mind and stepped around Delon, lifting his club. She unleashed her spell, aiming it to burst at chest level in front of the two. The small bluish-purple bolt detonated into the same flash of light and loud noise as before. All three of the men accosting her cried out. The two raithe dropped their clubs as their hands shot to their eyes and ears.

She jumped into motion, forgoing any hesitation, just as she had practiced against Cristole. She grabbed the first man by the shoulders and brought her knee up into his groin hard, eliciting a grunt as he collapsed. Sloane pivoted and brought her blade down on the bigger man's wrist as he started to reach out toward her.

The man screamed. The blade didn't cut through as Sloane expected, instead getting stuck in the bone. She bore down on the sword as she yanked it backward, slicing through the bone. The man's hand fell to the ground. She drew back her blade, grabbed his shoulder with her opposite hand, and thrust the sword into the man's stomach. His eyes went wide. Sloane pulled the sword from Delon and turned as he fell. She faced the telv instigator, who was just starting to get over his initial disorientation. Sloane channeled a [**Mana Bolt**] from her hand and prepared to fire it at the man.

She watched as he rubbed his eyes and looked at her. "You fucking bitch. Don't you know what you've done?"

"Yeah. This." She fired the bolt at him and hit him square in the chest. The bolt exploded through him and a flare of energy burst out of his back.

Sloane spun around, ready for anything else, but then paused and looked down at the whimpering raithe lying in a fetal position clutching his crotch. Delon, the bigger raithe, was bleeding out on the ground and didn't seem to have much longer. Dismissing the thugs from her thoughts, Sloane walked over and picked up her satchel. Crouching down, she opened it and verified the contents, happy that everything was still there, but frowned at the cut strap.

Going to need to fix that. I really like this bag.

She got up and turned around to leave, seeing Ismeld and Maud running by the alley. Maud did a double take and slid to a stop before calling back to Ismeld.

Sloane walked down the alley to the two knights. Maud called out to her first. "Sloane! Are you okay?"

"I'm fine. They're not."

Ismeld walked over to the last raithe who was alive. She kicked him and dragged him to his feet before slamming him against the wall. "Who sent you? What do you want with the baroness?"

"We-we were sent to grab the terran lady by Mister Rowe. He's been collecting all of them before someone else can."

"Who else is taking the terrans?"

"I don't know! All I know is Mister Rowe is trying to get whatever he can out of them before they're taken by someone else and never seen again. Someone with power."

Sloane stepped forward. "Who is Mister Rowe?"

"You don't—Mister Rowe is the boss. He runs everything that's outside central. He's the one really in charge of the city."

Ismeld looked at Sloane and Maud. "He sounds like the local underworld head."

"What do we do about him? Get the guards?" Maud asked.

Ismeld shook her head. "The guard won't care. They'll only care that he did this in the noble district. No, we'll need to—"

"Please! Don't kill me!" the man pleaded.

"We're not going to kill you," Maud said with conviction.

Sloane tilted her head. "Then what are we going to do with him?"

"We're letting him go," Ismeld stated. "You will take a message back to your boss, though."

The man stammered, "T-Thank you. Of course. Whatever you want."

Ismeld pulled the man close and spoke quietly. "You will tell your boss to stay away from us. If anyone else comes for the baroness, Tenera herself will not save him." The blond knight shoved the man as she stepped back.

He instantly ran, not even giving his companion's bodies a spare glance.

Taking a quick survey of their surroundings, Ismeld turned to Sloane and Maud. Her voice was steady. "Do you have all of your belongings, Sloane?"

Sloane confirmed with a nod, her eyes meeting Ismeld's.

"Good," Ismeld said, her tone decisive. "Let's go."

As Ismeld pivoted away, Maud moved closer to Sloane. "May I?" she asked, gesturing to Sloane's lip with a gentle hand.

A soothing emerald glow illuminated their faces as Maud drew on her magic. The pain that had lingered in Sloane's lip eased and then vanished completely. Satisfied with her work, Maud nodded and turned to rejoin Ismeld.

Feeling healed, Sloane made to follow the two women, their footsteps echoing lightly in the stillness. But as her sight lingered on the bodies of the men she had slain, her stride faltered and she stumbled.

Maud looked back. "Sloane, are you coming?"

Sloane raised her eyes. "Yeah. I'm right behind you." She didn't speak again as they walked back to the inn and the rest of their group.

Sloane closed her eyes as she sat down at a table. Ismeld and Maud were with the others, recounting what had happened. Her eyes welled as she went over everything again in her head.

I barely hesitated in killing them.

What is happening to me?

CHAPTER FIVE

THE LOGIC OF MANA

I t had been a few days since the incident with the thugs and Gisele had come by her room to talk to her about what had happened, but Sloane didn't want to think about it.

Especially the puking that came after.

Later, the knight-captain brought the entire gang along with the same questions, so she mustered up the courage and told them everything she knew.

Despite what some people may think or say, killing someone wasn't as easy as it sounded, and it shouldn't be easy. Anyone who said otherwise was lying to themselves.

With that thought, would she have resolved the situation any differently?

No, I can't say that I would have. She felt bad about the act, but she didn't regret having done it. Those men had wanted to kidnap her. She had defended herself. End of story.

But she *was* unhappy about how she handled the situation. Namely, how she had run off alone to chase after someone who had stolen her satchel. While the bag had everything, including her notes and journal filled with all her designs and work, in hindsight, it was not worth the danger. She had left two knights behind without thinking, and if they'd been with her . . . well, everything would have gone much differently.

She needed to stay in control and assess situations better. Especially now that she knew there were several factions looking to take advantage of her and other humans. So, if there was anything good about what happened, it was learning that.

She thought of the man they had let go. *The knights wouldn't kill someone in cold blood. Why would I? I'm not some mobster.*

She would handle any repercussions for that decision as it arrived. *That's a problem for future Sloane. There's no need to dwell on the topic. What's done is done.* Next time, she wouldn't stumble over her thoughts. And she would react appropriately.

In the end, Sloane remained free to continue her search, which now included people within the city. Now, she needed to find out if Gwyn had been in Thirdghyll and more about the humans who currently were. *Or, shit, if Gwyn is here now.*

One of the reasons for her talk with everyone had been so Deryk and Ernald could get as much information as possible so they could use it to help with their search for Gwyn.

She had wanted to help, to go out and look for her daughter, but they had firmly told her that since someone was trying to get to her, she should stay in the inn with at least two knights nearby in case anything happened.

So Sloane had taken a deep breath, calmed her nerves, and got back to work. While the knights were searching the city and doing their own tasks, Sloane was delving back into her crafting. Earlier, she had messed with the rings that she had crafted with Reanny and tested their limits, seeing how much the gems helped with magic and what all they could be used for. She'd gotten the knights to test them in their spare time, and it seemed they didn't have the same reaction she and Gisele had gotten before.

After that distraction, she pivoted to other ideas. First, she had drawn the overall schematic of her watch and was going over it again. Her watch had many things that needed to be explored and researched, such as all of the internal magic symbols that were etched as if by a computer. The gems were set up like a circuit board, and she knew there was something there, especially with the symbols, so she looked down at the picture she'd drawn in her notebook of the layout.

Sloane had purchased some paints just for this purpose, and smiled as she looked down at the beautiful, colorful rendition of the internal layout of the watch's mainboard.

While Gwyn's ability vastly surpassed her own even at ten, Sloane was a bit proud of her basic drawing.

Looking over the table she had made in her journal with Reanny the dwarf's assistance in Vilstaf, Sloane refreshed herself on the various purposes and functions of each gemstone.

Sapphires were the logic gems that handled both external and internal functions. The opal maintained a sort of magical connection to the user of the watch, and the topazes took the link from the input functions and displayed them on the outer glass. The pink sapphire drew and distributed power from the mana crystal, and the amethyst targeted the use of mana that the ruby manipulated. The emerald connected to the user's core; the various diamonds connected to mana and amplified its use; and, finally, the onyx was a massive sensor.

There were multiple runes on the onyx in particular that she suspected determined the type of things it would detect. Sloane reviewed the runes she had scribbled in her journal as she tried to suss out their purpose. So far, she had managed to glean the intent of a few by pushing her mana into them like Reanny had done with the gems. The more she did it, the easier the learning became, but still, many of the other runes or groupings were difficult to figure out.

The individual ones she was sure of were |Detect|, |Intent|, |Display|, |Use|, |User|, |Spell|, and |Amplify|. She could tell there was a simpler naming scheme associated with each rune within the intent itself, but she hadn't gotten that far. She decided to ascribe her own description to each character.

She noticed how some runes combined with others for a more specific purpose. There were symbols that she worked out as operators for those groupings. The two sapphires were an example of this—the one on the left had a combined rune she was calling |Intent: User| while the one on the right had |Intent: Spell|. Sloane took these to mean that one processed user-focused intent, and the other, spell-focused intent.

Some runework had a lengthy structure that seemed to follow a certain logic. The black diamond had complicated runework that she had started to decode. Its structure had something to do with spell intent and the user *doing* something

in order for the watch to trigger . . . something. Based on what she had learned
of the gem functions, Sloane theorized the runework had to do with storage and
the use of a spell. She wasn't sure how that corresponded to intent, however.

On the onyx, there was a runework chain—a group of runes that worked
together—that she thought translated to detecting mana use and then displaying the results. She figured it was how the screen showed mana use in her surroundings. There were also a few runes on the topazes that likely dictated *how* to
display the previous "data" gathered. That rune was the most complicated one
Sloane could figure out at the moment. Some were far more complex, and deciphering those would come in time. Plus, she would need to use a jeweler's loop
to even do so for some of them.

Looking through her journal, Sloane had some ideas about how to use runes.
She didn't think she would need gems for *everything*. She would need to test it,
but she figured she could etch runes directly into an object. Silver or a similar
metal was likely key in this regard. Some type of engraving ink. She had scribbled
some ideas of a silver-based ink and an engraving pen that could utilize it. Sloane
would need to try to build one soon.

For now, she put down her notebook and went back to her flashbang design.
She had originally kept it hollow, thinking she would put some type of explosive
inside. Now, Sloane considered a different design, one that would make full use
of runic chains. She would place a ball inside that she would engrave with runes.

She just had to figure out how to imbue her **[Flashbang]** spell into the object.
Wait . . . that one runic chain.

Sloane quickly scanned back to the black diamond runework that she had
been trying to puzzle out. It was obvious, now that she thought about it: the
gem's function was to store a spell and then use it. *So, if the second rune focused
on an action or requirement for use, that left a rune to determine what to store . . .*

With that thought, she wrote out what she suspected it did. She worked out
the translation for the gem's runework into a runic chain that read eerily like a
line in some programming language, and after she wrote it out, she smiled.

The final runic chain indicated that it would store a spell and then wait
until the user triggered the rune to cast it. The intent portion of the runework
probably referred to the user pushing the intent of which spell they should store
into it. With that thought, she wondered if the black diamond could do more
than just store spells. *Could it also store data?* It was something she would need
to test.

Going back to her working table of operators, Sloane updated the list and
scribbled in the logic. She added the two new runes to her running list and nodded—everything was looking good. She just needed to make the engraving pen
and she'd be golden.

Or silver, since that's what I'll need, she thought with a wry smile.

Based on the runes she now knew, Sloane believed she nearly had enough to test her grenade. Her only issue was figuring out a way to delay the use of the |Flashbang| spell.

She would also need to add a button to the grenade with a pin so that it wouldn't inadvertently go off. The button would trigger the runework and the spell. So, she needed to delay the cast. Which the handy |wait for| runic symbol could be used for.

Yet, then she had to figure out a way to add a timer after the operator. Thinking about it, with the plethora of runes she had seen just on the watch, there *had* to be a rune for *time*. Sloane would just need to figure it out.

She also needed to determine if engraving the runework on a ball or something protected by the outer steel casing would cast the spell inside or outside. If it was cast inside, she had to figure out a way to make a spell that separated the casing at the seam *before* casting |Flashbang|.

Or simply engrave the runework on the outside temporarily. Sloane sighed. There was so much to do and test, but that was enough "artificing" for the day. *Definitely a word.*

Actually, speaking of tests . . . maybe one *last thing.*

Sloane looked down at her watch as the rumblings of an idea hit her mind like the foreshocks of an earthquake.

The watch clearly had the capability to store and *use* spells, if her runic deciphering was correct. While she *wanted* to go hard in the paint and try to add a |Mana Bolt| to the storage, she figured the safest option would be to add the only other spell she had made. But how to do it?

The rune was about intent . . . so perhaps all she needed to do was push her intent and the spell into it?

Worth a shot.

Definitely a reason to use [Flashbang] over [Mana Bolt], because I don't want to damage the watch if I'm wrong.

With a deep breath, she placed her hand over her watch and channeled her spell through her hand into the device. She kept her mind focused on the spell and the intent of what she wanted, ensuring that it didn't actually 'fire'.

In the end, her hunch proved correct . . .

The screen glowed white before it pulsed several times and her spell channel ended. She looked down at the watch face and noticed a tiny rune that hadn't been there before, along the side of the screen, also glowing white.

The rune slowly pulsed, and she could feel a slight difference in the connection between the watch and herself—it was as if the spell was sitting there, queued up and ready. It also appeared that the watch might be able to hold only one runic version of a spell at a time.

She hoped that the opal's connection to her meant that the strength of the spell would be determined by drawing mana from her, instead of just from the mana crystal, because it would be weak if it used only the watch's power.

Sloane knew it wouldn't cause any harm, so she turned away and aimed her wrist at the back door of the wagon. Focusing on the watch, she thought: |*Flashbang*|. She watched the runic spell launch out from her wrist and burst against the door in a flash and a loud crack of sound.

Sloane instantly felt a rush of excitement. *Yes!* She jumped up and pumped her fist. "Hell, yeah!" *This adds so much versatility!* She had to show the knights. *They will get a kick out of this! There are so many things we could do with this.*

Then she froze. *Shit. I said I'd test my spells in a proper place.* "Ugh! Damn it, Sloane!" *Hopefully, no one noticed.* She sighed. *I really need runes to dampen the sound in the wagon.*

She looked down at her watch and saw that the rune was subdued. *Almost like it's recharging or on cooldown. I definitely need to test everything else I can do with this watch. I should have considered it before. There are so many available gems that the watch has to have additional capabilities.* Feeling both satisfied and embarrassed by her test, Sloane decided to clean up and go find the knights.

When she emerged from the wagon where she and the knights had set up a crafting workbench for her to use, she stretched and squinted her eyes in the bright light of the midday sun. Before stepping down the ladder, she looked around to determine whether anyone had heard her spell.

Satisfied that she hadn't seen anyone, Sloane stepped down . . . right into Cristole.

She jumped in surprise. "What the—? Where'd you come from?"

Cristole had a very unamused look on his face, and Sloane could feel the judgment wafting off him as if it were a physical thing.

"Sloane . . ." he started.

"Oh! Hi, Cristole. Nice to see you here!" She knew she had to take control of the interaction or she'd never hear the end of it. *Distract and redirect!*

"Sloane—"

"So, what do you say we head to the bar? I'll buy you a drink."

Cristole sighed. "Sloane, what—"

"I have so many great things to tell you about! Something new and exciting that will be a *huge* benefit to the group."

"Wait—"

"I also figured out how to make the flashbang!" she redirected.

Cristole did not look impressed.

Time to go for sympathy. She leaned close, placed her hand on the high elf's shoulder, and gently patted it. "Cristole, buddy. Let's not speak my shame into existence. Come. Join me. Together we shall rule the galaxy as Artificer and . . . uh . . . knight."

Cristole raised an eyebrow and tilted his head in confusion. "What the . . . Sloane, what in Relena's name are you talking about?"

"Exactly. Come along!" Sloane said, as she started walking back to the inn. She smiled as she heard the groan and footsteps coming from behind her.

Success.

Sloane and Cristole sat at the bar inside the inn. She had bought him *two* ales— one as a bribe to keep him from bringing up her spell, and the other to stop him from telling the others. Now that she actually *had* her own money . . .

Speaking of.

"So, Cristole. Before I speak on the new wondrous things I have discovered, let's discuss the Banking Guild."

"Sloane, don't think I'm letting you off the hook."

She pointedly looked at each beer and then back at him. "Sure. Whatever you say, my friend," she agreed with a smile.

Cristole groaned again as he threw his hands up. "Fine! Okay, so. The Banking Guild. Sure. Let's discuss it. What do you want to know?"

She ticked off the items on her fingers. "One: can we go? Two: what do I need to do to obtain an account? Three: how does the Guild track my money wherever we go?"

Cristole nodded as she listed her questions. "Alright. Yes, we can go. It's only midday, so we can actually go after we are done here. We will bring your patents of nobility that establish you as the baroness of House Reinhart. That will ensure you get a higher-tier account. Lastly, every month, the Guild will send out the updated ledgers in armed caravans from each regional headquarters—Thirdghyll is one of these. These travel a route that passes through each major branch, which in turn sends out updates to the smaller branches.

"It's a proven and secure system, but always make sure you track your purchases and balance so that you do not over-allot your account," he explained in between sipping his drink. "The Guild enforces harsh penalties upon anyone who does. You should never test them. They're a *very* powerful entity." He punctuated the last part by jabbing a finger on the table.

Sloane's eyes went wide as an idea slammed into her head like a sledgehammer. An idea that could be *very* profitable and right up her runic alley.

Thank you, fantasy, for your wonderful tropes that transfer to real life.

"Cristole. Where is the main headquarters of the Banking Guild for West Ikios?"

"Well, it's not just for West Ikios, but for the entire continent, and it's in Marketbol. A Sovereign City that the Guild itself funded and founded as a neutral location."

"Marketbol," Sloane deadpanned. "That name couldn't be blander and more cliche for a *Banking* Guild if they tried . . ."

Cristole chuckled. "You're not wrong. And Marketbol is only about one hundred and thirty kilometers from here."

Sloane considered her idea. "What is the likelihood the group could go there first? Not only does it give us another place to look for Gwyn, but also I think I can pitch a revolutionary idea to the Guild that will save them hundreds, if not more, in gold and ensure their ledgers are one hundred percent accurate. After that, they will start *making* gold."

Cristole tilted his head. "What is your idea, exactly?"

Sloane smiled. "So, this is something I'm shamelessly stealing from my world, but I want to create a membership card for the Guild that will allow you to synchronize your account balance no matter where you are. In the first version, you will simply go to the nearest branch when you go somewhere new and register your card for that branch. Once you leave, you update it. Or even if you forget to do that, when you get to the next branch and register it, your balance will update automatically. So instead of forcing the bank to constantly send out caravans to update ledgers everywhere, the new system will ensure the people do it for them. Each regional headquarters can maintain a runic system that creates a backup of the database for security purposes."

She watched as he fell into thought but didn't respond, so she nudged him back to the present. "What do you think?"

"That's . . . that's a lot. However, I certainly see the benefit. Why don't we meet with the guildmaster of the branch here in Thirdghyll? Instead of going today, let's go tomorrow. It will give me time to set up a meeting with him. You can describe your idea and maybe show him an example of what you're envisioning. It will allow us to see his response, and then we can go from there. If there is enough money in the venture, I'm sure we can convince Gisele of a detour before making our way to Swanbrook."

"A prototype? By tomorrow?" Sloane asked hesitantly.

"Yes, is that doable?" Cristole asked with a raised eyebrow.

"Yeah. Sure. No problem. Easy peasy," she replied, internally cursing.

It's going to be a long night.

CHAPTER SIX

THE BANKING GUILD

As discussed in other parts of this text, society was changed at all levels, no matter the nation. One of the earliest examples of this is evident in the various guilds. Their acceptance of magic and mana solidified the primacy of the guild system at large and even encouraged the establishment of new guilds. The three most prominent of these post-Flash guilds are the Artificer, Mage, and, of course, Adventurers Guilds. These three were humbly formed by trailblazers in their respective fields but developed into the influential continent-spanning organizations that we see today. However, one cannot discount the massive contributions that were made at the behest of the Banking Guild.

A History of Mana, 184 SA

It was very late, and Sloane was literally burning the midnight oil. Even though she was exhausted, she knew there was more to do. She had spent the last few hours sketching out various designs that the Banking Guild could use for currency tracking and purchases. Badges didn't work for her. She considered pen-like cylinders, but felt that was too *Empire.* In the end, she decided she would just go with what she knew.

Sloane was hard at work trying to design a card that the Banking Guild would be interested in. She had a general idea of what she needed to craft, but ran into a problem as soon as she considered the runework. First, she needed to make the card. The runes could come later.

Sloane grabbed a piece of steel and pushed her mana into it, shaping it into a small card. She left a slot for the "chip" that she would make from silver and some gems. Looking down, she considered the chip and what gems she would require. Sloane picked a sapphire, black diamond, and opal from her slowly diminishing stock and placed them in front of her. She also picked up a small coin of silver and started shaping it into the design she wanted. It looked almost identical to the ones back home, just silver instead of gold.

Now, time to fabricate the first true Manatech item. Oh, hey, I like that.

She picked up the gems and forced mana into them, keeping the shape and intent of what she wanted firmly in her mind. Gems were much more difficult to work with than metals, but she watched as the gems were slowly reformed—a square for the black diamond, and triangles for the opal and sapphire.

Sloane used her tweezers to gently place the gems into their slots in the chip. She manipulated the silver to carefully mold a lip that would hold the gems in place. Content that the MTC, or Manatech Chip, as she dubbed it, was done well, she proceeded to insert the chip into the slot on the card. Using a bit more Alteration, she melded the silver to the steel card.

The card looked great, even if it was currently blank. Considering the look, she smiled before altering it a bit more to add a slot for another gem. *A way to differentiate customer tiers.*

Sloane grabbed her journal and paints and designed what she thought the final product would look like, writing in placeholder runes. She would transfer the picture to a scroll later to present it to the local branch's guildmaster.

She was happy. Now, she needed to figure out the runework, *or* at least enough to make it work in a basic form. She knew she needed approximately four runic chains. She would need one to tell the black diamond what to store. Writing her thoughts in her notebook, she considered other requirements. A runic chain would be needed to act as a trigger when it contacted a terminal device that she would also need to design.

That's a headache and a half.

She would need to have the sapphire hold the intent of transferring data from the card to the terminal and back. And she needed some way to secure it all. Figuring out a way to have someone secure it with their mana signature would be the ideal way to do it. *If that is even a thing. I'll need to test later.*

The opal would allow the card to connect to the user, which should allow it to check their mana against the card's data to match them.

So, the runes she needed that she didn't know were |Secure|, |Mana Signature|, |Data|, and |Transfer|. |Data| and |Transfer| were the important ones. She had to figure those out before the card would work at all.

Why did I have to commit to something so soon? I barely know the runic language. Sloane banged her head gently against the table a few times. *Thiiink.*

She removed her watch and took it apart again. She looked at the runes, focusing hard on them, channeling her mana as she did. She *needed* to understand them. She had tried pushing her mana into the runes before, but now she would try more. She felt at each rune and channeled her mana through herself and the rune. She drew heavily on the blue mana her core was able to utilize, to help with logic and knowledge. She pulled the mana back from the rune and refocused through her ring that Reanny made her. Pushing herself, Sloane put her entire being into one simple concept: *learning runes*. She concentrated on the first symbol, trying to gain an understanding of its intent.

Sweat dripped from her brow as she pushed herself, and she became increasingly tired. It was as if she were mentally draining herself the more she channeled the mana. Just as she was about to give up on the current rune, Sloane felt something *click* in her mind, and a rush that seemed to start in her core then spread throughout her body. She instantly stopped channeling her mana and sat back. Something about the click she felt changed her, and now her mind was filled with all sorts of images. Where before she had been focusing on figuring out what runes meant, she now felt as if she had a connection to them. She looked at the runes again and sensed she could *almost* figure them out. She channeled her mana again and focused it on the feeling she had.

There was a difference almost immediately. She now felt her ability to read the runes had grown—in just a few moments too. *How does that work?* Sloane scrutinized one rune again and discerned its meaning nearly instantaneously. That rune stood for |**Repair**|, which was very beneficial to know.

Also, great to know my watch has a self-repair function.

She returned to the runework connected to the black diamond. The effect was the same. *Now, this is exactly what I need.* She had found the runic chain for |**Store: Knowledge**|. That alone solved a massive requirement.

With that success, Sloane continued. She located and deciphered runes for |**Combine**|, |**Mana**|, and |**Time**|. Her head was starting to throb, so she stopped channeling mana. Her pain lessened, which led her to believe there was a connection between mana use and mental strain.

She sat back and considered her options. First, she had just figured out how to finish her |**Flashbang**| grenades. Second, she had obtained what she needed for a prototype. While she didn't have a way to transfer yet, she figured she could try to figure that out on the way to Marketbol.

Grabbing her small set of engraving tools, she got to work. Sloane hadn't had a chance to create an engraving pen yet and didn't have silver ink, so she would have to use magic to alter some silver when she was done.

Before starting the engraving process, Sloane wrote out the runework she would need for the prototype. She needed the |**Store: Knowledge**| chain. Then she could use |**Combine**| instead of *Transfer*, which she hadn't found yet. So, the next she needed was the chain to send and receive data, which would work with the terminal, which would have a trigger that made contact with the chip.

Sloane nodded. *That's all I can do for now. Let's hope it works.* She got to work on engraving and performing the finishing touches on the card.

Sloane was roused from sleep by the insistent knock at her door. She grumbled under her breath, shuffling her way through the early-morning haze to answer it. Cristole greeted her from the other side, his cheerful smile far too bright for the unholy hour.

"You're not ready?" he asked, his voice brimming with the kind of early-morning enthusiasm she could do without.

"Hardly," she replied, stifling a yawn. "I was up all night. What do you want, Cristole?" She couldn't help the crankiness creeping into her voice. Morning person she decidedly was not.

At least I know where Gwyn gets it from.

"We need to leave soon. Given you missed breakfast, I thought I'd come and check on you," he told her, his cheer unabated. His gaze remained pointedly away from the bird's nest state of her hair.

Sloane let out another groan, then sighed. "I'll be down in a minute." Before he could respond with another of his cheerful remarks, she shut the door abruptly in his smiling face.

She stood there for a moment, gathering herself before beginning her morning routine.

Sloane and Cristole made their way down the city streets toward the Banking Guild. With the morning's grogginess banished, she felt revitalized, though a sense of anxiety persisted. They were on their way to meet the head of the local Banking Guild branch—an interaction that filled her with a blend of excitement and apprehension.

She was eager to find out if there had been any developments by Reanny and Mulinn in their mutual business. And the dwarf woman had promised she would find a way to get word to her if she heard anything about Gwyn. But the actual act of opening an account with the Guild was a stark reminder that she and Gwyn might never find a way back to Earth.

Basically, I'm on a roller coaster of emotions.

Cristole briefed her on the plan. "First, we'll meet the guildmaster. Once that's done, we'll proceed with setting up your house account. I've brought all the necessary documents."

"Alright," Sloane replied, her tone resolute. "I'm ready to commence Operation Noble Pretender."

Cristole shot her a serious look. "This isn't a game, Sloane. These meetings are crucial, even if it's just an informal discussion. Frankly, I'm surprised we managed to arrange an audience with the guildmaster this quickly."

Sloane met his gaze squarely. "I am taking this seriously, Cristole. I fully understand just how make-or-break this meeting is."

"Good," Cristole said, pausing as they navigated through a throng of pedestrians crossing the road. They emerged to face an imposing Romanesque-style stone building, its facade adorned with five towering pillars. "Because we're here. How did you say it before? Put your face game on?"

Sloane chuckled. "Game face on, and ready for action." She paused, grimacing inwardly. *That's what she said.* "So to speak . . . Never mind, let's do this."

Walking into the grand lobby, their eyes were drawn to a magnificent statue of an elegantly adorned telv woman, her gaze directed benevolently upon all who entered.

"That's the goddess Dylenia," Cristole explained. "She's revered as the goddess of commerce. The Guild says anyone who attempts to defraud them should pray that Dylenia strikes them down mercifully first, for the Guild's retribution will be far less forgiving. It's a warning they've upheld for over a century."

Sloane nodded appreciatively. "Impressive."

They proceeded toward a large central desk where both raithe and telv were serving customers. Cristole guided her to a separate queue where a moon elf couple, sporting far more luxurious attire than other patrons, stood ahead of them. The woman's eyes swept over Sloane before she returned to her hushed conversation with her partner.

Whispering to Sloane, Cristole explained, "This is the counter dedicated for nobles. The attending staff are specially trained to interact with the nobility and their retinue who come to conduct business with the Guild."

Sloane nodded. "Understood." She took a moment to survey the room, noting the cage with seven windows in front of a formidable vault door. Behind them, a series of offices lined the wall, and farther back, a staircase coiled up to another level.

After a brief time, the noble couple ahead of them completed their transaction and moved toward the offices. The raithe associate glanced at Cristole and Sloane and excused himself to confer with the telv who seemed to be overseeing the area. The telv studied them briefly, taking in their appearance before approaching.

"Good morning. How may the Guild assist you today?" he asked.

Cristole greeted him warmly. "Good morning. We have an appointment with the guildmaster. I am Ser Cristole Leblanc, and this is Lady Reinhart of House Reinhart of the Kingdom of Blightwych."

The telv remained professional and impassive as Cristole introduced them, his composure unflinching even at Sloane's baroness title. Sloane surmised he must have encountered far more distinguished individuals in his line of work.

"Welcome to the Banking Guild of Thirdghyll, milady and ser," he said. "I am Aimon Loderick." He consulted a log on the desk before him. "Ah yes, your appointment is listed here. Thank you."

Turning to Sloane, he inquired, "Milady, I note that you do not presently have an account with the Guild. Will you be initiating one with us today?"

"I intend to, Mister Loderick," Sloane confirmed. "After the meeting with the guildmaster, of course."

"Wonderful, milady. I'll ensure everything is ready once you conclude your meeting. May I provide an overview of our services in the meantime?"

Sloane turned to Cristole. "May I have the Guild's copy of the contract, please?"

Cristole obliged, pulling the requested document from the satchel he carried.

Taking the contract, Sloane focused her attention back on Aimon. As she handed him the document, she explained, "This is a contract I have with some merchants from Vilstaf. I'd like it reviewed and linked to my account. The Guild should already have the merchants' authorization and transactions pending for the creation of my account. Additionally, I'd like to deposit funds I've accrued so far."

Aimon quickly scanned the contract, then nodded in affirmation. "I'm familiar with this contract. Our liaison with Vilstaf arrived a few days ago, and we established the hold on funds for you. I'll make sure it's prepared for your review and approval upon your return."

"As for our services," Aimon continued, "we manage your account, ensuring its currency across all of West Ikios. However, we can also send a request to Marketbol if you require to go to any other region of Ikios, and they will ensure you are well taken care of. The guilds currently do not provide services within Loren, unfortunately. Now, for members of the nobility, we also offer our assistance as mediators or consultants for any transactions you might wish to undertake, for a nominal fee. Please note that our esquires are some of the best in the region. Lastly, we can manage your finances or assist you in hiring competent personnel to do so for your house."

Sloane absorbed the information, finding the services largely aligned with her expectations. She was confident she would learn more when she returned from her meeting.

"Thank you. I look forward to doing business with the Guild. I may even take advantage of the offer for financial consulting," she said.

Aimon flashed a professional smile. "The Guild looks forward to serving any needs House Reinhart may have." He made some notations on a form and placed the contract with other documents he had already set aside for her. Looking up, he smiled once more. "I will inform the guildmaster of your arrival. He will send an attendant when he's ready to meet with you. Please, feel free to take a seat over here." He gestured toward an inviting arrangement of cushioned chairs and small tables, accompanied by tastefully placed potted plants.

"Thank you for your time, Mister Loderick," Sloane said, reciprocating the smile.

The telv paused before returning her smile with a slow nod. Sloane noted the reaction with a touch of surprise. *Huh, who'd have thought being polite would elicit a reaction?*

Cristole glanced at her, one eyebrow raised in silent query, before leading her toward the seating area. They had barely settled into the plush chairs when an attendant arrived, carrying a pitcher of water and glasses.

Sloane turned to Cristole, her brow furrowed in thought. "Can you tell me more about the Guilds? They seem to be more prevalent than I had first thought."

Cristole nodded, appreciating her inquisitiveness. "Well, as kingdoms and nations began to rapidly rise and fall throughout Ikios to fill the void after the fall of the old empire, there was a growing need for institutions that could safeguard the interests of the masses. That's how the guilds came into being. Over time, they've evolved into powerful entities in their own right, especially as the region has grown in size and people. Most of the people on the continent are focused here and the south."

"Huh. Why are West and South Ikios the most populated regions?"

Cristole shifted in his seat, preparing for a brief dive into history. "These areas were primarily where the Loreni, my ancestors, decided to settle upon their arrival from Loren. This mass migration took place many generations ago, forever changing the demographic landscape of Ikios. There's a reason there are so many various kingdoms and city-states that dot the lands, but we are slowly reaching a point where the stronger nations expand and solidify their lands. The entire region is a spark away from a wildfire, and I fear that whatever is happening between the Empire of Vlaredia and the Sovereign Cities could spread. I sincerely wish to be out of the cities before it ignites."

Sloane traced the rim of her glass thoughtfully. "What prompted the Loreni to migrate here?"

Cristole shrugged, a far-off look clouding his eyes. "That piece of history is obscured, even to most of us Loreni. Ernald might know more, but it's generally believed that those who left Loren did not do so willingly, if the rumors hold any truth. What transpired after we arrived here . . . well, it's no coincidence the Church moved itself to Ikios and established its stronghold in Strathmore. I shudder to think of the secrets that lie buried deep within its vaults. There is very little contact between the continents, even to this day, and it's mainly done through the Church, as the archpriestess still presides over those who live in the old lands."

"This is all very interesting, thank you," she said.

Cristole nodded. "Of course. You'll need to know all of this as you navigate the intricacies of this shitstorm of politics and peoples. I can't imagine what it would be like to live in a world where there is only one people, like your Earth."

Sloane gave him a sad smile. "Just like here, but instead of focusing on entirely different species, we tend to focus on skin color and where you were born. In a way, I think that's worse."

They grew silent as each contemplated the revelations by the other, the air filled only by the low murmur of the guildhall around them.

Cristole switched the topic back to the upcoming meeting. "So, just remember, your goal is to make a positive impression. You don't need to strike a deal today. The actual negotiation will happen in Marketbol with those with more widespread authority. What you need from the guildmaster now is his recommendation so they take you more seriously."

Sloane gave a confident nod. "Understood. We've got this."

Cristole raised his hand, pointing a finger at her. "Correction. *You've* got this. I'll be waiting in the back as your escort. You'll be meeting the guildmaster alone."

Sloane raised an eyebrow, slightly taken aback. "I wasn't expecting that."

Cristole smiled reassuringly. "You'll do fine. Here, one second."

Their conversation paused as a moon elf woman descended the staircase and approached them. "Lady Reinhart?" she queried.

Sloane straightened and acknowledged her. "Yes?"

"Please follow me. The guildmaster will see you now."

Sloane looked at Cristole, who smiled at her and stood. He gave her an encouraging smile.

Steeling herself, Sloane mentally prepared for the upcoming meeting. She had ample experience with tech pitches back home. But here, in a fantasy world? This was entirely new territory.

She drew a deep breath and followed the elf, ready to navigate the uncharted waters of negotiation in this new reality filled with elves and magic.

I got this. All of this is for Gwyn. Any benefit I gain only improves my odds of finding her.

CHAPTER SEVEN

COST OF PROGRESS

The sun elf seated across from her wore a thoughtful expression. He bore the countenance of a modern CEO rather than the traditional banker image she'd anticipated. His physique hinted at regular exercise, though his age was betrayed by hair that held more silver strands than black, and his brown eyes bore an intensity that felt as if they could see through her.

Despite not being a noble, a detail Cristole had explained was intentional for such roles, he exuded authority. He was a man well aware of his position and the influence he held within it. From their brief interaction, she could discern that he was adept at wielding this power.

Sloane had just concluded her account of her journey to Thirdghyll and her understanding of magic and mana. She had to be vague about her origins, yet Guildmaster Lanthil Romaris had promptly discerned her terran roots and posed questions.

I really need to figure out where that 'terran' naming came from and why.

She maintained her gaze on him as he spoke. "So, allow me to express my understanding of what I have gathered so far. You claim to be a noble from your world. Which, in itself, isn't particularly intriguing. We have had a couple of ter-ran nobles visiting the city in recent weeks. One is even advising Count Kayser as we speak. However, your association with Blightwych makes your case more interesting and lends you some credibility. Without that link, I doubt I'd have had the time to consider any proposition you might have for the Guild.

"As for this matter of mana, it's disconcerting. I've never encountered any-thing quite like it. Rumors are circulating among Thirdghyll's high society, and I'm aware the count has launched an investigation. But that's neither here nor there. You propose that this mana can benefit the Banking Guild. You will need to elaborate a bit more, I think."

Sloane nodded in acknowledgment. "Certainly! From my understanding, mana innately seeks to be utilized. It possesses an inherent logic that can facilitate the transfer of knowledge and information if harnessed correctly."

"And you have uncovered this 'correct' method, I presume?" the guildmaster responded as if he had heard similar claims before.

Sloane was slightly taken aback. Most business professionals she had dealt with in the past had appreciated some background context. Not too much, of course, but enough to provide a framework for understanding.

It appeared Sloane would need to adopt a different approach with the guildmaster. "Indeed," she said. She delved into her satchel and extracted a card and several documents. She laid them on the desk before her and began to explain.

"This card, when linked to mana, enables information storage. It specifically retains details regarding the owner's identity and financial balance. It will also communicate with a terminal maintained by the Banking Guild, synchronizing data with the cardholder's account, which can be used to withdraw or transfer funds. In time, the Guild could establish a network of merchants who conduct transactions using this card system. The Banking Guild might even levy fees for such service."

The guildmaster reached out and picked up the card. "All of this is possible through this card?" He scooped up the schematic with his other hand, examining the real-life prototype against the design.

"Absolutely. This model is a prototype capable of accepting and transferring information. This will conserve—"

"Yes, yes, the Guild will conserve significant resources. Spare me the sales pitch, Lady Reinhart. I'm familiar with the routine. I grasp the implications of your proposal, and I don't need a comprehensive explanation of its workings. I need to understand why the Guild should collaborate with you, specifically. I'm sure others will inevitably decipher this technology, especially now that its existence is known. This would grant us a degree of control that I suspect far exceeds what you'll propose to our leadership in Marketbol. Is that your objective? A recommendation?"

Sloane took a moment to compose herself, sipping from the glass of water provided upon her arrival. "The Guild should partner with me because I offer something it lacks. I have extensive knowledge of how such a system functions and the optimal strategies for implementation, derived from a world's worth of practical use and experience."

Lanthil's eyes sparkled and a hint of a smile crept across his features. "That . . . that is the response I was seeking. Yes, we could likely find other terrans with similar knowledge, but that's irrelevant. You're here, now, with a tangible product.

One that, *on the surface*, appears beneficial enough to warrant consideration. You needn't convince me of its efficacy. I'm indifferent. I stand to profit regardless. So you desire my endorsement? How will you *and* House Reinhart reciprocate?"

She blinked, taken aback. *Did he just ask for a damn bribe?*

"What exactly are you asking for?" she countered.

His smile broadened. "I anticipated your shock. 'Dylenia! Did he just request a bribe?' No, I have no need for your money. In fact, if you're here pitching this concept to me, it's because you're in need of financial backing, not the other way around."

"I see . . ." Sloane nodded, recognizing the guildmaster's true interests: the intangible elements of power—favors, influence, backroom deals. He wanted a piece of the pie.

I can work with that.

"Tell me, Guildmaster, how would you rate your staff's competence?"

The guildmaster of Thirdghyll returned her question with an amused grin. "Now, *that* is an interesting question. I can proudly say my team is exceedingly professional and efficient. Even better, they are *loyal.* They excel at their tasks, notwithstanding the region's limited profitability."

Good. Time to go all in.

"In that case, I believe we can reach a mutual agreement. House Reinhart is currently aiming to extend its reach in the financial sector. However, we're short of key personnel to implement this practically. Your recommendation for specialists in the field could greatly assist my house in fostering a more effective collaboration with the Guild. Besides, House Reinhart always remembers its allies and their valuable assistance."

This decision would either set her up for success or result in failure, she knew. And the implications would be enduring. Her task was to ensure that his monetary aspirations remained foremost and outweighed any desire to undermine her.

"Indeed, I might have a few excellent candidates in mind. In fact, my niece could be an ideal fit for such a role. Since you're about to embark on a journey, I cannot simply let a family member accompany you without ensuring her safety. I have a man in mind who would serve admirably as part of your House Guard."

The man would clearly just be there to spy or act as a minder. *Probably both.*

"Guildmaster Romaris, I assure you that the order escorting me is capable of providing ample protection for an additional person. They are, after all, highly trained Blightwych knights."

"Certainly, certainly. However . . ." Lanthil shuffled a stack of documents on his desk, his eyes scanning the pages. "Recent discussions between the Order of Haven's Hope and the baroness Lady Reinhart suggest that they are soon to part ways. The baroness is currently searching for her estranged daughter, but no leads have emerged regarding her whereabouts or the reasons for their separation.

The Knights themselves are divided on the matter. Continued observation will be necessary to determine the order's future objectives and the individual members' aspirations. Lady Reinhart has entered into a lucrative contract with the siblings of the Farum Merchant Co. As per this record, the baroness's profit share is substantial, owing to the siblings' swift ascent in Vilstaf, and it even appears that the dwarven siblings are preparing to expand soon. Within a single season, they've had to hire ten additional staff members to cope with their escalating sales and increased business, which the designs provided by the baroness largely drive. The items sold exhibit faint signs of magical functionality; however, further observation will be required. As of now, these objects haven't spread to Thirdghyll, and we've observed no signs of magic use among anyone other than terrans. Yet, the siblings in Vilstaf are suspected of somehow having the ability to tap into this newfound phenomenon. It's recommended to increase surveillance on the baroness to determine whether she can provide access to magic.'"

He paused momentarily, studying her response. "Shall I continue?" he asked.

Sloane struggled to speak, a tight knot forming in her throat.

How has he managed to acquire so much information about me so swiftly? Is he looking for Gwyn?

She attempted to voice her thoughts, only to be interrupted by a hand resting on her shoulder. Glancing upward, she noticed Cristole standing by her side, the knight's hand gripping his sword's hilt. "Guildmaster, you ought to clarify your intentions. *Immediately.*"

A soft click resonated through the room, prompting Sloane to swivel around. Two men were stationed behind them by the door. The orkun, his hand on the doorknob, raised his voice. "Guildmaster, is everything in order?"

He's the first orkun I've seen in Thirdghyll. His tusks look fierce.

With a reassuring gesture, the guildmaster raised his hand. "Yes, everything is perfectly fine, Reji. Allow me a moment to explain."

As she returned her attention to the elf, Sloane realized he had known her identity for quite some time.

"I trust I need not emphasize that any information I share henceforth must remain confidential. You *will not* disclose it." He cast a pointed glance at Cristole, who was still visibly on edge. "This includes Ser Gisele and Lady d'Argin. If you breach this confidentiality, I assure you, I will not be pleased."

Before Cristole could respond, Sloane laid a calming hand on his forearm. He glanced down at her, and she found her voice. "We understand. We won't tell anyone. Now, tell us how you know so much about us."

Lanthil Romaris fixed his gaze on the pair, his stare unwavering for what seemed like minutes. Sloane couldn't decipher what he was searching for, but his scrutiny began to unnerve her. She was picking up undertones she hadn't anticipated from someone she had initially presumed was a regional bank manager.

"Before I delve into that, Lady Reinhart, I think it would be best to shed some light on the structure of the guilds in general. This might clarify a few things for you."

She gestured lazily for him to proceed, appearing disinterested on the surface, while internally her anticipation was palpable. "Go on . . ."

He permitted a slight smirk to grace his lips before diving in. "Let me begin by clarifying that the guilds remain politically neutral in this region of Ikios. We don't meddle in governmental affairs unless they pose a potential threat to the collective guilds. The unique political landscape of the Sovereign Cities encourages such a stance. Over time, the guilds have recognized the continent as being too vast for effective governance from a single headquarters. Consequently, we've partitioned it into sub-regions, such as West Ikios. While our region plays host to the majority of the headquarters of each guild, each region also has a guild council, chaired by the head of each respective guild. Our considerable influence is drawn from our unified purpose, our neutrality, and the extent to which we will go to preserve this influence." His tone sounded ominous.

Sloane narrowed her eyes. *Two can play at that game.* "Spare me the threats, Lanthil. I know the spiel: you're part of a formidable organization, one that transcends borders and possesses the resources and willpower to retain its societal standing. The subdivision of the continent is merely a strategy to manage control more effectively. I come from a world where organizations operate on a *global* scale, with corporations influencing *billions* of lives. I comprehend the dynamics. Now, please, get to the point."

In her peripheral vision, she noticed Cristole regarding her with unmasked surprise.

A smirk pulled at her lips, not going unnoticed by the guildmaster, who responded with a hearty laugh. "Well put. I trust you won't object if your revelations find their way to the ears they could serve."

Sloane shrugged nonchalantly. Knowledge was bound to spread eventually. The key was to control the flow at her own pace.

"Alright, then, to the point. Each major city, or sphere of influence, has a singular guild that oversees operations for all other guilds. Typically, this is the Banking Guild, thanks to our abundant resources and personnel. However, this isn't always the case. But it is here in Thirdghyll. Any noteworthy occurrence is reported by the other guilds, with information disseminated to the relevant parties. In this case, that would be me. The arrival of a new race to our world, or the emergence of a mythic phenomenon previously deemed divine or supernatural—these warrant our attention and demand our response.

"We would have approached you, had you not approached us. The count is gathering almost every terran he can find, and *I do not know why.* The Empire is moving against the Sovereign Cities, and *I do not know why.* Many things are happening that we are still collecting information on. You provide me with potential answers to one, plus you also potentially increase the influence of the guilds as a whole. I will put forth my recommendation if you accept my niece into your house, and hire the guard I've suggested. This guard would accompany you to your eventual meeting with Count Kayser, allowing him the opportunity to gather information for me. Do this, and you will get my recommendation before you depart, along with some guidance on your next steps."

Sloane nodded. She could see the man's practicality. *This could work. It's not like I have to do much else.* "Your man will not endanger my interests or *any* of the people close to me. If he does . . . well, that will be the *last* thing he does. I'm sure your spies know what happens to those who wish to harm me." *Ugh . . . smooth, Sloane. Smooth.*

His narrowed eyes conveyed his understanding of her warning. Still, he nodded. "He will follow your instructions, as long as they cater to my needs. Once you depart from Thirdghyll, he will protect my niece and you, as that aligns with my interests. However, you have quite a bit to demonstrate before we reach that stage."

"Certainly. Additionally, I would like my account to have the highest level of access the Banking Guild offers."

The guildmaster stood up and quirked his brow. He looked back down at the design she had given him. "You know, the Ruby Tier is actually our second-highest tier, typically reserved for individuals of a duke's standing. The highest tier is kept for royalty. I'll ensure that you're granted the tier you've so artfully represented in your example." He gestured to the two guards by the door, one of whom nodded and exited the room.

Sloane stood, extending her hand with a sly smile. "I look forward to our future dealings."

He shook her hand with a surprising gentleness. "The pleasure is mine, Lady Reinhart. I will arrange for my niece and my man to meet you at your inn."

Sloane acknowledged his statement, turning to Cristole. "Shall we proceed to open my account?"

Cristole initially appeared hesitant, but Sloane's eyes seemed to resolve his internal conflict. With a slight nod, he agreed. "Let's."

As Sloane made her way to the door, the guildmaster's voice echoed behind her, causing her to pause and turn. "Lady Reinhart, the next time someone attempts to exploit you, try not to leave remains. It's considered unseemly. However, you won't need to concern yourself with that any longer. Moreover, the involved parties haven't encountered, much less procured, any terran children. That would be deemed distasteful, and they're well aware that the guilds would disapprove. Consider this information a token of the Banking Guild's goodwill."

Sloane offered a simple nod of acknowledgment before resuming her path to open an account, sighing in relief at the indirect assurance regarding Gwyn.

It seems that House Reinhart is finally being established. One step closer to securing the means needed to maintain a search, no matter how distant I must go.

As the door closed behind them, Sloane reflected on the fact that the guildmaster had never truly explained how the Guild, *or guilds*, had acquired the extensive information they possessed about her group, let alone the thugs.

Lanthil Romaris sat in contemplation at his desk, reflecting on the intriguing meeting he had just concluded. While the baroness's proposals were groundbreaking and held substantial potential, the approach and underlying goals she displayed were not foreign to him. It was a familiar ploy to capitalize on the immense resources of the Guild. Had she not been a terran, he might have dismissed her overtures without much consideration. Yet, she brought forth opportunities that would otherwise remain unexplored.

When Lanthil had assured Lady Reinhart that he did not require an understanding of her object's workings, he was earnest. He planned to employ specialists who would dedicate their efforts to mastering the novel system. If it functioned as she suggested, it would generate massive profits for the Banking Guild, strengthening their grip on regional politics further.

He would have to continue the observation and information collection of the baroness and her house by the Blad—

His thoughts were interrupted by his guard. "Guildmaster, Stefan will be here soon. Elodie, however, will require another bell to arrive."

"Thank you, Reji. That is fine. Please allow Stefan in as soon as he arrives."

Reji acknowledged his instructions with a nod, but hesitated as he turned to leave.

"Is there something else on your mind?" Lanthil asked.

"If it's not too much trouble, Guildmaster, what are your thoughts about the noblewoman who just left?"

Lanthil consistently hired staff who possessed a keen sense of intuition. Having subordinates who could anticipate his needs was advantageous, but it was equally beneficial to employ individuals capable of discerning others' traits and motives. Such insights could provide valuable information, aiding in his dealings with various characters. Reji, in particular, exhibited an exceptional ability to gauge an individual's character upon a single interaction. His observations were always valued.

"What do you mean?"

"There's something peculiar about her, Guildmaster. I can't quite explain it, but she's . . . different. She doesn't give off the same haughty or superior vibes typical of nobility," Reji explained.

Slowly nodding, Lanthil contemplated Reji's observation. After a moment, he responded to the patiently waiting guard. "Your insight is noted. The next time she meets with me, let me know if your impression of her changes."

"Understood, Guildmaster."

A knock sounded on the door. Reji promptly answered, permitting Stefan to stride in before he himself exited.

Lanthil took a moment to study the raithe who had just entered. Tall by raithe standards, Stefan Stranca nearly matched Lanthil's own height. His slender frame bore an aristocratic air, and his smooth, gray skin hinted at a well-bred lineage. Shoulder-length white hair, that was tinged red at the tips, complemented his distinguished coat. In his ensemble, Stefan would blend in seamlessly at any noble gathering. His red eyes, almost glowing, rested easily on his face as he stood, seeming relaxed. Lanthil knew the man wasn't actually one of the nobility, but that didn't seem to affect his demeanor.

"Guildmaster, you requested my presence?" Stefan broke the silence.

Rising from his chair, Lanthil circled around his desk. "Stefan, thank you for coming promptly. I have an assignment for you, one that involves your guild as well. You'll be serving as a guard to a baroness who has attracted the interest of both the guilds and me."

For the next quarter bell, Lanthil outlined his plans and expectations for Stefan. They discussed his proposed role, the manner in which he should communicate any gleaned information back to the guilds, and other relevant details.

"I'll inform the guild and arrange for a support team. I'll make it a point to meet your niece before our rendezvous with the baroness," Stefan confirmed.

"Take this. It should give you a more comprehensive understanding of whom you'll be working for." Lanthil handed Stefan the dossier on Sloane he had meticulously assembled.

A knock resounded in the room before Reji peeked in as he cautiously opened the door. "Guildmaster, your niece has arrived," he announced.

"Excellent, show her in," Lanthil said, beckoning from his plush chair near the liquor cabinet.

Elodie entered, her pants and tunic notably professional in the Guild's colors. Her braids had been painstakingly redone, a sign she anticipated business. Lanthil admired her astuteness.

He'd miss her financial expertise, but an alliance with a potentially ascendant house through a family member promised greater long-term advantages.

"Uncle, did you call me to discuss the reports I submitted?" she inquired.

"Not at all. Can't an uncle simply desire to see his favorite niece?" he retorted with a chuckle, gesturing toward the bar.

Unfazed, Elodie strolled over to pour herself a measure of the finest whisky, barely a finger's depth, then turned to face him. "I'm your only niece," she replied with an eye roll that made him chuckle again. "Uncle, let's be frank. You haven't invited me for a casual visit since I was a child. It's always business with us. That's fine. I like business."

"Alright, you've got me. I do have something for you, and no, it's not your report. Though, while your financial acumen displayed in the report has something to do with that, it's your connection to the family that is equally important," Lanthil confessed.

Elodie's face assumed a dry expression. "Uncle Lanthil . . . you're not trying to arrange a marriage for me, are you?"

Taken aback, Lanthil nearly choked on his drink, almost wasting a good vintage. "What? Why would you . . .? We aren't nobility."

"So you're not planning to engage me in a political marriage to further our family's interests?" she clarified.

Studying her, Lanthil asked, "Is that what you think I'd do?"

She tilted her head slightly. "Isn't it?"

"Of course not! However, I do have a job for you. That has the potential to become highly political."

Elodie's gaze hardened. "So, a job. Are you reassigning me?"

Thinking through his words carefully, he replied, "In a sense. There's a new house—House Reinhart of Blightwych. You'll join them and manage their finances, which could involve considerable travel."

"To what end?" she queried.

"This house aims to establish extensive business ties with the Banking Guild. Besides, this move will foster certain other connections and facilitate information gathering. You're aware of my role within the guilds here in Thirdghyll. This is a means to further those aims."

Elodie nodded thoughtfully. "I understand. When do I start? And do you have more details?"

"Immediately. You'll first meet your bodyguard, who also belongs to the guilds. While he will report directly to you on guild-related affairs, he'll also keep an external line of communication open with us. Subsequently, you'll meet the baroness, Lady Reinhart, at her inn. Her dossier is on my desk—peruse it before your meeting. Notably, she is a terran."

Her eyes widened in surprise. "A terran? She's the second terran noble I've heard of. So she has business with us rather than Count Kayser?"

"Thirdghyll is but a stop in her travels. You will accompany her to Marketbol if she proves herself and gains my recommendation. Otherwise, we will consider a resolution to the matter," Lanthil explained.

Elodie nodded in understanding. "I look forward to this assignment. Could you elaborate on your expectations from my role within the house?"

"Of course. Here's what I envision . . ."

CHAPTER EIGHT

TINKER, NOBLE, ACCOUNTAN,TSPY

S loane and Cristole arrived back at the inn after her meeting and setting up the account with the Banking Guild. The high elf knight had been extremely helpful in navigating the minutiae of what was required, providing documentation, and explaining contracts and forms she needed to fill out.

To Sloane's surprise, the Guild operated with standardized forms. This revelation didn't align with her initial understanding of the society's progress since her arrival. Then again, she reasoned, this was an entirely distinct civilization, and certain disparities were to be expected.

Now seated at a table in the tavern, she sifted through the documents related to her new account, studying the badge that would serve as an additional form of identity at any branch location. It was a palm-sized, round coin, with "The Banking Guild of Ikios" inscribed in elegant script along the top edge. The front side of the badge was dominated by a scale with a ruby inlaid at its base. Above the gemstone was a small engraving of the crest of Thirdghyll, with Sloane's name and title featured beneath. Flipping the badge over, she noted her account identifier etched in a compact space. One of the benefits of the Ruby Tier membership was the ability to have her house crest engraved on the badge. If she desired this service, all she needed to do was return the badge to the Guild for their jeweler to work on it.

Satisfied, she stowed the items back in her satchel and surveyed the nearly vacant inn. Given the Guild's apparent surveillance, it was prudent to inspect each remaining patron. Cristole, nursing an ale across the table, had been unusually quiet on the return journey, but she had refrained from probing him then.

Now, though, it seemed an opportune moment. "So, Cristole," she ventured in a hushed tone, "what's on your mind?"

He sighed, focusing his gaze on her. "I'm startled by the depth of information the guilds have on you and, consequently, us. We must tread carefully."

"I agree, but—"

"Cristole, Sloane. Good to see you're back," Gisele's voice echoed across the room.

Sloane reciprocated Gisele's greeting with a smile and wave before turning her attention back to Cristole. "But we can only do so much to maintain privacy. If I can secure the Guild as an ally, it's a win for us. We *should* bring Gisele into the loop," she concluded just as Gisele, Deryk, and Ernald approached their table.

Cristole nodded in agreement before greeting the newcomers.

"Good afternoon," Gisele said, settling into a chair. "How did your meeting with the Banking Guild go?"

"It was both productive and informative," Sloane replied.

Cristole subtly shook his head at Gisele, indicating a need for discretion. "We should discuss the specifics later. In private."

Ernald, situating himself next to Sloane, glanced at the two as Deryk dragged another chair to the table, placing himself between Sloane and Cristole. Gisele, who had taken the seat next to Cristole, examined the pair. "Why the dire expressions? Do we need to have a private conversation right now?"

Cristole met Sloane's glance and shook his head. "It's not urgent, but I must stress that sensitive matters be discussed privately."

Deryk bobbed his head in agreement. "Yes, it seems my suspicions were correct. Thank you for the confirmation."

Sloane shot Deryk a quizzical look. "If you've already guessed what we are going to say, I'm going to be impressed."

He offered her a slight smirk in response but remained silent.

Ernald reclined in his chair, adopting a serious tone. "Sounds ominous. Did you at least manage to open an account?"

Sloane retrieved the badge from her satchel and placed it on the table. "I did. Cristole was a huge help. The meeting, I think, was also beneficial."

Both Ernald and Gisele turned their attention to the badge. While Gisele's eyes narrowed, Ernald let out a low whistle. "Ruby Tier? How in Dylenia's name did you manage that?"

Cristole tilted his head toward Sloane. "She made a deal with the guildmaster. One that is quite dangerous."

"What did you do?" asked Gisele.

"Not much," Sloane replied nonchalantly, "Just agreed to add two potential members to my house. One being the guildmaster's niece—"

"And the other one is likely a spy, or worse . . ., a Blade," Cristole interjected.

Deryk leaned forward. "Are you certain?" he asked in a low voice.

Cristole nodded, his expression serious. "I can't be entirely certain, but it's a strong possibility. We know their guild operates in Westaren and the Sovereign Cities. We'll discuss it in more depth when we're alone."

"Understood," Deryk said, settling back into his chair.

"What's a Blade?" Sloane asked.

Deryk and Cristole shared a look. The elf answered, "A member of a more . . . grey oriented guild. We'll discuss it more later."

She nodded.

So maybe like an assassin? Are they the Assassin's Guild?!

Sloane observed Ernald and Gisele, but they seemed to be lost in their thoughts. "Cristole can explain a bit more later, but for the time being, we will have two members joining us. This leads us to the next point. I would like to request you all to accompany me to Marketbol. Cristole and I discussed an idea I have that will be revolutionary for the Banking Guild and I would like to ensure your order can take advantage of it."

Sloane placed the Guild badge back into her satchel and grabbed the card. "This would replace the badge. It will also hold information that would allow the Guild to know exactly how much in funds you have available, regardless of your location."

Ernald picked up the card, examining it with a curious look. "So, this relies on mana and magic to function?"

Sloane nodded as Ernald passed the card to Gisele. "Yes, it would save the Guild considerable amounts of money that they currently spend on maintaining their network, along with *making* them money in the long term."

Gisele, holding the card, nodded. "That sounds intriguing. I can see how that would be something they'd be very interested in."

Sloane explained her idea a bit more, leaving out any exact details in case they were being spied on. Fortunately, Gisele seemed genuinely interested. Ernald posed numerous technical and theoretical questions, which Sloane promised to answer in detail later in private.

She noticed Gisele giving Cristole a prolonged look. The knight-captain then turned her gaze on Sloane, her eyes narrowing. After a moment of contemplation that left Sloane feeling a little uncomfortable, Gisele finally broke the silence.

"Fine. We'll accompany you to Marketbol."

Sloane smiled broadly. "Great! You won't regret it."

Gisele exhaled slowly. "I certainly hope not."

Sloane leaned forward, beckoning Gisele closer, and whispered, "Now, we just need to help this guard spy on the count and get information on terrans who are supposedly in the city. Then hope that the guildmaster will give his recommendation to use when I meet with the Banking Guild's leadership. Oh, and I have a few things I want to make! Easy peasy!"

Gisele furrowed her brow. "What do you mean, *spy on the count?*"

Cristole placed a hand on her shoulder. "Later."

Gisele frowned as she leaned back in her chair, her stern gaze fixed on Sloane and Cristole. "I don't appreciate making decisions without all the relevant information."

Sloane's expression softened. "I'm sorry. It will be worth it, and you'll understand everything once we can discuss it in more detail. I promise."

Gisele nodded, albeit reluctantly.

"Oh, and Gisele," Sloane continued, "would you mind being here when I meet with the two representatives the guildmaster is sending? I'd greatly appreciate your insight."

Gisele's frown deepened even further.

Ernald leaned forward and with a serious tone, added, "Gisele, that scowl will be perfect to intimidate anyone Sloane meets with. Excellent work."

Gisele turned to face the scholar, her expression unchanging. "I will end you, Ernald."

A hushed silence fell over the table, only to be shattered by an unexpected snort from Deryk. Sloane glanced over to see Deryk break into uncontrollable laughter.

"'End . . . you . . .' Oh, Gisele, that's a good one," he managed to say between bursts of laughter.

Gisele just stared until she, too, couldn't suppress her laughter anymore. Sloane looked at Ernald, who still wore a terrified expression. She had no idea what was so funny to the two orkun knights. She had to admit, even if she could speak the same language, a lot of their cultural quirks still confused her. Some were awkward or just not funny; others were hilarious if only in the responses of others. After looking around and seeing everyone's looks, she knew which this situation fit into.

Their reactions were infectious, and, despite her initial confusion, she soon found herself laughing along with them.

The only one who didn't join in was Ernald, whose awkward expression never left his face.

"So, you were told in no uncertain terms that we are being spied on," Gisele repeated, seeking confirmation after Cristole and Sloane revealed everything that had transpired during the meeting.

They had congregated in Sloane's room, the largest of their accommodations, retreating to the bedroom rather than the sitting area for added privacy. Deryk and Maud had opted to remain outside to keep watch for anyone trying to listen in. Sloane had taken a seat on her bed while Gisele and Cristole stood in conversation. Ismeld had claimed a small desk chair in the corner of the room.

"They didn't blatantly say, 'Oh, we're spying on you and we're going to continue.' The guildmaster directly read from a report that explained broadly everything we've done in and since Vilstaf," Cristole elaborated, the strain evident in his voice.

Sloane released a sigh. "Should we really be so surprised? You all practically warned me that this was basically the City of *Secrets*. The fact that we're being spied on is a given. Our challenge is to flip this situation to our advantage."

Ismeld interjected with a slight cough. "She's right. The guildmaster perceives us as potential assets. We can exploit this. We still need to secure an audience with the Westari Order of Secrets at the Ghyll Academy, and the guildmaster may be able to help us with that as well."

From his post against the wall, Ernald nodded in agreement. "He may well be our only hope, and if Sloane is aiding the guilds in their surveillance of the count, we may be able to press on that. Deryk and I have been having trouble locating any leads, which is frustrating. We must ascertain where the Order of Secrets stands and who they're backing in this clandestine power struggle. We have 'Mister Rowe,' mentioned by the thugs Sloane encountered, the guildmaster, and the count—all of whom are vying for information and access to the terrans. The Guild seems to be the underdog in this race."

"Which could work to our advantage, and likely explains why the guildmaster is keen to cooperate with Sloane," Gisele chipped in. She turned to Sloane and continued, "I will accompany you to meet your potential house members. It's important that we display unity. Regardless of their awareness of our eventual departure, there's still considerable time before that happens."

"I'm also available to join and provide any necessary insight or support," Ismeld offered.

Gisele looked around and then nodded before addressing the group, "Let's do that. Cristole, take Maud and subtly try to figure out who is spying on us. Check our things in the wagon and ensure nothing has been stolen or tampered with. The inn *should* have it secured, but we can't be sure. Ernald, work with Deryk and look into the Ghyll Academy. If you can secure a meeting without any outside help, do so. If you can meet immediately, you know what we need. Do it *quietly*. We do not need any further parties to know our interest in finding Gwyneth. In the past, we may have been too aggressive. We need to ensure we do not give any groups leverage over us."

Sloane looked up at Gisele. "I know this goes without saying, but even if these two do end up working with us, we have to have conversations in private. We cannot expect anything we say to stay private if they hear. There's a saying in my world: 'loose lips sink ships.' It means that careless talk can be pieced together and make up enough information that an enemy can learn what you are planning. We need to treat them as spies until they prove otherwise."

"Well said, Sloane. I agree. Now, do you know when to expect them?" Gisele asked.

"Yes, an attendant slipped me a note before we had left the Banking Guild. It said to expect them at the eighth bell."

Cristole gestured to gain Gisele's attention. "I will also speak with Deryk about the potential origins of our spy. We'll look into more after we meet him."

Gisele nodded. "Then let's get to it. We have a few hours to prepare."

Sloane, Gisele, and Ismeld occupied a table in the back of the inn, patiently waiting for their impending rendezvous. The tolling of the eighth bell had marked their anticipated meeting time, and they were primed to encounter whoever might appear.

"So, how long do you think they'll make us wait?" Sloane queried, glancing at her companions.

Ismeld shook her head thoughtfully. "They'll be here shortly. The guard—if we can call him that—is likely checking the area before they approach."

Gisele nudged Sloane subtly. "In fact, look over there. I believe that's them."

Following Gisele's gaze, Sloane observed a male raithe and a female sun elf entering the premises. The elf was darting furtive glances around the room, making no effort to hide her scrutiny. The raithe, on the other hand, was attired impeccably, seeming more befitting of high society than a personal guard. He paused to whisper something in the elf's ear, causing her to abruptly cease her surveying and focus solely on the path ahead.

The spectacle elicited a soft chuckle from Sloane.

She suspected she didn't have to worry overmuch about the elf spying on them, except for maybe on their finances.

However, it could just be an act. Gotta stay vigilant.

Ismeld had barely taken a step forward when the raithe registered her presence. He glanced in her direction, a flicker of recognition illuminating his features. He leaned over to whisper something to the elf before advancing toward them.

Upon reaching the table, the raithe initiated the conversation. "Lady Reinhart of House Reinhart accompanied by Knight-Captain Gisele and Lady d'Argin of the Order of Haven's Hope, I presume?" His tone carried a hint of formality.

Without missing a beat, Ismeld retorted, "Guildmaster's niece and the Guild's spy? Yes, please sit." She gestured toward the vacant chairs across from Sloane and Gisele, before reclaiming her own seat.

The elf was the first to sit, followed by the raithe and finally Ismeld. Once everyone was comfortably settled, the guildmaster's niece broke the silence. "Thank you for granting us this meeting, Lady Reinhart. I am Elodie Romaris, and with me is Stefan Stranca." She gestured to the raithe, who acknowledged with a subtle nod.

"You may call me 'guild spy', as the lady so eloquently identified," Stefan said wryly. "However, that is not my sole function."

"Whether it is or not, it is how we shall treat you. Your presence here is tied to Lady Reinhart's agreement with the guildmaster. We're here to discuss the terms of that arrangement," Gisele stated plainly.

Sloane directed her attention to the elf. "First, let's discuss what you believe you can contribute to the house, Miss Romaris."

Elodie appeared energized by Sloane's question. "Please, call me Elodie, milady. I can oversee your house's finances and protect your interests in any investments you plan to undertake. With my access as part of the Banking Guild, I've taken the liberty of reviewing your contract and your account status. Your agreement with the Farum siblings should provide a decent income stream. While I respect your ambition to expand your holdings, the Farum Merchant Company's business model is still in its nascent stage. However, I believe with your support, their business could expand significantly."

Ismeld interrupted her. "So, you've exploited your position to access confidential information about Lady Reinhart's finances before she even confirmed your position within her house?"

Flustered, Elodie stammered, "B-but, Uncle Lan—I mean, Guildmaster Lanthil assured me I already secured a position in the house. Was he wrong?"

Sloane narrowed her eyes at Elodie's admission, Stefan's dismissive eye roll not going unnoticed. "While I appreciate the guildmaster's support, it doesn't grant me the obligation to accept anyone into my employ without due diligence. You must demonstrate your competence. Your presumption marks your first mistake. Consider this your only warning. I will not accept such behavior from anyone within my service, especially those forced upon me by external parties."

Sloane turned her focus to Stefan, the amusement dancing in his eyes met with a steely gaze. "And you," she began. "You are here as a guard. You will perform that role under the supervision of Ser Gisele or whomever she appoints. However, we both understand that you are here for more than just protective duty. You and I both know you will be collecting information on my house in addition to your primary target. If I discover that any of the information you relay might jeopardize me or my interests in any way, then, regardless of the nature of those interests," she leaned in, lowering her voice to a deadly whisper, "I will end you. Do not fuck with me. I do not care if you are a Blade or not."

Are you an assassin, buddy?

Stefan's eyes widened, and she knew she had guessed right.

Good instincts, Cristole. That could have been embarrassing otherwise.

Having laid down her warning, she sat back, waiting for his response. Stefan seemed to ponder her words, his gaze sweeping the room. When his eyes landed on Deryk, posted near a pillar, and Cristole, standing by the stairs, he visibly registered the situation he was in. Reevaluating Ismeld and Gisele, he conceded to the conclusion they had expected. Stefan positioned his hands on the table, leaning back with a newfound respect.

"Well played, Lady Reinhart. Well played," he acknowledged. He looked at Elodie, sitting next to him, for a few seconds before refocusing on Sloane. With a respectful nod, he said, "It seems I was not as prepared to act as a guard as I had thought. I let my charge distract me from what I know. Allow me to explain my current assignment, and please, let's not bring up my origins again. This is already not good for business."

Sloane nodded and gestured for him to continue.

"My task involves gathering information about Count Kayser and his dealings. Following that, my duty will be to assist you. Should your house align with the guilds, I am to serve as one of the assurances offered to protect that investment. The guilds look out for their own," Stefan explained. What he left unspoken was what his purpose would be if the house's and the guilds' interests did not align.

"Then your job, from now on, is to be the best damn spy in the entire city," said Sloane. "That includes the Order of Secrets." He snorted at this as if there was some joke she wasn't privy to, but a scowl convinced him of her seriousness. "You will relay any and all information that might help further the interests of the Guild, which currently means sharing everything you know with me. I need this information to position you close enough to acquire what you need from the count. His ball is at the end of the week. You must brief me on every detail prior to the event. I need to be prepared for all possibilities."

Stefan nodded his understanding. "I'll provide you with the necessary information."

Sloane scrutinized Elodie and Stefan, her gaze narrowing. However, after a moment of contemplation, she returned her attention to the woman. "You. We need to discuss the finer points of what I plan to introduce to the Banking Guild in Marketbol," she said. "I assume you're informed enough to assist in crafting a strategy for its implementation?"

Elodie quickly nodded. "Indeed, milady. My being a Romaris was, of course, important, but my uncle valued my ability and effectiveness within the Guild significantly. The guildmaster wants you to succeed, not least because it will bolster our family's influence within the guilds and consolidate his position."

"As expected," Sloane acknowledged. "Mister Stranca, please join Ser Gisele to discuss your role within our group further. I wish to speak alone with Miss Romaris."

Gisele and Ismeld stood, and Sloane noted that the raithe was shorter than Ismeld.

Stefan exchanged glances with the women before nodding at Sloane. "Milady, perhaps we can also speak later in a more private setting."

"Of course. I look forward to working with you, Mister Stranca."

As the others walked away, Sloane refocused on the fidgeting woman in front of her.

Elodie was a sun elf about Ernald's height, with curly, dark-brown hair that was pulled back into a tight braid that fell to just below her shoulder blades. Her eyes, a bright yellow-orange rimmed with brown, were filled with unease. She looked as if she'd rather be anywhere else.

Sloane broke the uncomfortable silence. "Elodie, I hope you comprehend my reluctance to place trust in you immediately. Especially given the revelations about your companion."

If Elodie was a six on a scale of nervousness before, now she was a solid nine. "M-milady, I swear, I had no idea that . . ." her voice lowered to a whisper, "he was a Blade. My uncle simply said he'd be my protector."

"I believe you," Sloane reassured her. "What are you aware of regarding my plans?"

Elodie's response was immediate. "Nothing, just that it was potentially revolutionary."

"The guildmaster said this?" Sloane mused. "Interesting. Correct, of course, but still interesting. Yes. We will go more in-depth later, but it has the potential to completely change the financial sector of the entire region. However, given that you've already perused my private accounts, what financial endeavors can my house currently support, based on your understanding?"

Elodie contemplated for a moment before she began outlining the current financial status. "The Guild currently covers the employment costs for both Mister Stranca and me, a responsibility that the house will assume after we leave the city. However, at present, your funds aren't sufficient to acquire any land or a residence befitting your rank. You have enough to sustain yourself and us for approximately seven months, an estimate that will undoubtedly increase as your income source grows. Do you have other pressing needs? The Guild provides certain discounts to its members that I could leverage."

Sloane thought for a moment, retrieving her satchel from the floor and placing it on the table. She took out the nonoperational flashbang prototype and the card. Elodie's attention immediately focused on the one pertaining to her role.

"I do have a few purchases in mind," Sloane said. "I need to acquire light armor and attire for a ball. An expanded wardrobe would be beneficial but isn't critical. Also, I need supplies for crafting . . ."

"May I examine that before we discuss your needs further?" Elodie interrupted, pointing to the card.

Sloane pushed the card toward her, allowing the elf to scrutinize it, her brow furrowed in concentration. Just when Sloane started to grow concerned, Elodie looked up, a sense of awe in her eyes.

"This small thing will revolutionize the Banking Guild?" she asked.

"Yes, it's designed to securely hold account information, allowing updates to balances and statuses anywhere," Sloane explained. "The card features dual-layer security: one implemented by the Banking Guild to safeguard against balance manipulation, and a user-authentication layer to ensure its use is restricted to the account holder."

Elodie's eyes widened in realization. "Incredible. Let's revisit the specifics later, as you suggested. Now, about your needs, the house can manage these purchases. I would like to accompany you during any purchases, if you don't mind. This will allow me to ensure you're getting not only the best prices but also the highest quality goods, given your Ruby Tier status within the Banking Guild."

Sloane nodded her agreement. "That would be helpful, thank you."

The ensuing conversation delved lightly into the house's finances and how Sloane could best utilize them. Elodie seemed to relax considerably when the conversation shifted to economics and trade, and before long, the sun elf appeared as comfortable as if she'd been working with Sloane for months, not a mere hour.

Sloane smirked. *Get people talking about the things they love and they open up.*

CHAPTER NINE

DID YOU ASK HER?

Ser Sabina Dominis, knight in service to House Reinhart, stood patiently in the hallway, awaiting Princess Gwyneth's emergence from her suite.

Emma, the royal's handmaiden, and the other attendants were getting the girl ready for the day, a task Gwyn had finally permitted them to undertake over the past week. Sabina found herself smiling at the girl's fierce independence, a trait that never ceased to amuse her.

Gwyn and other terrans had arrived like a sea storm of disruption that had demanded rapid adjustments to the status quo of society.

Already, Sabina and her fellow knights were doing everything possible to ensure the house was positioned as well as possible to weather the inevitable storm. Avoiding the worst aspects of the Polite War was critical, which is why the majordomo had pressed them into forging ahead with the force of a rogue wave.

The initial days in Strathmore had been a whirl of activity for Sabina and her fellow knights. Their time was filled with meetings and interviews with staff, followed by discussions with various agencies and influential individuals. Plans were already in motion for Gwyn to meet with the daughters of their newly subordinate noble families, to determine if they would join the main house as ladies-in-waiting.

Ser Taenya had placed Sabina in charge of information gathering and control, a role she had embraced with enthusiasm. Her evenings were spent compiling and updating files on personnel and key figures. One such individual was scheduled for a mid-morning meeting with Taenya and Majordomo Siveril Norric.

Siveril had provided Sabina with the names of two potential candidates who could assist the princess in acclimating to Aviran high society. While Gwyn undoubtedly possessed class within her own culture, her knowledge required refinement for the Kingdom of Avira.

Sabina had been able to accomplish only a topical investigation thus far on the two scholars the majordomo had contacted. The brief information she gained pointed to two professors who were both highly accomplished and seemed to be fierce rivals.

She wasn't sure what Siveril had planned.

If the meeting proceeded as anticipated, the princess would have a brief introduction and session with the scholars in the afternoon. Siveril would then arrange a future schedule to accommodate the princess, during which Sabina could meet with Taenya.

She sighed. The pace was more hectic than she had ever imagined.

Can't say I don't enjoy the challenge, though.

Sabina was in her element. She was an excellent judge of character and being placed in a position that leveraged her skills was hugely fulfilling. It was almost as if undertaking this responsibility had honed her instincts. Her intuition had been instrumental in identifying several staff members who intended to sell information about the princess and even Lord Iemes. Sabina swore she could somehow sense people's emotions just by looking at them. It was as if she could interpret their feelings, and when she concentrated, it felt like she could almost read their minds.

It was as Lord Iemes said: *Many will try to exploit the young girl simply because of her title.*

Sabina's thoughts were interrupted by the opening door and the emergence of Gwyn, with Emma trailing closely behind.

That woman is starting to prove her worth. I may have to train her in the use of a dagger soon. She was *very* attentive to the princess' needs. Sabina felt a twinge of guilt for having intimidated her.

As Princess Gwyn noticed her, Sabina greeted her with a warm smile.

"Good morning, Your Highness. How are you on this fine day?" Sabina asked, injecting her voice with an appropriate level of enthusiasm. Her words were slightly strained due to fatigue, but the young girl's optimism and kindness were infectious.

"I'm great, Sabina. How are you?" Gwyn replied.

"I am well. Are you ready for the day? Majordomo Siveril wished to speak with you over breakfast."

"Okay! Let's go."

Sabina smiled and led them to the dining hall.

Ser Siveril Norric sat and watched as the princess conversed with the other . . . *human*, as Gwyn called herself, in a language from their world.

After he'd inquired around his various sources in the city, it seemed that the young girl was the only one to call them that. Others had taken to calling them *terrans*, and it seemed they had appeared everywhere. Most by themselves, but there were even reports of small groups that had materialized together. Siveril knew the duchy was taking a wait-and-see approach based on how the situation developed.

I wonder how the Crown will react. I need to figure that out for the princess's sake.

What he did know was that the terrans had brought with them a diverse array of knowledge and backgrounds, and his people were only beginning to understand the implications. To his knowledge, no one had encountered anyone resembling the description Gwyn had provided of her mother, let alone another royal.

Aside from the man currently speaking with the princess, there were no reports of other nobles. Given Gwyn's unique position as potentially the only terran of high peerage within Avira, she was poised to become a pivotal player in the Game.

The situation had complicated his role significantly since the princess's arrival at what was now House Reinhart. Siveril needed to solidify the house's standing before others attempted to exploit both them and the princess. Fortunately, there had been only one such attempt so far, when a disreputable baron had audaciously proposed a match with the young princess.

Avira was not the barbaric Empire in the northwest or one of the uncivilized kingdoms in the southern part of the continent. Siveril had promptly quashed the proposal and shared the details with his contacts in the ducal court.

House Reinhart needed allies. His first contacts were the guilds and a few houses indebted to him. It certainly helped that while they desired influence, the family heads were simple hangers-on. Siveril knew he could use this to his and House Reinhart's advantage and had arranged a meeting between the princess and three potential ladies-in-waiting in two days' time.

If this man Friedrich was indeed a knight, it would provide even more influence to the house. The princess could vouchsafe such a thing, and he would speak to Ser Sabina about meeting with the man more to determine his goals as he mastered the language.

Siveril had to admit, the man was making impressive progress. In just seven days, his proficiency had improved remarkably. Siveril refocused his attention on the pair as Friedrich attempted to converse in Common.

"I want to thank you for you—your . . . *sacra nochma* . . ." Friedrich paused to collect his thoughts.

Siveril raised an eyebrow at the apparent curse, but chose not to interrupt the man's heartfelt moment.

The terran knight continued, "P-patience and help with me, my lady," he concluded with a respectful bow of his head and a hand over his heart.

The princess, however, was effusive in her response. "*Prego,* Friedrich! You're welcome. You're so nice, and doing really well too."

Siveril watched with a small smirk as Friedrich processed Gwyn's words, then broke into a broad smile. "*Dankeschön! Grazie!*"

Siveril chuckled politely at Friedrich's excitement. Clearing his throat to regain their attention, he addressed the princess. "Your Highness, with your permission, I must meet with a potential tutor for you. Afterward, I will coordinate with Ser Taenya to arrange your meeting with Mister Fenren tomorrow—"

"Oh! I finally get to go see Onas's family tomorrow?" the princess interjected eagerly.

Siveril smiled. The bond she had formed with the merchant would undoubtedly benefit the house, much as it had with Lord Iemes.

"Yes, of course. We've taken care of all the other immediate necessities, and it was only proper to give Mister Fenren time to reunite with his family," he explained.

"I can't wait!"

Taenya found herself deep in thought as she waited in the room Ser Siveril had designated for meetings with potential house members. The space was a cozy sitting area, furnished with four chairs arranged for conversation, each pair flanked by a small table. A telv woman sat at a desk, prepared to transcribe the meeting's notes, while Niles Balfiel, the house's esquire, was stationed at another desk, armed with contracts and other employment documents for joining the house. The high elf was currently engaged in conversation with the majordomo, who had arrived a few minutes earlier.

Joining a house could be achieved in several ways. The most obvious were through birth or marriage. Another method was to become a retainer of the family, a role typically assumed by nobles who would forfeit any benefits or lines of succession from their previous house. This act didn't make them part of the immediate family, but rather distant cousins, complete with the responsibilities and prestige that came with house membership. While retainers could exercise the family's authority, they held none of their own. This method of joining a house was commonly seen among knights sworn to a lord or minor nobles serving a higher peerage.

Lastly, there was fostering. Fostering could be either permanent, or for a set time period, and was usually done if a retainer died and left children behind. A child could not be a retainer, so they could be fostered to a house until the age of majority. Most of these children were eventually adopted into the family.

However, another use of this form of joining a house was for political alliances, and typically only with royals. While marriage was seen as the ultimate way to unite two houses, others could commit a member of their family to cement a political bond. It was a binding of service rather than of matrimony or family—a prospective retainer pledging their fealty and service in return for prestige and support.

Siveril seemed adept at navigating the political intricacies involved in this process, which made sense given what Taenya had learned about him from Sabina. He had once served as an advisor for the duke's house and had joined Lord Iemes as part of a deal made in response to the baron's rapid rise in influence within the duchy. The baron's willingness to release Siveril to House Reinhart indicated a significant bet on the princess.

There was a single knock on the door before it opened and one of the servants stepped in, followed by an older sun elf. Taenya stood and watched as Siveril stepped forward and addressed the man.

"Professor Branigan, it's a pleasure. Please, come in." Siveril reached out and clasped the elf's hand.

"Thank you for having me, Ser Siveril. How have you been? It's been far too long since we last spoke," the professor replied.

Taenya raised an eyebrow at yet another connection Siveril had leveraged.

"I am well! Allow me to introduce Knight-Captain Taenya Shavyre, also of House Reinhart. She is here to ask questions regarding the position. Please," the majordomo gestured to the chairs. "Have a seat. We have some tea prepared. Hopefully, my memory of your tastes is correct!"

"It's a pleasure, Ser Taenya. I'm sure you have the tea correct, Ser Siveril. We both know your memory hasn't dulled." The professor shook Taenya's hand and then moved to the chair next to the servant waiting with his tea.

Taenya heard him whisper appreciative comments to the servant. The sun elf took a sip of his tea, savored it, and then smiled.

"As expected. So, based on the presence of your house's esquire, you're expecting a lot, Siveril," he commented with a small smile.

Taenya raised an eyebrow at their familiarity.

"Of course, Quinn. I believe this is something you'd be interested in," Siveril responded.

"Your message was enticingly . . . vague. Can you explain what you want?" Professor Branigan asked.

Siveril nodded at Taenya, indicating that she should take the lead. She tilted her head in consideration, deciding to start at the beginning.

"What have you heard of recent events concerning the blue flash?"

The sun elf looked at the two of them and sat a bit straighter before responding. "I have heard of the new people who appeared randomly all over the region and beyond, and who are outwardly similar to telv but with round ears. I . . . heard a *rumor* . . . that your new house, Siveril, was established by one."

Taenya glanced at Siveril, who maintained his characteristically composed demeanor. "Yes, the rumor is essentially correct, and it is the reason we have requested you," she said. "We would like for you to join House Reinhart as a tutor for our lady, and to assist other humans—or rather, terrans—in familiarizing themselves with the customs of our kingdom, and society at large."

The old elf's eyes widened, but Siveril spoke before the professor could interject. "We would also primarily like you to serve as the house researcher, compiling information gained from these people for the benefit of the house. There are wonders you can only imagine. As the house grows, so too would your team."

Taenya observed the professor as he leaned back, rubbing his chin. After a couple of minutes, during which they patiently waited for him to consider their proposal, he turned to Siveril. "Did you ask her?"

Taenya was confused. *Ask who?* She focused on Siveril and noticed a slight smile gracing his face.

"I asked you first," he replied.

The professor's smile broadened slightly before he burst into laughter. "Serves her right! I suspect you'll be meeting with her soon?"

Taenya looked at the two Loreni, puzzled. "I'm sorry, who?"

Siveril turned to her with a grin. "Quinn's academic rival. We want them both. She would focus on material research, while the professor here will focus on the people."

Branigan snorted. "I can most certainly perform 'material research' just as well as her."

Taenya rubbed her head. "But . . . who is she?"

The elf professor laughed. "My wife."

Taenya gave the two men a blank stare. "Seriously?"

Siveril laughed. "Yes. They long ago decided that the only way they could ensure one would not sabotage the academic efforts of the other was to get married."

Taenya shook her head, incredulous. "I just . . . I can't. Professor, would you like to discuss the position more in-depth, and then we can get to the contract?"

He nodded. "Yes. That would be lovely. Would I be able to meet the lady of the house today? I'd like to make some initial assessments to ensure I have adequate material for when we begin."

"You've decided?" Siveril asked.

"This sounds like a splendid opportunity, especially if I can write on my findings. Now, what can you tell me about the lady?" Branigan asked.

Siveril looked as if he were about to respond, but Taenya lifted a hand to forestall him. She smiled at the professor. "Allow me to tell you about Princess Gwyneth."

The old elf froze. "Did you say princess? The girl is a royal?"

Siveril's smirk returned, but Taenya continued. "She is. We need you to help prepare her for the Royal Academy and the inevitable meeting with the royal family. Oh, and meeting with the duke and his family in the near future."

Branigan looked up thoughtfully and then turned to his friend. "Siveril, I am absolutely delighted you came to me first. I can't *wait* to see Maya's face."

Taenya slowly shook her head. "That's a meeting I will *not* take part in. Now, Professor, let's discuss the finer details. Ser Siveril?"

Siveril cleared his throat, "So . . ."

The three proceeded to discuss the terms of the professor's joining of the house, and nearly a bell later, the contract had been signed. Afterward, Taenya stepped out to fetch Gwyn.

Things were starting to come together. Gwyn would meet with the professor, and then they would go see her old friend Onas the next day.

First, Taenya needed to speak to Sabina about two more people the burgeoning spy mistress would have to maintain information on.

Taenya navigated the manor's corridors, her mind going down the list of things she needed to do next. The ornate tapestries lining the walls seemed to blur into a riot of colors as she passed, her focus elsewhere.

She needed fresh air, a change of scenery to help her process everything, as she found the manor stuffy. It was why she would often walk through the small gardens on the estate. After asking one of the servants if they knew where Sabina was, the man had told her that the knight was out on the training circle near the small barracks of the House Guard.

Lucky.

Stepping outside, she was greeted by the view of the sprawling estate bathed in the soft glow of the evening sun. The cool air was a welcome relief, carrying with it the scent of the surrounding greenery. She made her way toward the training grounds, where eventually the rhythmic clashing of steel grew louder with each step.

Sabina and Theran were in the center of the grounds, their bodies moving in a deadly dance of steel and skill. Sabina, her raven-black hair tied back and blue eyes focused, moved with a fluid grace that was mesmerizing. Her every move was a blend of agility and power, her sword a blur as she parried and attacked.

Opposite her, Theran, his brown eyes intense and his brunette hair slick with sweat, was a picture of controlled power. His movements were precise, each strike and parry a display of his technical prowess. His sword seemed an extension of his arm, moving with a speed and accuracy that was impressive.

Several groups of house guards watched the spectacle, their eyes following the pair's every move. The air was thick with anticipation, each exchange drawing gasps and cheers from the onlookers.

They're learning from this. Every move, every strike, it's a lesson for them.

The spar was a dance of contrasting styles that showcased their respective skills. Sabina was like water, flowing around Theran's attacks, countering with quick, unpredictable strikes. Theran, on the other hand, was like a mountain, his defense unyielding, his attacks precise and powerful.

Taenya settled in and observed as the match continued, neither giving an inch in a thrilling spectacle that pushed each of them to their limits.

In the end, it was Theran who emerged victorious, his final strike catching Sabina off guard, but it was a close match. Sabina had clearly pushed him and tested his skills to the limit.

Taenya found herself clapping along with the other onlookers, impressed by the display. She enjoyed sparring with the two, and found it amusing how vastly different their three styles were. Compared to the two knights, Taenya's own was more . . . practical in nature. She fought to win, not to impress or fulfill some code.

"Well done, both of you," she praised as the two wiped their faces with towels provided by a guard. Theran thanked her, a modest smile on his face. Turning to Sabina, Taenya asked, "May I have a word with you, Sabina?"

Sabina, still catching her breath, nodded. She and Theran clasped wrists and spoke quietly about their spar, before Theran walked off to the gathering of guards. As he joined them, Taenya could hear him discussing the spar, asking what they would have done better, or explaining how they could learn from it. She was impressed, and gladdened that he was the one in charge of increasing the readiness of their people.

As Taenya walked away with Sabina, she filled her in on the meeting with Quinn Branigan and his upcoming meeting with Gwyn, as well as the appointment with Branigan's wife, Maya Rolfe. She asked Sabina to delve deeper into their backgrounds and expressed her surprise that she had missed the fact that they were married.

"I'm not surprised," Sabina said. "I only managed a cursory look yesterday, and they are very private people outside the realm of academia. The outcome of your meeting was to determine how much further effort would be required."

Taenya nodded. She hadn't been aware that Sabina had already looked into them, but was pleased about her initiative.

Sabina assured her that since Branigan would be joining the house, she would gather more detailed information on him. She also wanted to have regular meetings with Taenya in a more official setting so they could discuss findings and expectations, but also mentioned that she would need more help soon. Taenya agreed wholeheartedly and was glad for the suggestion.

"I have an idea on that," Taenya said. "But give me some time to think about it more and to determine the feasibility. It will affect all three of us."

She meant the three knights. Her current idea involved not only increasing their numbers but also creating specialized teams assigned to each of the three knights for support. These wouldn't be squires exactly, but skilled men-at-arms.

Eventually, Sir Friedrich would integrate fully, but for now she wanted him to focus on learning the culture and norms of Avira. She envisioned him following a path more akin to Siveril's, a civil position rather than a martial knight role like hers and that of the others.

Sabina agreed to her plans and promised to provide an update on the scholars as soon as she had one. Taenya was well aware that Sabina needed help, and she was surprised to see the woman not showing signs of fatigue, despite hearing from several servants that she had been out late the previous night.

If she can give so much effort, so can I.

She advised Sabina to rest after cleaning up. Sabina reluctantly agreed after Taenya assured her that she had everything under control.

As they parted ways, Taenya found herself looking forward to the challenges ahead. A sense of satisfaction began to settle within her.

Things are starting to come together.

CHAPTER TEN

WORDS ARE POWER

G wyn followed Taenya into one of the house's offices. It was a spacious room, featuring a large bookshelf that spanned an entire wall. An older sun elf with dark skin sat at a table on the left with a notebook and various books in front of him. Cabinets lined the wall opposite the bookshelf, while a small fireplace with two chairs in front of it occupied the right side of the room. However, the room's most prominent feature was the large desk situated at the rear.

Upon their entrance, the old man rose to his feet, and Emma positioned herself quietly by the door. Gwyn flashed a smile at her.

I like her.

Gwyn's attention returned to the room, her eyes widening as she realized Taenya had stopped. She narrowly avoided colliding with her, grimacing in embarrassment at her distraction.

Taenya, smirking slightly, stepped aside before introducing her. "Professor, allow me to introduce Her Royal Highness, Princess Gwyneth Reinhart."

Gwyn looked up at the elf, who offered her a small bow. "Your Highness, it is a pleasure to meet you. I am Scholar Quinn Branigan, formerly a professor at the Strathmore branch of the Royal Academy," he said. He paused for a moment, then added, "I will technically still be a professor, but I will be taking an extended leave of absence to assist you and your house."

Gwyn tilted her head slightly, giving a small nod as she and Siveril had practiced. "Good afternoon, Professor Branigan."

"Please, join me," he said, with a gesture to the chair across from him. "Would you like some tea, Your Highness?"

Gwyn nodded and took a seat at the table. "Please, thank you. I'm Gwyn."

His eyes crinkled in amusement, almost as if she had said the right things. He nodded in approval. "Of course, Miss Gwyn. This is appropriate when we're in a session or place of learning."

Taenya gave her a small nod and excused herself from the room. Gwyn noticed Emma still standing by the door. "Emma?"

The high elf handmaiden instantly moved forward. "Yes, Your Highness? Do you need something?"

Gwyn looked at the professor. "Will we be here long?"

He nodded approvingly. "We will be here for one bell."

Gwyn returned the nod and turned her attention back to her handmaiden. "Emma, please sit down so you don't have to stand the whole time. That's too long!"

"Your Highness, it's quite alright, I—"

"Please?" Gwyn interrupted, causing the woman to start slightly.

Defeated, Emma replied, "Yes, Your Highness."

Gwyn smiled as her handmaiden moved to sit in the chair in front of the fireplace. Emma still maintained her formal posture, hands crossed in her lap, keeping a watchful eye on Gwyn.

I can live with that. At least she's comfy.

She turned back to the sun elf professor and watched as he poured her tea and opened a small pitcher. He used tiny tongs to pick up some white cubes. "Sugar?"

Gwyn smiled. "Please, Mister Branigan. Only one."

After preparing the tea for both of them, the elderly elf opened the notebook on the table next to him and folded his hands together.

Gwyn, meanwhile, reached for her tea and gently stirred the sugar until it dissolved, steam wafting up from the cup. She hesitated for a moment, then subtly channeled her blue magic, directing it to cool the beverage just enough to make it more enjoyable.

She took a careful sip, her eyes lighting up at the taste. "This is quite delicious, Mister Branigan."

He looked pleased. "I'm glad you enjoy it. It's from the Lymtoria Republic, a particular brand favored by their aristocracy. I always bring it with me to initial meetings such as this. I find that sharing tea with a potential pupil is more telling than any other method in determining compatibility."

As he reached for his own cup, he paused, pulling his hand back as the heat of the tea seeped through the porcelain. He looked at Gwyn, a hint of confusion in his eyes as he noticed she was unaffected by the temperature.

Gwyn hid a small smile, pleased with her subtle use of magic. She had to remember Taenya's advice about not revealing her abilities unnecessarily, but in this case, it had made her tea-drinking experience much more enjoyable.

"Now, Miss Gwyn," he said, as she held her cup with two hands. "Allow me to tell you a little about myself." He chuckled, his eyes twinkling with the memories of his past. "I am originally from the Kingdom of Rosale, but I moved to Avira and joined the Royal Academy in the capital many years ago. I had a passion for learning and discovering new things, which eventually turned into a passion for teaching."

He took a sip of his cooling tea, his gaze distant as he reminisced. "The scholarly field can be quite cutthroat, you know. In fact, my rival once tried to steal something from me at knife point. Of course, I had stolen it from her first. All's fair in love and war, as they say."

Gwyn's eyes went wide. "What happened after that?"

Mister Branigan smiled. "It grew into a grand game, and we both enjoyed it immensely. We would often choose to go on academic excursions to other nations or explore old ruins, just to ensure the other wouldn't gain more prestige. Ours was a rivalry for the ages. She would publish something that would garner her accolades and then rub it in my face, and then I would finish my work soon after just to revel in her scowls. We went back and forth like this for ten years, trying to sabotage each other in a way that wouldn't actually ruin any of each other's hard work."

He chuckled, his eyes sparkling with amusement. "I remember one time I had written the results of a particularly difficult excursion, and well . . . I didn't realize that she had slipped a page into it. When our director reviewed it in front of all of us . . . he found the picture she had drawn."

Gwyn tilted her head, curiosity piqued. "What was the picture of?"

A blush creeped up the professor's cheeks. "N-nothing. Needless to say, it was childish, and the director finally reached his limit. He assigned us to another excursion that brought us to the Duchy of Tiloral and demanded we not return until we figured it out. Well, we came to an agreement there. Eventually, I was transferred to Strathmore, which is when I first met Ser Siveril Norric. "

"What was the agreement?" Gwyn asked.

Mister Branigan chuckled again, shaking his head. "That's a story for another time, Miss Gwyn. For now, since you know a bit more about me, and if you are amenable to it," he began, "I would also like to learn more about you so that I may assess how I can best assist your learning. Could you tell me a little about yourself and where you come from?"

"Of course!"

He asked her about her life in Italy, her mom, school, friends, and interests. She told him about her love of art and history, her fascination with the ancient ruins scattered around Italy, and her passion for pasta and gelato.

I miss gelato.

The professor paused in his notetaking. "And your father?" he asked gently.

Gwyn's smile faltered slightly. "He . . . he died when I was little. I didn't really know him."

"I see," he said, his voice soft. "I'm sorry for your loss, Miss Gwyn."

She shrugged, a small smile returning to her face. "It's okay. Mom has always been there for me. She's the best."

The professor nodded, scribbling something in his notebook before changing the focus. "And how are you finding the adjustment to an entirely different culture?"

Gwyn thought for a moment before answering. "It's not too bad. I mean, I moved from Michigan to Italy when I was little, so I'm used to big changes. But this . . . this is different. Everything is so . . . old."

"Old?" he asked, tilting his head slightly.

"Yeah," she said, struggling to find the right words. "Like, back home, we have cars and computers and stuff. Here, it's more like . . . like the old days, you know? Like in the history books from like a thousand years ago."

The professor's eyes widened slightly, a spark of interest flickering in his gaze. "Fascinating," he murmured, jotting down more notes.

Throughout their conversation, Gwyn was struck by the professor's kindness and intelligence. He listened attentively, asked insightful questions, and seemed genuinely interested in her experiences. It was clear to her that he was a scholar through and through, his curiosity and thirst for knowledge evident in every word he spoke.

She watched as he wrote notes about the things she said. After they'd talked back and forth for a while, he held up a hand and paused for a moment. His eyes darted back and forth over his notebook for a minute before he looked up and asked, "Miss Gwyn, you speak another language, correct?"

"Yes. I speak Italian. Why?"

"Can you write it?"

"*Si*. I mean, yes . . ."

Mister Branigan grabbed another notebook he had and placed it in front of her with one of the feather pens everyone seemed to like using.

He tapped the page. "Please write a sentence in Italian."

"Oh, okay." She picked up the quill, examining the ornate metal nib at the end, before lightly dipping it into the inkwell. With *careful* strokes, Gwyn wrote out her sentence in Italian: *Io amo scuola e la mia materia preferita è la scienze!* Upon finishing, she set down the quill and turned the notebook back toward the professor.

"Thank you, Miss Gwyn," he said, studying her handwriting. He squinted at the sentence, looked up at her, and went back to the notebook.

"Hmm. This is fascinating. Now, could you write the same sentence in . . . what do you call the language your people use for what we refer to as Common?"

"English."

"Perfect. Please write the same sentence in English."

Gwyn took back the notebook and carefully scribbled out: *I love school and my favorite subject is science!*

She watched as he compared the two sentences. "Fascinating. Not only do you know two languages, but you also know two entirely different alphabets. One for Common and one for Italian."

Gwyn tilted her head in confusion. "What do you mean?"

The professor paused, glancing back down at the notebook and then at Gwyn. "Do these two look the same to you? The letters?"

Gwyn looked down. "Um . . . yes?" *Is there something wrong with me?* She looked back down at the notebook, her eyes darting over it until she was interrupted by him turning it to face her again.

"Write one more thing for me. Please write the English alphabet as you know it. Take your time and *think* about it."

She slowly picked up the pen and started writing the alphabet. *A-B-C-D-E-F . . .*

Gwyn said each one in her head as she wrote. When she finished, she looked back up. "Done."

The sun elf looked over her work, his poofy eyebrows scrunched up in thought, and began tapping his finger against the table, causing Gwyn to worry even more.

"Is everything okay?" she asked hesitantly.

He looked up and pointed at what she wrote. "This is the English alphabet?"

"Yes. It's also the Italian one. They're the same, just pronounced differently. Oh, and in a different order."

"Does this look the same as the sentence you wrote in English?"

She looked back and forth, then had an idea. She *reached* for her magic, trying to use it to help her. *I need to focus! Come on, magic!*

Slowly, she felt her magic swirl around in her head, as it had only a few times before. It made her thoughts really clear, and Gwyn **[Focused]** on the letters. She gasped, as suddenly, the words looked completely *wrong* to her. "Th-that's not English. Why did I write that?"

Gwyn still knew what they meant, but she could definitely tell they were completely different letters. *That is so weird.* Her head started to get a bit stuffier, so she let go of her magic and allowed it to settle back inside her.

Almost instantly, the letters looked correct again.

What? "They look fine again!" she exclaimed.

The sun elf sat back, rubbing his chin thoughtfully. "This is fascinating. I have one more thing I would like to try. I am going to write a sentence in the language of my people. It is called Stel'loreni."

She watched as he wrote a sentence in pretty, flowing letters that looked nothing like any language she had seen back home. His handwriting was perfect, and she thought it looked almost as if he had used a computer and printed it.

When he was finished, he rotated the notebook and showed her the sentence.

"Wow, that's beautiful, Mister Branigan! What does it say?" she asked.

The professor snorted. "I guess that explains whether or not you can read a language other than Common. So, I suppose the phenomenon that brought you here allowed only for the translation of the predominant bridge language— which, I presume, is the role English filled within your world?"

She shrugged. *I have no idea what that means.*

He smiled, then took on a look of concentration again. He looked up at the door, then paused, glancing at Emma. Leaning toward Gwyn, Mister Branigan quietly asked, "I was told that you have certain . . . abilities. Could you explain them to me?"

Do I tell him? Taenya told me—actually . . .

Gwyn looked at Emma, who noticed the attention and stood. "Yes, Your Highness?"

"Could you please go get Taenya? Actually, maybe Sabina. Whoever isn't busy. I don't think Sabina is doing anything right now. Taenya said she had some stuff to do."

Emma nodded. "Of course, Your Highness. I will go retrieve one of them for you."

Gwyn watched as she left the room. *Either of them will be able to cover for me if this goes bad.*

She turned back to the old elf, meeting his orange eyes, which were filled with a knowing look she had often seen in her mother and others.

I think Mom called it . . . cursed with knowledge. Whatever that means.

Feeling a spark of mischief, Gwyn smirked, then called to her magic, channeling it to bring fire to her eyes.

The sun elf's eyes widened in surprise, but he quickly regained his composure and leaned forward. "Your eyes. How?" he asked, his voice filled with curiosity.

Gwyn fixed him with a look as serious as she could muster. "Magic," she stated simply.

"What else can it do?" He leaned in closer, his interest clearly piqued.

She pondered how to respond. With a slow nod, she replied, "It's everywhere around us. It sings to me. The magic shows me how to do the things that I want. Like the letters." She gestured toward the notebook. "I wanted to understand what you meant, so magic helped me [**Focus**]. It also helps me protect people. Like this."

She lifted her fist and opened it, the fire coalescing into a ball.

A tiny sun.

* * *

Quinn Branigan was captivated by the miniature sun hovering over the young girl's hand. The princess had summoned the celestial body that was the namesake of his people with a mere thought. For the first time in many years, Quinn found himself speechless.

He peered into the fiery irises of the girl who must surely be Alos's Chosen and saw an intensity that hadn't been there before.

Just as he was beginning to regain his composure and find his voice, the young terran did something that completely shattered his previous assumptions.

He watched in awe as her eyes transformed into an icy blue, appearing as though they were filled with mist. The radiant sun hovering over her hand was gradually consumed by ice until the fire was extinguished and a small frozen solid sphere fell into the girl's hand.

With a mischievous smirk, Princess Gwyn held it out to him.

Flabbergasted, he reached out and allowed her to place it in his hand. Instantly, he dropped it due to its intense coldness.

"H-how?" he stammered.

"I told you. Magic sings to me, and I listen," she declared with a sense of finality.

Quinn pondered what he had just witnessed, considering how it related to everything that was happening in the world.

She knows exactly what she's doing.

His thoughts were interrupted by the door opening. Ser Taenya entered, with the servant, Emma, trailing closely behind. Emma positioned herself next to the door, ready to assist her mistress. Taenya approached the table and immediately frowned at the sphere lying on the floor.

Ser Taenya regarded the princess with the expression of a disappointed mother, not a retainer. Quinn raised an eyebrow as she sighed and placed her hand on her hip.

"Gwyn. What did we discuss?"

Quinn observed the princess's reaction and was pleasantly surprised to see her looking suitably chastised. "Not to show off my magic to others we've just met. I'm sorry, Taenya. I thought it would be okay, and I wanted to ask you first. That's why I asked Emma to get you or Sabina. I just . . . um . . . got excited."

Taenya's face softened, and she placed a hand on the girl's shoulder. "It's okay this time, Gwyn. We informed Professor Branigan of the circumstances and the need to maintain secrecy." Quinn's eyes narrowed slightly as the knight gave him a pointed look.

I can take a hint, young lady.

He looked at the two of them. "Of course, my ladies. I won't tell a soul. However, I've had some time to think. Ser Taenya, with you here, perhaps your insight will be beneficial. Could you please sit with us for a moment?"

"Certainly."

After she sat down, he collected his thoughts and asked, "Ser Taenya, how long after the Flash did it take for you to meet Miss Gwyn?"

The telv looked up for a moment as she considered. "Not more than a quarter bell."

He nodded. "Now, for both of you. Was there any misunderstanding in your conversation with each other?"

The girl shook her head slightly. "I don't remember. I was really upset. My mom was not there."

Taenya, on the other hand, was nodding. "I recall not being able to understand Gwyn immediately. I initially thought that it was because she was upset, and after learning she could speak another language, I considered that maybe she was just mixing the two."

Quinn nodded along and made notes. As he tapped the top corner of the page, a habit he had when deep in thought, he tilted his head and lifted the quill. The ink had spread, creating a circular blotch. He recalled something the princess had mentioned earlier—that magic was all around them.

"Gwyn, you said the magic is everywhere. It helps you. It also seems to be aiding you in reading and even writing in Common," he said, then turned his attention to Taenya. "Do you think the magic is assisting her spoken language as well? Also, you've been near her since the Flash. Have you felt any different?"

Taenya seemed to fidget. "I . . . have. But I didn't know what it was. I will reflect more on this, and maybe we can discuss it another time."

She paused, then redirected the conversation. "You said magic is helping her with our language?"

Quinn nodded, understanding that the telv knight would seek him out when she was ready. "Yes. I observed her writing two different sentences and not being able to distinguish between them until I had her physically write out each letter used in the alphabet of her people's English and Italian."

Taenya crossed her arms. "But why wouldn't it help Friedrich? Or why doesn't it translate Italian?"

Quinn pondered the various reasons and settled on one that seemed plausible. "The trade language of Ikios, known as Common, is designed to be widespread and used by everyone. Perhaps English serves the same function among her people? There have been instances of terrans appearing all over the region. Even Friedrich knows some English. Perhaps . . . it was simply the most common language among those who were transported to Eona."

"Poor Friedrich," Gwyn murmured, her lips pursed in a sad expression.

Taenya looked at her. "Why's that?"

"He was brought here, and the magic didn't even help him communicate with us. He must be so scared and confused right now. He doesn't have any family. At least I know my mom is out there somewhere."

Quinn smiled, feeling increasingly confident in his decision to join this young girl. He exchanged a glance with Taenya, not wanting to bring up anything about the girl's mother.

That is a hope that cannot die.

He'd seen it before in many. It would crush her, and she wouldn't be the same person afterward. He looked at her and gently patted her small hand. "At least he has someone as caring and protective as you to assist him."

Taenya nodded and pulled Gwyn into a comforting hug. "Professor Branigan is right. You are remarkable. Your mother is going to be so proud of you."

Gwyn offered a small smile, though she didn't seem entirely convinced. "Thanks. I really do need to help him more. Mister Branigan? Could you assist him in learning too? Now that you've explained it, I think you may be right. I believe the magic is aiding him in learning . . . Common."

"I will certainly help him. I believe this is the beginning of a wonderful opportunity," Quinn replied, aiming to reassure the young princess.

He took a deep breath. *Maya, I may need your help more than I first thought.*

His wife was never going to let him live this down.

CHAPTER ELEVEN

WAKING UP AND CHOOSING VIOLENCE

O nas Fenren stood at the counter in his store while his daughter Kerala engaged in a lively discussion with several staff members. He should have been paying attention, but his thoughts were elsewhere.

The past week and a half had been filled with family time and handling the aftermath of Raafe's death. Raafe's remains had arrived in Strathmore before Onas had, leaving him to meet with the deceased guard's family. They were understandably upset, but the time between arrivals had allowed the most acute grief to subside. Onas had managed to speak with an aunt and hand over Raafe's remaining effects, but she kept insisting that Raafe's family was gone. The woman seemed to be grappling with her own issues, so Onas didn't press further.

Later, Taenya had approached him about arranging a visit for Princess Gwyn to meet his family and see him again. Apparently, the young princess had been asking about him. He had to admit, he missed the girl.

With a sigh, Onas refocused on the conversation his daughter was having, earning a mild glare from her before she turned back to the man she was speaking to.

"So, Ricard, I need you to meet with the Smithing Guild. We fulfilled their purchase request, but there were some errors in the funding approval," Kerala explained, handing over documents to one of the company's esquires. "Essentially, they didn't specify any quantities for the items we purchased, nor did they attach the required ducal forms. These are the documents from the approved purchase request. Miss Sheya over at the Guild is the contact."

Onas watched as his daughter navigated one of the company's common issues—documentation. The Artisan Guilds facilitated purchasing for all their affiliated tradesmen—in this case, blacksmiths. Unfortunately, these guilds were often short-staffed, leading to numerous administrative errors.

After Ricard left, Onas turned to leave, but Kerala placed a hand on his shoulder, turning him back to face her. "Father . . . you weren't paying attention at all, were you?"

"You did wonderfully, my dear," he reassured her.

She sighed. "Come on, what's got you distracted? Is it because Taenya is coming over today?"

"How did you know she was coming?" Onas asked, his eyes narrowing in surprise.

"Dad, you know I have been taking a larger role here." Kerala replied, rolling her eyes. "Gods, you gave it to me, remember. Not that I'm complaining, but knowing when we're getting important clients is *literally* my job now."

Onas groaned. "Of course, you're right. You really have been doing wonderfully. And yes, Taenya is bringing the princess today. Admittedly, I am a tad nervous."

He felt hands slip around his waist and turned to see his wife peeking around from behind him. "Why would you be nervous, my love?" she asked. "She's just a child, and from what you've told me, I think everyone is going to love her."

"Mother is correct," Kerala said. "Plus, it's Taenya. We all know her. There's nothing to be nervous about. Well, except maybe Kalen embarrassing us."

"Kerala, your brother will be fine. Be nice," his wife gently admonished as she came up beside him.

Onas smiled. "Of course, you are both right. Kerala, speaking of your brother, could you please go retrieve him, and your other one?"

Kerala looked at each of her parents and sighed. "I'll get them." She turned to a staff member at the other end of the counter. "Jasmin, I'm stepping out for a bit. Can you cover the counter, please?"

"Sure, Miss Kerala! I'll handle everything," the short sun elf responded.

Their daughter gone, Onas's wife looked up at him. She peered into his eyes and raised an eyebrow. "Onas. Let's go somewhere private."

He sighed, but let his wife lead him to his office. Onas shut the door behind them as they entered and took naught two steps before his wife rounded on him.

Talani studied her husband, her turquoise eyes softening. "Onas, how are you really doing?" she asked, her voice gentle. "I know you've lost guards before, but this . . . this seems different."

Onas moved to pour two glasses of liquor, then guided his wife to a pair of chairs. She accepted the glass he offered and sat, her eyes never leaving him.

He sighed, his gaze falling to the amber liquid in his glass. "I'm managing as well as can be expected, my love," he admitted. "Raafe was so young, full of hopes and dreams. He was training the princess in swordsmanship, and she was a natural. Took to it like a fish to water, that one. It's hard not to dwell on what could have been."

He paused, his fingers tracing the rim of his glass. "I met with an aunt of his, whom I honestly believe may have actually been just a family friend. She was evasive about his family, and I think . . . I think something happened to them. Raafe never mentioned anything, so I'm not sure."

Talani's brow furrowed in concern. "Are you going to search for them?" she asked.

Onas shrugged, a weary sigh escaping him. "I'm not even sure where to start. I've done what I can, but if I hear anything, I won't ignore it."

Talani nodded, her hand reaching out to cover his. She took a deep breath. "Onas," she began, her voice again steady and sure. "It's time you told me what's going on with this princess and why you and Varciel are so interested in her. I've been patient, but there's something you're not telling me."

Onas shared a long look with her that held more emotion and thoughts than could be expressed by mere words. He could see that Talani was barely containing her pent-up frustrations. He couldn't keep her in the dark any longer. She deserved to know the truth—the whole truth.

He took a deep breath and proceeded to tell her everything about Gwyn. He started with how the girl had arrived, and how Gwyn had saved them after Raafe died. He told her about Gwyn's unique abilities, and the profound impact the girl had already had on their lives.

As he finished speaking, his wife drained her glass, rose, and poured herself another. She stood before him and asked, "So, this girl is capable of casting magic, and you believe magic is going to become a reality?" She shook her head. "How does this affect us?"

Onas went to his desk, retrieved a key, and unlocked a drawer. He inhaled deeply and pulled out a small case.

"Onas?" his wife queried, her tone laced with curiosity and a hint of concern.

"This is how," he responded, opening the case and turning it around to reveal its contents. Inside were glowing orbs that immediately caught Talani's attention. Her breath hitched, and she looked up at him.

"What are those, Onas?" she asked in a low voice, almost whispering as the glow lit their faces.

"*These* are from animals. One of our agents purchased them from a local hunter. They emit a feeling, a certain . . . energy. I've had some experts look at them. One of them was able to use the orb to cast magic as Gwyn can. However . . ."

He retrieved another case from the same drawer and opened it. Inside was a larger orb, glowing with a swirling yellow mist. He took another deep breath.

"This one . . . this one came from a telv who was injured. It was discovered during an attempt to save his life. The surgeon removed it, and the man died instantly."

Talani gasped audibly. "Onas, why do you have this?"

"The duke asked me to use my connections to investigate it. He has more."

His wife stood aghast. "Why? Did he desecrate bodies?"

Onas sighed. "He needed to know. I am told the bodies were chosen carefully. There were experts from the Royal Academy and priests of Relena on hand to ensure everything was done properly and with respect. They believe it's widespread and that the Flash is what caused it. There have been tests . . . No one else has been found to utilize magic naturally yet. Certainly not like Princess Gwyn. However, there seem to have been physical improvements. The Scholars theorize that most changes are physical rather than magical in nature."

"Naturally?" she echoed.

He nodded. "The orbs allowed a few individuals to use weak magic. Those who were found were invited to the Royal Academy for further research. One woman in particular was already a scholar, and made some sort of shimmering barrier made of magic."

"Then why—" Talani shook her head, a strand of hair falling in front of her eye. She brushed it away. "Why does the duke need *your* connections?"

"I have connections throughout Meris, some in Lymtoria, and even Lehelia. You know this. I can have our people interact more discreetly than any official means," Onas explained.

His wife scrunched her nose up and raised a hand. "But that still doesn't explain the princess. How does she figure into this? Does the duke know you have made our family and business beholden to a foreign royal?"

He let out a heavy breath, feeling a bit exasperated. "Of course he knows, Tali. But the princess? She's something else. She allows our family to expand outside of this small part of the kingdom. The company can expand throughout the entirety of the kingdom, and I can do it without resorting to immoral means. The princess is at the forefront of this new magical world we live in. She can do things that *no one* else can right now. Varciel and I are betting that her influence will catapult her to a level that a mere baron and merchant would never even hope to reach."

The disappointment on his wife's face made him hesitate. "So it's just about greed? It's not about the girl? A girl who lost her mother? Have you even looked into where her mother could be? Or did you leave that to Taenya? Are you only riding the coattails of a child because of what she can do for you?"

"No—Ta—no, of course not. I decided to help her before I knew of the potential," he stammered, trying to defend himself.

His wife scoffed. "It sure sounds like it, Onas. That girl is not a tool, because

Alos knows everyone else is going to be trying to use her as a puppet for influence." Talani stepped forward and jabbed a finger into his chest. "You need to sort this out. We're tied to this girl now, and I swear to Tenera, Onas Fenren, that there will be a *reckoning* if you attempt to use her for your own gain."

"Tali—"

"Do. Not. Tali. Me. That girl will be here soon. You will get your shit together. We will welcome her, and we will treat her as if she were our own child. We will help her as if she were our own child. *Any* benefit you gain will be a result of her own free will. Do you hear me?"

"Yes."

"I'm sorry?" she pressed.

Onas sighed and leaned back against his desk, running his hand through his hair. "Yes. You're right. I-I let my excitement cloud my judgment."

"That had better be all it was. Now, you're not a bad man, my love. You've made a mistake. You're going to rectify it."

"Yes, dear."

His wife smiled. However, it did not look pleasant and did not rise to her eyes. "Speaking of, dear, we have enough employees—hundreds, in fact. You should not be going on your nostalgic routes each year. Clearly, they are too dangerous. Perhaps you need to be here preparing *our* business for all the changes you say are coming. Oh, and use all these *connections*, that *we* know about, to locate this girl's mother."

Onas took a deep breath, then responded, "Yes, dear."

Talani perked up. "Good! Now, come help me prepare for the princess's arrival."

"Let me put everything back up. I'll be right there," he told his wife.

"Good. I'll see you shortly." Talani patted his cheek gently, then added, "We will talk more of magic and Eona-shattering revelations later, and why you've kept them from me, your partner in life and business."

Perhaps Onas hadn't thought everything through as thoroughly as he should have.

Gwyn was excited. She and Taenya were in a carriage on the way to Mister Onas's shop. She glued her eyes to the window next to her, taking in all the sights of the bustling city. There were so many elves and telv going about their day in the streets and on the sidewalks. The buildings, all so much different from back home, were made of stone, and most had vines or other decorations on them. She thought it looked like something straight out of a movie.

"Gwyn?" Taenya's voice interrupted her thoughts. "What are you thinking about?"

"Huh? Oh, just about how pretty the city is. It's *so* much different from back home. Are we almost there?"

Her knight smiled and nodded. "Yes, we're almost there. The guards will stay outside, but you, me, and Keston will all go in to meet Onas and his family."

Gwyn nodded, her mind already anticipating the meeting. Sabina and Theran had stayed back at the house, busy with other things they had going on. However, the more she thought about it, the more it seemed as if Theran was *always* busy. She barely got time to talk to him since he was constantly working with the guards and going out to look for more people to hire for their house.

Maybe I can get him to teach me how to use Raafe's sword.

As the carriage rolled through the city streets, Gwyn's gaze remained fixed on the outside world. They eventually entered a plaza, where a large building dominated one side. A steady stream of people flowed in and out of the grand doors at the front. The building was impressive, with five large columns supporting the front facade. Above them, in big letters, was "Fenren Trading House."

In the Common alphabet. That's still so weird.

The carriage came to a halt, and one of the guards, Liam, stepped up to open the door. Gwyn smiled at Taenya, who gestured for her to exit. As she descended the carriage steps with Liam's assistance, she spotted Keston standing off to the side.

"Thank you, Liam," Gwyn said, offering him a warm smile.

"My pleasure, Your Highness," the elf replied, returning her smile with a nod.

Gwyn waved at Keston. "Keston! Are you ready? Excited? We haven't seen Mister Onas in so long. It feels like ages."

Her cooking partner laughed. "It's only been a week and a half! But, yeah, I'm excited," Keston chuckled.

Taenya stepped up next to Gwyn. "Let's go, you two."

Gwyn followed them toward the doors, where two telv guards in what Sabina had referred to as light armor stood watch.

They don't look nearly as cool as my guards.

One of the telv opened the door and gave Taenya a bow.

Wait. That was for me. Crap.

Gwyn quickly turned to the man and offered him a nod and smile, which he returned with a warm grin of his own. "Welcome to Fenren Trading House, Your Highness," he said.

"Thank you!" Gwyn replied, her voice filled with enthusiasm.

As they stepped through the door, Gwyn's eyes widened at the sight of the interior. It was impressive, to say the least.

If my whistle didn't sound like a dying bird, I would definitely whistle right now. Nice job, Mister Onas.

Inside were tables and displays showcasing a variety of items. There were glass cases filled with fancy plates and glassware, and a central area that had a big case and a counter filled with jewelry.

Oh, my gosh. It's like the fancy stores from Milan back home, but bigger.

At the back of the room, a long counter seemed to be the hub of business discussions. A spiral staircase to her right led to a second floor, where she could just make out what appeared to be bookshelves filled with books.

Gwyn's mind was already racing with possibilities. She loved shopping for new things—they would absolutely have to shop when they were done.

Oh! Maybe they have art supplies! I love drawing!

She was so engrossed in her surroundings that she didn't notice Mister Onas and his family approaching until Taenya nudged her.

Turning her attention to the family, Gwyn offered them a warm smile. Mister Onas had a big family. His wife, a beautiful high elf with blond hair, had linked her arm through his. His children, whom he had mentioned before, were a diverse trio, but they didn't really look like kids. Well, one did.

The youngest one looked *maybe* a little bit older than her. He also looked like he did *not* want to be there. The oldest had dark hair and bore a striking resemblance to her dad. She was also ridiculously pretty. The middle child was a boy who, funnily, looked just like his mom. He even had long hair pulled up into a bun.

Ha! A man bun, like Aunt Katie's boyfriend.

"Princess Gwyn! It is a pleasure to have you here. We are so happy you could visit us. Taenya, Keston. It's good to see you both," Mister Onas greeted, his smile welcoming.

"Thanks, Mister Onas!" Gwyn replied, her smile mirroring his own. Taenya and Keston also exchanged greetings with their former boss.

Mister Onas then stepped forward, placing a hand on his wife's shoulder. "Allow me to introduce my family. This is my lovely wife, Talani." He gestured toward the elegant high elf woman standing beside him. Her blond hair was neatly arranged, and her turquoise eyes sparkled with warmth as she curtseyed to Gwyn.

Her eyes are so pretty.

"Your Highness, it's a pleasure to meet you," Talani greeted, her voice soft yet firm. "My husband has spoken highly of you."

Gwyn acknowledged her formal address with a gentle incline of her head, as expected. "Thank you, Missus Talani. I have to say, your eyes are so pretty! My people don't have eyes your color."

Talani Fenren blushed mightily at that and quickly thanked Gwyn for her kindness.

Mister Onas, turned to his daughter. "This is Kerala, my oldest," he introduced. Kerala stepped forward, her eyes reflecting a mix of curiosity and respect.

"Your Highness," Kerala greeted, offering a slight bow. "I've heard so much about you, and how impressive you are. I cannot wait to work with you. It's an honor to meet you."

Gwyn blushed slightly at the compliment, but quickly regained her composure. "Thank you, Kerala. I'm happy to meet you too."

Mister Onas gestured to his older son, who seemed the most excited of the three at meeting her. "This is Relas," he said.

Relas stepped forward, his eyes meeting Gwyn's with a friendly sparkle. "Your Highness," he greeted, his voice carrying a hint of excitement. "It's a pleasure to meet you. Our father has spoken of your adventure since arriving, and I must say it sounds fascinating. I wish I could have been there, and I can't wait to hear about it from you."

Gwyn laughed, her eyes twinkling with delight. "Thank you, Relas. I'm sure we'll have lots to talk about."

Finally, Mister Onas gestured to a younger boy with blond hair like his mother's, but with blue eyes that mirrored his own and Kerala's. "And this is our youngest, Kalen," he introduced.

However, despite the nudging from his brother, Kalen remained silent, offering only a shy nod in greeting. Gwyn chose to ignore the slight awkwardness, her excitement undiminished.

For her part, she was excited. She had hoped to make more friends around her age. "I'm so happy to meet all of you! Mister Onas talked *so* much about you—"

"Mother, do I even need to be here? It's boring, and I don't want to meet her," Kalen interrupted with a frown on his face.

Onas and the rest of his family froze. Gwyn's eyes shot wide.

What was it that Aunt Katie would say all the time that irritated Mom? Oh yeah . . .

Gwyn placed a hand on her hip, and with a scowl, addressed the rude boy.

"*Excuse me*, kid? Are you courting death?"

CHAPTER TWELVE

HOPEFUL MEETINGS

T aenya winced inwardly at Gwyn's words. She took a deep breath, schooling her features into a neutral expression as she turned to regard the
young girl beside her. *Are all ten-year-olds like this?*

Are you courting death? The phrase echoed in her mind, and she had to suppress a grimace. *What even is that?* It was a rather dramatic turn of phrase, and she
hoped that it wasn't common where the princess was from. Taenya decided then
and there that she would need to have a serious discussion with Gwyn about the
appropriate ways to express herself in public.

Definitely, something for her tutor to help with.

Her gaze shifted to the Fenren family, who had formed a huddle around
their youngest member, whispering what seemed like threats at the boy. Taenya
noticed a small smirk playing on Gwyn's lips and shook her head slightly.

"Gwyn," she began, leaning toward the young girl. "I think we both know
that was not the best choice of words."

"He was rude!" Gwyn protested, her eyebrows furrowing in indignation. She
opened her mouth as if to argue further, but then seemed to reconsider. "But . . .
maybe you're right. Ugh. Alright."

As the Fenrens continued their hushed discussion, Gwyn approached them.
"Mister Onas," she began, her voice gentle. "If Kalen doesn't want to be here, it's
okay. I just wanted to meet your family. I was just kidding. He didn't actually
upset me."

Taenya exchanged a look with Keston, who had been observing the exchange
with a bemused expression. She gestured subtly with her head toward the group.
"Come on, let's join them."

Onas's wife, Talani, smiled at the princess. "Thank you for your understanding, Your Highness, and we apologize for any offense given."

Keston chuckled. "Missus Fenren, I think I can speak for the princess when I say we're all friends here. No need for excessive formalities."

Gwyn nodded eagerly in agreement. "Yeah! Mister Onas, you said you'd have some food when I came over." She turned to the children. "Let's grab some food and you guys can tell me all about what you do here. Then I can tell you about how great your dad has been."

Taenya couldn't help but smile at Gwyn's enthusiasm.

Kerala laughed. "Our father? He really was great? Now you *must* tell us all about it."

"What? I *am* great," Onas protested, feigning offense.

Talani patted her husband's shoulder, her eyes twinkling with amusement. "It's okay, my love. You're great to me."

"Ugh, Mother," Relas, the middle child, interjected, his face scrunching up in a playful grimace.

Taenya glanced at Gwyn, noting the broad smile that lit up the young girl's face. It was a welcome sight. Gwyn needed these moments of lightness, especially given the challenges that lay ahead in their quest to find her mother.

Catching Onas's eye, Taenya received a slight nod from him. He cleared his throat, drawing everyone's attention. "Alright, why don't we go and have our lunch? Afterward, we can discuss future plans. Such as the princess being enrolled in the Royal Academy!"

Gwyn's face scrunched up in confusion as they all started walking. "The Royal Academy? Like school? But what about Mom?"

"You'll need to attend the Academy to assist with maintaining your house and to create connections. It will also protect you from anyone wishing to do you harm," Onas explained.

Kerala chimed in, "It's an honor to be able to attend the Royal Academy, Your Highness. I only attend the Strathmore Ladies Academy. It's much smaller."

"But what about Mom?" Gwyn repeated, her voice laced with worry.

Taenya placed a comforting hand on Gwyn's shoulder. "Onas and Siveril will be working together to search on your behalf. Your job will be to focus on being strong and making the house strong. Can you do that?"

Kerala stepped forward, offering a supportive smile. "We will help you, Princess."

Gwyn scrunched her face up. "Gwyn."

Relas chuckled. "Yeah, we'll help you . . . Gwyn."

"Thanks, everyone," Gwyn said, her voice soft and tinged with sadness.

The group made their way into a room set aside for staff meals. An array of food was spread out on plates and trays on one of the tables. Some of the company staff stood by, ready to serve. Kalen rushed over to grab a plate, eagerly lining up to fill it. Taenya followed Gwyn, chuckling softly as she overheard the young girl whispering to herself about which items didn't look appetizing.

Talani clapped her hands together, drawing everyone's attention. "Alright, for now, let's focus on what we can do. Let's eat!"

Gwyn stood next to Siveril while they waited on the nobles and their daughters to arrive. They were the same ones who had been sitting and talking with the elf majordomo in the dining hall when she had arrived for breakfast.

Sensing her restlessness, Siveril cast a comforting smile down at her. "They should be here shortly, Your Highness."

Gwyn winced, her fingers fidgeting with her dress. *It's just so boring!* If she'd known how tough being a princess would be, she would have never pretended to be one.

She hadn't meant to be so visibly anxious. Being a princess was proving to be more challenging than she had ever imagined. Now, she was about to meet three girls who were destined to shadow her, assist her in everything, and essentially become a part of her life. They were not much older than her, and their roles would evolve as they grew up together.

The thought was overwhelming. These girls would live in the house with her, sharing her life for a long time, unless they did something that warranted their return to their families. Siveril had explained all this to her, and it was a lot to take in. For instance, the house was obligated to allow at least one of them to visit their families on every holiday.

I don't even know the holidays here yet!

Gwyn's tutoring session with Professor Branigan the previous day had been a whirlwind of information. The focus had been on her sharing what she knew from her schooling back home, but the conversation had quickly veered toward the calendar they used in this world.

The professor had explained that their calendar was divided not into months, but seasons. There were four major divisions, each symbolizing one of the four main gods. This was another peculiarity she would have to adjust to. The calendar was further broken down into weeks, with nine week-long holidays scattered throughout the year, each dedicated to a minor god. The system was complex and confusing, and Gwyn knew she would need Professor Branigan to go over it several more times before she could fully comprehend it.

Her thoughts were interrupted as the door swung open, revealing a guard who held the doors wide for the incoming guests. The first to enter was a noblewoman Gwyn recognized from the group she had seen earlier in the dining hall. The woman, an older elf who nevertheless looked younger than Siveril, was accompanied by a girl who appeared slightly older than Gwyn.

The girl was a touch taller than Gwyn, her long, sharply pointed ears a distinctive feature. Her light brown hair was intricately braided, starting from the top of her head and cascading down her back in an elaborate weave.

I would hate to sit through having that done.

The Loreni girl had a soft face, and she looked very kind.

I hope she's nice.

The two women approached and curtsied, prompting Gwyn to respond with a slow, practiced nod of her head. As each noble was introduced, Siveril discreetly whispered their names into Gwyn's ear. With this prompt, Gwyn greeted them in the formal manner she had been taught: "Welcome to House Reinhart, Lady Olacyne. It is a pleasure to have you return."

The elder elf rose from her curtsy, addressing both Gwyn and Siveril. "Thank you for having us again, Your Highness. Allow me to introduce my daughter, Lady Aleanora Olacyne."

The younger elf lifted her gaze, a faint smile gracing her lips. "It is my pleasure to meet you, Your Highness. Thank you for the honor of inviting me to join your house."

An immediate scowl marred Lady Olacyne's face at her daughter's words, and Gwyn noticed a similar frown on Siveril's face. Deciding to defuse the tension, Gwyn offered a friendly smile to the young elf. She understood the difficulty of navigating formalities, especially in a new environment.

"Thank you for coming, Lady Aleanora. I look forward to talking with you! I look forward to seeing if you will stay or not."

There! Nice and hopeful.

Gwyn hoped her words conveyed optimism without overstepping Siveril's authority in making the final decision. She didn't want to put him in a situation where he *had* to say yes.

However, the reaction she received was not what she expected. Lady Aleanora looked slightly scared, and Lady Olacyne's eyes darted toward Siveril, as if she had a question she was hesitant to voice.

Did I say something wrong?

Gwyn looked at Siveril. The elf who helped manage the house wore a small smile on his face, adding to Gwyn's confusion.

If he's in a good mood, why are they looking scared?

Siveril subtly cleared his throat, drawing attention back to him. "Lady Olacyne, please follow our staff to the hall. We will convene there to discuss matters further, and then the ladies and Her Highness can speak more privately."

The noblewoman nodded, whispering something to her daughter that made the girl straighten her posture. The two followed a telv maid who had been waiting to guide them.

"Well said, Your Highness," Siveril commended quietly once they were out of earshot.

Gwyn leaned a little closer to him, her voice hushed. "I was just trying to be nice. I didn't want to upset anything for you."

Siveril paused, turning fully toward her and bending slightly to meet her at eye level. "Your Highness, why would you think that anything you did would upset me?"

"Because you have to choose whether or not they join our house. Right?" Gwyn asked, her head tilting inquisitively.

"Princess, the decision is yours. I am just here to assist and guide you," Siveril clarified.

"Oh. So, when I said that, she thought that I may not want her here?" Gwyn asked, trying to understand the implications of her words.

"I would not presume to know exactly what she thought, but to me, it seemed as if you were lightly rebuking her presumptions of joining the house. I commend you for how you handled it," Siveril explained.

Gwyn frowned, troubled. That hadn't been her intention at all. She nodded and turned back to the door as the next pair of nobles entered. Gwyn and Siveril welcomed the two barons, Lord Camus of House Trenlore and Lord Hagen of House Urileth, and their daughters, Lady Ilyana and Lady Lorrena. After they were guided to the hall, Gwyn followed Siveril, her mind preoccupied with his words.

He's just here to help me? I really *need to learn more about this princess thing.*

As they entered the hall, Gwyn noticed the three adult nobles huddled together in conversation, with Taenya standing among them. Sabina was off to the side, engaging the three young girls in light chatter. As Gwyn and Siveril made their full entrance, all eyes turned toward them, and a hush fell over the room.

Gwyn inwardly groaned. The formality of it all was starting to weigh on her. Everything was so stuffy.

If Siveril was being honest about helping me, *then I also need to set some ground rules around this house.*

Siveril paused, and Gwyn halted beside him, giving him the cue to address the room. "My lady and lords," he began, his voice carrying a formal tone. "Allow me to welcome you again to House Reinhart. We are here to forge connections between our houses, and I look forward to a long, mutually beneficial relationship, regardless of the outcomes here today. Though, I have faith that all parties will leave with a positive impression. Now, without further ado, Her Highness, Princess Gwyneth Reinhart."

Stepping forward with a warm smile, Gwyn gave a respectful nod. "As Ser Siveril said, welcome to House Reinhart! I look forward to getting to know all of you. Now, would you please join me for tea?"

A circular table was set up to the side, with four chairs arranged around it. Each place was set with tea cups and a selection of small cakes and bite-sized pastries. Gwyn was particularly excited about the pastries, though she knew she wouldn't be able to indulge as much as she'd like. Sabina had promised to sneak her some extras after the formalities, reminding her that this was more of a show than a meal.

The girls all moved toward the table, finding their designated seats by the beautifully written name cards in Common. Gwyn took her place and sat, prompting the others to do the same. The formality of it all was still so strange to her, but she was determined to navigate it as best as she could.

Gwyn swept her gaze over the trio of high elf girls seated before her. High elves, as Mister Branigan had explained, were the most prevalent among Avira's nobility. The house staff was a diverse mix of telv and Loreni, but the key figures Gwyn interacted with were predominantly high elves, with the notable exceptions of Taenya and Mister Branigan.

She recalled Mister Branigan mentioning that the Kingdom of Meris and Lymtoria Republic were primarily inhabited by telv, and that Taenya's family still lived in Meris. As for Mister Branigan, he was from the Kingdom of Rosale, home to a significant population of sun elves. There was also an island kingdom to the southwest known for its sun elf inhabitants.

Oops, got distracted again.

Gwyn shook herself from her reverie, refocusing on the task at hand. She turned her attention to Aleanora Olacyne, the light-brown-haired girl she had met first. According to Siveril, Aleanora, at thirteen, was the most likely candidate to assume a leadership role among the three girls, though ultimately, the decision was Gwyn's. Aleanora's demeanor was calm and composed, her eyes attentive and curious.

Next was Ilyana of House Trenlore. At fifteen, Ilyana was the eldest of the group. She stood a head taller than Gwyn, with her blond hair elegantly coiffed into a bun. Her eyes were a striking shade of gray tinged with a hint of blue, and her ears were slightly shorter than Aleanora's. Ilyana wore a beautiful white and lavender spring dress adorned with intricate patterns. Despite her cheerful demeanor, Gwyn noticed her casting occasional glances at Aleanora, her expression betraying a hint of unease.

I know I would be upset if I was the oldest and had to listen to someone younger than me.

The last girl was Lorrena of House Urileth, who was the youngest and seemed to be the happiest to be there. Lorrena had dirty-blond hair and hazel eyes, which Gwyn thought was fascinating only because she was the first elf Gwyn had seen with them. Being eleven already, she was a little bit older than Gwyn.

I should be turning eleven soon! I need to talk to the others about that. Maybe they can help me figure it out.

Gwyn observed the girls, noting their initial hesitation. Deciding to break the ice, she introduced herself.

"It's wonderful to meet all of you! I'm Gwyn Reinhart," she began, tucking a loose strand of hair behind her ear. "As you may know, I'm what's referred to here as a terran, though back home we just call ourselves humans—the name that I prefer. My arrival in Avira is still a mystery to me, but I'm determined to make the most of it! Ser Siveril has assured me that you are trustworthy, and that I can rely on you to help me navigate the craziness of Aviran society."

She offered a warm smile to Aleanora. "Maybe we could start with you, Lady Aleanora? Could you share a bit about yourself and your interests? Then we'll move on to Lady Ilyana, and finally Lady Lorrena. In the meantime, let's enjoy some tea."

I'm going to have to give them nicknames. Their names are far *too long.*

The staff—Gwyn still wasn't comfortable calling them servants—stepped forward to pour tea for each of them.

Once everyone had been served, Aleanora began her introduction. "Thank you, Your Highness. I am Lady Aleanora, the third child of House Olacyne," she said, her gaze flitting between the other two girls. "I was previously attending the Strathmore Ladies School, but my family deemed this opportunity more significant. I look forward to continuing my studies with the tutors of your house." Aleanora concluded her introduction, lifting her teacup for a sip.

Ilyana nodded respectfully at Gwyn. "I am honored to be here, Your Highness. As you know, I am Lady Ilyana of House Trenlore. I am the sixth child—"

"Hmph, sixth . . . House Trenlore sends someone so low?" Aleanora muttered under her breath.

Ilyana shot a scowl at Aleanora but chose not to respond to the interruption. "I am the third daughter of my family. However, my eldest sister is already married, and my second sister, Laura, is recently engaged, though we have yet to announce it publicly."

Gwyn smiled. "Oh, congratulations to her! That's wonderful news. I'm delighted to have you here, Ilyana—or should I say, Lady Ilyana."

"Oh, Ilyana is fine, Your Highness," the elf quickly interjected.

"Wonderful! So, what are some of your interests, Ilyana?" Gwyn inquired, hoping to put the girl at ease.

"Well, I enjoy dancing and painting mostly, Your Highness," Ilyana replied, her voice slightly tremulous.

Gwyn, sensing Ilyana's nervousness, sought to reassure her. "I love to paint and draw too. I can't wait to see your work."

Ilyana visibly brightened and sat straighter in her chair. "Thank you, Your Highness. I look forward to sharing it with you."

Aleanora was wearing a scowl, but Gwyn couldn't discern the reason. Turning her attention to the youngest girl, Lorrena, she saw her sit up straighter and flash a smile, clearly ready for her turn.

"Hello, Your Highness! I'm Lorrena . . . and you can just call me that, Princess. I love spending time by the lake, being around animals, and painting by the shore . . ." she said, glancing at Ilyana before adding, "oh, and I love to dance as well! I also play the viol, and I'd be thrilled to play for you sometime, Your Highness." She spoke so rapidly that she was slightly out of breath by the end of her introduction.

"Thank you, Lorrena! I'd love to hear you play. I'm looking forward to getting to know all three of you better," Gwyn responded, her smile unwavering.

She understood the importance of what their alliances meant for her house. The support of them and their families would be invaluable in her dealings with the duke, whom Siveril had mentioned she would be meeting soon.

Gwyn picked up her tea, allowing herself a small sigh. The weight of her new responsibilities was beginning to sink in. That said, if she could also gain a friend or two in the process, all the better. *I could really use a friend right now.*

CHAPTER THIRTEEN

A FIERY INTRODUCTION

S abina stood at a respectful distance, observing as Emma and the newly appointed ladies-in-waiting assisted Gwyn with her preparations. It had been a mere four days since the young ladies had been integrated into the princess's retinue, and they had worked daily with the professor and majordomo to become acquainted with House Reinhart and further their education. Siveril and Taenya had determined that the youngest, Lorrena, would join Gwyn in the Academy.

Today, they were all in a flurry of activity, preparing to present House Reinhart at the duke's court later in the afternoon.

Siveril had been a whirlwind of efficiency, meticulously planning every detail, with Taenya shadowing him closely. The long-term plan was for Siveril and Theran to remain in Strathmore to manage the house's affairs while Gwyn attended the Royal Academy the following year. Taenya would assist the princess in securing a residence within the capital, after which she would take over the management of the house's affairs there. As for Sabina, she found herself increasingly by Gwyn's side during the day, and fulfilling her other duties at night.

I really need to find some subordinates to delegate to.

Sabina had been assisting Gwyn with her magical training, a process she found utterly fascinating. She was intrigued by the possibility of wielding such power herself and had taken to observing Gwyn's practice sessions and asking questions whenever the young human sought to expand her understanding of magic.

A soft knock at the door interrupted her musings. Sabina turned and opened the door slightly to see Siveril standing outside. After a moment, he asked, "Is she ready?"

Sabina glanced back into the room. Ilyana was just finishing pinning up

Gwyn's dark-brown curls. The princess turned around, her vibrant blue eyes sparkling with excitement and joy.

"Oh my gosh! I love it, Ilyana!" the girl gushed. "And thank you, Nora and Lori. You all did a wonderful job. You too, Emma!" Gwyn's voice was filled with genuine appreciation, her smile radiant.

Turning back to Siveril, Sabina said, "She's ready now, ser."

"Good. The carriage is out front. I would like you to be at her side. Ser Taenya and I will be there, but we may have to meet others. I know it's last-minute . . ." Siveril's voice trailed off.

Sabina nodded in understanding. "I understand. I will stay near her."

Siveril sat in one of the house carriages with Princess Gwyneth and Lady Aleanora, the wheels crunching on the gravel as they made their way to the ducal palace. They had just passed through the grand gates and were now approaching the main entrance. A second carriage followed closely behind, carrying Sabina, Taenya, and the other two ladies-in-waiting. The princess had yet to make a firm decision on which of the two older girls would take the lead, a matter Siveril knew he would need to discuss with her privately.

Ser Taenya, still in the process of learning the intricacies of her position, was proving to be an eager and quick study. Siveril found himself impressed by her dedication and aptitude, trusting her to handle tasks with minimal guidance.

As the carriages drew to a halt, Siveril turned to the girls, his gaze steady. "We're here, ladies. Lady Aleanora, remember, you're here to support the princess. Don't interrupt." He waited for her nod of understanding before turning his attention to the young princess.

"I'm ready, Siveril. Let's do this." Gwyn's voice was filled with determination, her eyes sparkling with anticipation.

The carriage doors were opened by the ducal guards, and the group disembarked. Siveril stepped aside, allowing the princess to take the lead. Ser Sabina followed closely behind, her armor gleaming in the sunlight. Taenya, too, was resplendent in her new armor, the silver and blue fabric accents and ornamentation signifying her status as knight-captain. Clearly, Lord Iemes had spared no expense in outfitting Gwyneth's first knight.

As they entered the grand hall of the palace, Siveril felt a flutter of nerves. He knew Dasron, the Duke of Tiloral well, having served as his close advisor for two decades before moving to work with the baron. Yet, this was the first time Siveril would be presenting someone to the court.

The weight of the responsibility was not lost on him. The young royal walking next to him held her head high and looked as if she were in her element. But Siveril knew better. Gwyn's bravado was a carefully constructed facade, a lifeline she clung to amid the stormy seas of uncertainty. All it would take was one rogue wave to wash away all that confidence. Her hope of finding her mother was the beacon guiding her through the tempest, and her shrewd understanding of the need for allies in this quest was nothing short of impressive.

Their guide stopped them at the door to the court, and the guard at the door peeked inside before returning and nodding to them.

As Gwyn would say, it's go time.

The grand double doors swung open, revealing the opulent Tiloral ducal hall and the assembled nobility. Their guide, a telv man Siveril had seen only in passing, led them toward the duke, stopping at the appropriate distance before announcing, "Your Grace, presenting House Reinhart." With a respectful bow, he stepped aside.

Siveril stepped forward, bowing formally before straightening to address the duke. "Your Grace, it is my honor and privilege to present before you and your court, Her Royal Highness Gwyneth of House Reinhart. A terran, hailing from a faraway land and displaced to our world by the same event that brought so many others. Her lineage is without doubt and her house has been established within all prescribed laws enforced within your duchy."

Stepping aside, he allowed Gwyneth to step forward. The young princess offered a slow nod of respect, as was customary. "Thank you for inviting me to your court, Your Grace. I look forward to a positive relationship between our houses."

The duke reciprocated the gesture with a slight bow, then addressed her, his voice resonating through the hall. "Welcome, Your Highness, to the Duchy of Tiloral. There have been many rumors and reports about your people. I hope that we can both learn from each other in a mutually beneficial way. Please, be welcome within my court. I acknowledge your house and wish you good fortune." He paused, his gaze sweeping over the court. "Your people have been an important topic of note within this court for some time now. In fact, your very house has come up in numerous discussions."

Siveril felt a twinge of unease at the duke's words. His gaze flickered to the right as the crowd shifted, and his eyes narrowed at the sight of Lord Angwin stepping forward.

The marquess strode confidently into the open space and bowed to the duke. "Your Grace, if I may. Now that House Reinhart has been acknowledged within this court, I believe we should discuss its status." He turned to Gwyn, his head dipping in a curt nod that lacked the respect due to her station. "Welcome, Princess, to our kingdom."

His attention returned to the duke, his tone carrying an air of self-importance. "With respect to the majordomo, Your Grace should appoint a noble with the appropriate station to manage the house of a foreign royal minor child. There are intricacies and nuances that a knight simply cannot navigate. Further, it would only be in the princess's favor, as it would be primarily for her protection. Someone of a higher peerage would be able to shield her as no simple knight could."

The duke's eyes met Siveril's, a subtle nod passing between them.

So, you're throwing me to the wolves, you sly dog.

Siveril composed himself, ready to counter the marquess's thinly veiled power play. "Your Lordship, with respect, that is up to Her Highness. As you stated yourself, she is a *foreign royal*, and thus, the duchy cannot impose a minder of lower status."

His gaze flicked to the left, where Lady Olacyne stood. The viscountess inclined her head subtly, a silent show of support.

With that, the majordomo readied himself for a fight.

Gwyn found herself slowly retreating as Siveril and the other noble engaged in a verbal duel before the duke. The duke, for his part, seemed intrigued, allowing the exchange to unfold without interruption.

As the crowd began to encroach on the open space, Gwyn noticed Taenya had moved to the side with the other girls, leaving her and Sabina alone in the center.

Lady Olacyne approached, offering a warm greeting. "Welcome to the ducal court, Your Highness. I trust Aleanora has been helpful?"

Gwyn smiled. "Nora is great! She's really nice to me and helps me with everything I need," she said, wanting the viscountess to be proud of her daughter.

"Nora?" Lady Olacyne smirked at the nickname. "I am glad she has been beneficial to your house. Please excuse me, Your Highness. I should assist your majordomo before he slaps that poor marquess."

Gwyn giggled. "Good luck! I think Siveril is doing alright, though."

As she scanned the room, Sabina moved closer, placing a comforting hand on her shoulder. "Your Highness?"

Gwyn turned to see Sabina standing with an older high elf man and a telv woman. The man offered a respectful bow, and the woman curtsied before speaking. "It is an honor to meet you, Your Highness. I am Lady Racine, and this is my husband, Lord Alec."

"Your Highness," Lord Alec greeted with a nod of his head.

"I especially wanted to make your acquaintance because I would like to introduce you to a young woman we recently took into our estate," the countess continued. "She too is a terran who is lost and far from home. Perhaps it is someone you know. If not, perhaps our houses can simply come to an arrangement that would see her helped."

Gwyn instantly became more interested. "A woman? What is her name?"

"Her name is Amanda. She says she hails from the country of Canada," the countess explained.

"Oh! She's Canadian? That's great! I would love to meet her," Gwyn responded, her eyes lighting up with excitement.

Sabina, ever the protective knight, interjected, "My Lady, perhaps this evening your house can send a formal invitation to tea? Her Highness, of course, maintains a busy schedule. The majordomo and Ser Taenya will ensure we can coordinate an adequate time to meet. I am sure Her Highness would love nothing more than to meet another member of her people."

Lady Racine's face softened into a smile. "Lovely. I look forward to a more private setting, Your Highness. And don't you worry about all the nonsense going on over there. Old Ser Siveril can handle an uppity marquess like it is nothing."

"Thank you, Lady Racine," Gwyn replied, looking back at the heated exchange between Siveril and the other elf. Even Nora's mom had joined in, and it seemed they had gotten closer to where the duke now stood near his throne.

A group of young elves were seated behind the duke's throne. Gwyn turned to Sabina, curiosity piqued. "Sabina? Who are those kids behind the duke's throne?"

"I believe they are the duke's grandchildren. Probably here to observe the court."

Gwyn looked back and saw one of the younger girls staring at her. From what she could see, the girl was quite pretty. She had blond hair in a fancy style, just like Gwyn's. Her dress was also really beautiful. It was a pretty red color, with a curvy-diamond pattern in the fabric, decorated with gold accents and stitching. There were a bunch of gold buttons on the bodice and two rows of them going down the middle of the skirt. She looked like a character straight out of a fairy tale.

Gwyn's brow furrowed slightly as the girl covered her mouth with a delicate hand and giggled. It was then she realized her own hand was raised in an awkward wave. With a start, she quickly pulled it back to her side.

The young girl smiled at her. She returned the smile awkwardly, and the girl responded with a friendly wave.

"Sabina? Can I meet her?" Gwyn asked.

Sabina didn't respond immediately. Gwyn looked around in a slight panic. She spotted the knight a few steps away, engaged in conversation with another noble, which made her feel better.

As Gwyn was about to turn back to the girl, an older elf with gray hair and a stern expression approached her. She glanced around quickly, confirming that he was indeed heading her way, before facing him again.

"Princess, I am Count Telford of House Telford. I would like to present you with an opportunity. One that would be beneficial to you," he stated, his tone serious.

Gwyn tilted her head, puzzled by his words. "What do you mean?"

The man glanced over at Siveril, who was still engaged in a heated discussion with the marquess, and then at Sabina. He stepped closer, causing Gwyn to instinctively take a half step back.

"The marquess is right about one thing. You need protection. Your knights cannot protect you, and an old knight such as your majordomo will not either. It is in your best interest to find an ally. My son is such an ally," he explained.

Gwyn's confusion deepened. "Your son? He can help me?"

The man smiled, a hint of satisfaction in his eyes. "Yes, of course. Your knights have to listen to you, correct?"

"Yes? They're very helpful," Gwyn replied, still not understanding his point.

"Exactly. They will listen to you when you tell them that you wish to do something. My son can protect you more than they can, you see, because others will have to listen to him."

"I don't understand what you're saying, Mister . . ." Gwyn trailed off, her eyebrows furrowing in confusion.

The elf's frown deepened. "That is *Count* Telford, Princess. Show me the respect I am due. As I was saying, my son is the heir to my house's county. You currently have very little land. It would behoove you to strengthen your position, don't you agree?"

"Yes . . .?"

"And having more people who will listen to you will help you as well?"

"Of course. Taenya and Siveril are looking for more people now," Gwyn explained, her confusion only growing every time he spoke.

Of course, having more people to help me is a good thing.

The older elf's countenance softened, and he leaned in slightly, his voice dropping to a conspiratorial whisper. "Exactly, Princess. Now, imagine if you had a powerful noble at your side. Someone who could command respect and obedience from others. My son can be that person for you. To help you find your mother."

Gwyn's heart skipped a beat. "My mother? What do you know about her?" she asked, her voice wavering slightly.

The count waved his hand dismissively, as if brushing off her concern. "It is nothing. Simply a rumor I heard. My house is considerable, much larger than your own, Princess. We have authority over many. Would you like our help?"

Gwyn hesitated, her mind racing. *I do need help . . . but why is he talking like this? Does he think I'm younger than I am?*

"If you want to help, I would like that. Thank you, Count Telford." She made sure to emphasize his title, hoping to assert some control over the conversation.

His smile widened, revealing a row of perfectly white teeth. "Perfect. Princess, perhaps we could step aside, and we can simply sign a contract. This will give us both protection as we work together for a long time."

Gwyn scrunched up her eyebrows. "A contract? Why do we need a contract?"

"Of course, the best way for House Telford to assist you is for you to be pledged to marry my son when you come of age in a few years. You're what, twelve?"

What? Did he just say marry?

"I'm *ten*," she snapped. "I'm a bit young to marry anyone."

The count appeared slightly surprised by her response, but continued undeterred. "Nonsense. You simply need to be pledged to marry. This can be done as early as ten, and you will be engaged at thirteen. You would not formally marry until sixteen. That gives us time to prepare you for what will be required."

Gwyn's fear was quickly replaced by a rising tide of anger. "I don't want to marry anyone. I don't even know your son."

She looked around, her eyes landing on Sabina, who was gesturing at someone. She turned her head the other way and saw that Siveril was still busy. Taenya and her ladies-in-waiting were nowhere to be found.

Gwyn looked over at the girl from before and saw her looking at her with concern. Next to her was a guard in red armor leaning over and talking. The girl was pointing at Gwyn.

Gwyn refocused on the count, who spoke again. "It would be in your *best interest* to marry my son, Princess. Unfortunate accidents happen. My house can ensure no accidents happen to anyone close to you. We will provide you with true strength."

Her eyes narrowed, and she felt her neck heat up. Any previous fear was burned away. "I am not going to marry *anyone*, Telford. Please leave me alone."

Gwyn turned to walk toward Sabina but was suddenly jerked back. She looked down to see the count's hand gripping her wrist tightly.

"Girl, do not disrespect your betters. I am doing *you* a favor. Come with me and sign this contract. Now."

Gwyn tried to pull her hand away, but his grip only tightened. She was about to respond when the sound of a sword being unsheathed echoed through the hall. She turned to see Sabina striding toward them, her sword drawn and a furious expression on her face.

"Let go of her," Sabina said slowly and deliberately, emphasizing each word. Her voice was a low growl, her eyes locked on the count.

Gwyn jerked her arm again, but the elf's grip remained ironclad. "The girl has agreed to and accepted my house's assistance. Now she is trying to back out of a verbal contract simply because I want her to sign a physical one. She will sign this contract, and if you do not put that blade down, I will have your head, woman."

No! No one else I care about will die.

Gwyn pulled on her magic in a way she hadn't before, using her **[Pyromancy]** to directly control fire.

If the elf wouldn't release her, she'd force him to.

In an instant, Gwyn's arm was ablaze, a living torch that seared the air around it. The elf's scream echoed through the hall as his arm was engulfed in a maelstrom of heat, the skin blistering and blackening in an instant. His sleeve disintegrated into a cloud of ash, carried away by the heat waves radiating from the flames. He recoiled, clutching his scorched arm with his other hand, his eyes wide and filled with a primal fear.

Gwyn turned to face him fully, the fire on her arm coalescing into a sphere of pure flame. With a flick of her other hand, she summoned a twin orb, and with a mere thought, set them to orbit around her. They spun in a mesmerizing dance, casting flickering shadows and bathing her in a warm, fiery glow. The orbs served as a barrier, a clear warning to those who dared approach.

The crowd around her took heed, swiftly retreating from the spectacle.

Good.

After a few moments, Gwyn drew the fire back to her right hand, letting the orbs settle into a lazy co-orbit. They hovered above her palm, a duo of miniature stars that pulsed with raw energy.

She tilted her head, her gaze fixed on the floating spheres of fire, refusing to acknowledge the whimpering elf. "Come near me or any of my people, and your hand will be the least of your worries."

The fire was a living entity, its surface roiling and churning, casting an intense light that made the count's face look ghostly pale. The flames danced and flickered, bathing Gwyn in a warm, orange glow. The sight was mesmerizing.

The count, still nursing his burned arm, could only watch in stunned silence as Gwyn demonstrated her power.

The message was clear. Don't mess with her.

Gwyn's gaze swept across the room and landed on Sabina. The knight's face was a mask of fierce pride, her eyes gleaming with admiration. Siveril, on the other hand, looked as if he had swallowed something sour, his brow furrowed in deep thought, likely trying to figure out how to navigate the political fallout of her display.

A sun elf guard, clad in vibrant red armor, had edged forward, his eyes locked on to the fiery spectacle. His hand was half-raised, as if he yearned to touch the flames, his expression one of deep longing.

Behind the duke, the young girl had risen to her feet. Her eyes were wide, filled with fascination as she watched the magical display. There was no fear in her expression, only pure, unadulterated awe.

Gwyn smiled at her. With a final pull on her magic, she forced the two orbs together, their fiery bodies merging into a single, larger sun. She turned to face Count Telford, her gaze hard and unyielding as she stared into his whimpering eyes.

The authority and strength he had boasted of were nowhere to be seen. All that remained was a pitiful display of weakness.

Shaking her head, she spoke, her voice echoing through the silent hall, "Threaten me or mine again, and I will show you what *true* strength looks like."

With that, she closed her fist, and the sun in her hand responded.

It flared brilliantly, a blinding burst of light that filled the room, before disappearing as if it had never been, leaving only the echo of her words and the memory of its brilliance.

CHAPTER FOURTEEN

MAGICAL EXPOSURE

Aleanora found herself standing shoulder to shoulder with Ser Taenya, Knight-Captain of House Reinhart, amid a flurry of activity. A sudden, brilliant flash of light had sent the court into a state of disarray, and the nobles were buzzing with speculation and concern.

"Damn it. Gwyn . . ." Ser Taenya muttered under her breath, her gaze scanning the crowd with a furrowed brow.

Aleanora followed the knight's gaze before turning to look up at the taller telv. "Princess Gwyneth? What's happened to her? Can you see?" She craned her neck, trying to catch a glimpse of the young princess through the sea of bodies, but to no avail.

From the knight's other side, Lady Ilyana chimed in, her voice laced with worry. "I can't see anything either. Where is Her Highness? Ser Taenya, do you have a better view?"

Aleanora suppressed a sigh. *I was speaking to the knight, not you . . .*

Ser Taenya shook her head, her expression grim. "No, but I'd wager my last copper coin that flash had something to do with her. Lady Lorrena, are you with us?"

The youngest of their group, Lady Lorrena, nodded her affirmation. "Yes, Ser Taenya."

The telv knight turned her attention back to them, her gaze steely. "Alright. Lady Ilyana, your task is to keep Lady Lorrena close. Do *not* lose sight of her. Understood?"

Lady Ilyana nodded, her face set in determination. "I will do my part for the house, Ser Taenya."

Aleanora rolled her eyes at the older girl's eagerness. *There's no need to seem so desperate* . . . She almost chuckled when she noticed Ser Taenya's subtle shake of her head, clearly sharing her sentiment. The princess was far above any petty rivalry between the two of them. The daughter of a viscountess and a baron were so far beneath her that she hadn't even bothered to designate a lead among the three of them. Aleanora respected that and was determined to prove her worth by simply being superior.

"Ladies, stay *close*. We're going to find the princess and Ser Sabina," Ser Taenya instructed, her voice firm.

As Lady Ilyana dutifully kept Lady Lorrena close, Aleanora found herself begrudgingly admiring her rival's competence. It was a relief, really, knowing she wouldn't have to shoulder all the responsibilities alone. Lady Lorrena, being the youngest, was primarily there to be a confidante to the princess and was too young to take on any other roles that Aleanora or Ilyana could handle.

The trio navigated their way through the throng of people, moving steadily toward the front. As they drew closer, they could see the Ducal Guard attempting to push the crowd back. The air was thick with tension, and the volume of the crowd's chatter escalated into a cacophony of raised voices. Suddenly, the crowd began to retreat more rapidly, and Aleanora found herself being swept along in the tide of bodies.

Ser Taenya halted abruptly, and Aleanora narrowly avoided colliding with her. Lady Ilyana's hand was her shoulder, her voice barely audible over the din. "I have Lorrena. Stay close to Ser Taenya. People are giving her room."

"I know what to do," Aleanora retorted, her voice laced with irritation and embarrassment.

Before Ilyana could respond, Ser Taenya was already engaging with a member of the Ducal Guard. "Let us through. We are Her Highness's retainers." Aleanora peeked around her and up at the telv guard, whose armor gleamed in the well-lit hall. "Stay back. I don't care who you are," he retorted, his voice cold and unyielding.

Ser Taenya didn't budge. "Let us through. Now. I will get to my liege, or we will have issues. You are doing your job. Allow me to do mine."

A wave of unease washed over Aleanora. She had no desire to be caught up in a confrontation with the duke's guards.

But Gwyneth is a princess.

"If you do not back up right now, you will all be arrested. I don't care who your liege is," the guard repeated, his voice causing the bystanders around them to go silent.

Summoning her courage, Aleanora stepped up beside the knight. "You may not care, but the Duke of Tiloral will when he hears that you accosted the retainers of Princess Gwyneth. I am Lady Aleanora and I will personally make it my life's goal to ruin yours if you do not let us pass."

The telv's scowl deepened as he regarded her. "Your *princess* is the one who started this mess. Last warning. Back up or—"

His words were abruptly cut off as Ser Taenya's fist connected with his face. The knight's punch was so forceful that the telv simply crumpled to the ground, his armor clattering against the stone floor.

Aleanora stared at the telv woman, her eyes wide with shock.

Ser Taenya turned to them and spoke with a commanding voice that they heeded immediately. "Ladies. Stay together, and give me a bit of space."

Aleanora's eyes met Lady Ilyana's, the other girl's face a mirror of her own shock. A silent understanding passed between them, and Ilyana gave a small nod and placed a hand on Lorrena's shoulder. Aleanora moved closer to the older girl, their shoulders brushing lightly. As a unit, they retreated a few steps, giving Ser Taenya the space she had requested.

The crowd around them seemed to hold its collective breath.

What did Mother get me into?

Taenya watched as two guards drew their weapons, a sigh escaping her lips as she rolled her shoulders, loosening the tension coiling in her muscles.

Scanning the area, she noticed Sabina standing protectively near Gwyn, sword unsheathed and ready. Gwyn was scanning the semicircle of guards surrounding her, a look of determination etched on her face. A noble lay on the ground nearby, clutching his arm in pain, while another guard stood over him in a protective stance.

The duke was shielded by two guards, and Siveril seemed to be in a heated discussion with him and another noble. Aleanora's mother was also present and stood next to Siveril in solidarity.

Taenya's attention snapped back to the immediate threat before her. The two guards had spread out, and the high elf woman on Taenya's left brandished her blade.

"Ser Knight, you have attacked a member of the Ducal Guard. Lay down your weapon and surrender," the woman ordered, her eyes glinting with a mix of anticipation and disdain.

"Yeah, that's not going to happen. You two are going to step aside and let me get to my liege or you're going to end up like that guy," Taenya retorted, jutting her head at the unconscious telv she had just knocked out. She flexed her fingers, feeling the familiar grip of her weapon in her hand. She didn't want to draw her blade, but if it came down to them or her princess, she wouldn't hesitate.

Without another word, the telv man lunged at her, blade swinging. She stepped forward, catching the blade on her bracer and sliding down and seizing his wrist. A quick jab to his side made him wince, and she followed it up with a hook to his temple. His head jerked back, and she released his wrist, grabbing his breastplate at the neck opening to keep him upright.

The guard woman, who had initially frozen in shock, suddenly sprang into action. She charged at Taenya, but Taenya simply flung the man she was holding into the woman's path. The two guards collided, their bodies tangling as they fell into a heap on the ground.

Two more figures emerged from the group of guards, their swords gleaming ominously in the court's light. Taenya's eyes narrowed, her grip tightening on her own weapon. She was outnumbered, but not outmatched.

The first of the new challengers, a burly high elf with a scar running down his cheek, lunged at her with a roar. Taenya sidestepped his attack, her hand shooting out to grab his extended arm. With a swift, practiced move, she twisted his arm behind his back, forcing him to drop his weapon with a grunt of pain. Before he could recover, she shoved him forward, sending him sprawling to the ground, gasping for breath.

The second challenger, a lithe telv woman with a determined glint in her eyes, was more cautious. She circled Taenya warily, her sword held defensively in front of her. Taenya mirrored her, keeping her own weapon ready. The two women waited for the other to make the first move.

Finally, the telv woman lunged, her sword slicing through the air. Taenya parried the attack, her blade clashing against the woman's with a loud clang. She pushed back, forcing her opponent to stumble backward. Seizing the opportunity, Taenya swept her leg out, knocking the woman's feet out from under her. As the guard hit the ground, Taenya swiftly kicked the sword out of her hand, sending it skittering across the floor.

With the immediate threats neutralized, Taenya turned back to the other guards, her eyes scanning for any other potential challengers. Her heart pounded in her chest, battle fervor coursing through her veins. She was ready for whatever came next. She had to be. For her princess.

Stepping past the fallen guards, Taenya found herself facing a fresh set, their bodies tense and their eyes wary. Sabina met her gaze and gave a curt nod of acknowledgment. Taenya turned her attention to Gwyn, raising her voice to cut through the commotion. "Your Highness!"

At the sound of her name, Gwyn's head snapped up, her body visibly relaxing at the sight of her. "Taenya!" she exclaimed, starting to move toward her.

Taenya raised her hand in a halting gesture, and Sabina quickly stepped in front of the princess, her arm barring her way.

"Wait, Your Highness. Let Ser Taenya come to us," Sabina advised, her eyes never leaving the guards.

Casting a glance over her shoulder, Taenya saw that the ladies-in-waiting were still at the edge of the crowd, their expressions anxious. They were safe for now. She locked eyes with Ilyana and gave a reassuring nod, which the girl hesitantly returned.

Turning back to the guards, Sabina addressed the one who seemed to be in charge. "Are you going to tell your people to stand down? Or are you going to continue protecting someone who tried to harm my charge?"

Taenya looked down at the high elf on the ground, who was being examined by a medic. His hand and forearm were severely burned where his tunic had charred against his skin.

She took a step toward him, but the guards shifted in response, blocking her path. She turned to Sabina for an explanation. "What happened?"

Sabina's gaze was fixed on the injured noble. "That noble had one of his guards distract me by arguing with me, and then he—"

"He tried to force me to marry his son! When I said no, he tried to pull me with him to sign a contract. He hurt me and wouldn't let go, so I *made* him let go," Gwyn interjected, her voice seething with anger.

Taenya narrowed her eyes as she turned to the guard Sabina had addressed earlier. "He attacked my princess and you have the *audacity* to defend him?" She stepped forward, her voice ringing out in the tense silence. "Your Grace, is this how the duchy handles affairs such as this? Do you condone a noble attacking and attempting to force a ten-year-old child into marriage?"

"Move. Now!" a commanding voice echoed from the direction of the duke and Siveril.

Taenya watched as the Duke of Tiloral pushed past his guards, Siveril following closely behind him. The viscountess, too, began moving toward her daughter and the other two girls.

Good. She's prioritizing correctly.

The duke, now in control of the situation, addressed his men. "Captain, stand everyone down. And for Alos's sake, get the count to an infirmary. Post a guard. I will speak to him later." He looked at Gwyn, his expression unreadable. "Your Highness, could we please retire to my private study?" He cast a pointed look at Siveril. "I do believe we have much to discuss."

Siveril stepped forward, his agreement clear. "I too believe it would be of benefit, Your Highness. Especially now."

Taenya watched as Gwyn gave a nearly imperceptible nod, her response carrying a fraction of the anger she had previously displayed. "Fine."

"Let's go, everyone," Taenya said loud enough for both the young ladies' benefit and Gwyn's.

Just as they were about to move, Lord Angwin stepped forward, his face a mask of concern. "Your Grace, surely you can see that the princess is a danger. She—"

But the Duke of Tiloral silenced him with a wave of his hand. "Enough,

Angwin. Your audience has ended." His gaze returned to Gwyn, his expression softening slightly. "After you, Your Highness."

Lady Ilyana stood alongside Ser Sabina and her fellow ladies-in-waiting, their collective gaze fixed on the closed door of the duke's private study. The princess and her two lead retainers were inside, engaged in a private discussion with the duke. The absence of any commotion or guards rushing in suggested that the meeting was proceeding smoothly.

The two Reinhart knights had left a profound impression on Ilyana. Both women had been prepared to face off against the entire Ducal Guard for the sake of the princess.

Yet, it was the princess herself who had truly astounded her. The royal had performed some form of magic that had caused the flash of light that had startled everyone. The details remained a mystery, as Sabina had quickly silenced any speculation until they returned to the house.

Leaning toward the knight, Ilyana whispered, "Ser Sabina, how much longer until they are finished?"

The knight closed her eyes briefly, then opened them again. "They are nearly done. Please be patient, Lady Ilyana."

Ilyana nodded and resumed her silent vigil. Lady Aleanora, usually so aloof, seemed more approachable, keeping the younger Lady Lorrena close.

As if on cue, the door to the study opened not long after. *How did she know?* Ilyana wondered, marveling at the knight's intuition.

The duke emerged from the study, flanked by the three heads of House Reinhart. Ilyana strained to catch their conversation, then felt a sort of *click* in her head as she **[Focused]**.

"Thank you for your understanding, Your Highness," the duke was saying. "I will send couriers with what we discussed as recompense for this situation. Siveril, old friend, don't be a stranger. We live in fascinating times, and I could use your advice again. With your leave, of course, Your Highness."

Siveril bowed his head slightly. "I will be back soon, Your Grace. We have much to discuss concerning Her Highness."

The duke sighed. "Of course."

The princess then looked up at him. "Your Grace?"

The old man smiled. "Yes, Your Highness?"

"Was that your granddaughter sitting behind you?" she asked.

The duke squinted in thought. "Yes, it was. Would you like to meet her?"

"I would! Is that alright?"

"But of course. I will work with Ser Siveril to set up a meeting," the duke promised.

The princess nodded, satisfied. She turned to the waiting group of ladies. "Let's go home, everyone."

Ilyana caught Lady Aleanora's eye, and they exchanged a slight nod.
A new rival appears.

Roslyn sat in a separate office while waiting for her grandfather, her gaze fixed on the polished red armor of the paladin, Khalan. The sun elf was an elite warrior of the Church who had been assigned to her by the archpriestess herself after discussing the matter with the duke.

The archpriestess, who was a longtime close friend of her grandfather, had revealed during a private meeting that Roslyn was one of the two subjects of a divine Seeing.

The revelations from that meeting had been vast and overwhelming, but the most significant outcome was Khalan's pledge to protect her from anyone who posed a threat.

The office door creaked open, and her grandfather walked in. His usual jovial demeanor was replaced by a look of exhaustion and emotional drain. Roslyn immediately rose from her seat.

"Are you okay, Grandfather?" she asked, her voice laced with concern.

The duke took a deep breath, running a hand through his hair. "We did not need that to happen, but yes, I am fine. The princess is fine, as well. I deeded her some land in the city and two smaller plots for her knights. That was the least I could do. I also pledged to ensure such a thing did not reoccur."

He looked at Khalan. "Thank you for standing at my granddaughter's side, Evocati."

The paladin nodded in response. His stern face softened as he addressed the duke. "I am here to protect her, Your Grace. However, it is important that I meet with the archpriestess. Tonight. The princess may be the other subject of the Seeing, making her as significant as Lady Roslyn."

Roslyn's heart skipped a beat at Khalan's words. The implications were monumental—that the other subject of a Seeing was a *terran* . . . it boggled her mind. However, she knew having one of the infamous Paladins of Alos at her side would ensure her safety despite the potential for danger.

Her grandfather took a deep breath. "I will summon the count before me and pass judgment. I would request a member of your order to be present. As a witness of what occurred, you would be preferable. However, I understand your primary duty."

Khalan nodded firmly. "I will ensure one of my brothers or sisters in Alos is present."

The duke seemed satisfied with this, and he turned to Roslyn. His eyes softened, and a smile finally graced his weary face. "Also, the princess would like to meet you."

Roslyn's heart gave a leap, and she gasped, her eyes widening in surprise.

* * *

A knock echoed through the room, pulling Roslyn from her studies. Before she could respond, the door creaked open to reveal her grandfather. She pushed back her chair and rose to her feet, a smile lighting up her face. "Grandfather! What brings you here?"

His eyes crinkled as he returned her smile. He was holding a small card. "We received an invitation for you."

Roslyn's heart fluttered with anticipation. "She sent one for me, finally?"

Her grandfather chuckled, his laughter a comforting sound that filled the room. He extended the card to her. As she took it, her eyes quickly scanned the elegant script. It was an invitation to the princess's celebration of her eleventh year.

A week from now. That's not nearly enough time!

She looked at her grandfather in alarm. His amused expression only deepened her scowl. "I need a gown, a gift, I-I need—"

Her frantic words were cut off as her grandfather placed a calming hand on her shoulder. "Whatever you wish to get her as a gift, we will see it done. It pleases me to finally see you this excited to meet someone your age. I will send a messenger to inform Ser Siveril of your attendance as the representative of House Tiloral and the duchy."

Roslyn nodded, her mind already racing with ideas for the perfect gift. *What does a princess even need?* She thought back to Gwyneth, her attire, her demeanor. An idea sparked. Her lips curved into a smile. She knew *exactly* what to get the princess.

She looked at Janine, who sat at a table with Roderick. Her knight met her gaze, a warm smile on her face. Roslyn returned the nod before turning back to her grandfather.

"Grandfather? I need access to the vaults and a letter."

This will be perfect. I hope she likes it!

CHAPTER FIFTEEN

CRAFT TIME

In the cramped but quiet confines of the knights' wagon, Sloane gazed at the chaos of the workbench they'd set up for her. Notes, metal scraps, and various parts littered the surface, remnants of past projects and experiments. Now, on the cusp of attempting rune engraving, she picked up a scrap of metal she had set aside solely for the purpose. A pair of gleaming silver ingots also lay close at hand, waiting to be molded for the engraving. She still needed to commission an engraving pen, but for the time being, she hoped that the silver would suffice for the runes. Once engraved, she could alter the silver into the desired form.

She reached for her makeshift engraving tools. With a deep breath, she focused on her goal of carefully engraving the runic chain that would serve as a storage system for a spell. In theory, at least. Her experiment aimed to evaluate how long a spell could be held within the confines of plain metal, in contrast to a gem. This was a critical part of making her grenades functional.

She scanned over the varying runic chains inscribed in her journal till she found the one she planned to etch into the metal. Using the tool as a conduit for her mana, she **[Altered]** the metal, making it a bit more malleable as she etched the runes. Once the final link in the runic chain was in place, she scrutinized her work, ensuring all the minute details were accurate.

Satisfied, she gave a curt nod and reached for one of the silver ingots. She hovered the tiny block above the engraved runes, channeling her focus into subtly altering the material enough to fill the engravings so that it filled the grooves almost like putty.

The ten-minute process left her panting, sweaty, and far more fatigued than usual from the prolonged magic use. Nevertheless, she admired her handiwork, the hint of a smile gracing her lips. "Here goes nothing . . ." she murmured to herself.

She placed a finger against the runes, accessing her Artifice domain and channeling the [**Flashbang**] spell into the engraved chain. The casting process left her winded, her breaths heavy and irregular as she fought to regain her composure. A soft blue glow emanated from the silver, which gradually faded. Her gaze remained fixed on the silver, tracking its transformation back to its original color.

Well, shit. That didn't work at all.

She tried again, this time trying to channel as slowly as possible. After only five minutes, the glow was completely gone, and Sloane found herself looking at the scrap metal with some nonmagical silver inside of the large runes.

Why is it doing this?

Notebook in hand, she carefully transcribed her observations, trying to glean insights from the lack of a lasting interaction. Resolved to persist, she decided on an added complexity: an additional runic chain to her enchanting, one that would pause until manually activated by the user before unleashing the stored spell. The new runework felt promising and filled her with a renewed sense of optimism.

I hope, at least. I just need to take this to the area set aside for my testing.

A bell later, Sloane was on the training grounds, a veritable laboratory of open space and solitude. A quick glance confirmed she was alone, allowing her to continue her experiment without interruptions or unwanted observers. With a deep breath, she channeled [**Flashbang**] into the runes again. The resulting blue glow was familiar, but this time she didn't wait for it to dissipate. Instead, she carefully set it on the ground, steeling herself to activate the stored spell.

With a simple flick of her will, the rune-engraved piece sprang to life, triggering the |**Flashbang**| runic spell.

The resulting display, however, was far from what she'd anticipated. Instead of the explosive burst she was expecting, it was more akin to a firework—visually appealing, but disappointingly harmless. The sight of a small, blackened spot in place of the storage rune only compounded her frustration.

I'm glad I wasn't holding that. Holy crap.

She was once again thankful that she seemed unaffected by her own magic. That was something else she would need to experiment with, *carefully*, at another time.

Sighing, she slumped against a nearby bench, already beginning to formulate her next strategy.

Now, what can I—

But her thoughts were rudely interrupted when the bench tipped over, sending her sprawling backward. The back of her head struck the ground with a sharp crack, eliciting a string of curses. "Fuck! Ow, damn it! Shit!"

She sat up and groaned, nursing her sore head. "Can this day get any worse?" she grumbled.

"From the looks of it? Not really," a voice answered.

Sloane jerked in surprise and looked for the source of the voice. Gisele stood nearby, an irritatingly amused smirk gracing her features, with Maud beside her.

Approaching with the calm assurance of a seasoned healer, Maud knelt beside Sloane. "Here, allow me," she offered, laying a gentle hand on the back of Sloane's head. A wave of [**Heal Wounds**] flowed from her fingertips, instantly dulling the throbbing pain.

The humiliation, however, remained as stark as before.

Gisele extended a hand, rough yet oddly comforting, to Sloane, to help her up. Though the pain had receded, Sloane absently rubbed the back of her head.

The orkun woman patted Sloane's arm. "Are you okay?" Gisele asked, her voice carrying an undercurrent of amusement thinly veiled by concern.

"Yeah. I'm good now. Thank you, Maud," Sloane assured, meeting Maud's bright green eyes.

The redhead beamed. "Of course! I'm glad I was here to see that. I mean, to help you!"

Sloane squinted at the woman, a faint thread of irritation running through her. *Someone who is supposed to heal shouldn't take such pleasure in embarrassing accidents.*

"So, what were you working on?" Gisele shifted the focus, distracting Sloane.

"I'm trying to work with runes, but they aren't cooperating," Sloane confessed, her frustration evident in her tone. "The spell dissipates way too quickly and doesn't hold at the right strength."

"Interesting. Do you have any thoughts on why?" Gisele asked.

"Not really. At least, not yet," Sloane said. "I need to go back over my observations and figure it out."

Gisele's brow furrowed, arms crossing as she slipped into contemplative silence.

Maud's gaze, meanwhile, strayed to the piece of scorched metal on the ground. "Is this the result of your experiment?" she asked.

Sloane confirmed, an idea igniting. "I chose something expendable for a first test . . . but what if the material's quality determines how well it holds the spell?"

Maud nodded and reached down to pick up the scrap metal with a curious look on her face. "Also, your silver here looks different from when you showed me the inside of your watch."

"Of course. It's not glowing," Sloane responded, not understanding her statement.

The knight-medic shook her head. "No, that's not it. The silver in your watch isn't *just* silver. It's not even a solid metal."

"What are you saying, Maud?" Gisele asked.

Maud explained. "Back home, some of the finer artisans used metallic fila-ments in their works. The material within your watch resembles that more than plain silver." Maud handed the metal slab back to Sloane.

A new avenue opened in Sloane's mind. "So, I originally thought to use silver-based ink. Maybe that's the direction I should explore. It will probably be useful for the Banking Guild runecard as well."

Gisele perked up, eager to contribute. "There's a stationery store in the nobles' market that might have what you need. They cater to high-class scribes and nobles, selling a variety of papers, waxes, and inks. They even make custom stamps for house crests. It might be worth checking out."

Sloane shrugged, her enthusiasm sparked by the promising lead. "Worth a shot. Let's go!"

Accompanied by Gisele and Maud, Sloane ventured through the bustling streets of the central district. She'd traversed this locale several times since her unforgettable first visit, each time flanked by her friends for extra precaution. Always keeping her hood up, she hoped it would serve as a cloak of anonymity, though it did little to tame her unruly curls.

As if she were reading her mind, Maud leaned in. "We need to visit this place next time," she whispered, point out a small, white and gold-fronted storefront. "They have just the thing for your hair."

Sloane peered at the seemingly ordinary building. *There is an actual hair salon!* She looked at Maud's impeccable curls. "Are these places common?"

Maud nodded. "Of course," she said, her voice holding an air of surprise. "A woman needs to take care of her hair, after all. I purchase solutions in every city we visit. It's why my hair looks so fabulous."

Sloane couldn't help but agree. "It does. It really does."

Gisele's snort broke through their light-hearted exchange. "Why does that surprise you, Sloane?"

Sloane lowered her voice a bit. "In my world, during our equivalent devel-opment period, we didn't have anything like this. It's so strange to me. In some areas, you are centuries ahead of where we were, and in others, you're right on track. I don't have the background to guess at the reasoning, and I haven't studied your history enough . . . but it's quite interesting to me."

Maud chuckled. "That sounds like something Ernald would love to discuss. It's beyond me."

Gisele shrugged, her expression thoughtful. "I don't think it's *that* compli-cated. We have many types of people. Your world only had terrans. We have a single pantheon of gods. Yours had many. Our two worlds are different. What we place value on is different. How we live is different. All of this?" She gestured around. "It is pretty recent. My people had it rough. Maud's as well. The Loreni migrated and invaded Ikios hundreds of years ago. They never left, but most of us adapted. Those who didn't . . . well they found a new path. We carved new societies out of it. We improved and learned that if we all worked together, then we could be better than before. What is now known as Ikios looks nothing like what existed during the Old Empire, or like what exists today in Loren."

Maud nodded. "Well said, Gisele. I don't think about it much, personally. It's all I have ever known. It's all my parents have ever known. Some places are worse than others. Westaren is one of them, for instance . . . at least mainly restricted to the nobility in the kingdom . . ." She trailed off and went silent.

Concern washed over Sloane as she watched Maud. "You okay?"

The redhead simply nodded, a distant look in her eyes. "Just thinking. I miss home."

Gisele, catching the vulnerable moment, moved closer to Maud, wrapping her arm around the healer. "We all do, Maud," she said softly. "We all do. But we know why we're here."

Maud wiped her eyes and nodded. "The store's right there. Let's go. I'm fine."

Exchanging an understanding look with Gisele, Sloane acknowledged the silent conversation between them. Maud needed them, and they were there for her. Gisele gave Maud one last squeeze as they made their way to the store.

As they neared the stationery shop, Sloane's eyes were drawn to the elegant wooden facade and large windows showcasing the interior. Rows of bookshelves and tables laden with various supplies beckoned to her curiosity.

The jingle of a small bell welcomed them as they stepped in. An elderly raithe man appeared from behind a stack of notebooks. "Welcome, welcome. How may I assist you?"

Gisele looked at Sloane and stepped aside. Getting the hint, Sloane rolled her eyes and stepped forward. "I am looking for a type of ink that has silver inside of it. Maybe powdered? I am not entirely sure. If you have multiple types, I'd like to try them."

The old man paused and rubbed his chin. "I have some silvered ink right over here."

They wove through the labyrinth of shelves, each filled to the brim with notebooks, document folios, envelopes, and intricate writing paper. Sloane found herself drawn to a display of exquisite pens and quills, adjacent to a collection of various ink wells. Among them, a leatherbound journal, adorned with an intricate floral design on the front, captured her attention.

"Maud, look at this." She pointed out the leatherbound journal. "Isn't it simply beautiful? Oh my gosh . . . and these pens! I need to buy some supplies. Stat."

Gisele and Maud exchanged amused glances. "Gisele, I think we've stumbled upon what Sloane likes to shop for."

"Sloane, I never realized you had such an . . . exciting . . . hobby," Gisele teased, her lips curling up and around her tusks as she glanced around the shop.

Sloane crossed her arms. "What? Gisele enjoys massive swords. I like office supplies. We all have our thing. Maud likes . . . being fancy."

Maud mimicked a motion Sloane would only describe as meaning, "touché." "You're not wrong, Sloane."

Their congenial banter filled the shop as the old man, with a soft chuckle, led them toward a cabinet brimming with glass bottles filled with an artist's palette of inks. He rifled through the multicolored collection and then shifted his attention to the adjacent cabinet.

"Aha," he murmured finally, retrieving three containers filled with a distinct, silvery liquid. He guided the group to a nearby counter and selected a piece of paper and a quill. "I have three different types. The first is a new product and contains some new materials. It's quite expensive due to the rarity of the ingredients." He moved to the next. "This one is simply silver powder, some oil binders, and a solvent. And this one is silver-colored, but doesn't have silver in it."

"That one won't work. Containing silver is a requirement," Sloane said.

The shopkeeper nodded in understanding. "The first is probably the one you want, then. It is a new product that arrived only in the last couple of weeks. It has a higher silver powder content and similar oil binders, but the organic solvent is from a newly discovered plant called the silden fern. I don't know the specifics, only that it is similar to a type of fern that is prevalent in these parts, but seems to grow at night under the moons rather than through the day."

Intrigued, Sloane inquired, "The plant was only discovered recently?"

"Yes, it was found a few weeks ago. The alchemists who chanced upon it were studying the Flash's effect on the local flora," the shopkeeper confirmed.

Sloane looked at her companions, silently sharing her curiosity.

It was just discovered. Could it be a magic plant?

She turned her attention back to the shopkeeper. "How popular is this ink?" she inquired.

The shopkeeper hummed in thought. "Well, quite in demand, I must say, but its premium price deters excessive purchases."

An idea sparked in her mind. "First, I would like two bottles of this ink. Second, could I possibly get in touch with these alchemists?"

"A fine choice!" he said, clapping his hands once. "But do keep in mind: they exclusively sell their products through our shop."

"That's perfectly fine. I'm more interested in other finds and alchemical creations they have made. I guess you could say I am something of an alchemist myself," Sloane explained.

Gisele, standing off to the side, stifled a snort of amusement. Sloane sent her a reproachful look.

"Ah, a fellow lover of the alchemical arts. Very well," he conceded, "let me pack up your ink and I'll get you their information."

"Oh! As you do that, there are a few other items that have caught my eye," Sloane said, her attention already drifting back to the shelves of office supplies.

The shopkeeper chuckled good-naturedly, accompanying her as she made further selections. With her bounty gathered, Sloane finally approached the counter. The old raithe began to diligently packed her purchases, reciting the cost of each as he placed them in a fabric bag.

"And here are your two bottles of ink," he announced. "Fifteen silver each."

Maud choked on her breath beside her, and Gisele raised a questioning eyebrow. "How much silver is in them?" she queried.

The shopkeeper chuckled once more. "While these contain more silver than any other ink we stock, the quantity remains minimal. It's the production process and the rarity of the silden fern that inflate the price."

Sloane chewed on her lip as she mentally tallied up the day's expenditures, cross-checking with what she knew was in her Guild account.

I may want to stockpile this. Especially if it works like I think it will. If not, well, then I have a pretty ink.

"How many bottles of this ink do you have on hand?" she inquired.

The shopkeeper appeared to do a mental inventory, eyes fixed on the ceiling in concentration. "After these two, I believe there are still . . . eleven bottles left."

Sloane mused for a moment before asking, "Would it be possible to charge my purchase to my Banking Guild account?"

"Certainly, my lady," the shopkeeper said with a nod, professionalism etched in his every word. "Being a member of the Scribe and Merchant Guilds, I maintain my own accounts. I'll require your badge, and you'll need to stamp your seal on the bill of sale," he explained methodically.

Sloane reached into her satchel, drawing her badge with its gleaming ruby set in it. As she placed it on the counter, she began, "Here's my badge. If you give me a moment to . . ."

The shopkeeper's eyes widened as they fell on the badge. "M-my lady, I had no idea . . ." He stuttered in surprise. "Please, just have one of your attendants deliver the bill of sale to the Guild at their earliest convenience. The Guild will manage the rest."

Bemused, Sloane raised an eyebrow and glanced at Gisele, who seemed equally taken aback. "You know, Elodie would be perfect for this sort of task," Sloane mused aloud.

Gisele's lips curled into a knowing smirk. "She did mention her usefulness in handling purchases," she concurred.

Sloane shrugged, storing this new insight in her mental notes.

The shopkeeper attentively followed their conversation. When they finished, he said, "Furthermore, as a token of gratitude for your patronage, I'd like to offer a twenty percent discount on your purchase. Would you prefer for us to deliver your goods?"

"I believe we can manage to carry our purchases for now," Sloane said. "Thank you for your kindness, Mister . . ."

"Keenley. Mister Keenley," he responded promptly.

"Well, thank you for all of your assistance today, Mister Keenley," Sloane said with a smile.

The shopkeeper nodded. "Thank you kindly, my lady. If you'll excuse me, I'll package the rest of your supplies."

Mister Keenley busied himself with carefully packaging Sloane's office supplies, then paused. He slid open a drawer under the counter and pulled out a small notepad and pen, a thoughtful look on his face. His hand moved with swift precision as he jotted down something on a piece of paper, ripped it from the pad, and folded it.

"These are the contacts for the alchemists who concocted this unique ink," he explained, his fingers delicately holding out the piece of paper. His voice held a note of respect and admiration for the craft. "They're a pair of remarkable individuals. They continue to make strides in alchemy, and I highly recommend them."

Sloane accepted the note and opened it to find two names and an address written in elegant, looping script. She looked up at Mister Keenley, her eyes shimmering with curiosity and excitement.

"Tell them Mister Keenley sent you," he added with a knowing smile, the hint of a shared secret in his eyes. "They'll understand."

With a sense of anticipation bubbling in her chest, Sloane gently folded the note and placed it safely in her satchel. She took in the collection of all her new office supplies. A slow smile spread across her face, satisfaction making her eyes shine, a spark of joy kindling in her heart.

You can never have enough.

CHAPTER SIXTEEN

UNLEASHING CHAOS AND COUTURE

A few bells later, Sloane found herself back at the comforting familiarity of her workbench. Gisele sat adjacent to her, her curiosity evident in the thoughtful expression she wore. Meanwhile, Maud, ever the social butterfly, had returned to the company of their friends, the detailed intricacies of Artifice holding little appeal to her.

Beneath the warm glow of the overhead lantern, Sloane's workbench was a controlled chaos of tools, materials, and plans. In the center of it all sat one of the steel balls she planned to embed within the grenade's casing. The cool metallic surface waited to be etched with powerful runes, its potential almost palpable.

Sloane held a piece of white chalk, her hand hovering above the steel ball as she envisioned the placement of the runes. There would be a specific spot where the button would activate the functions, with a dominant area on the side dedicated for the |Storage| rune.

Just like a blueprint coming to life.

Gisele broke the silence, her voice brimming with interest. "So, how does this all work? Can you explain as you do it?"

Sloane nodded, maintaining her attention on the task as she started drawing her reference lines. "Sure thing." She lifted the chalk and pointed at the white lines. "I'm making a reference of everything I want to do, so that when I start engraving I can just follow the lines."

"That seems sensible. It will help you not make a mistake?"

"Yup!"

She [**Focused**] as she began the meticulous process of drawing out the runes. "When this is done, I'm going to engrave the various runic chains that make up the overall runework of the grenade. Each chain performs a separate function, translating my intent into tangible magic." She completed the reference of the |Trigger| rune, the symbol standing out sharply against the steel, before moving to the next one.

"The runic language functions like an extremely basic programming language my people used back home. It's not too robust, but that could just be me. Maybe I can even learn enough to create my own runic language in the future. But that's a long way away. I'm barely scratching the surface as it is. One thing I have learned is that runes will *not* function if you just etch one out. You have to have the Artifice domain for the runes to work, as that type of magic is what will properly imbue the runes with intent. This is a good thing: it means that only other Artificers can copy a design. I'll need to work with the Merchant Guild or some other to work out a way to ensure my designs are my own and aren't stolen."

"I understand," Gisele responded, absorbing the information. "Perhaps, when the field expands enough, you could contribute to establishing an Artificer's Guild," she suggested.

"That's a great idea, Gisele. I'll have to pick your brain about it later." Sloane finished the same |Storage| runic chain that she had designed previously.

"What is the difference between runes and runic chains or the like?" Gisele asked.

"Too bad Ernald isn't here. He'd love this part," Sloane mused out loud. Moving on, she picked up her engraving tool, ready to carve life into the bare metallic surface. "The runework consists of various runes, each associated with a distinct function. For instance, this one," she gestured with the tool, "is the rune for |Detect|. Its primary function is to sense or perceive something."

She etched the rune carefully, using her alteration to gently manipulate the metal as if gliding through putty. "However, on its own, it's pretty much useless. It needs to be coupled with an operator, or a directive that guides its function. In this context, we're adding a specific symbol because we want it to |Detect| when the |Trigger| rune is activated. This activation occurs when the rune on the button of the casing comes into contact with the rune I've placed on top. So, this specific rune translates to |Detect: Trigger|."

Her tool danced across the steel, etching a new rune. "Then we need it to wait. We want the grenade to wait for a certain duration after detection—say, three seconds. This can be achieved with the |Intent| rune, which, as far as I've figured, is a bit of a wild card. This might be why an Artificer's presence is so crucial—I'm not certain if anyone else can infuse their intent into the runes. For this rune, we're going to project the intent of a three-second delay."

Sloane then moved to the final steps, her movements steady and focused. "Finally, we instruct it to |Use| the |Spell| that was previously |Store|'d, and we amplify it. I got that idea after our earlier experiment didn't quite meet my expectations." The steel ball now bore a complex network of runes. "So, the final runic chain manifests as this," she said, pointing at the long sequence.

Throughout the explanation, Gisele watched with rapt attention, her keen eyes tracking Sloane's every move. After a thoughtful pause, she asked, "The |Flashbang| spell seemed to be emitted from the runes earlier. If you insert this ball into the casing you've designed, won't the spell detonate inside?"

Sloane shrugged, her brow furrowed in contemplation. "Honestly? I have no idea. I'm hoping it will see the casing as part of the overall design. If not, I'll probably need to use the |Separate| rune somehow."

Gisele considered this, her forehead creasing slightly. "If you don't mind my saying, I think . . . logically, you should go ahead and try it. Based on what we saw earlier, I don't think your spell will work as you intend it to. You have that one rune that waits for a trigger. Maybe just copy that but instead of triggering the spell, it triggers the |Separate| rune."

Sloane tapped her etching tool against her notebook, amazed by how quickly Gisele had picked that up. *It wouldn't hurt to do it that way.* If anything, it might make her grenades slightly more expendable. Which was the reason she hadn't already done it.

I think I'm making enough to commission a decent number of them. Four or five, maybe, should be enough for each knight. She looked at Gisele. "Okay. Let's give it a shot."

Sloane got to work finishing everything up, etching the new runic chain and then using the new ink in the runes and pushing her mana to help it set. When she was finally done, she slowly channeled **[Flashbang]** into the storage rune, then her intent into the timer. She watched as the silver started glowing, then seemed to sit well. After five minutes, it still hadn't dimmed.

"So, think we're good?"

With a smile, the knight nodded. "It's go time."

Sloane snorted. "Alright. Let's put it all together, then test it."

She placed the steel ball into its slot in the bottom casing, then carefully set up the oversized button she had fabricated before she carefully inserted the pin that would keep the trigger from accidentally triggering the grenade. She fastened the top half of the casing on the bottom and smiled.

"I think we're ready," she said.

"Okay, let's go test it!" Gisele said excitedly.

The two gathered up all their things and made their way to the training courtyard. Cristole and Ernald were already there.

Sloane instinctively rubbed the back of her head as she saw them. They were both sitting on the *evil* bench and talking. Gisele noticed and Sloane ignored her light chuckles.

"Alright, we're here. Should we tell them?" Sloane asked.

Gisele smirked. "They'll figure it out quick enough."

Sloane held out the grenade. "Do the honors?"

Gisele smiled. "Gladly. I just pull the pin, press the button until it makes contact, then toss it?"

"Yup!" Sloane was getting excited.

She watched as Gisele smirked, turned slightly, and pulled the pin. She took a deep breath, then pressed the button and tossed it. *Right* onto the half of the courtyard where the two were sitting.

Sloane's eyes went wide. "Wait!"

Shit. Well . . . moment of truth!

The grenade bounced several times before it settled and Sloane mentally counted in her head. She misjudged the time because right before she hit three, the grenade separated, both halves flying apart. The steel ball inside glowed blue. Then, the runic |**Flashbang**| went off with a loud crack of sound and blinding light.

It didn't affect Sloane as it had done before, but Gisele instantly reacted by shielding her eyes. The other two were not as lucky. The men both screamed and instantly grabbed at each other as they toppled over the bench to the ground.

After a moment, Sloane saw Cristole's head peek above his legs, which were draped over the fallen bench. "What?!" The elf's eyes caught sight of Gisele and narrowed. "Gisele? What did you do?!"

Ernald rolled over, groaning and rubbing his head. "Why . . .?"

Gisele smirked. "That, you two, is for what you both did in Parholm."

Cristole's eyes widened. "That was *two* years ago! We apologized!"

"And now we are even. I told you I would get you back one day."

Sloane looked between the two men stumbling to their feet and the woman with an overly satisfied expression on her face. "What happened in Parholm?"

"They ran off with my clothes from the bathhouse. I ran around that city with barely a *towel* after those two for a whole bell."

Sloane snorted. "So, you used a flashbang on them because they made you *flash* the entire town? I can respect it." Ernald groaned. Sloane gathered up all the pieces of the grenade. Everything seemed to be in decent shape.

Gisele smiled. "Well, at least we know your grenades work."

"Luckily, these aren't nearly as debilitating as they are back in my world. I'll need to work on that. Well, and you tossed it sufficiently far away from them. Next, I'm going to work on some that will explode."

Cristole's eyebrows shot up. "Not near us, you won't!"

Gisele's grin grew predatory. "See you two back at the inn. Sloane, shall we?"

Sloane laughed. "Let's go." She called back over her shoulder, "Don't take too long, gentlemen. I have to teach you all how to use these!"

* * *

In the aftermath of her testing, Sloane had envisioned a tranquil afternoon of respite, tucked away in her quarters with a mug of hot tea, her newly acquired office supplies, and the comfort of solitude.

However, like a relentless tide, Maud, Gisele, and Ismeld had swept her away, whisking her off on an unanticipated shopping expedition for the imminent ball. Sloane then ensured that Elodie, too, had been conscripted into this mission, and as an inevitable consequence, it meant Stefan was also roped in.

What had started as an innocent venture had snowballed into an extravagant spectacle. The event quickly mutated into an ordeal that had Sloane questioning her life choices.

Finding herself in a sumptuous boutique nestled within the heart of the central district, Sloane was awash in a sea of nobility. The shop was abuzz with elegant women of varying ages and races, each engrossed in their quest for the perfect dress. Raithe ladies, telv debutantes, and elf matrons swarmed the shop, their chatter merging into a cacophonous symphony.

Stefan stood sentinel near the entrance. His placid expression belied the amusement lurking in his eyes.

Meanwhile, Gisele, Maud, and Elodie had established a command center of sorts, huddled together on plush velvet seats with Sloane's lone ally in this arena of haute couture, Ismeld, as they appraised her current dress with analytical eyes.

I wish I hadn't waited until the last minute. Fuck.

The garment in question was an exhibit of intricate craftsmanship. It boasted a tight bodice, meticulously laced up, constraining her form like a bird caged within an ornate, gilded prison. The skirts were voluminous, cascading down in a waterfall of velvet, the fabric heavy and cumbersome. Billowing sleeves, trimmed with extravagant fur, hung from her shoulders, lending her an appearance more akin to a monarch from a bygone era rather than the modern, practical woman she identified as.

The painstaking embroidery, the glinting precious stones sewn into the design, and the overwhelming majesty of it all were undeniably impressive—as a museum piece, she thought. Thus, along with the tangle of hoops underneath that supported the skirt it was a stark mismatch to her disposition. She was a woman of practicality and comfort, not an ornament to be displayed.

Expressing her dislike, she quickly cast off the medieval relic, and reluctantly slipped into the next offering from the raithe attendant—a gown with decidedly Renaissance flair, or, as they called it, Sovereign.

This dress bore a lower neckline, revealing her décolletage in an unabashed display of femininity. The bodice was snug, accentuating her curves, and the skirts were a little more manageable, flowing down in softer waves of lustrous fabric. The sleeves, less extravagant but still ornate, complemented the overall look.

The switch seemed to ignite a spark among the onlooking women. The transformation was undeniable; she looked every bit the stately woman they'd envisioned, her exposed cleavage and the dress's enhanced silhouette eliciting their collective admiration.

Maud was the most starry-eyed and excited, and the first to express her opinion. "Sloane, that is *gorgeous*. Absolutely stunning. I can't wait to see how many heads you turn."

Sloane rolled her eyes. "You're just saying that because you can't wear a dress, like you want."

Gisele, ever the tease, was quick to follow, a sly grin tugging at the corners of her mouth. "Well, if anything, you'll give the ball a much-needed shock. And if all else fails in what we need to do, you can distract everyone with that cleavage."

Sloane responded with a glare, her expression a mix of annoyance and discomfiture. "You're not helping, Gisele."

The orkun woman merely shrugged, her smile deepening. "Just saying."

Elodie chimed in next, ever the consummate employee speaking to their boss. "Regardless of your discomfort, Lady Reinhart, you do look quite regal. But it is important that you feel comfortable and like yourself."

Ismeld, in contrast, snorted, seemingly unimpressed by the spectacle. "She looks silly," she declared with a dismissive wave of her hand. The armor-clad woman had been visibly relieved that she'd been exempt from the dress-fitting ordeal.

She's not wrong.

Sloane sighed, her fingers twitching against the rich fabric. "I look like someone cosplaying in a Ren faire. I've never done that before. I have to say . . . I don't like it," she admitted aloud, a rueful smile tugging at her lips.

Maud gasped in response, clutching her chest dramatically. "But you look amazing, Sloane!"

Gisele, though, raised an eyebrow. "What is a Ren faire?"

Sloane smiled. "Well, you see how all of you dress now?"

They nodded.

"Remember the clothing I wore when I arrived?" she continued.

Gisele nodded again. "Of course, it is so . . . different."

"Well, we have these events where people dress up like you do, sort of, just for entertainment," she explained. "This dress is kind of similar to dresses worn in my world almost six hundred years ago."

A smirk played on Ismeld's lips. "And now you get to wear it here. What's the phrase you like to say? Ah, yes. 'Sucks to suck.'"

Sloane scowled.

I wish there was somewhere to hide a grenade in this dress.

She sighed as she looked down at herself.

I could probably fit at least one there.

* * *

Her outfit and other accoutrements now safely stored in her room, Sloane sat at a large corner table with the knights, Elodie, and Stefan.

Inns have really become our go-to spot—not that there's a plethora of other options around here. She was definitely going to find a nice spot to settle with Gwyn. Maybe Avira, if it was as nice as the knights suggested.

"Elodie, have you ever been to Avira?" Sloane asked the young high elf woman sitting a couple of seats down, at the end of the table.

The elf looked up from where she was awkwardly observing her hands. "Me? No, I haven't been that far. I've been as far as Laudenwych in the central plains. I've been to Marketbol many times, though. So I can certainly help us navigate the city when we arrive. It's a much nicer city than Thirdghyll."

"I've heard good things about Marketbol—aside from the fact that its name is a travesty," Ernald chimed in. "Leave it to the guilds to have no sense of flair. That said, it's undoubtedly the crown jewel of the guild system as a whole."

Elodie nodded. "It is indeed a key location. It is also home to the regional offices of numerous minor guilds, in addition to the headquarters of the Banking Guild. I was born there, and would much prefer to live there. However, with Uncle Lanthil setting up here, the family relocated to be of assistance."

"If you have questions about any of the other Sovereign Cities, I have been to many of them. Including the Empire and Rosale," Stefan offered.

"The Kingdom of Rosale will probably be a key stop along the way to Avira, Sloane," Gisele helpfully added.

Sloane nodded, making a mental note for the future. She had a thought. "Sorry to switch topics, but what about the ball? It's in two days. Are we ready? Stefan, are *you* ready? What can you tell me since we last spoke about it?"

Ismeld gestured between herself and the rest of the knights. "We're ready. I believe you are too. I also would like to know what we're getting ourselves into with you, Stefan. We need a plan to exfiltrate the area if the worst happens and whatever they tasked you to accomplish is discovered."

"I have learned that there is another terran noble working with the count. His name is William Bolton, a baron, and he apparently comes from the land of England?"

"He's British? Interesting. I didn't realize they still had barons there, but I'm not up-to-date on their nobility. Do you have any other information about there being other, uh . . . terrans?" Sloane asked.

Stefan shook his head. "No. That's still the primary goal of what I am to figure out. I have found out that terrans have been seen entering his estate. Beyond that, nothing. I simply need you to keep the count occupied long enough for me to slip around. If you can create a distraction of some type, that would be even more ideal."

Gisele narrowed her eyes. "There will be no distraction."

Stefan sighed. "Fine. I'll figure it out, but Lady Reinhart, I will need you to hold Count Kayser's attention at least a little while." She nodded. He pulled out a map and lay it on the table. "Here are the grounds of the count's estate. Here is the hall where the ball will be held," he said, pointing out the location. The raithe circled several more key points. "And these are exits."

"Where are the guards typically posted? What is their response time when alerted?" Cristole asked.

"And how are they alerted and from where?" Deryk followed up.

Sloane swapped seats with Ismeld to be near Elodie and then watched as the rest of the group discussed the specifics of their attendance and exit if anything negative were to happen. Stefan would attend as her direct guard, while the knights would attend as part of their order. Elodie would join as Sloane's assistant.

"Lady Reinhart?" Elodie whispered from next to her.

Sloane looked over at the woman, who looked as if she'd just won an internal war with herself about whether to speak or not. *She looks worried.* She didn't want to cause any undue stress to the elf, so she leaned in closer to her. "Is everything alright, Elodie?"

"I'm sorry. I thought we would have time to talk before retiring for the evening," she said, without explaining anything at all.

"Go on . . ." Sloane pushed.

"I know what my uncle wants you to do to get his recommendation, but I have to say . . ., I'm worried about going up against the count," she said. "He's not one to be underestimated."

Sloane rested her hands on top of each other and tapped a finger. "I understand, Elodie. But I need to do this." She paused, considering. "I need all the help I can get to find my daughter. If things get bad, your uncle *should* be there. Get to him. I have a feeling he can protect you. The knights and I will be fine."

"I sure hope so."

"Me too, Elodie."

The discussion wound down, and Sloane went back to her room. She looked over everything, trying to determine what she would bring to the ball. She would need to spend the day preparing. A few flashbangs to give to the knights would go a long way toward arming them for any potential outcomes.

Sloane looked longingly at the grenade sitting there, ready to be used, before placing her knife next to her dress. That was something she couldn't forget. Her options were limited, but at least she'd chosen a dress that would be easier to maneuver in.

She sat on her bed cross-legged, thinking about what else she could do to ensure everything went well. *There is one thing I can bring with me that others can't.*

Sloane focused inward and, with a smirk, felt mana coursing through her as she drew on it.

CHAPTER SEVENTEEN

CASANOVAS AND ESPIONAGE

The arrival of Sloane and her companions at the ball was a decidedly understated affair: Stefan's whispered conversation with the gate guards, a cross-check against an opulently illuminated guest list, and they were admitted. Elodie was at Sloane's side, a comforting presence in the midst of the growing grandeur, while Stefan took up a watchful position behind them.

The knights would make their entrance separately—a plan designed to portray an image of growing separation between the two groups. This ploy might not fool many of the attendees, but it should help disperse the attention their group invariably drew.

Stepping into the expansive courtyard of the count's estate was like stepping into another world—one teeming with gaily dressed nobility and affluent commoners, holding court at the multitude of standing tables that were strategically scattered across the verdant expanse. Groups of elves, raithe, and telv huddled in close-knit clusters, their low murmurs punctuated by the delicate clinking of glasses of what looked like sparkling wine.

Uniformed guards, resplendent in their finest ceremonial attire, stood at attention, their presence a seamless part of the landscape. It was curious, Sloane noted, that all the guards were either raithe or moon elves.

As they approached the stately manor, an attendant stepped forward to greet them. After a brief exchange, they were allowed to proceed. As they passed, the attendant turned away, disappearing into the depths of the estate.

Perhaps reporting on my presence?

Everywhere she looked, the surroundings dripped with opulence, an ostentatious display of wealth and power. This was nothing new; she had seen such extravagance among the privileged back on Earth. But the count seemed to be doing it to the detriment of those he governed. Sloane would hold her opinions until she met him, but, thus far, she saw no reason for any nation to allow such blatant corruption to continue.

Caught up in her observations, Sloane turned to Elodie. "Have you been here before?" She waved a hand, encompassing the gold-trimmed frames, the ornate vases, the imposing marble columns—objects more suited for a royal palace than the home of a ruler presiding over a largely poor region.

Elodie's gaze swept over the decor before returning to Sloane. "Here? No. Never." Her voice held a note of understated surprise. "It's . . . remarkable, isn't it?"

"How can he afford all of this? The central district is reasonably well-off, but the rest, well . . . everything seems to not support this," Sloane mused aloud.

Stefan's voice interjected from behind them, crisp and clear. "It's because the count prefers to bleed his people and businesses dry with exorbitant taxes rather than improve his dominion. All that wealth? It ends up here."

Sloane, her gaze lingering on the extravagance around her, murmured, "Why does the kingdom allow it?" She looked at Stefan.

He lifted his shoulders in a casual shrug. "I don't know. Perhaps the guild-master has some insights into that." His tone was noncommittal, leaving Sloane with her unanswered question.

Sloane simply shrugged and led the way, guiding her group along a grand corridor. They navigated past knots of nobles engaged in private conversations, their voices hushed, heads bending together in conspiratorial whispers. Their path led them down another hallway, this one lined with an imposing array of guards. One particular moon elf guard stepped forward, his stance authoritative yet courteous, and ushered them into the main hall.

As they passed through a pair of ornate double doors, the sight of a sprawling ballroom unfurled before them, down a staircase that seemed to invite them into its festive throng. Spread throughout the hall were tables, each a hub of chatter and laughter, around which servers moved like agile dancers, balancing platters laden with sumptuous food and exquisite drinks. Standing sentinel just inside the doors, at the top of the staircase, was a raithe guard of remarkable stature. His white hair, meticulously braided, was draped over a shoulder and contrasted sharply against his scarlet doublet.

Once the grand doors had thudded shut behind them, the raithe surveyed them with a look of mild disappointment, his eyes glazed with indifference. "Your name, my lady?" He drawled the question out lazily, as if it were a chore to inquire.

Elodie, a single eyebrow arched in mild annoyance, answered on their behalf, announcing her title and house with a note of defiance.

The raithe seemed unimpressed, turning away to proclaim in a voice laced with boredom, "Presenting Lady Sloane of House Reinhart from the Kingdom of Blightwych." Swiveling back to face them, his voice dropped to a more conversational tone as he drawled, "Lord Kayser sends his regards, my lady terran. Enjoy the ball."

Sloane shook her head at the strange comment, deciding to dismiss the attendant rather than engage in fruitless bickering. Elodie, however, shot the man a scathing glare as they began their descent down the majestic staircase.

Sloane took note of the many eyes that had settled on her small group as they made their way down. Several even seemed as if they would step forward the moment they set foot at the base. She sized up the crowd and immediately zeroed in on the one person here already she knew. Standing at the bar and talking with a group of Loreni was the sun elf guildmaster of the Banking Guild and Elodie's uncle, Lanthil Romaris.

Turning to Elodie, Sloane inclined her head toward Lanthil, keeping her voice low as she whispered, "Could you please go and meet your uncle? See if he might be available for a conversation?" The subtle movement of her head in Lanthil's direction ensured Elodie understood precisely who she meant.

"Of course. You do not need assistance?" the young financial advisor asked.

A smirk played at the corners of Sloane's mouth as she shook her head.

You are way out of your element here, girl. I just have to pretend they're all CEOs and politicians.

She had learned to navigate such spaces with a simple mantra—smile and nod. Aloud, she simply responded, "I'll manage."

Elodie offered a nod of understanding, moving away gracefully as they descended the final steps and reached the base of the grand staircase. Stefan, silent until then, stepped forward to stand beside her. Sloane cast him a quick, curious glance. "Are you off to do your thing, or will you remain by my side to maintain appearances?" she asked, sotto voce.

Stefan met her gaze, replying in an equally hushed tone, "Let's get through the introductions first. I'll slip away afterward."

They had barely taken a few steps further when a pair of moon elf men sidled into their path. The first—a purple-skinned elf with a fragrant cloud of cologne, or perhaps perfume, wafting around him—caught her attention. His closely shaven beard framed a receding hairline that nearly met his ears.

He seemed middle-aged and instantly—"A new face! Glorious, splendid!"—came off as a pompous prick.

Patience, Sloane. Patience. Alos? Eona? Anyone?

"Greetings?" she asked, not wanting to say much else.

"Ah, I was just telling Lord Andrei here that Ghyll's high society was due for another terran noble. The other one is such a bore," he elaborated, gesturing at his companion.

Sloane's gaze shifted to the other moon elf, a man with bluish skin and an impressively full head of hair. His sharp jawline and narrow nose were accentuated by a pencil-thin mustache that traced his smirk as he appraised her. In turn, she evaluated him, her gaze sliding over his black vest adorned with gold trim and intricate embroidery, and the form-fitting pants bloused above a pair of shin-high leather boots, also trimmed with gold.

Much better looking than his friend, she acknowledged to herself, surprised to find the appraisal wasn't entirely begrudging.

"Lord Andrei, is it?" Sloane ventured, deftly sidestepping the boisterous moon elf.

At the mention of his name, the man straightened, offering a bow. "Indeed. Lord Andrei of House Vasile. My somewhat rude companion is Lord Leon of House Iliescu. A pleasure to meet you, Lady Reinhart." He paused, tilting his head slightly as he recalled her introduction. "It was House Reinhart, yes? Did I hear it correctly?"

"Quite so," Sloane confirmed, her gaze flickering between the two men. "But please, let's not be so formal." A wave of Lord Leon's excessive perfume hit her, nearly overpowering, prompting her to subtly draw back.

Less is more, my dude.

Taking Sloane's response as an invitation to rejoin the conversation, Lord Leon swiftly interjected, "Why, we simply wanted to acquaint ourselves with you, Lady Sloane! *Sloane* is correct?" She nodded and he smiled a bit too wide. "Splendid. It's not every day we have the delight of welcoming a new noble to our modest circle. Are you planning to stay long in Ghyll? We must certainly arrange for a social gathering, perhaps over drinks or some other amusement."

Sloane raised an eyebrow.

Ah, these two are running game. Oldest trick in the book, Andrei.

She put on her best smile and looked straight at Andrei. "Oh, that does sound *splendid*. Regrettably, my schedule is rather packed. In fact, I am only here for a short while for business before I must continue on my journey. I am only here tonight to meet with the *bore* you mentioned earlier and, if time permits, Lord Kayser."

A flicker of interest sparked in Andrei's eyes, though it was quickly replaced with a guarded expression. "Leon," he started, his gaze never leaving Sloane's, "didn't we observe Lady Ansley earlier? Weren't you keen to discuss the new play she's sponsoring?"

Lord Leon's eyebrows knitted in momentary confusion before recognition dawned. His nostrils flared slightly, perhaps a sign of annoyance. "Oh, yes! I absolutely must confer with Lady Ansley." As he pivoted toward Sloane, he extended his hand, palm upward.

Really? She resisted the urge to roll her eyes.

"My lady, it has been a splendid pleasure meeting you . . ." he drawled.

"Likewise," she replied, allowing a warm smile but avoiding his outstretched hand. She swiveled her focus back to Andrei, catching the fleeting scowl on Leon's face as he pulled back his rejected hand and stalked off.

"Don't mind him. He's an only child and can't help himself," Andrei said, in an attempt to smooth over his companion's demeanor.

As they began to weave their way around the crowd, Sloane subtly guided their trajectory toward the location she knew Elodie to be. "Oh? That's quite unfortunate that his parents would allow their only child to act in such a way."

Andrei gave a resigned shrug, the movement stirring the folds of his elegant attire. "The perils of overloving a child, but what can you do? It's why I tend to be by his side. He's a good man, just a bit over the top. I tend to stay close to him, try to curb his flamboyance a little, ensure he doesn't cause too much disruption."

"That's rather noble of you, Lord Andrei," Sloane replied, her words laden with subtle sarcasm that Andrei seemed to blissfully miss.

With a soft chuckle, Andrei extended a hand to intercept a passing server, procuring two glasses filled with sparkling wine. Handing one to Sloane, he indulged in a small sip from his own. "What do you make of our city? Quite the jewel in the kingdom's crown, don't you think?"

Sloane fought the expression that was threatening to show on her face. She nearly raised a single eyebrow, the same one Gwyn always called her out on when she was dealing with someone without sense.

Sloane calmed down by remembering what her daughter would say: *Mom, put that brow away. It's a deadly weapon.*

"Your city is certainly something. I have been all over the district while we have been here, and there are many things to see and do. Great people to meet. It feels so safe and calm," she ground out.

"Exactly! I am gladdened you think so, Sloane. Is it alright if I call you Sloane? Please, call me Andrei. I would be happy to show you some of the lesser-known locations that are to die for," he said, then began talking about some of his favorite spots they both just had to see.

"Well, I can confirm I've encountered at least one spot that meets that criteria," Sloane added with a sardonic smile.

Intrigued, Andrei turned to her. "Oh? And where might that be?" Genuine curiosity illuminated his eyes.

Catching sight of the bar where Elodie was engaged in conversation with her uncle, Sloane tilted her head toward Andrei and replied, "Somewhere along the main street. I simply can't remember. I was in a rush, and almost lost my bearings amid the side alleys. Luckily, it was all over in a flash, and I made my way back to where I am staying."

"Indeed, it can be quite overwhelming," Andrei replied, his words veiled in condescension. "All the enthralling stores, the rush of the unfamiliar, it can sometimes cause a lady to lose her way. Perhaps, if you'd allow, I could serve as your guide during your stay?" As they continued their meandering progress, Andrei filled the air with his self-praise and lofty propositions of how he could enhance her visit to the city.

Meanwhile, Sloane noted the reactions of the crowd: women glancing at them with disdain, men ogling her with scant regard for discretion. It was a predatory environment, and the stench of lascivious entitlement in the air tested her patience.

In his attempt to charm her, Andrei broached another proposal. "I would be honored to host you at my manor for tea. Perhaps I could give you a private tour of my esteemed art collection?"

Calmly, Sloane declined. "Your offer is generous, Andrei, but my schedule here is rather packed. My sincere apologies."

Spotting their arrival at her intended destination, she continued, "Speaking of obligations . . ." Turning to face Lanthil, she greeted him. "Guildmaster! What a delightful coincidence to find you here. Elodie and I were just discussing when we might have the pleasure of your company again."

Lanthil looked at her and Andrei before turning back to the group he was with. "A moment, please." The group said some last words and politely excused themselves from the area.

Sloane looked at Stefan and gave him a subtle nod. His eyes hardened as they landed on Andrei, but he acknowledged her with a succinct nod before melting into the crowd. Sloane surveyed the room as Stefan retreated. As her gaze swept over them, several nobles hastily averted their eyes. Evidently, she had already earned a reputation as a figure to be wary of. Though not to the Casanova-wannabe at her side, of course.

At the far end of the bar, a cluster of young nobles appeared to be indulging in a toast with grappa or some similar clear spirit. The sparkling wine she was drinking was lacking, and she wished there was either a good red or even a dry white wine to drink. Living in Italy had definitely spoiled her.

I would kill for some prosecco right now.

Realizing she had exhausted her patience for her current companion, Sloane turned to Andrei, her tone polite but firm. "Andrei, dear, I appreciate the cordial welcome. However, I must now direct my attention to the esteemed guildmaster. Please excuse us."

Andrei, visibly taken aback, protested. "Lady Reinhart, we were having a lovely discussion."

At this, Sloane swiveled to fully face him. She paused, making a show of contemplating her next words while scrutinizing him. She saw the barely hidden frustration on his face and a bit of . . . *excitement.* She wondered how he perceived her—as a conquest, perhaps, made all the more enticing by her apparent disinterest. Judging by the haughty expressions she had seen on the faces of the other women in attendance, Andrei wasn't exactly a crowd favorite.

How men like this always find more and more women willing to sleep with them, I'll never know.

Andrei scrunched up his eyebrows as he took in her unimpressed gaze. He opened his mouth to say something, but she leaned in close and whispered into his ear, "Look, I know the game. I know how you simply wanted to make yourself more interesting by having your pompous friend introduce himself first. You're so transparent it hurts. Now, excuse me." She stepped back and watched a whirl of emotions play over his face.

Surprisingly, he wore a smile. He leaned toward her as he made a rather audacious request. "Might I request a slap before I depart?"

Her eyebrows shot up, an incredulous chuckle slipping past her lips. *Is this guy for real?*

With a dismissive wave of her hand, she retorted, "Look, I have actual business with actual adults. Please, run along now." Without affording him a chance to rebut, she turned around to be met with the expressions of surprise on Elodie's face and amusement on the guildmaster's.

In the corner of her eye, she saw Andrei retreat, his pride battered.

That will probably come back to haunt me somehow.

Looking to defuse the awkwardness that hung in the air, she offered the guildmaster an apologetic smile. "I beg your pardon, Guildmaster Romaris. It seems some members of this gathering are a touch *too* welcoming."

Lanthil met her comment with a hearty laugh, motioning to the bartender as he turned to the bar. "Two glasses of your sesora." He quickly turned toward his niece and asked, "Elodie, would you like a glass?"

"Please, thank you."

He promptly amended his order, raising three fingers for the bartender to see. "Make that three!"

Sloane waited as the bartender grabbed a bottle of something and poured a yellow-gold liquid into three glasses and then set them on the counter for Lanthil. The man picked up the glasses, handed one to each of the women, and then raised his slightly. "To future business."

Sloane repeated the gesture and took a sip.

Ah, that's good wine.

"This is excellent, Guildmaster. Thank you."

"Lanthil, please, my lady. After tonight, I believe we shall have a long-lasting, mutually beneficial relationship between my family and your house. Now, Elodie here has told me some of your progress and how she is quite interested in continuing under your employment. I must say, I am pleased to hear that."

Sloane sipped her drink and smiled at the elf woman. It seemed that she had been correct in assuming the sun elf would tell her uncle of what was occurring in her house, and she was glad that she and the knights had been cautious about what the two new members of the group had seen or heard.

"Elodie has been a wonderful asset. I look forward to working further with her. I wanted to ask you, however: Have you seen the other terran noble tonight?"

Lanthil confirmed that he hadn't and lifted a hand. An elf seemed to materialize from the crowd and stepped forward. Lanthil whispered into his ear, and the man leaned forward and replied. With a nod from the guildmaster, the man melded back into the crowd, and Sloane quickly lost sight of him.

Her surprise must have been apparent, because the guildmaster answered her unspoken question. "My position requires me to have protection. I bring a suitable number for everything I attend. The count and I have an understanding on the matter."

She just nodded, and they spoke of various business topics while listening to the music that was playing in the background. A group of raithe were on a stage playing what looked like cellos and lutes. The sound of their songs was melodious and soothing, and just loud enough to fill the room over the sound of people talking.

Lanthil asked how guilds were in her world, and she explained superficially about banks and corporations. The entrance doors opening interrupted them and the raithe at the doors called out an introduction. "Introducing Lady Ismeld of House Argin and the Knight Order of Haven's Hope, representing the Kingdom of Blightwych."

I really *need to learn more about Ismeld's past.*

Sloane watched as the group descended the staircase. The crowd all turned and started whispering about the knights who had entered the ball. It seemed that the previous attention on her was already forgotten.

Good job, Gisele.

Sloane was about to turn back to the guildmaster when she caught sight of a man with rounded ears. She narrowed her eyes, watching him, and then quickly glanced at the guildmaster and Elodie. "I'm sorry to leave suddenly, but there is someone I wish to meet."

Lanthil put a hand on her arm as Sloane started to step away. "I'll have some men watch over you," he said quietly. Sloane nodded absently.

She moved through the crowd, avoiding catching anyone's eye as she zeroed in on the other terran. He was talking with a group of raithe and moon elf aristocrats as if he had done the same song and dance many times before.

Maybe he has?

As she got closer, she managed to get a better look at him. He wore a navy blue coat with golden buttons on either side. The back of the coat had a tail that draped down below his rear. Under his coat he wore a ruffled shirt and a vest. His white pants ended just below his knees, and he wore what seemed to be stockings with boots that came just above his shins.

What is he wearing? I haven't seen anyone else wear anything like this. Sloane tilted her head in confusion as she watched him.

He did a slight double take when he saw her, then smiled and walked up to her. The man was nearly a head shorter than her. "My, you're a tall one."

She raised an eyebrow at that. "You are Lord Bolton, I presume?"

The man laughed, and replied in a distinctly British accent, "I see that my reputation precedes me! Why, how does a lovely woman such as yourself know of me?"

"You are apparently the only other terran noble in the city. I would be surprised if you hadn't heard of me yourself," she said.

Lord Bolton made a subtle gesture toward a nearby door, and, following his lead, Sloane stepped out onto an elevated balcony that commanded an impressive view of the city. Below them, the garden was alight with well-heeled attendees immersed in their own little worlds of conversation.

In the far reaches of her vision, Sloane could discern a stark contrast. Past the brilliant incandescence of the central district lay a constellation of rundown edifices and plumes of smoke billowing from countless chimneys. An imposing inner wall stood guard between these two disparate worlds. Like night and day, they coexisted side by side in jarring juxtaposition.

Turning her head, she noticed yet another enclosed area of the city, an expansive labyrinth of buildings, green spaces, and winding trails. She recognized it as Ghyll Academy, which she would need to visit soon. The state of the city was appalling, and that no one had stepped in to intercede baffled her.

As though sensing her internal disquiet, the British man's voice broke into her thoughts. "This world seems quite primitive to your eyes, I presume. The city is but a cesspool hidden beneath layers of aristocratic sheen." He paused, turning his gaze on her. "The *terran* woman—yes, the rumors do speak of you. A *noble*, they say."

Sloane regarded him with narrowed eyes, yet she chose to keep her tone casual. "I have made do. I arrived in the middle of nowhere. Alone. Luckily, I came across some helpful people." She decided not to mention anything about Gwyn. She was sensing some weird vibes coming from him.

He narrowed his eyes too. "Where would you say you hail from? Your accent eludes me. Your command over the English language is quite fluent, yet you clearly do not belong to the Empire."

Sloane's eyebrows arched in bemusement at his comment. "Empire?" she echoed, a hint of perplexity creeping into her voice. "I am from the US, although I lived in Italy for half a decade before I arrived here."

"The you-ess? Where is that?" he questioned.

The unexpected query set off a silent alarm in her mind. "What do you mean, 'Where is the US?' The States? Aren't you British?" Sloane's voice registered a note of disbelief.

"Of course," Lord Bolton responded, a clear edge to his tone. "However, I must object to falsehoods. What are these 'states' you speak of?"

"You're really telling me you've never heard of the United States of America?" The confusion in Sloane's voice was unmistakable.

The baron's eyes narrowed and he physically withdrew a step. "United States of *America*? Do you refer to the colonies? No matter our location, speaking such words is dangerously close to treason."

Sloane was left momentarily speechless. *What the actual . . . What is he playing at?* She shook her head. "Are you joking with me?" she challenged, her tone swinging between disbelief and irritation. "You can stop now."

As her gaze swept the area, she spotted a guard seemingly eavesdropping nearby.

Is he doing this for their sake?

His indignation palpable, the baron gripped his cane more firmly, raising it slightly off the ground as if offended. "I assure you, I am not jesting. We suppressed that silly rebellion three decades ago. Who are you?"

His brow furrowed as he scanned Sloane, an analytic gaze that seemed to pierce through her. "You carry the name Reinhart. You claim residency in Italy, yet profess to be born in America, the term rebels used for the colonies. Your entire persona is filled with contradictions. I seriously doubt your nobility."

The baron's scrutiny sent a jolt through Sloane.

Oh really? You're going to say I am not a noble?

She was starting to get angry. There was clearly something off about the man. His snobbish demeanor, the arrogance. It was like he was playing a character in an exaggerated manner, and she didn't like it.

You're the first human I've seen and you're acting this way?

She scoffed. "Oh, come on, we are literally in another world and what you're saying is more fantasy than the elves around! Why are you acting this way? What is your deal?"

The grimace on Lord Bolton's face deepened, his chest heaving in measured breaths as he prepared to unload another barrage of accusations. Anticipating the impending argument, Sloane cut him off abruptly. "You know what? I'm done with this."

As she turned away, a vice-like grip on her wrist spun her back around. But before the baron could utter another word, she fiercely tugged her wrist back, pulling him off balance. "If you do not let go of me, you will have something other than nonsense to worry about," Sloane threatened icily.

His face twisted into a resentful scowl, but he released her, nonetheless. His eyes, however, grew wide in what seemed to be a sudden realization. "You are an agent of Napoleon, aren't you? Your backstory is a convoluted mess—a tale spun too far, spy!" His laughter echoed around them, a self-satisfied smirk on his face as though he'd just solved the mystery of the century.

Ignoring Sloane's stunned silence, he scanned the vicinity, catching the attention of one of the nearby guards. "Guard! This woman is no noble—she's a fraud! We must inform the count immediately!"

Sloane's mind whirled as she pieced together his words.

Put down that silly rebellion? Thirty years? Napoleon? Where the hell is this guy from?

As several armed guards approached, she found herself utterly bewildered, her thoughts spiraling around how this could disrupt her quest for Gwyn. But she shook it off—this man was crazy.

I hope the next human I find makes more sense.

The moon elf leading the guards spoke with firm authority. "You will accompany us to the count."

Taken aback, Sloane demanded, "For what reason?"

"For the charge of falsifying noble patents," the woman sneered in reply.

To her right, she saw Lord Bolton's smug grin.

I need Gisele and Ismeld.

She frowned at the woman, irritation seeping into her tone. "I haven't committed any wrongdoing. You're merely relying on this man's false accusations."

The raithe guardswoman scoffed in response. "The count trusts his judgment, not yours. You will come with us peacefully, or we will ensure compliance."

Sloane's eyes flickered between the guards, her mind assessing the odds.

Well, Stefan needed a distraction.

"Fine," she conceded, "Take me to the count."

She turned her head toward the smug baron.

"We *will* get to the bottom of this."

CHAPTER EIGHTEEN

BALLROOM CONFRONTATION

S loane followed behind the lead guard and the Baron of Lunacy, William Bolton, through the bustling ballroom. As she forced herself to calm her breathing, she considered everything the man had said and how he'd acted. His odd behavior and mannerisms appeared, at first glance, like someone attempting to respond to the traumatic experience of arriving in an entirely new world significantly behind their own.

That has to be it. He saw how civilization is here, and adopted a persona he thought would fit.

Finding more humans was now higher on her list of priorities; hopefully, the next ones would be easier to interact with. But for now, she had to deal with this shit.

Her thoughts swirled like leaves in an autumn breeze, eventually landing back on the immediate predicament at hand. Elodie had been trailing behind her at a cautious distance but was smart enough to separate from the group as the guards approached. A well-timed glance from Sloane had warned her younger companion against entangling herself in this predicament.

As they traversed the grand ballroom, Sloane could feel the collective gaze of the crowd swiveling toward her. Whispers trailed in their wake like wisps of smoke; pointing fingers traced her journey through the sea of aristocrats. She cast a surreptitious glance over her shoulder, searching for Elodie, only to find that the clever girl had melted into the crowd.

A further scan of the room for her knights yielded nothing but more staring faces.

Stefan had better be gathering the intel we need. Almost everyone is focused on me.

Upon entering another grand space, smaller than the first but dripping with ostentatious decorations, Sloane's attention was caught by the intricate design of the pillars. A mass of serpents appeared to be coiling upward, reaching for the lofty ceiling in an eternal chase.

The echo of a different set of musicians wafted through the room, their harmonious chords weaving an almost sacred hymn.

The room was alive with a sophisticated court dance. The central space was filled with around thirty pairs of what appeared to be moon elves and raithe. The dance floor was a swirl of color and elegance, the partners rotating in a beautiful symphony of movement, their actions mirroring the enchanting cadence of the music. The vibrant swirls of the ladies' dresses seemed to dance alongside their owners, a vivid contrast to the stern formal attire of the men, painting a mesmerizing tableau of rhythmic coordination.

The graceful choreography of the dance, the twirling gowns and the harmonious ebb and flow of the music, all begged for Sloane's attention. She would have reveled in the chance to observe and enjoy the spectacle. Alas, she was instead being paraded along the periphery of the room, her destination a raised dais where five moon elves reclined in a mixture of apathy and silent judgment.

Her gaze fixated on the elder moon elf occupying the tallest chair in the center, his garb a riot of red and gold—a grandiose display of power. His focus was unnerving. The cool gray of his eyes bore into her from across the room, the lines on his face as harsh as the contempt she saw reflected in his gaze.

Shit. This doesn't seem promising.

The small procession came to a halt at the base of the platform, and the moon elf guard leading them took it upon herself to address the count.

"My Lord, this terran is accused by Lord Bolton of masquerading as nobility. He claims she's a spy."

The elder moon elf's gaze turned steely, but then his attention drifted back to the ongoing dance. After a brief moment of contemplation, he waved a dismissive hand. "Captain Lars, deal with this. I am otherwise engaged." The contempt was palpable as he disregarded the unfolding drama, choosing instead to immerse himself in the elegant dance unfurling behind Sloane.

A formidable moon elf—who was she kidding, the man was *built*—emerged from the shadows cast by the dais. His gaze was probing, assessing her with a disquieting intensity. He gave a dismissive glance at Bolton before turning his attention back to her.

"Who are you?" the captain asked.

Sloane took a breath, remaining calm and in control of her emotions. *This isn't the time to panic. It's just some misunderstanding by a crazy guy.*

"I am Lady Reinhart." She looked pointedly at the British buffoon before continuing. "*This man* is clearly insane. He is spouting nonsense before spewing even more about my status. *My* peerage is without question, and I have not only proper documentation to prove it, but also recognition from the Kingdom of Blightwych."

She looked around the room in a desperate search for her knights, finding none. She also noted the carefully averted gazes of those within earshot of their conversation, their polite pretense of ignorance almost comical. She couldn't help but feel a knot of frustration tighten within her.

The captain's scoff was as dismissive as his attitude. "And what if you falsified your documentation or deceived the Blightwych representative? I'm not certain about their procedures, but around here, we don't simply hand out titles and patents of nobility to every random passerby who claims one."

Sloane arched an eyebrow, a subtle show of defiance. "Well, it's fortunate then that I'm not from around here."

His sneer was palpable, even as he retorted, "That much is abundantly clear, terran."

"She is a French spy and clearly an imposter," Bolton chimed in, further muddying the waters. "Nothing about her fabricated story makes sense."

Sloane's patience was wearing thin, and she scowled directly at him. "You are seriously crazy. Nothing *you've* said makes any sense. Why are you continuing with this charade?"

Bolton ignored her question, lifting his chin haughtily and turning away from her in dismissal. Sloane scoffed, irritated by his theatrics.

The moon elf guard captain, seemingly unimpressed by the exchange, addressed the guards surrounding her. "Take her to the dungeon. A week in isolation might make her more willing to cooperate."

"Gladly," the raithe guardswoman growled, stepping forward, her sword still unsheathed.

Sloane scanned her immediate surroundings, noting the sparse guard presence. She couldn't afford to be detained, especially not for an extended period.

Nothing, absolutely nothing, can prevent me from searching for Gwyn.

She looked at the baron, who had a smug look on his face. "Are you really going to continue with your lie?" she asked.

"Do not speak to me, *spy.*"

Looks like we're going with plan GTFO a bit earlier than planned.

"You are really beginning to piss me off. Anyway," she started, and lifted her fist and pointed her watch at the guards. "This isn't going to work for me. You really just throw people into a dungeon based on the unfounded words of another? Yeah, no. We're not going to do that, and I don't give a fuck what you have to say on the matter. Do not come closer, or you will force me to defend myself."

The captain maintained his silence, simply motioning for another guard to proceed with the capture. As the man advanced, bearing manacles, Sloane turned to face him. "This is your last chance," she said.

"Do not resist. You are coming with us," he replied.

Sloane shrugged, triggered her watch, and cast a |**Flashbang**| at the approaching guard. The bolt burst right in front of the man with its trademark flash and resounding bang, enveloping the immediate vicinity.

Chaos ensued. Surrounding bystanders screamed and recoiled, covering their eyes and ears. Somewhere in the background, the discordant screech of a snapped string from one of the musicians added to the pandemonium.

In the midst of the disarray, Sloane took advantage of the momentary blindness and disorientation of her captors, backtracking toward the entrance. The captain was the first to recover, drawing his blade and furiously rubbing his eyes in an attempt to hasten his vision's return.

The baron yelled out. "A witch! Count Kayser, she uses witchcraft!"

Sloane looked back up to see the count standing beside the table with a cold expression. "You dare assault my people with your witchcraft?"

Raising an eyebrow at the accusation, Sloane retorted, "Witchcraft? Where have you been for the past two months since the Flash? What I'm doing isn't witchcraft, no matter what this man has told you. I am not going to some dungeon."

"Your actions are unnatural. You will reveal your secrets—"

"Lady Reinhart!"

The interruption was a welcome distraction.

Gisele and Ismeld were pushing through the crowd, the rest of the knights parting the throng of onlookers in their wake. The two women took up positions on either side of her, a united front against the accusations.

"What is happening here?" Ismeld demanded, her voice echoing through the now quiet room.

Lord Bolton moved to stand next to the count, hands on his hips, the smug expression still plastered on his face.

I really want to punch that look off of his face. What an absolute lunatic.

Count Kayser fixed his gaze on his captain, then shifted his scrutiny to Ismeld. "Lady d'Argin, I presume?" He pointed an accusatory finger at Sloane. "This . . . woman assaulted everyone present with witchcraft, completely unprovoked. Step aside. My men will take her into custody and deliver her to the dungeon. Should you interfere, you will all share her fate."

The room seemed to hold its breath in the ensuing silence, the tension palpable. Ismeld, holding herself tall, met the count's cold gaze with a steady one of her own. Her voice, when she spoke, carried the weight of her station and the conviction of her defense for Sloane.

"Count Kayser, you would be wise to consider your next actions very carefully," Ismeld began. Her voice echoed in the room, commanding the attention of everyone present. "Accusing a recognized noble from the Kingdom of Blightwych of such a crime is a severe overstep of your authority as city lord. I *personally* acknowledged her status. Detaining Lady Reinhart, let alone any of us, without concrete evidence would trigger a diplomatic incident that, I assure you, your *nation* would rather avoid. Blightwych will not stand for baseless accusations against its representatives." Her tone was a potent mixture of warning and defiance, challenging the count to reconsider his reckless course of action.

"Lady Reinhart."

She jerked her head back and looked at the rest of the group. Deryk drew one of his two shortswords, flipped it around, and extended it to her. Sloane smirked as she accepted the blade, before turning back around and facing the count.

"I will not allow myself to be taken simply for the *word* of a man who is spouting nonsense. Every story he has told is not true. *Hell,* his fictional setting is two hundred years old."

She wasn't sure what she said that finally caused the smug look to fall, but the surprise on Bolton's face was apparent. The count did not seem fazed at all. "I tire of this distraction upon my ball. Captain, detain them. I will be down to speak with the terran later."

Ismeld's eyes flickered between Sloane and the knight next to her, her voice dropping to a murmur barely audible amid the tension-filled silence. "We can use the grenades for a diversion, and the shield to narrow their approach."

Gisele's nod was solemn, her hand unsheathing her sword from her hip with a swift and practiced grace. The sight triggered a wistful thought in Sloane's mind. *I wish she had her big sword tonight.*

In response to their silent accord, Gisele pivoted, her hand thrusting out toward the guards on their right. A luminous barrier, almost three meters wide, sprang into existence, shielding the group's flank. The shimmering shield had grown noticeably larger since Sloane had last seen it.

She's been working on it.

The crowd recoiled at the magical manifestation, their startled cries punctuating the charged air. Count Kayser's eyes narrowed further in an icy stare as he stepped back slightly. Meanwhile, the guard captain roared out, "Capture them! The orkun is also a witch!"

Motivated by their captain's command, a swarm of moon elf and raithe guards advanced, their drawn weapons glinting in the ballroom's light. Sloane reacted with a defensive cast of **[Mana Bolt]**, altering it into a less lethal version this time, which collided with a guard's breastplate and sent him sprawling backward.

I need to defend and disable, not kill.

The knights had drawn their swords and formed a defensive formation.

The ballroom erupted into chaos, the grandeur of the night marred by fear and uncertainty. High-pitched screams rang out as nobles and attendants alike scrambled for safety. Amid the chaos, Gisele barked orders.

"Maud, hold the center. Focus on providing support. Cristole and Ernald, right side. Deryk, keep Sloane in your sight. Move. Backward."

Gisele dipped her hand into her pouch, revealing a familiar spherical object. Her eyes met Sloane's for a moment, certainty and a bit of excitement held in their depths.

"Shield your eyes in three seconds!" Sloane called out to the knights, preparing for the imminent burst.

With an expert flick of her wrist, Gisele lobbed the grenade toward the cluster of guards and their captain. The innocuous object bounced a few times before settling at the feet of an unsuspecting raithe. The sight of the grenade seemed to puzzle him as he nudged it with his foot, his confusion soon replaced by a wave of shock as the device exploded into a blinding light and cacophonous noise.

There were even some guards who had heeded her warning, but luckily still found themselves disoriented and stunned by the force of the blast.

Should probably train with the knights more. Calling out a strategy is clearly just something you see work well in movies and books.

The count recoiled, his startled cry echoing across the grand chamber. Taking advantage of the momentary chaos, Sloane called upon her magic, conjuring a trio of [Mana Bolts] that orbited her like celestial bodies. Each homed in on a different guard, erupting upon contact and scattering them like leaves in the wind.

Gisele and Ismeld acted as a seamless unit on the front line, their expertise clearly on display. Gisele danced around her raithe opponent, a blur of motion. With a quick flick of her wrist, she disarmed him, sending him sprawling to the ground with a swift kick.

Beside her, Ismeld stood firm, the epitome of stoic resolve. She engaged a moon elf guard, her defensive strategy turning swiftly offensive. With a calculated thrust, she disarmed him, pushing him backward and to the ground.

In the midst of this, the whistling of airborne projectiles filled the air. Three crossbow bolts sliced through the commotion, two of them colliding against Cristole's shield with loud clanks. The third, however, found its mark, piercing Cristole's side through a gap in his armor.

Maud's voice rose above the clamor. "Cristole!"

Her focus shifted to the oncoming bolts, her shield deflecting two more as she stepped in front of the wounded knight. Sloane responded in kind, directing a |Flashbang| from her watch toward the crossbowmen and effectively disarming them as it burst.

Swift and precise, Maud reached down to the embedded bolt and closed her hand around its shaft before pulling it out in a swift, fluid motion. A green mist enveloped the wound, its soothing glow signaling the onset of a healing spell.

Sloane watched the scene unfold. Count Kayser's expression had turned to shock, the previously haughty man now lost in the spectacle of power and defiance they were putting on display.

Her hand rose again, conjuring another swarm of [Mana Bolts], ready to strike. As they hovered in anticipation, a strange sensation rippled through her. The magical energy within her spell seemed to warp, transforming her [Mana Bolts] into a vibrant purple hue. She let a whisper of her intent seep into the spell, surprised by the newfound degree of control it seemed to offer.

More things to experiment with.

Meanwhile, the guards regrouped, their collective gaze flickering nervously as they saw their compatriots laid low by Sloane's magic. The captain helped the count to his feet, the elder elf appearing visibly shaken by the unexpected onslaught.

The scene settled into a tense stalemate as both groups stared down the other. The knights, poised like a drawn bowstring, were ready to strike or retreat based on the merest hint of hostility from the guards. Their ranks were closed tight, their faces etched with determination. Amid them, Sloane felt her spell pulsing with lethal potential, held taut by her will alone. Its release was a hairbreadth away; a breath too sharp or loud could set it loose.

Suddenly, a voice thundered through the chaos, every syllable filled with righteous indignation. "Count Kayser! Enough of this farce. I suggest everyone stand down and discuss this when tempers have cooled."

Sloane craned her neck, her eyes finding the source of the commanding tone. Guildmaster Romaris emerged from the fray, backed by an intimidating band of eight, a mix of telv, raithe, and elves, all radiating an aura of menace that held the room's guards at bay.

Count Kayser's eyes narrowed, his nostrils flaring with barely restrained fury. "Guildmaster Romaris. This does not concern you. This is a situation among the nobility."

"From where I stand," retorted Romaris, his gaze sweeping the room, "I see a corrupt noble exploiting his power against a crucial ally of the guilds." The sun elf's gaze fell on Sloane, and a barely perceptible nod of acknowledgment passing between them. Among his retinue stood Elodie, her worried eyes darting from Sloane to the knights.

Cristole broke the tense silence with a chortle. "Took you long enough to join us, Guildmaster."

Romaris's eyes twinkled. "The other areas seem terribly dull in comparison."

The count erupted, "Enough! This doesn't involve the guilds. This terran and her foreign knights attacked my guards!"

Sloane swept her gaze across the room, noting the guards back on their feet, albeit some wincing from her previous spell attacks. Her lips curled into a dry smile. "Your guards seem fine to me, Lord Kayser. In the future, instead of instantly moving to accost someone, perhaps speak to them first."

Kayser seethed. "You dare blame me? You invade my house, assault my guards, and now claim moral superiority?"

I suppose it looks bad from his perspective, Sloane mused. *Still, he crossed a line.*

As silence fell, Kayser sneered, "Nothing to say?"

Time to pull out some bullshit.

Her eyes flashed with defiance. "Your man slandered my honor, Lord Kayser. You let him threaten to imprison me and the knights of Blightwych without even hearing my side of the story. And you dare to lecture me on morals! I do not know how things are done here in Westaren, but nobles should be treated with the deference due their station."

The tension spiked anew as the captain of the guards shifted, his blade reflecting the light ominously. But before the threat could materialize, a crash reverberated through the hall. The doors burst open, revealing a fresh troop of guards led by the same captain Sloane had encountered in the courtyard.

"Another squad incoming. Brace yourselves." Cristole's words were an undertone of steel in the mounting tension.

The knights and the Banking Guild's guards swiftly reoriented, the ambient energy of their readiness permeating the room. But surprisingly, the newcomers were not charging them. Rather, they were rushing toward the count.

The captain at their helm gave Sloane a fleeting, questioning glance before his focus snapped back to the irate noble. "Lord Kayser! There is an urgent matter we must discuss!"

"Can't you see I am occupied, Captain Jorin?" The count's tone was frosty, dismissive. "Assist with this current situation, not with whatever trivialities you've brought."

"My Lord, I perceive nothing more than the usual squabble between nobility here. The news I bear is far more dire," he replied with some urgency.

Kayser's expression turned sharp. "Speak then, Captain."

Sloane heard the echoes of more footsteps, more voices rushing in from behind. Captain Jorin cast a glance over his shoulder at the incoming crowd before meeting the count's gaze again.

"I have convened all those of significance who need to be informed. My Lord, it concerns Valesbeck."

"Valesbeck?" A voice rose from the newly arrived group, a raithe man cutting through the crowd with brisk strides.

"Lord Hirothe, I am grateful for your timely arrival," acknowledged the captain. Turning back to the count, he took a deep breath. "Two riders have brought word from Valesbeck. The town . . . it has been destroyed."

A ripple of shock swept through the hall, gasps filling the air like a chilling breeze. Sloane herself felt a wave of surprise, her hand reflexively rising to cover her mouth.

The count's eyes widened, his attention fully on Captain Jorin. "What happened?"

The captain looked at a raithe man Sloane hadn't noticed until then. He was clad in ragged, torn clothing, the kind she'd seen worn by the Valesbeck militia. "Creatures, My Lord. Scores of wolves, bears, and other wild beasts descended upon the town a week ago. They wreaked havoc, feasting on the fallen. These were no ordinary beasts—they were larger, fiercer. Some wolves were as large as horses. We were five when we set out to bring this news, and only two of us have survived to deliver it, My Lord."

The throng of figures continued to flood into the room, clustering around the captain and the count. As the man went on unfolding the harrowing tale, a shared sense of dread hung in the air, thickening with each successive detail. It appeared the wolves that had been causing problems were just precursors to a larger, devastating wave of attack. The defenseless town hadn't had the chance to complete its walls before this onslaught.

I hope the blacksmith and his son made it out.

Amid the chaos, Guildmaster Romaris managed to maneuver himself next to Sloane. His voice was a murmur, a private undertone amid the clamor. "While their attention is elsewhere, you and the knights should slip away. I will stay. Please take Elodie with you."

Gisele nodded in agreement. "Indeed. Let's move. Slowly, subtly through the crowd."

Sloane cast a final glance at Lord Bolton. Fear was etched clearly on his face, as he absorbed the implications of the captain's report.

You and I will have a conversation later, Bolton. I'm going to figure out your story.

With a surge of unease, Sloane turned and navigated her way through the crowd, wary of catching the count's attention again. The knights followed her lead, carefully picking their way through the huddled assembly. The air was thick with fear and trepidation. Whispers of war and attacks spread like wildfire, igniting concerns among the crowd.

When they finally emerged into the open, Sloane drew a deep, liberating breath. A sense of relief washed over her as they left the confines of the estate. She noticed Stefan in the periphery of her vision, engaged in animated conversation with a group of elves. As they passed, he flashed a smirk, winking at her before seamlessly merging with their group.

"Most excellent distraction, my lady." His voice was a bit too enthusiastic. "I look forward to a future filled with such excitement as part of your house."

"Did you find what you were looking for?" she inquired.

"Indeed, I did. I'll fill you in on the pertinent details before I pass this information on to the guilds."

"Then let's head back to the inn," she decided, eager to put the day's events behind her.

Later that night, two men sat at a small table in an empty café in the central district. Ghyll was abuzz with the news of Valesbeck's destruction. The City Guard and the count's personal forces were busy mobilizing and preparing the city. The two men calmly drank tea and spoke of unimportant things as if it were simply any other day.

They most certainly didn't broach the topic of monsters or beasts that were at that very moment moving toward the city. They didn't discuss how they expected that same horde to arrive in a few short weeks.

No, the shadowy men didn't even focus on the new knowledge their organization had gained of the secret activities of the count or the guilds, and the possible shadow war that could erupt among the factions of the city.

They finished their repast without debating what to do about a certain baroness and the magic her group had displayed. Nor the new race of people with whom the count seemed to have an obsession.

The two men from the Ghyll Academy stood up and parted ways without another word. It was simply another day.

CHAPTER NINETEEN

THE DEMANDS OF PROGRESS

After returning, the group gathered in Sloane's large room in the inn. To maintain appearances, she had been staying in one of the nicer rooms since being in the city. Currently, her companions were scattered about in the sitting area of her suite, which felt a little too tight for the nine of them to comfortably inhabit.

Sloane, Gisele, Stefan, and Ernald sat in the only four chairs. They had been discussing the evening and what could have gone better.

Everything could have gone better.

Sloane listened as Stefan explained what he had learned.

"Lord Kayser has been collecting terrans to learn how to utilize their magic. To date, he has managed to . . . detain nine of them. Apparently, Lord Bolton has been actively assisting the count in this endeavor. I found detailed documentation—"

"Was there anything about the ages? Any children?" Sloane asked.

Stefan shook his head in response. "No, there were only adults. He's been frustrated because only two of them have exhibited any use of magic."

Ismeld considered this, tilting her head thoughtfully. "That does make sense. Among us, only three individuals have shown magical capabilities so far. It might be that it's rarer than we presumed and not everyone possesses a core."

Stefan's expression darkened. "That's the thing. *Everyone* appears to have one. The count has recovered cores from a number of the terrans, even from those without any manifestation of magic."

A gasp from Maud punctuated the chilling revelation. Sloane looked at the other knights. Deryk leaned against the wall by the door, his stoic form a pillar of silent support, while Maud, Ismeld, and Cristole sat clustered on the floor beside him. Maud's hand flew to her mouth, her eyes brimming with distress.

Sloane felt a cold shiver course through her. *Extracted the cores? Hold on . . . That would mean . . . no, that can't be right. What the fuck?*

Locking her gaze with Maud, Sloane found a mirror of her own disbelief and distress. She knew exactly what the man had done.

"He killed them," Sloane stated simply.

Maud nodded. "It's the only way he could have retrieved them."

"I imagine the process to remove one would kill someone," Cristole added.

Sloane heard a small whimper on her right. She shifted to see Elodie where she had awkwardly sat off alone in the corner.

"Why? Why would he do that? What could he hope to gain?" the elf questioned.

"Several of the people fought him and were killed for the trouble. One of the two with magic was killed while trying to escape. The other was moved out of the city." Stefan shrugged. "But as for why he's doing this in the first place. I have no idea. Power? Influence? It could be any number of things. This has consumed his entire purpose since the Flash. Everything he has done in the past month has been to figure out magic and how to exploit it." He looked at Sloane. "He believes it is something your people brought with you, and that your people are innately magical."

Sloane scoffed. "That's preposterous. Our world had—*has*—no magic either. Maud and Gisele can use magic. Hell, Maud used magic before any of us."

"So, you didn't give them the ability to do so?" he pushed.

She shook her head. "No. I don't even know how anyone could give that ability."

Stefan's gaze was unfocused as he thought.

Sloane continued. "Was there anything else? You mentioned he had kidnapped nine people too. Does that mean there are some being held prisoner?"

"Yes. Several have been relocated out of the city. But there's a woman. Other than you and Lord Bolton, she is the last one in the city. Apparently, several made it out of the city in time to avoid capture. Again, no children. I'm sorry." Sloane searched his face and saw no signs of deception. He meant it.

"Would the kingdom intervene?" Elodie posed the question timidly.

"Perhaps. It certainly accelerates our timeline for contacting the Order of Secrets here," Gisele suggested.

"I think I need to work on more tools for us to use as well," Sloane added.

Ismeld smirked. "Yes. If only so Gisele can use them. She is obsessed."

"They are a force multiplier. Why would I not want to utilize every tool at my disposal?" Gisele asked her fellow knight with a quirked eyebrow.

"Oh, I agree. I just think you should share with the rest of us," Ismeld said with a chuckle.

"Sloane, what else can you make?" Ernald asked.

She considered the question.

Sloane had several ideas. But she likely would need to learn more magic before she could make an explosive grenade. For the time being, she needed to consider what options would benefit the knights and herself. There was one project she really needed to start.

"I would like to try to enhance your weapons and shields, perhaps your armor. However, there is another thing I want to work on first." She turned again and looked at her financial advisor. "Are you still willing to assist with purchases for the house?"

The woman sat straighter. "Of course, my lady. Allow me to be of service."

"Perfect. After this, I have a list of supplies I would like for you to acquire tomorrow. I have a big project, and I wish to get started and then finish it before we leave the city." She looked at Gisele. "Speaking of, we should likely move up our timeline."

Gisele nodded. "I agree. I don't believe we can stay longer. How long will this . . . project take to complete?"

Sloane tapped alongside her mouth as she considered. "No more than two weeks."

The knight-captain looked away, considering, then back up at Sloane. "That will work."

Sloane slapped her hands on her thighs. "Okay, if no one else has anything—"

"What of the attack?" Deryk posed.

Gisele shrugged. "There isn't really anything we can do about it, my friend. The count has to send soldiers to handle it. We would not be able to join them."

"What if they come here?" Elodie asked.

Cristole shook his head. "That is a long distance. I think we're safe here."

"I hope so," the woman murmured.

Sloane looked down at her work. There were plates of metal, a pile of gems to the side, and a blue core that had been found in some animal. Elodie had impressed her by completing every task she had asked of her, and procured every one of the supplies on the list. She had even given Sloane a paper with the details of the order from the smith she had used, along with his contact information.

I will definitely utilize her for future transactions.

Sloane hoped to meet with the guildmaster to discuss another business venture she had thought of—one that would be highly beneficial to the Smith's Guild.

She grabbed her journal and opened it to the page where she had started sketching and writing down ideas for the project. Ever since the knights had committed to moving on after escorting her to Swanbrook, she had been considering what she could do or make that would help her. She needed ways to defend herself.

Her grenades were the first step, and of course, her magic. Sword training with the knights helped, but she knew she would never be a master swordsman.

The next thing she needed was a way to be aware of her surroundings. She had considered several solutions, and none seemed to help when she was on the move. Stefan would be a huge help, but she still wasn't sure how effective he'd be in the guard role. He was more of a "sneak in the night and stab someone in the neck" person.

So, that brought her to what she was working on. She was going to build a manatech bird, one that utilized runes, gems, and a core to function. Her original idea had called for something far smaller, but the core that Elodie had obtained was double the size Sloane had imagined.

So instead of something small and cute like a sparrow, she was going to design something fierce and regal, like a falcon.

It fits the whole nobility theme too.

Sloane sat down and started sketching out a design, quickly coming up with a form that would work. It would take a prodigious amount of alteration to fit everything, and she would need to include gems to help the bird move.

When it came to how to power the thing, the blue core was *exactly* what she needed, even though it was bigger than she had imagined. It would draw in blue mana at a much higher rate and it would vastly increase the bird's capability to perform autonomously.

The crown, legs, and feet would be made of steel, and she would also make the skeletal structure out of steel. She would look into using something else for the body or just paint the steel. *Mainly for the aesthetic. My birb boy has to look good.*

The chest cavity would be where the core was held, while the cranium would hold most of the gems. She had already shaped and cut two onyxes to use for the eyes.

Her biggest hurdle was that the bird would need to be made of stainless steel. She was going to be outside constantly and having a material that would weather the elements well would be ideal. The problem was, stainless steel hadn't been invented until the twentieth century—in her world. Luckily, she knew, roughly, how it was made and the materials it would need to have. Namely, chromium.

A few hours later, Sloane had selected the gems that she would use and had started fabricating the skeletal structure with steel. She looked over the work she had done. She had finished everything except for the wings, neck, and head. Those could come later. In the meantime, she put the bird away and placed the gems she had selected for use into a small case she would keep separate from her stash.

She looked down at her notebook and the paper from the smith next to it. She needed to meet with Guildmaster Romaris. His role as head of the guilds in Thirdghyll would give her an in with the smiths and possibly help with what she planned. Plus, she had another small idea that she could use to entice him. Namely, the concept of subsidized research.

With a smirk, she gathered up her things and walked out in search of Elodie.

Approaching the front of the inn, Sloane found Elodie and Stefan hunched over a scatter of documents sprawled across a table. They were so engrossed in their conversation that they didn't notice her until she was close. Stefan was the first to acknowledge her presence, his eyes flicking up to meet hers. He gave her a subtle nod.

Sloane responded with a congenial smile before claiming a seat opposite them, joining the council of her only two house members. "How's everything looking?" she asked, her eyes roving over the clutter of documents that resembled a makeshift war map.

Elodie flinched, evidently startled by Sloane's sudden appearance. Stefan's laughter filled the air, a light moment amid the serious task at hand.

"We're sifting through potential strategies to enhance the stature and influence of House Reinhart," Elodie began after recovering from her surprise. "Right now, you bear a closer resemblance to a merchant house than a noble one. If you wish to be accorded the respect due to your title, you'll need to acquire land."

Sloane shrugged nonchalantly. "Acquiring land isn't a priority for me at the moment. I'm not planning to settle down until after we've found Gwyn. But I know of one avenue we can utilize." She turned her attention to Elodie. "We're going to ingratiate ourselves deeper with the guilds."

Elodie looked confused. "My lady? How are we going to do that?"

Sloane pulled out her notebook and turned to the page with everything she knew about stainless steel. She rotated it slightly so they could see as she explained, "This is everything I know about something my people called stainless or *rustless* steel. It is vastly superior to carbon steel in many aspects. Primarily, the fact that it does not corrode and takes much longer to rust. Further, there is a simple concept in my world. We call it subsidized research."

Elodie narrowed her eyes. "Do you mean like when a kingdom researches various subjects for some goal?"

Sloane considered. "Yes. For us, it definitely started with governments funding projects for specific goals. From what Ernald has told me, the Royal Academy of Avira works similarly. What I want to propose to the guildmaster is setting up a deliberate function within the guilds to fund and support research and development. Possibly even set up research centers that provide a single location to create new technology. This will allow the guilds to stay at the forefront of technological advancement. Especially since this world is at the cusp of a drastic societal shift with the introduction of magic."

"You intend to intertwine your relationship even further with the guilds?" Stefan asked.

Sloane nodded and explained, "Due to my unique circumstances, our house will not have a set place to work from. The guilds are everywhere. I believe forming a lasting connection with them will benefit us more in the long term."

Seeing the confusion etched across Elodie's face, Sloane leaned back in her chair, crossing her arms. A contemplative silence fell over the table, the clatter of the passersby and the hum of the city fading into the background. "Before we proceed," she began, her voice adopting a more serious tone. "I need to ask you both something. How far are you willing to go with me on this?"

The two exchanged glances, communicating silently in a manner only close allies could. Stefan took the lead, the man slightly more confident in his opinion than the young woman. "Our immediate plan was to head to Marketbol, Lady Reinhart. We understand your urgency to go farther, due to your quest, but as of now, you haven't even secured the recommendation from the guildmaster."

Sloane shrugged, an impish grin tugging at the corner of her mouth. "And isn't that the purpose of the information you gained?"

Stefan's responding nod was slow and deliberate. "Indeed, of course. However, I believe it would be prudent to concentrate our efforts on what you intend to accomplish in Marketbol first."

Elodie, agreeing with Stefan, leaned forward across the table, her voice dropping to a whisper. "Your house needs resources, Lady Reinhart. Let's focus on your strategy for Marketbol. This is not an endeavor you can launch and then abandon without substantial plans in place to manage it."

Sloane narrowed her eyes at Elodie, a certain determination glinting in her gaze. "My initial plan was to sell everything to the Guild. Everything."

Elodie recoiled, shaking her head vigorously. "My lady, if I may speak frankly, that is a terrible idea."

Caught off guard, Sloane tilted her head, curiosity piqued. "Explain."

Elodie looked at her and then Stefan. "First, allow me to ask: Would you be willing to purchase land and establish a business, or perhaps even one of these research centers yourself somewhere? The house could grow in this way while you continue your search."

Sloane tapped her lips as she sat in thought.

The idea had merit, and it would further her own influence in a way she hadn't really considered. Her entire focus was currently on locating Gwyn. If she had more soft power, perhaps she could use it to lean on others during the search. Growing the house and forming a deeper connection with the Guild would provide this. The guilds were everywhere she would go; it only made sense to utilize them as much as possible.

When the knights left, she would likely need more than just Stefan as a guard; he was currently assigned only to protect Elodie. Sloane didn't even know how far the sun elf would go. No more than one or two guards would be required, she suspected, as large groups attracted too much attention.

Thirdghyll would be a terrible place to recruit more people, and she didn't want to become a tool of the guilds by continually accepting their people. She needed to find people on her own who would be loyal to her first.

She also would need craftsmen and researchers to work on these projects.

Wait, the alchemists who made the ink. I wonder if I could meet with them.

With her mind made up, she answered, "Yes. That's something we can do. First, let's meet with your uncle and the Smithing Guild. Perhaps, if we have time, we can go meet with the alchemists I learned about."

"The ones who made the ink you had me pay for?" Elodie clarified.

"Yes. I believe they would be a great addition to any research center we can make. However, we need to discuss a location for such a facility and how much it would cost us to see if we can afford it."

"I think the location is obvious, my lady," Elodie said. "Marketbol. Not only is it close enough to ensure a constant update of funds from your connections in Vilstaf, but it will also ensure you gain enough funds to continue immediately. We can return to the financial benefits later, but if it is okay, let's discuss your ideas of the Smithing Guild first. I think it would be best if we were reading from the same scroll before approaching them. Along with the alchemists. There is some potential here that we should definitely exploit, if possible."

Stefan released a protracted sigh, his fingers running through his white hair as if trying to sift out the unnecessary complexities from the looming conversation. "This seems like a subject that isn't for me."

Elodie chuckled warmly. "Don't worry, Stefan," she said, her eyes twinkling as the conversation turned to a subject that she clearly felt confident in. "You can go play with the knights. This is *precisely* why I am here."

Sloane swiveled her notebook back toward herself and grabbed her quill, ready to take notes. It was time to force some progress.

Walking into the grand building of the Banking Guild, Elodie assumed the lead with an effortless grace, her steps sure and confident. Sloane was just a step behind, absorbing the rich, polished aura of the building, while Stefan brought up the rear, his eyes scanning their surroundings with practiced ease.

Their path veered toward a grand staircase, its marble steps whispering stories of countless sojourns. Upon reaching a central counter, Elodie raised her voice, calling out to a familiar figure. "Aimon! Is he in?"

Aimon, the telv Sloane had previously encountered at the Guild, blinked at the three of them, rapidly shuffling through a stack of papers on his desk. After his eyes scanned the written details, he looked up, a curt nod accompanying his words, "He's available until next bell, Miss Elodie."

"Perfect! We're heading up," Elodie's voice chimed, the edges of her words touched with an enthusiastic lilt.

"I'll annotate your appointment to ensure no one disturbs you," Aimon replied, already engrossed in his task.

"You're the best, Aimon," Elodie called over her shoulder, her words hanging in the air like a well-deserved compliment.

She's much more comfortable here, Sloane observed, an inward chuckle surfacing at her own understatement.

As the women ascended the stairs, Stefan detoured toward a plush chair, settling himself comfortably while the ladies proceeded. The duo traversed the corridor, their destination the guildmaster's office, situated at the end of an ornate hallway. Upon their approach, a guard standing sentry observed their advance, respectfully knocking and peeking into the office before swinging the door wide open for them.

The orkun guard smiled at them as they stepped across the threshold. "Miss Elodie, Lady Reinhart," he greeted them, nodding respectfully.

Guildmaster Romaris stood as they entered, and walked around his desk to greet them. He gave Elodie a hug and a kiss on each cheek. "Welcome, Elodie. Lady Reinhart. To what do I owe the pleasure of this visit?"

The intricate dance of their plan had been rehearsed thoroughly, with Elodie fully aligning herself to Sloane's ideas, having even devised the most effective methods for implementation. Today, Elodie would take the reins of the discussion.

Nonchalantly, Elodie gestured toward the inviting couch and chairs positioned to the side of the room. "Please, Uncle. Let's sit. Shall I get us a drink?" Her voice held a warmth and familiarity that only close relations could harbor.

The guildmaster shook his head genially as he ushered them toward the tastefully arranged seating area. "It's a bit early for a drink, don't you think?" His words drifted through the room, lightly laced with amusement.

Sloane let out a rich chuckle, her own humor sparkling in her eyes. "You're not wrong. However, I think we'll let you be the judge of that when we're done," she retorted playfully, her gaze firmly meeting the guildmaster's.

A quizzical eyebrow ascended on the guildmaster's forehead. "You have another idea for the Banking Guild?"

Quick to dispel any confusion, Sloane shook her head slightly. "Overall, not quite. Except I believe this one should interest you first." Her words, clear and precise, carried a note of intrigue, causing the guildmaster to lean in, his interest now visibly piqued.

Sensing Sloane's silent cue, Elodie adeptly took over the reins of the conversation. "Yes. Lady Reinhart has a twofold proposition. One that will benefit everyone, and the guilds, and you, by being the first to take advantage. She has given me notes on how to make a revolutionary new metal alloy from steel. One that is much better for many applications. Also, one that is evidently the result of over four hundred years of technological advancement beyond our own civilization's current progression." She paused, her eyes seeking Sloane's for validation of her words.

Sloane mirrored her nod, adding her own insights to Elodie's revelation. "Your civilization is roughly equivalent to a period of development that occurred around our year fourteen hundred. My world developed this type of steel over time, starting in our early eighteen hundreds. For reference, it was the year two thousand twenty-four when we were transported here."

A ripple of surprise shuddered across the guildmaster's face, his eyes wide with a sudden realization. "I had not been aware of that fact." The implications seemed to resonate with him, his usual calm demeanor replaced by a thoughtful frown. Murmuring under his breath, he appeared to be grappling with the new information. Suddenly, he got up and moved to his desk, and began rifling through a stack of papers he had set aside. He plucked one from the pile, his eyes hungrily scanning the words sprawled across the parchment.

"Lord Bolton. The terran toadstool the count has," he said finally. "I have a report from my people that states he is from the year eighteen hundred and nine."

Sloane shrugged. "There's no way. Either the man is having some type of traumatic response to leaving everything he knows or he's crazy."

Lanthil tilted his head. "Is it crazy? Some magical event brought you here. By your admission, our civilization is centuries behind yours. Is it so hard to imagine it ripped him away from his own time?"

Sloane squinted her eyes. She was ready to deny it; it was just too . . . fantastical. But she found herself unable to refute it completely. The guildmaster was right. She couldn't discount the possibility.

The only point of contention was that Bolton thought the colonials lost the American War of Independence. Napoleon was still doing his whole "conquer Europe" thing, and apparently the French either didn't help the colonials as much as they had—at least, in her world?—or they simply lost to a stronger British presence.

Does that mean the multiverse exists? Fuck. I swear, if a strange doctor pops up, I'm gonna just give up.

She took a deep breath. "Fine. I can't deny the possibility that the man is actually from where, and when, he states. That brings up a lot of potential issues and complications that I am not sure I am prepared to handle or discuss at the moment, though."

Like how does that affect my finding Gwyn? She's here. She's here . . . I will find her.

He nodded. "Very well. We will look into the matter further. Including the report that Stefan provided that indicates that the count has terrans held prisoner. Now, I apologize for the distraction. Please. Continue."

Elodie proceeded to carefully unpack their grand proposition, elucidating the intricate details and potentials. She discussed the conception of research centers, the benefits they carried, and the tangible impact they could have on society and their status. She proposed establishing one such center in Marketbol, under a synergistic partnership between Houses Reinhart and Romaris.

Elodie dove into the realm of material sciences, an area where Sloane, with her knowledge, could provide a significant leap forward. The conversation also touched on potential advancements in alchemical studies, particularly given Sloane's intent to connect with the runic ink alchemists. As the pieces of the plan fell into place, Guildmaster Romaris's demeanor changed from his initial nonchalant curiosity to intense interest.

The discourse unfurled, absorbed as they were in the exchange of ideas, questions, and answers that spanned well over the time they had allotted—at least two bells had rung in the distance.

Interrupting their meeting, Reji, the guildmaster's guard, poked his head into the room. "Boss, Aimon sent a message. Your next appointment is here and waiting. He already rescheduled the previous one."

Romaris sighed, the sound heavy with reluctant acceptance. "Fine. Sorry, ladies. As much as I think this meeting deserves that drink, I will have to pass for now." With swift movements, he scribbled a note on a piece of parchment and handed it to Elodie. "Here, give this to Aimon. He will give you what you need for the Smithing Guild. They will work with you after my request."

A radiant smile bloomed on Elodie's face. "Thank you, Uncle."

Following her lead, Sloane expressed her gratitude as well. "Thank you for your time, Guildmaster Romaris."

Thoughtfully, Romaris looked at the two women. "Hire a Guild-sanctioned esquire to draft up the paperwork," he said to Elodie. "I'll approve it. I want in on this, especially the center in Marketbol."

At this, Sloane flashed a triumphant grin. "Perfect. I am happy to hear that." Extending her hand to him, she continued, "I look forward to a profitable partnership. I suspect that this is enough for my previous request for a recommendation?"

Lanthil responded with hearty laughter. "Of course! I will draft it up and have a messenger deliver it to Elodie. Now, please excuse me."

Their exit from the Banking Guild was marked by shared smiles and the satisfaction of a job well done. Aimon promptly drafted the necessary documents for their presentation to the smiths, marking another step toward Sloane's project. As they stepped out into the bright light of day, a smirk played on Sloane's lips.

The next step toward her future economic victory was complete. *Sid got it wrong: domination isn't the only way to play here.*

CHAPTER TWENTY

PIECES OF THE PUZZLE

While many debate the exact moment that the early Contemporary Era began, it is an accepted fact that the arrival of the Displaced was the impetus that brought it about. What seemed like fanciful concepts and ideas at the time began a drastic change within all facets of civilization. The early attempts to marry Displaced technological knowledge with magic and mana were fraught with trials and tribulations. Several individuals stand out during this period as the most instrumental in bringing change; for gain or naught

In the next section of this text, we will focus on those who would one day establish organizations that last until this day.

Mana and Industry: The Early Contemporary Era, 522 SA

The Smithing Guild was nestled in the merchant district, a stone's throw from the central nobility area. The building projected a sense of humble charm, an unassuming facade hiding a bustling heart of activity. As they stepped inside, a moon elf woman welcomed them from behind a desk, strategically placed to command the entrance. Surveying the interior, Sloane noted three more desks scattered around the room, a door left ajar revealing a glimpse of a private office, and another door shut, its purpose concealed, but likely leading to storage or rooms tucked away in the back.

The moon elf's gaze fell upon the trio, a warm smile gracing her lips as she recognized Elodie. "Welcome back to the Smithing Guild, Miss Romaris," she chimed, her voice echoing a certain familiarity. She regarded the two strangers accompanying Elodie with a friendly nod. "And what brings you and your company here today?"

Taking the lead, Elodie reciprocated the elf's familiarity with a smile of her own. "Good day to you too, Imala. This is Lady Sloane of House Reinhart and along with our guard, Stefan. I have a request here with authorization from Guildmaster Romaris about a project for the Smithing Guild to undertake for Lady Reinhart and our house."

Imala's eyes widened slightly, intrigue piquing. "Oh my. May I?" she asked, extending her hand toward the document Elodie held.

With an affirmative nod from Elodie, Imala quickly unfurled the document, her gaze dancing over the words penned on the parchment.

The quiet rustle of paper was disrupted as a man emerged from the office in the back. "Imala, what have we here?" he asked, curiosity playing in his eyes.

The moon elf turned, grinning at the approaching figure. "Guildmaster Darius," she greeted him, then gestured at Elodie and her company. "Look who's here. Romaris . . . I mean Guildmaster Romaris—"

Elodie chuckled. "It's quite alright, Imala. You know my uncle isn't hung up on formalities."

Sloane raised an eyebrow. That didn't sound like the man she'd met.

Her financial advisor turned to the man and greeted the guildmaster with a friendly nod. "Always a pleasure, Darius."

With the familiarity of an old acquaintance, Darius returned the nod and smiled at Elodie. "Elodie, causing us headaches again? Another audit?" His tone was light, their shared history reverberating in his jesting words.

"The intention is far from causing distress, Guildmaster," Elodie countered, her tone congenial yet firm. "On the contrary, this project holds promise to profit the Smithing Guild immensely."

Darius's eyes narrowed in interest as he accepted the document from Imala. He perused it with a furrowed brow, then looked up at Sloane, disbelief coloring his words. "You intend for us to fabricate a new type of steel? For you?"

With an assertive nod, Sloane answered, "An alloy, to be more precise. The Smithing Guild will secure a license to the process, the alloy composition, and any derivative compositions born from my knowledge. Your Guild will select two smiths who will be taught on the specific metals and their respective percentages. This knowledge will be a Guild secret. Furthermore, I intend to employ one of these smiths to join me on my trip to Marketbol, where they will be instrumental in the creation of more novel materials. In return, I request a modest fraction of this alloy for personal use."

The depth of Sloane's proposition, coupled with Guildmaster Romaris's endorsement, triggered a sharp intake of breath from Darius. His disbelief evident, he protested, "You can't just force one of the smiths to leave their home."

Sloane raised a placating hand, her tone patient and assuring. "That's not my intent, Guildmaster. I'm seeking a volunteer, someone who harbors a desire to glimpse and shape the future of material science and technology."

Darius gave a slow nod as he digested Sloane's words. "So, what exactly do you propose?"

Seizing the opportunity, Elodie gently interjected, "Guildmaster, perhaps it would be best to discuss the details seated? There's much to unpack."

Thus, the ensemble found themselves seated around one of the unoccupied desks. Imala diligently jotted down the critical points as Elodie and Sloane expanded on their ideas, the specifics of the metal they wished to make, and its advantages. As the conversation unfurled, the initial disbelief on Darius's face gradually gave way to budding excitement. In a brief interlude, Imala rose to prepare a round of tea for the group.

Sloane delicately sipped at her tea, observing as Elodie and Darius negotiated the finer points of the licensing agreement.

"You want fifteen percent of every sale using this stainless steel that the Guild brokers? Plus, a monthly fee from any smith who uses it. That's excessive. One percent of every sale will still net you a very healthy sum. We could simply roll the monthly licensing fee for each smith into their Guild fees. Though, I think a two point five percent increase on Guild fees that we would then pass on to you is more than fair."

Sloane raised an eyebrow. It *was* fair, but Elodie had gone high for a reason.

The pair had already established their minimum acceptable terms, aware that the present agreement would not necessarily cover the entire Smithing Guild. Today's final terms would be used by Elodie to instruct an esquire who would negotiate with the Guild's headquarters after they had established their research center and demonstrated the viability of their unique product.

Although this contract would extend to the entire region under Guildmaster Romaris's stewardship, which was by no means small, Elodie aimed for an initial agreement significantly higher than what they anticipated to settle for with the larger Guild.

Elodie's response to Darius was imbued with her customary charm yet also a trace of assertiveness, reminiscent of a chess player countering a strategic move. "Your counter proposal might be equitable if this were just another carbon steel production method, Guildmaster. However, House Reinhart is offering an advanced product, backed by centuries of research. The amount you suggest does not reflect that disparity. We propose twelve percent on Guild brokerage. For the Guild fees, a different structure could be considered: a five percent increase passed on to our House. Then, we can consider it a deal."

Darius balked at this, countering, "That's still considerably high, given that the majority of the work, including the complexities of producing an advanced alloy, would be on our part."

Elodie's smile was unwavering. "A fair sentiment indeed, Guildmaster. If you believe the smiths in Thirdghyll are not up to the task, we can postpone this agreement until we reach Marketbol. There, we can collaborate exclusively with the smith who chooses to accompany us."

A hint of surprise flickered in Darius' eyes. "Let's not make hasty decisions here. Implementing this project would yield significant benefits for our city. I must remind you, it's *your* city too."

Clearly not a man good with deals. Elodie has him right where she wants him.

Elodie made her final plea with a soft, unwavering determination. "Indeed, Guildmaster. It is due to our common roots and shared interests that we approached you first, demonstrating our willingness to compromise. However, the figures I've proposed are the lowest we can accommodate. Shall we make this deal?"

Guildmaster Darius fell into a thoughtful silence. His gaze floated upward, as though seeking guidance from the intricate, wooden ceiling patterns, before trailing back to his interlaced fingers resting on the desk. Sloane watched him, her mind silently calculating.

Five percent might yield them only around two and a half gold a month from each smith, but collectively, this would build a significant stream of income. She had no desire to rob the smiths; her plan was built on a mutually beneficial partnership. She realized that brokering sales of metal was not as frequent as it might appear, but she expected a future surge in demand. She wanted to establish this deal now, ahead of the Guild fully recognizing the potential windfall it was stepping into.

After what seemed an eternity, Darius's contemplative expression morphed into a resigned frown. He turned to his moon elf assistant, who had been quietly observing the negotiation. "Imala, let's prepare the contract. I believe we've reached an agreement."

Elodie's smile mirrored her victory. "There's no need for that, Guildmaster. I've brought a contract with us. If you'll allow me, I'll fill in the agreed-upon amounts . . . and there. We are set."

Darius laughed, the tension in the room dissipating with his amusement. "You are definitely a Romaris. Alright! Lady Reinhart, I will set you up with the two smiths. They should be able to get you your requested amounts quickly." He looked at the notes Imala had taken concerning material requirements. "We have everything listed here available in the city. If your alloy works as predicted, the first batch should be ready within a week."

As they all rose from their seats, Sloane extended her hand to the guildmaster. "I look forward to it, Guildmaster Darius. Thank you for your business today."

Two bells—or about two hours—after their successful negotiation at the Smithing Guild, Sloane and Elodie found themselves in an unfamiliar part of the city. Despite having received directions to the alchemy shop, they had somehow gotten lost in the various streets.

The city district they were in was noticeably more worn down, a sharp contrast to the prosperous and bustling central district or even the merchant district they had just left. Buildings in varying states of decay lined the streets, and the cobblestones underfoot were uneven and poorly maintained. The smell of poverty hung heavy in the air, mingled with the earthy scent of age-old brickwork.

While Stefan sought directions from the district's inhabitants, Sloane and Elodie stood to one side, waiting. Sloane couldn't help but wonder if the stationery shop owner had deliberately provided convoluted directions to protect his alchemical suppliers, or if it was simply a testament to his poor sense of direction.

She smiled as she watched two young telv girls hold hands as they skipped together down the sidewalk, their hair blowing in the wind behind them. They swung their arms and giggled as they spoke animatedly about something only they knew. Two women followed them, and she heard one of them comment on needing to tie the other girl's hair up again. Sloane chuckled. The sight was reminiscent of Gwyn and her best friend as they played in the park near their school. Gwyn's hair would always be "wild and free," as her daughter liked to say. With a soft sigh, Sloane shook her head to clear the nostalgia, her gaze returning to Stefan. Elodie threw her an inquisitive look, which she decided to ignore.

Stefan returned, expressing gratitude to the elf he had been speaking to before addressing Sloane and Elodie. "Their shop is just a few blocks from here. Apparently, it's tucked away in an alley."

With a nod of acknowledgment, Sloane cast one last glance at the telv girls before turning to follow Stefan. The guard guided them through the winding streets and narrow alleyways of the district until they reached a particularly run-down street. Graffiti colored the stone walls of the buildings, and Sloane saw her first penis art since arriving in the new world. She shook her head, an amused smirk on her lips. *Not impressed, elves. Not impressed.*

Ahead, the cobbled path led between two buildings, with an overhang joining them. At first glance, Sloane thought it was just an architectural quirk. But as they drew closer, she realized an alleyway extended beyond the sheltered section. They walked through the entrance and down the winding alley that had graffiti all along the buildings on either side of them. The windows were all boarded up and there wasn't a single door on the road that didn't have wrought iron bars in front of them. Frankly, it was all creepy as hell, and Sloane was thankful she had magic.

And Stefan, I guess. He can be a distraction.

She looked around again, hearing what sounded like crows cawing in the area.

Yeah. A distraction while I run away from this place.

The alleyway eventually widened, forking into two paths separated by a quaint wooden shop. The sign swinging gently above the door bore the unusual inscription "Kemmy's Mixers and Elixirs."

Stefan snorted. "That's a unique name."

Sloane chuckled in agreement. "Yeah, for sure. Alright, let's—"

The front of the store exploded.

A violent blast of heat, dust, and shards of wood and glass shot outward. Stefan reacted instinctively, a startled curse escaping his lips as he twisted and threw himself against Elodie. They collided with the hard ground, his body forming a protective shield over the startled elf. Elodie's breath hitched as a startled cry tore from her throat, terror spiking in her wide eyes.

Sloane, in the split second the chaos unfolded, threw herself downward, arms raised protectively over her head. A scream perched precariously on her lips, yet she managed to strangle it before it could surface. As quickly as it had happened, the tumultuous calamity abated, leaving an eerie silence to blanket the alleyway.

What the fuck was that?!

Sloane's mind reeled, her heart pounding against her ribs like a frantic drumbeat.

As the dust settled, Stefan was the first to regain his bearings. Gently gripping Elodie's arm, he encouraged her to move, his voice barely more than a whisper against the eerie silence. The raithe guided her to crawl further away from the wreckage of the shop, which smoldered ominously, a symbol of destruction etched starkly against the urban backdrop.

Sloane lingered on the ground, eyes wide with the adrenaline that coursed through her. But when she realized no further disaster was imminent, she clumsily clambered to her feet, knees shaky from the shock. Her gaze swept across the alleyway, taking in the havoc left in the wake of the blast.

The shop was a heartbreaking sight. Where a quaint storefront had stood just moments ago, there now was a gaping maw in the building. The explosion had eradicated the glass windows, and as she watched, the front door groaned and fell with a crash, the final hinge surrendering to the force of the blast. Scattered embers glowed ominously among the rubble, though the structure itself seemed stubbornly resistant to catching flame. Yet the pall of smoke that seeped from the windowless void and crumbled sections of the wall posed a different threat.

As if to punctuate her thoughts, Elodie yelped as the hanging sign tumbled to the ground, dragging along with it a portion of the damaged entryway.

Sloane felt a hollow echo of shock reverberate within her. Instinctively, she drew upon her mana, her senses heightened in preparation for any unforeseen threats. Yet, in the wake of the catastrophe, the alleyway fell into an unnatural stillness.

Stefan was silent, scrutinizing in their surroundings, while Elodie seemed stuck in her shock, her gaze fixed on the charred remains of the shop.

Sloane approached the ruined building, her voice loud in the hush. "Hello? Anyone in there?"

Edging closer to the gaping hole that was once the entrance, she saw nothing but a thick wall of smoke. Yet, she felt an odd sensation in the air, like a residual echo of the explosion. She glanced down at her wrist, where her watch face showed swirling white and blue mist in the direction of the building. She looked back at Stefan.

"I think I'm going to go in. Do you have any cloth I can tie around my face?"

"You shouldn't go in, Lady Reinhart. It's too dangerous," he replied hesitantly.

"Someone needs to. There may be—"

A rasping cough, muffled by the smoke, caught their attention. "You should listen to your man."

Whirling around, Sloane was met by the sight of two women, a raithe and an orkun, stumbling out of the smoking building. Her heart lurched with relief and apprehension. There were survivors.

Springing into action, Sloane dashed over to the two women. "Let me help you!" she said, reaching the orkun first. She slipped under the smaller woman's arm, helping support her weight as she carefully wrapped the arm around her neck.

Almost simultaneously, Stefan darted forward, lending a hand to the taller raithe woman. A part of Sloane's mind filed away the oddly comical sight of the shorter man supporting the taller woman, but the gravity of their situation muted any potential laughter. Together, they guided the two women away from the damaged building, steering clear of the rising tendrils of smoke.

As they moved to a safer distance, the orkun woman let out a low groan of pain, her body sagging against Sloane's. With the utmost care, Sloane lowered her to the ground, her fingers gently releasing their grip.

"Thezmos's sack, that hurts . . ." the orkun muttered, grimacing.

The raithe woman shrugged off Stefan's help, choosing to crouch down in front of the other woman. "Rel, you okay, my love?" There was an urgency in her voice as her eyes roamed over Rel's form, scouring for visible injuries.

Rel groaned again, her hand batting away the concerned inspection. "I'm fine! I told you that elixir was too potent!"

The raithe woman groaned in turn, collapsing onto her backside in defeat. "Oh, come on! How was I supposed to know it would channel that much arcane!"

An exasperated sigh escaped Rel. "Maybe—and hear me out—because I *told* you it would! Clearly, you put too much silden extract into it!"

"If you hadn't used so much of *your* arcane flows, it would have been fine! You know you're only supposed to push a smidgen to activate the elixir!"

Sloane paused, a realization dawning on her.

Are they talking about . . .?

"Hold on, are you two talking about magic and mana?" she interrupted, eyes narrowing slightly.

The effect was immediate. The women seemed to suddenly recall they weren't alone. Their eyes went wide, a shocked silence hanging in the air. The raithe's hand flew to her mouth in apparent horror.

"We . . . we were just speaking alchemy talk. It's just shop terms," Rel stammered, her gaze darting nervously between Sloane and Stefan.

A small smirk tugged at the corners of Sloane's lips. She extended her hand, allowing a petite sphere of mana to coalesce above her palm. The two women gasped in unison, their eyes going wide as they beheld the display.

"It's okay. We're friends," Sloane said, her voice softening. "Are you both alright? Is there anything you need?"

The raithe woman sighed, casting a woeful glance at the remains of their shop. "Unless you can fix our shop, I don't think so. Our entire livelihood was in there."

"Perhaps introductions are in order," Sloane suggested. "I'm Sloane, and these are my companions: Elodie, the shy, shell-shocked one, and Stefan, our guard. We actually came here hoping to speak with you."

The orkun woman made a move to stand, but a pained grunt escaped her lips and she sank back down. "I'm Rel." She gestured toward her raithe companion. "And this is Kemmy, my partner." Sloane reached out to shake the offered hand, noting the firm grip.

"Nice to meet you both," she returned, her tone sincere.

Kemmy sighed deeply, her gaze traveling from the destroyed shop to the strangers standing before her. "Well, I apologize that you've found us in this state, but unfortunately I don't think we'll be able to assist with whatever you wished to meet us for."

Sloane gave them a warm smile, attempting to instill a spark of hope. "Let's see what can be salvaged first. Then we can discuss how I might be of assistance."

Rel's eyes narrowed slightly at Sloane's words. "Why would you want to help us?"

Sloane's response was candid. "I recently purchased some of your products and, well, let's just say I see potential for a fruitful investment in your future."

Kemmy's gaze ping-ponged between the ruins of their shop and Sloane, her eyes thoughtful. After a moment of contemplation, she seemed to come to a silent consensus with Rel. "Alright. Let's see what can be salvaged. But Rel, you stay here for now. I'm going to check the shop before doing anything else."

It was nightfall when they finally made it back to the inn. Rel and Kemmy had agreed to join them, and Sloane had secured a room for the two women. Maud and Deryk had helped them up to their room, and once they were in a more private setting, the knight-medic used her magic. It was no surprise that the two women were shocked by the healing spell.

Sloane could tell they wanted to ask many questions and discuss magic, but Maud firmly insisted they rest and recover before delving into such matters.

Sloane would need to speak to them about the elixir they spoke of and the potential reactions with mana. That could wait, though. First, she needed to ensure the women were cared for, extending the same helping hand the knights had once offered her. The business talk would follow later, at a time when they wouldn't feel obligated to her out of gratitude.

I know how that can feel. I won't take advantage of them. If they didn't want to make a deal with her, she wouldn't press.

Sloane looked at her mechanical bird, still a work in progress, and the notebook filled with meticulous notes by her side. With just the steel required for the joints and external covering yet to be procured, her creation was nearing completion. She set her focus on the chest cavity of the bird, carefully positioning the core within its cradle. Almost as if acknowledging its rightful place, the core responded with a brighter glow, its ethereal blue light swirling tantalizingly beneath its surface.

She grabbed the head and looked into the two onyx eyes she had made. Everything was coming together, and her tools had really started taking shape. As she reached for her inscribing tool, a fleeting memory ambushed her.

A quick flash of herself standing in a vast workshop, crafting—

Huh. That's some strange déjà vu.

Shaking off the peculiar sensation, Sloane returned her focus to etching the runes into her mechanical bird.

It's probably nothing.

She thought of the way forward. She just needed to avoid the count and then meet with the spy organization within the city. She narrowed her eyes. It wouldn't be much longer. Then they could move on and she could continue her search for Gwyn.

CHAPTER TWENTY-ONE

IMPRESSIONS

Sabina tried to force herself back to wakefulness as a building sense of terror, not her own, pulled her deeper into somewhere . . . else. The transition was disorienting, a violent upheaval that threatened to shatter her reality.

The pain that accompanied this shift was unlike anything she had ever endured. It felt as though an invisible force was prying open the very fabric of her mind, tearing apart the threads of her thoughts one by one. Each thread that snapped sent a jolt of agony through her, a searing pain that reverberated in the hollow recesses of her consciousness.

Sabina battled against the onslaught, her mental defenses straining under the relentless assault. She endeavored to anchor herself, to cling to the remnants of her mind, but the terror was unyielding, dragging her deeper into its alien world. Her thoughts, once coherent and structured, began to splinter under the strain. Ideas, memories, and emotions were ripped from their roots, leaving behind images and feelings that were not her own. The pain that followed was all-encompassing.

And then, even that was gone.

The last vestiges of her consciousness were swept away, leaving her adrift in a sea of black, glowing mist filled with . . . *power*. The foreign terror won over. It was as if both hers and the foreign thoughts had been forcibly laid bare, a door wrenched wide against her will, allowing the outside force to pull her in. Sabina was swallowed whole, consumed by an alien world that left her disoriented and adrift in its depths.

But then her mind *opened*.

* * *

It was a scene of a town quite unlike any I had seen.

The architecture around me was a stark contrast to what I was accustomed to, with smooth walls of solid stone, glass panes so clear they were almost invisible, adorned with colorful lettering and vibrant images. Everywhere I turned, there were people dressed in peculiar attire, and vehicles, which I later learned were called cars, whizzed by. I took a moment to absorb the sights, sounds, and even the unique smells of this new environment. The people seemed to radiate happiness, their faces free of worry or stress. Families strolled leisurely, their children darting about in playful abandon.

Across the road, a young girl walking with a couple caught my eye. Upon seeing me, she waved enthusiastically. *"Ciao, Gwyn!"*

I returned her greeting with a wave of my own. *"Ciao, Francesca! A lunedì!"*

"A lunedì!" she echoed, her voice trailing off as she continued on her way.

Children ran around in groups, their laughter filling the air, while others navigated the streets on their . . . bicycles, my memories told me.

Everything is so peaceful. So safe.

It was a stark contrast to what I was used to.

"Andiamo, mamma!" I called over my shoulder, eager to explore more.

Let's go!

Just as I was about to step forward, a firm hand pulled me back. "Gwyn, pay attention."

I looked up just in time to see a car zoom past the spot I had intended to cross. My heart pounded in my chest. That thing could have hit me.

Wait, a car? That's what a car is?

I turned back to see a tall, beautiful woman looking down at me, an unamused expression on her face, and concern in her piercing blue eyes that looked so like . . . my . . . own. There was something familiar about her, but I couldn't quite place it.

Why does *she seem so familiar?*

"Scusa, mamma. I'll make sure to look both ways," I promised, feeling a bit chastised.

"Please do. Now, let's get some gelato, shall we?" Mom suggested, offering her arm for me to hold.

We made our way to a quaint shop overlooking a serene canal. A large fabric awning, supported by a single pole with metal ribs fanning out from the top, provided welcome shade from the sunlight. Mother—*Mom*—ordered two cups of a *frozen* dessert from the woman behind the counter. I listened intently as she ordered two different flavors, the foreign words rolling off her tongue with ease.

It was beautiful.

As the woman behind the counter scooped the dessert into two cups, I watched with rapt attention. The first cup was filled with a vibrant pink concoction, the unmistakable hue of strawberries, while the second held a rich, brown dessert—the chocolate Mom had requested. Once our treats were ready, we moved to a table on the terrace, the cool breeze from the canal a welcome respite from the warmth of the day. Mom handed me my cup of strawberry . . . *gelato*, and I took it with a sense of anticipation.

The moment the gelato touched my tongue, a burst of flavor exploded in my mouth. It was unlike anything I had ever tasted before—sweet, creamy, and refreshingly cold.

How do they make this and keep it so cold? The sensation sent a jolt of delight through my system. It felt like a treat fit for royalty, yet all around me, ordinary people were enjoying the same indulgence.

I looked up at my mom, and while I could feel my excitement building, *I— the one behind the eyes*—couldn't help but feel a chill roll down my mental spine.

My vision lingered on my mom, committing her to memory as I did every night because I didn't want to forget. Warmth, love, and pride filled my chest as I memorized every feature of her.

She was a towering figure, her height surpassing that of most people around us. Her hair, a cascade of brunette curls, fell just below her shoulder blades, catching the sunlight in a way that made it seem like it was threaded with gold. Her eyes, a striking sapphire blue that mirrored my own, held a depth of intelligence that was both comforting and awe-inspiring. I glanced down at my arm, comparing my pale skin to her slightly tanned complexion. The differences were subtle yet noticeable.

I wished I would look as gorgeous as my mom one day. *I wished I could see—* The thought stopped in my mind as I fought to maintain separation.

I took another bite of my treat of the gods, the taste of strawberries filling my senses. A giggle escaped my lips as I noticed a smudge of chocolate on Mom's chin.

"Mom! Your chin!" I exclaimed, pointing at the offending spot. Her reaction, a mixture of surprise and amusement, only made me laugh harder. This was a moment I wanted to remember, a moment of pure joy and contentment.

Mamma was the *best.*

My mother's laughter was a melodious sound that filled the air around us. She reached for a napkin and wiped the smudge of chocolate from her chin with a playful roll of her eyes. Then, with a mischievous glint in her sapphire eyes, she reached out and tapped my nose with her finger.

"*Grazie*, Gwynnie!" she said, her voice filled with warmth.

I wriggled my nose as she pulled away, and smiled when I saw her nails, which were glossy and beautifully painted. The almond shape of them was really pretty, and I definitely wanted to get my nails done like that one day. I would love it if Mom and I could go to the salon together for mani-pedis.

Wait, I do? I don't even know what those are.

We sat in companionable silence, our attention drawn to a group of ducks swimming lazily in the canal. There was something inherently peaceful about these moments, just watching nature with Mom, a tranquility that seemed to seep into my very bones.

It really is peaceful here.

Suddenly, the serenity was shattered by a chorus of screams echoing from a distance.

I jerked upright, my gaze darting around as I tried to locate the source of the commotion. Everyone around us was looking up, their faces a mixture of awe and fear. Following their gaze, I tilted my head back and saw the sky lights . . . *no*, the *aurora*, painting the sky in vibrant hues.

"*Mamma!* I'm scared!" I cried out, turning to her. Her face was calm, her eyes devoid of the fear that was gripping me.

"Why be scared? It's going to take you away, and you'll never see me again. Goodbye, Gwyn," she said, her voice devoid of any emotion.

What!?

"No! Mom, *mamma!* Don't leave me! *Non andare!*" I pleaded, tears welling up in my eyes. The fear was a tangible thing now, a cold knot in my chest that made it hard to breathe.

"Goodbye," she said again, turning her back to me and starting to walk away.

"*Mamma!*" I cried out, reaching out for her. But it was too late. I tried to move, but I couldn't. It was like I was frozen in place. And then my world, my heart . . . collapsed.

No! Gwyn!

A bright blue flash filled my vision, blinding me.

Then the world around me seemed to dissolve into an inky blackness, yanking me away from the terrifying void and back into my body.

A wave of profound sadness and pain ripped Sabina from her sleep, causing her to bolt upright in her bed. Her heart pounded in her chest as she frantically scanned the room, her mind struggling to reconcile the dream world she had been pulled from with the reality of her surroundings. Her fingers came away slick with sweat as she touched her forehead. She sat in the darkness, her breaths coming in ragged gasps as she tried to piece together the fragments of her dream.

Then, like a bolt of lightning, realization struck her. She knew what had happened.

Gwyn!

With a sense of urgency propelling her, Sabina leaped from her bed and hastily threw on her clothes. She didn't understand what was happening, why she was experiencing these strange dreams, but one thing was clear.

She needed to get to Gwyn.

As she sprinted through the corridors of the house, the few servants and guards who were still awake performing their nighttime duties quickly stepped aside to let her pass. Her heart pounded in her chest, each beat echoing the urgency of the moment.

As she neared Gwyn's room, she skidded to a halt, her eyes scanning the area for any signs of danger. She turned to one of the guards, her voice urgent and commanding. "Tell everyone to stay back! There might be fire!"

Upon reaching Gwyn's room, Sabina threw caution to the wind and barged in, propriety be damned. Her eyes darted around the room, but all she was met with was an oppressive darkness. Her voice echoed in the room as she called out, "Gwyn? Are you okay?"

But instead of the heat and fire she had been expecting, a bone-chilling cold greeted her. It was as if winter had descended upon the room, filling it with an icy chill that seeped into her bones.

The air was so cold it was almost tangible, like a physical entity that wrapped around her, making her shiver. The sudden drop in temperature was disconcerting, adding another layer of unease to the already tense situation.

Sabina moved farther into the room, her breath visible in the frigid air. She felt as though she had stepped into a different world, one that had been replaced by the harsh cold of winter. The chill was so intense it felt as though it could freeze her very thoughts. But she pushed through it, her concern for Gwyn overriding her discomfort.

Sabina heard the girl before she saw her. But when she did, she immediately noticed Gwyn lying down, crying into her pillow. The waves of sadness emanating from Gwyn were so intense they felt almost tangible, suffocating Sabina with their intensity.

"Gwyn?" Sabina called out softly.

Gwyn's response was a series of muffled sobs, her words lost in the fabric of her pillow. Sabina moved closer, sitting down on the edge of the bed. She tentatively placed a hand on Gwyn's back, an unfamiliar gesture for her. Sabina had never done especially well with children before, but this sadness . . .

I have to do something.

"Gwynnie? Can you talk to me?" Sabina asked, using the affectionate nickname she knew Gwyn's mother in the dream used.

Gwyn stiffened at the sound of the nickname, but after a moment, she slowly rolled over to face Sabina. In the dim light filtering in through the windows, their faces were barely visible to each other.

"My mom calls me that," Gwyn whispered through her tears, her voice barely audible.

"I know. I know she does. I am so sorry, Gwyn. I know you miss her," Sabina responded softly, her heart aching at the raw pain in Gwyn's voice.

"She's gone, Sabina. I'm never going to see her again. I-I should have held her hand like she told me to. I let go. I let go, and she's gone. It's all my fault. I shouldn't . . . I shouldn't have—" Gwyn's words trailed off into a series of hurried breaths, her body shaking with the effort of trying to hold back her sobs.

"Shh, shh. Gwyn, please. Don't talk like that. It's not your fault. I know it's not. You're going to see her again. I promise," Sabina reassured her, her own eyes welling up with tears. The sadness was still there, but it had shifted, morphing into a sense of hopelessness and anguish that was almost unbearable. "Come here, sit up for me."

With gentle hands, Sabina helped Gwyn sit up and pulled her into a comforting embrace. Gwyn's breathing was rapid and shallow, but as they held each other, her breaths gradually slowed and synced with Sabina's own.

No one her age should feel this.

Sabina tried to channel thoughts of hope and love, humming a soft tune as she held Gwyn close. She thought of the strength and resilience Gwyn had shown, the pride she had seen in Taenya's and Siveril's eyes whenever Gwyn interacted with others. She thought of the joy that lit up Keston's face whenever he spent time with Gwyn. She thought of the deep love that radiated from Gwyn whenever she spoke of her mother, a love so profound that Sabina found herself yearning to experience it herself.

This girl is amazing. I will support her until my last breath. I will follow her anywhere, do anything to help her find her mother.

As she channeled these feelings, Sabina felt the waves of emotion emanating from Gwyn begin to calm. The girl was still crying, but the intensity of her sobs had lessened. Gwyn was gripping Sabina tightly, as if she feared that letting go would cause her to disappear, to lose everyone she knew once again.

Sabina held her, providing a steady presence in the midst of Gwyn's turmoil. She realized then that Gwyn was not just a princess to her, but a girl who loved her mother deeply and was loved in return.

A girl who had made a mistake without realizing the consequences until it was too late. Sabina would keep this secret, for Gwyn was her princess, and she would always stand by her side.

"Gwyn?" Sabina said softly.

"Yes, Sabina?" Gwyn's voice was small, hesitant.

"I will do everything I can to make it better. Alright? I will be right here, and if you ever need to talk or cry, I will always be available. I will never tell a soul any secret you share with me," Sabina promised, her voice steady and sincere.

"You promise?" the girl asked hesitantly.

"I promise," Sabina affirmed, her words echoing in the quiet room.

Sabina watched as Gwyn took a deep breath and pulled away, her small frame seeming even smaller in the dim light of the room. The silence that followed was heavy, but Sabina didn't rush her. She knew Gwyn needed time to gather her thoughts, to process the whirlwind of emotions that had swept through her.

She needs time. And I will give her all the time she needs.

As she waited, Sabina made a silent vow to herself. She would never again intrude on Gwyn's thoughts without her permission. She would not betray the trust that Gwyn had placed in her.

Suddenly, a small light appeared over Gwyn's shoulder, startling Sabina. Upon closer inspection, she realized it was a tiny orb of fire, no bigger than a gold coin. Gwyn offered her a small smile, a faint glimmer of her usual spirit shining through her tear-streaked face. "Sorry, I just couldn't see you."

"It's okay, Gwyn," Sabina reassured her.

"So. I . . . you *do* promise you'll never tell *anyone?*" Gwyn asked again.

"I do. I promise to keep your secrets to myself and never betray the trust you have placed in me. I will defend both you and your thoughts from anyone who would do harm to you or anything you claim as your own," Sabina swore.

Gwyn placed a small hand on Sabina's and squeezed gently. "Thank you, Sabina. I am so lucky to have you. I can't wait until you can meet my mom."

"I can't either, Gwyn."

"So . . . my secret," Gwyn began, taking a deep breath. But Sabina interrupted her gently.

"Gwyn, if it makes you feel safer, or better, you can keep this secret. It's alright. Whatever it is, it's from before. Who you are now is an amazing princess. One who has been acknowledged, and that cannot be taken away. Taenya, Siveril, and I won't let it be. You're alright. I promise."

"Are you sure? You won't get upset if you find out?" Gwyn asked quietly.

"Never."

Gwyn's eyes welled up with fresh tears, and she threw herself back into Sabina's arms for another hug. Her small arms wrapped tightly around Sabina, and the knight couldn't help but feel the waves of love and acceptance radiating from the girl.

I will need to teach her how to control the emotions she lets out.

Sabina smiled. She was happy and thankful that they had chosen her to join Gwyn's house. It was a kindness she would have to repay Lord Iemes for one day.

Sabina gasped as the light suddenly died out. The girl froze again, and then giggled. "Oops! I forgot about it for a second there. Sorry I scared you."

Sabina shook her head as she laughed and patted the girl on the back.

"Come on, you should get back to sleep."

"Sabina? Can you sit with me for a little while? Just until I fall asleep again? I always feel calmer when you're around."

"Of course. I will be right here." Sabina couldn't help but smile.

I will hold the nightmares at bay.

Several days passed, and Gwyn noticed she was starting to feel better. She hadn't had another nightmare yet, and she was just glad to be able to sleep. It was as if a calming influence had settled over the room each night, and she was so grateful for it.

Other than that, there wasn't much to do except continue with her tutoring. She had met with Mister Branigan each day, but today was special—she would meet his wife.

She walked down the halls, occasionally twirling around. It felt like it would be a good day. Gwyn waved and said hello to the guards and servants as she skipped past them.

Oh, wait! I'm going to be late!

She rushed around the corner and almost smacked into Friedrich, who was walking with Keston. "Oops! Sorry, Friedrich!" she apologized as she quickly moved around him.

"It's nothing, Your Highness. How are you doing today?" the German knight asked her.

"I'm great! Sorry, can't talk. I need to meet with Mister Branigan!" she said hastily.

"You'd better hurry. You know how he is about punctuality. Don't be late!" Keston called out after her.

She hurried down the halls and finally reached the library. She burst through the door in a huff like Kool-Aid Man. *Ohhhh yeaaaaah!* "I'm here! I'm here!"

Her sun elf tutor, Mister Branigan, was standing next to the table where they worked, holding a book against which he tapped his hand. "Miss Gwyn. Punctuality is the most effective approach to establishing a positive first impression."

Okay, Mister Grumpy-pants.

"Mister Branigan, 'a queen is never late; everyone else is merely early'" Gwyn said, quoting a movie she'd watched with her mom. There was a snort from the side, and Gwyn looked over to see a high elf woman with an amused expression on her face.

"She's got you there, Quinn." The woman focused her gaze on Gwyn. "However, luckily for us mere scholars, you are only a princess for now."

"Please, allow me to introduce my wife." Mister Branigan gestured to the elf woman, who joined them. "This is Professor Maya Rolfe. She works at the Strathmore Academy, like me. However, she deals with topics such as the historical development of civil infrastructure and techniques."

Gwyn squinted and was about to ask what he meant when Mister Branigan's wife explained. "What my husband means is, I look at how different cultures and nations made things and learned how to make new things."

"My mom does that! Sort of. She's in charge of a lot of people who make new things. Right now, she's working on a new watch. It's really fancy. It's kept her busy a lot, but she always finds time to do things with me . . ." Gwyn paused. *Oh* . . . "Or she did. You know, before we came here."

"It is quite alright, Miss Gwyn. I think I would *love* to hear all about some of the things your mother had people make. Perhaps we can speak about all the fascinating things from your world in the future? Then I can help teach you about the world you have found yourself in. Things you may experience that you are probably not used to."

"I would like that, Miss Rolfe."

She turned her attention to Mister Branigan. "No Lorrena today?"

He shook his head. "Not today. Since it's Maya's first day, we wanted to just have you for this session."

That made sense to Gwyn. They were here for *her*, after all, but she didn't want Lorrena's learning to fall behind either.

Miss Rolfe gestured for them to sit, and asked, "Tell me, what has my husband been teaching you this week? What's the most interesting thing?"

"He's mainly been teaching me about Avira and its history. Like when King Revish made a deal for the Kingdom of Tiloral to join, or when he made a deal with the dwarves that live in Dorn Loder—"

"Dirn Loduhr, Miss Gwyn," Mister Branigan corrected.

"Right. Yeah. Thank you, Mister Branigan. We also talked about the Kingdom of Meris, the Lymtoria Republic, and the Queendom of Lehelia. *Which is really cool!* Lots of history. We also talked about the Loreni diaspora. Oh, and we started going over the various customs and etiquette of Avira and the other areas I may travel to."

"History and ways to act as a noble, Quinn?" Miss Rolfe raised an eyebrow. "May as well teach her the migration patterns of the *Bisoprocta induus*. At least the etiquette will have immediate uses. She's not from our world. No one expects her to know that Queen Ismeyra signed the Recognition Act of Eight Fifty-One, which allows her to even establish a house in the kingdom as a foreign noble in exile. Which is most assuredly the route Siveril has taken."

Mister Branigan groaned. "Maya, history is important. It allows her to understand the kingdom she is now part of. It shows her *why* we do the things we do. Before you can understand the present, you must understand where we've been. Speaking of dates, one thing that *is* relevant is that there are talks of establishing a new calendar era. One based on the Flash."

Miss Rolfe looked up at the ceiling for a few seconds and then back at her husband. "Husband of mine. She is not one of your students. That information is relevant *to us*, and of *course* I knew that. I received the same missive. Like everyone else in the Academy," she said.

Mister Branigan looked at Gwyn before sighing and picking up the book he had placed on the table. "Why don't we get started for the day, Miss Gwyn?"

"Sounds great, Mister Branigan."

"You get one hour, Quinn. I will teach the next subject. We're going to learn something interesting." Miss Rolfe glanced at Gwyn and gave her a quick wink.

I think I'm going to like her.

CHAPTER TWENTY-TWO

JUST ANOTHER DAY, EH?

A manda Levings was nervous.

Lady Racine had told her about the meeting that had been set up, but then Amanda had completely forgotten about it until this morning. She was on the way to meet a young girl who was apparently also human but evidently a princess. Amanda definitely wasn't sure how to feel about that, but she was ready to see another person from Earth. No matter what country they were from.

The last human she had met was much different, and that was when Amanda realized that things weren't as they first appeared at all. The other human had been a kind man. Yet she remembered how mistrusting of him she had initially been when he had mentioned being from the Terran Solar Republic, and how confused she felt after he presented knowledge that seemingly proved it. Now, she was going to meet another human, who could be from literally anywhere.

If humans were from the future, *or a parallel universe,* who knew where this girl could be from?

Too bad the man wasn't here anymore to meet the girl with her.

Gwyn had nestled herself in the tranquility of the gazebo, situated amid the verdant gardens that sprawled behind her house. A book lay open in her lap, its pages whispering tales of far-off lands and heroic deeds of a hero from Eona's distant past. Around her, Lorrena, Nora, and Ilyana were engaged in their own quiet pursuits. Nora and Ilyana were engrossed in a hushed conversation, their heads bent together as they discussed the tasks assigned to them by Siveril and Taenya. Lorrena, on the other hand, appeared to be in the throes of a peaceful slumber, her chest rising and falling rhythmically as she dozed off.

Gwyn couldn't help but snort in amusement as she observed Lorrena's peaceful state, her nose twitching as she shifted to find a more comfortable position. The sound drew the attention of Nora and Ilyana, their eyes flicking up to meet hers. A smile tugged at the corners of Gwyn's lips as she noted the camaraderie between the two girls. Their initial bickering had given way to a mutual understanding, much to Gwyn's relief.

She didn't like when they fought over her.

It's funny how they remind me of my friends back at school. Always fighting yet inseparable.

"Is everything okay, Your Highness?" Nora's voice broke through Gwyn's reverie, pulling her back to the present.

Gwyn let out a groan of exasperation. "Nora! I told you guys: there's no one around but us. Please, call me Gwyyyn," she protested, dragging out her name for emphasis. It was irritating how proper they acted *all the time.*

Nora merely bowed her head in response, a hint of a smile playing on her lips. "As you say, Princess Gwyn."

Throwing her hands up in defeat, Gwyn turned to Ilyana, hoping for a different response. "You'll at least listen, right?"

"Of course, Your Highness," Ilyana replied, a sly grin spreading across her face.

Gwyn let her head drop in resignation. *Why is it so hard to make friends who see me as just Gwyn, not a princess?*

She looked at Lorrena, who was still peacefully asleep. *Eh, she's too quiet. She seems almost scared to talk.*

Her thoughts wandered to the blond elf girl she had seen at the duke's court. *I hope I get to meet her soon. Maybe she'll be different.*

"Your Highness?" A voice interrupted her musings, causing her to look up. One of the guards was approaching them, a sense of excitement in his voice. "You have a guest. Ser Taenya is meeting her now," he explained.

"A guest?" She perked up. *Is it her?*

"Yes, Your Highness. It's the terran from House Racine. She's here to meet you," he elaborated.

"Oh . . . okay. Thank you!" Gwyn responded, trying to hide her disappointment. *Drat. Not who I was hoping for.*

Amanda waited in a parlor of some sort while the guards went and fetched one of the knights. She sat and sipped water from the small glass they had given her, and looked around the room. It was well decorated and seemed to be situated in a way to make the guest feel at ease and comfortable. She could appreciate that. The chairs were disappointing, like anywhere else she'd been since arriving in the world. She was lucky to have run into Lady Racine's carriage after . . . after events.

Amanda finished her water and rose from her seat, her curiosity piqued by the bookshelves lining the room. She traced the spines of the books as she perused the titles.

A bell chimed in the distance as she was reading about two elf houses from competing Sovereign Cities. The story was amusing, and seemed centered on the two heads of the houses, a man and woman. The man and woman wanted to put aside their disagreements and fighting. They fell in love, but because of their houses' rivalry, they were forced to sneak around. The children and other members of the families discovered the secret and tried to stop their respective family heads from committing "treason."

Amanda snorted. *Sounds like a version of* Romeo and Juliet.

She was just about to delve into the book's climax when a throat-clearing sound startled her. Amanda spun around, the book slipping from her grasp as she came face to face with a telv woman. An amused smile played on the woman's lips.

"Good story?"

A wave of embarrassment washed over Amanda as she fumbled to close the book and return it to its place on the shelf. "Oh, uh . . . sorry!"

The woman's chuckle filled the room. "No, it's alright. I apologize for the delay. There was an issue I had to take care of. Welcome to House Reinhart. I am Ser Taenya Shavyre. We appreciate you accepting the invitation to visit Her Highness."

"So, she's an actual princess, then?" Amanda asked.

The woman squinted her eyes, and Amanda thought she looked more like a traditional elf to her than the actual elves, at least from the media she had seen back on Earth. She hadn't really been into fantasy, though, so her knowledge of the subject was lacking.

"She is. Is there some concern?" Taenya responded, her tone laced with a hint of caution.

"No concern," Amanda replied hastily. The knight's astute gaze didn't miss her quick response.

"Could it be because you may be from a different Earth? Or *Terra*?" Taenya ventured, her words causing Amanda's eyes to widen in surprise. Before Amanda could formulate a response, Taenya continued.

The room seemed to hold its breath as she revealed the existence of another human from Earth residing within their house. Amanda's mind spun, her thoughts a whirlwind of questions and speculations.

"May I meet him as well?" she asked.

"That can be arranged, if he agrees," Taenya responded, her tone becoming more serious. "Do you swear to not cause harm to Her Highness or her interests, even if anything she reveals causes undue stress for you? Do you swear to not seek to take advantage of her kindness and not attempt to influence her unduly because of your shared circumstances?"

Amanda blinked, taken aback by the sudden barrage of questions. *What could a child possibly reveal that would cause me undue stress?* she wondered, a sense of unease creeping in. "No, of course not. Is she okay?"

A sudden thought ignited a spark of anger within Amanda. She straightened, her gaze meeting Taenya's. "Are you holding her here against her will? Are you afraid I'll convince her to want to leave you?"

Taenya's chuckle defused the tension. "No, nothing of the sort. Be at ease. A noble at court attempted to force her into a situation that she did not wish to be in." Her expression hardened. "I will not see such an occurrence happen again while I am around."

Amanda considered how to respond. "I . . . heard something about that. I wasn't sure what to make of it. However, yes, I swear not to do anything to harm a child."

"Thank you," Taenya responded, her demeanor softening. She excused herself, and left Amanda alone with her thoughts.

The idea of meeting royalty was a foreign concept to Amanda. Back on Earth, royalty were distant figures, seen only on news broadcasts. The possibility of the princess being from a different version of Earth was a disappointing prospect. She yearned for a familiar face, someone from her own world.

Her musings were interrupted by a knock on the door. An elf, unlike any she had seen before, entered the room. She was tall, though not as towering as Taenya, with almost black hair and a striking blue crescent painted over her eye. Amanda couldn't help but admire her. *She looks like a badass elf warrior.*

A pang of jealousy hit her. Lady Racine's entourage had no one quite like this, except for *him*. Definitely a bit jealous.

The elf's smirk was a silent challenge, her gaze appraising as she took in Amanda's appearance. Just as Amanda was about to respond, the elf turned and opened the door, revealing a young girl, and Ser Taenya trailing behind her. The girl was tall for her age, though thankfully still slightly shorter than Amanda.

What the hell? Is this a house of Amazons?

Amanda could only imagine how tall the girl's mother was—though, everyone was tall compared to her own one hundred and sixty centimeters. Amanda guessed the girl's age at around eleven or even twelve. She was striking, with curly dark-brunette hair and piercing blue eyes that seemed to scrutinize Amanda in return. Her build suggested athleticism, perhaps a gymnast or a runner. *She must have been active back on Earth.*

Unsure of the proper etiquette in this situation, Amanda opted for a friendly approach. "Hello! It's really nice to meet you. I am Amanda! Amanda Levings."

The girl's face lit up with a smile. "Hi, Amanda! I'm Gwyn. Are you from Earth?" She paused, her eyes closing for a moment before refocusing on Amanda. "Sorry, of course, you're from Earth. You're human! Are you from . . .

my Earth? Wait. No. You wouldn't know that either. What year is it on your Earth? Oh my gosh."

Ser Taenya leaned in, whispering something into Gwyn's ear. Amanda suppressed a smile as the young princess straightened, her face taking on a serious expression. "My apologies. I got a bit excited."

Amanda glanced at the two women and the young girl, a strange feeling settling in her gut. The dynamic between them was unusual, and she couldn't help but wonder what exactly she had walked into.

She mustered her most reassuring smile, aiming to put the young girl at ease. "It's quite alright! Excitement is only natural when you meet someone with whom you share a connection. Let me answer your questions first, and then maybe we could sit and have a more relaxed conversation? As for whether I'm from your Earth, I can't say for sure." Amanda chuckled lightly, hoping to lighten the mood. "On my Earth, it's the year nineteen eighty-four."

Gwyn's face fell instantly, and Amanda felt a pang of disappointment.

So, we're not from the same Earth after all. That's a shame. But her reaction suggests our timelines aren't too far apart. Concern gnawed at her. *Is she okay here? Are they taking good care of her? Do they even know how to care for a human child? Where are her parents?*

A sudden shift in the room's atmosphere caught Amanda's attention, and she glanced at the two women. The elf's eyes were narrowed, her expression far from friendly.

Did I say something wrong?

She turned her attention back to Gwyn, leaning forward slightly. "Is everything okay? Your expression suggests we're not from the same place. Shall we sit and talk?"

I need to find out if she's safe here.

They moved to a set of chairs and a couch, the latter of which reminded Amanda of the old-style French furniture she'd seen in museums. It was an elegant piece, likely expensive, and yet another reminder of how different this world was from her expectations.

Amanda and Gwyn settled on the couch, leaving a polite space between them, while Ser Taenya and the elf took the chairs opposite them. Amanda turned her attention to the elf, whose stern expression hadn't softened.

"I apologize, I've been rude," Amanda said. "What was your name again, Miss . . ."

The elf's eyes narrowed further. "With respect, it's *Ser* Sabina."

"Oh, I'm sorry, Ser Sabina. It is lovely to meet you." Amanda managed a polite smile, but inwardly she felt a twinge of unease.

She seems rude. Hopefully, she doesn't act that way toward a child.

Amanda adjusted her position on the couch, angling herself toward Princess

Gwyn to give the young girl her full attention. "Now, where were we? Oh yes, Earth. May I ask why you think we came from different places?"

Gwyn exhaled a soft sigh. "Because, on my Earth, it's the year two thousand twenty-four. I heard you're from Canada, which is cool. I'm from Italy."

Italy? They're not a monarchy . . . What is going on?

Amanda's gaze flickered between the two knights, her mind racing to piece together the puzzle of the girl's situation. "Oh, Italy! That's so amazing. It's really beautiful there. I didn't realize Italy was still a kingdom. Is it in your world? It's a republic in mine. I'm from Ontario!"

Gwyn seemed to fidget slightly under Amanda's gaze, prompting the elf, Sabina, to shift her attention.

"Yes. It is a kingdom," Ser Sabina interjected.

Uh, no. Unacceptable. Amanda directed a scowl at the knight. "With all due respect, I was asking her."

Gwyn looked at Sabina, her expression softening. "It's okay, Sabina." She turned back to Amanda. "That's another reason I'm upset. We're from such different worlds. Sir Friedrich, he's from an Earth almost like this one. He's a knight, from a time when they still used armor and swords. Everything is so different, you know? I really miss showers." Gwyn chuckled lightly. "So silly. And YouTube and movies."

Amanda nodded. She was filing away information about this Friedrich being from what sounded like the *actual* Middle Ages and not whatever amalgamation of development this world had. Focusing back on the present, she realized what was wrong.

These women can't properly care for a child of modern sensibilities. They're much too primitive . . .

Suddenly, Amanda felt like she was getting a migraine. She had the sense of someone forcing their way through a door, but the door already had a broken handle and couldn't keep anyone out.

She winced and rubbed at her head. She thought she heard whispers, but the blond knight was just watching her, while the other seemed to have a look of pure confusion on her face.

Amanda shrugged slightly, her eyes softening as she empathized with the young girl. "I can certainly understand that! I miss fast food and cars. Oh, and Tim Hortons coffee and doughnuts! How has everything been here for you? It's quite a departure from what you're used to, eh?"

Gwyn's face scrunched up into a small frown. "It's very different, but everyone has been really nice." Her frown deepened into a scowl. "Well, except for that jerk at the duke's court."

Amanda's heart clenched at the mention of the incident. "I heard about that. I am so sorry that happened to you. It's unimaginable that anyone would try to put a child in such a situation. Personally, I don't think you should have been there at all at your age."

Gwyn shrugged, a small smile playing on her lips. "It's alright. I'll be going to school soon. They're planning to take me to the capital so I can attend the Academy."

Amanda's eyebrows shot up in surprise, and she turned her gaze to Ser Taenya. "You're just sending her away? Now that you've gotten what you needed from her?"

Taenya jerked her head up, her eyes flashing with indignation. She leaned forward as if she were about to stand up, but stopped herself. She glanced at Gwyn before placing her hands on the armrests of her chair, gripping them tightly.

"That is not true at all, Miss Levings. You seem to have misunderstood something here. We are not taking advantage of Her Highness. We are helping her, and attending the Royal Academy is the best opportunity for her."

Amanda frowned, her mind racing. *So they're sending her to boarding school? That doesn't seem right. Something's off. If it were up to me, I'd keep her close, so we'd both be safe. I need to get that girl away from them, no matter what it takes. They are clearly not fit to—*

Actually . . . they don't seem too bad.

Wait . . . no.

She shook her head, clearing the fog away.

"I'm sorry to hear that! Having to go away again can't be what you want," she said with concern, looking at the young princess and the stern knights.

Traveling in this society has to be dangerous. This city is relatively safe, and I'm sure more humans will come here. She should stay here.

"The princess's education is our highest priority," Ser Taenya interjected.

"Yeah . . . it's okay. I can learn a lot," Gwyn chimed in, her voice small but determined.

Amanda's eyebrows knitted together in a scowl. *A medieval school is not what I'd call an institution that will let someone learn a lot. If she went there, she would never fit in when we return home.*

"I don't know, sweetie." She shot a pointed look at the two knights. "The people here aren't used to what we are. Our schools are much different. You know, if you wanted, I could teach you. You wouldn't even have to leave—*ow!*" A sudden jolt of pain shot through her head, cutting her off mid-sentence.

What the hell?

Gwyn's face contorted with concern. "Are you okay? What's wrong?"

This migraine is excruciating. What I'd give for some Motrin . . .

Amanda winced again, rubbing her temple as she tried to alleviate the pain. She reasoned that the strange whispering was just a symptom of the severe headache. "I'm okay, just a headache. Sorry. Where was I? Oh yes. I think—"

Another jolt of pain hit her, this time so intense she nearly doubled over. The unintelligible whispers in her head grew louder.

This headache is so bad, it's making me hear things. Okay, I can get through one meeting. Then I can rest.

Ser Sabina looked at her, her eyes filled with a mix of concern and confusion. "Perhaps we can reschedule this meeting for another time when you are well. Maybe you should return to House Racine and rest. I assure you, we have Her Highness' best interests in mind."

Amanda's mind was whirling, a storm of thoughts and suspicions brewing within her. She couldn't shake the feeling that these women were exploiting the young girl, possibly even fabricating her royal status for their own gain.

"I am fine. Thank you for your concern. I also only have Princess Gwyn's best interests in mind. She is from a society much different from your own. She has things she is accustomed to, and has a right to, that you simply cannot provide in your level of development."

Amanda was baffled by their blatant disregard for her valid concerns. It was glaringly obvious that these women were failing to comprehend the fact that Gwyn required more than what they could offer.

They don't even have working plumbing! We humans have to stick together. Then we can figure out a way to make everything right.

Ser Taenya's eyes narrowed, a spark of defiance igniting within them. "And you can provide these? After one meeting?"

A wave of frustration washed over Amanda. Clearly, they were manipulating Gwyn. Why else would they be so resistant to the idea of someone else from Earth assisting her? "Gwyn? Where is your mother? Your father?"

I need to get this girl away from here. Maybe Lady Racine will send her guard and the knight. He was so strong, powerful. He would make sure everyone was—

Pain shot through her head again. The whispers sounded more like her own voice.

No, she's fine. Taenya and Sabina just want to help her.

Shaking her head to clear the intrusive thoughts, Amanda turned her attention back to Gwyn, who seemed on the brink of tears. "Gwyn? Are you okay? What's wrong, sweetheart?" Amanda reached out, but halted her movement when Taenya leaned forward in her chair.

"I don't know where my mom is. We were together, but then I got here alone. Taenya and Raafe went and looked for her, but they couldn't find her."

They were together? And then Taenya took her away? Did she do something to the girl's mother? Oh, my god. They've kidnapped her. Gwyn needs to get away from—

Another wave of pain washed over Amanda, and she doubled over, fighting the urge to vomit. The whispers returned, and she found herself inexplicably agreeing with them.

She's fine. Everything is fine. I'm just having a moment and overreacting. I really need to go home to rest. Take a deep breath and tell them goodbye.

Amanda took a deep breath, trying to regain her composure. "I'm sorry, Gwyn. That all sounds really horrible. I am glad Ser Taenya was able to help you. However, I am not feeling well. I think I should retire for the day. Maybe we can meet again soon?"

The girl nodded her head slowly, and the two knights stood up. Amanda stood as Ser Taenya stepped forward. "I am sorry you don't feel well. Please, reach out when you feel better. I will have someone escort you back to House Racine to ensure you are well. Thank you for coming."

But Gwyn, she isn't safe—

She's safer than anywhere I could take her. Amanda felt herself relax slightly.

"I'm sorry again. I'm not sure what's come over me. Maybe I ate something that didn't agree with me. I can't wait to see you again, Princess Gwyn. Please tell Sir Friedrich I'm sorry I didn't get to meet him."

Gwyn nodded. "It was nice meeting you."

Amanda caught Gwyn's concerned look at the knights.

She smiled as she walked out of the mansion, content that the little girl was safe and well cared for. She pushed away the nagging doubts and focused on the relief that washed over her.

Several hours later, Amanda was sitting in the house drinking tea with Lady Racine. The noblewoman had asked her to come by and talk about her meeting. She was excited to hear about the young royal, who had been the talk of the city's high society.

"It was a good meeting, then? Was she from your Earth?" Lady Racine asked.

"No, unfortunately not. Her version of our world is much different, it seems. Starting with the fact that her year is forty years later than mine, and the nation she comes from is a kingdom, whereas in my world, it is a republic."

"I'm sorry to hear that she isn't from your world. I know how hopeful you were, but . . . she *is* a princess?"

"Oh, absolutely. There isn't any doubt in my mind," Amanda replied with surety.

"How was her situation in the house? Do you still have any of the concerns you voiced when we discussed meeting her?"

"No, none at all. I had some initial hesitation, but I wasn't feeling well, so I think it caused me to overreact a bit. Thinking about it, it seems everything was perfect and the people there are very attentive to Princess Gwyn's needs. I believe she's in great hands, and she's very lucky they're on her side. It could have gone very poorly if that noble from the court had taken advantage of that poor girl."

"On that, I agree. I'm glad everything is as it seems, though. I was worried they wouldn't be enough to protect a princess, but it seems my fears were unfounded. Ser Siveril seems to have everything in hand."

Amanda smiled and nodded. "They definitely do. That girl is loved there. Which is important. I'm happy for her."

I can't wait to meet them all again. Especially Ser Sabina. She was great.

As she looked down to pick up her tea, she caught sight of Lady Racine giving a subtle nod to the knight in the room.

Just another day in this backward world, eh?

She was glad House Racine was so safe.

CHAPTER TWENTY-THREE

REVELATIONS AND PREPARATIONS

S abina winced as the door slammed shut behind her, the sound echoing in the room like thunder. Taenya followed her in, her face a mask of barely contained fury. Sabina knew she had given the woman plenty of reasons to be upset, but the intensity of her anger still took her by surprise.

She halted mid-step, turning to face Taenya. The woman's expression was a storm cloud, dark and foreboding. Sabina opened her mouth to speak, but quickly thought better of it. Silence, she decided, was the safer option.

"What was that, Sabina?" Taenya's voice was deceptively calm, a stark contrast to the anger simmering in her eyes. "You're overtly doing it now?"

Sabina's heart skipped a beat. "How . . . how long have you known?" she stammered.

"I've known for weeks," Taenya replied, her tone growing sharper with each word. "You're not the only one capable of reading people. You were too obvious, picking up on things that most wouldn't have noticed. Not to mention the incident with Gwyn that had you sprinting across the house. And the fact that I can feel it when you use your magic!"

Sabina blinked in surprise. "Y-you felt it? How?"

"That's not important right now!" Taenya snapped, her patience clearly wearing thin. "Do you want a fucking inquisition to come down on us? Mind-fucking someone? Physically harming them with insidious magic?" Her voice rose. "If you continue to use your magic without restraint in ways that go against the Decrees, *expect* it. Because this is how one is formed!"

Sabina recoiled, taken aback by the intensity of Taenya's words. The ferocity of Taenya's feelings was potent, but she did not direct them at *her*, just her *actions*. That small distinction offered a sliver of comfort, but it did little to lessen the sting of Taenya's rebuke.

"I . . . you're right," Sabina admitted, her voice barely audible. "I went too far."

"No shit, Sabina," Taenya retorted. "Alos save us, because I can't keep Gwyn safe alone. Tell me. Right now. What is the extent of your magic?"

Sabina took a deep breath, steeling herself for the confession. "You know about the emotions. I can't stop that. I just feel them. That's how I can tell most things. I can also hear surface-level thoughts if they're strong enough. It's like the person is speaking them out loud." She hesitated, her heart pounding in her chest. "I . . . I was pulled into Gwyn's nightmare."

Taenya's eyes widened in shock. "Does she know? Have you—"

"No! She doesn't. That was the first time I'd actually been inside someone's mind, and I did it while I was sleeping—"

"You are going to fix that. You need to—"

"I know, Taenya. I know!" Sabina interrupted, her voice rising in desperation. "I swore to myself I would never betray her trust like that, especially after that happened. I will *never* influence or listen to her thoughts. I swear it. I want to protect her. If she doesn't trust me, I can't do that."

Taenya scoffed, her disbelief evident. "Sabina. She will not trust you if she thinks you can enter her mind at any time and change things. *If . . .*" Taenya paused, taking a deep breath to calm herself before continuing, "if you let her find out on her own. We will need to inform her. You will swear to her that you will never do those things before the thought even comes up."

"I will."

"Good. Now, what in Relena's name was that? What did you do to Miss Levings? You *physically* harmed her. Then she acted as if everything was fine and completely changed her mind."

"You don't think I know that?" Sabina snapped back.

"Sabina, tell me. *What* happened?"

Sabina hesitated, grappling with how to explain her actions. She had overstepped, pushed too far. Amanda's thoughts had been overwhelming, a whirlwind of suspicion and mistrust. She spoke of taking Gwyn away. Then she subtly tried to influence the princess into leaving them. Sabina had felt it, heard it in the woman's thoughts. There was something about the absolute certainty in what Amanda had believed.

It had surprised her. So it was simple. Amanda was never going to believe them. The terran had arrived with preconceived notions and biases. She had formed a conclusion from the moment she saw them—one unlikely to change.

It had been so easy just to nudge her in the right direction, whispers in her mind mistaken for her own thoughts. But in her fear, Sabina had pushed too far. Instead of a gentle nudge, she had slammed her desired outcome into Amanda, hammering it home with a force that was far too strong.

How does Gwyn make magic seem so easy?

Taking a deep breath, Sabina began to explain. "I tried to steer her thoughts in a different direction. I don't think I can actually change someone's thoughts. At least not at this point. I essentially whispered in her mind, sowing seeds of doubt and suggesting alternative thoughts. I was trying to guide her toward what I wanted. But I-I pushed too hard. She was far too receptive to it."

Taenya looked up at the ceiling, letting out a deep sigh. She brushed her hair out of her face and tugged at it, lost in thought. The utter lack of any leakage of the woman's thoughts impressed Sabina.

She is exceptional at keeping her thoughts to herself.

"Amanda wasn't a threat, Sabina. She was just another human who had the same experience as Gwyn and Friedrich. She's not handling it well. She saw Gwyn and found something familiar she could latch on to. She wasn't *malicious*."

"You didn't hear her thoughts, Taenya. She was determined to take Gwyn, no matter what it took."

"And how would she do that, Sabina? We literally just stopped a marquess from doing anything, and let's not forget the *count* that Gwyn literally burned. How will some *commoner* human manage it?"

"But . . ." Sabina's words trailed off as she deflated, her chin dropping to her chest. Taenya was right. Sabina had overreacted and caused harm to Amanda. Tears welled up in her eyes and trickled down her cheeks, but she made no move to wipe them away.

She felt a hand on her shoulder, then another lifting her chin. Taenya's hazel eyes met hers. "Sabina, I am frustrated and angry, but not with you. I'm angry with how you reacted with such immediate aggression to the situation. We can't afford to do that. We're under too much scrutiny. We need to set some rules, and we're going to do that right now. Come, let's sit."

Sabina obediently followed, sinking into the seat next to Taenya. Her gaze remained stubbornly fixed on her hands, the weight of her embarrassment too heavy to lift. The soft sigh from Taenya made her flinch. "Sabina. Look at me."

The command was gentle, yet firm, filled with an undercurrent of compassion and resolve. It wasn't a reprimand, but a plea. Sabina felt a fresh wave of tears threatening to spill over.

I really messed up.

Summoning her courage, Sabina lifted her gaze to meet Taenya's. The woman's eyes were filled with a caring warmth, her expression resolute. Taenya was a protector, a guardian who would do anything for Gwyn. And in that moment, Sabina realized that the same protective instinct was directed at her. Taenya embodied the very essence of what it meant to be a knight, and Sabina wanted nothing more than to live up to that ideal.

Taenya was everything she wanted to be.

"Sabina, first, I will say just the *thought* of what your magic can do is honestly terrifying. However, I *trust* you. I need to trust you and I need you by my side, so please . . . please, do not give me a reason to fear what you can do with that magic."

Sabina quickly nodded.

Taenya took a deep breath. "Second, do *not* use any of your magic against anyone in the house unless I directly order it and am with you. Continue listening to the surface thoughts and feeling emotions in others. We will figure out a way to restrict the staff's thoughts or something. I'm sure you're not the only one with this ability. I just have zero clue how we'll accomplish that without them learning about the reason or you planting it in their head . . ."

Taenya's voice trailed off as she mumbled the last part to herself, but she quickly regained her composure. "That ability is beneficial in dealings with external agents. However, do not invade the thoughts of anyone who is not physically hostile to the house or the princess. Even then, do not harm their mind."

Taenya paused, shaking her head before continuing, "Actually, we cannot have knowledge of your ability to get out. It *must* stay a secret. Try to use that ability as only a last resort. That said, if anyone ever invades our House, do *whatever it takes* to ensure the princess's safety. You are the last line of defense for that girl."

Sabina's eyes widened in surprise. "Me? You trust me with such a task? Why? Why not yourself?" Her curiosity overpowered her embarrassment, prompting the question.

"You are not the only one to gain magic since the event, Sabina. Just the only one who apparently cannot keep it a secret." Taenya's words were sharp, and Sabina winced but didn't protest. She knew Taenya was right.

Wait. "You—" she began, but a stern look from Taenya silenced her.

Taenya glanced back at the door, then leaned forward slightly. "I know our roles. I will be the one to hold fast against any force that comes against us. You will be protecting the princess while disrupting our enemies. And Gwyn will rain fiery death upon them."

With that, Taenya abruptly stood up. "Now, enough of that. We can discuss more later when we have an even longer heart-to-heart about your magic and what it means. That discussion though . . . it's going to require some alcohol. A lot of it."

Sabina nodded mutely.

Taenya forced a smile. "Now, we need to prepare for the princess's birthday tomorrow."

Sabina blinked in confusion. "It's her birthday?" She tried to recall if she had been informed about this before.

"It is! And we only found out last week. I apologize, we have both been so busy that I did not inform you. Wonderful timing, right? She and Maya worked it out. Siveril coordinated invitations already."

Sabina groaned as she followed Taenya out of the room. They were going to be up late arranging everything. Yet, despite the impending workload, she couldn't help but smile as she felt the eagerness radiating from Taenya.

I won't disappoint you again.

Gwyn was a bundle of energy as she skipped down the hallway toward the quarters of her three ladies-in-waiting, a group she had affectionately started calling "the crew." As she neared their rooms, a servant caught sight of her and, with a warm smile, knocked on one of the doors before pushing it open. Almost immediately, Nora emerged, impeccably dressed as always.

She may have someone to help her like I do. So, not a big deal, Gwyn.

"Good morning, Nora!" Gwyn greeted, her voice ringing with cheer.

Nora responded with a quizzical look, her eyebrows scrunching together in a way that Gwyn had come to recognize as her version of an amused or "really?" expression. It was cute that she wasn't able to raise just one brow like Gwyn. *Or like the brow master, Mom.*

"Good morning, Your Highness," she said with a cheerful tone.

Gwyn let out an exaggerated sigh, throwing her head back for added effect. "Must we do this every day, Nora?" She longed for the day when they would address her by her name.

Nora chuckled softly. "Please allow me just one more day, Your Highness."

Which is what you say every time!

Next to emerge was Ilyana, the oldest of her ladies-in-waiting. "Your Highness! It is a beautiful morning. I wish you a pleasant Day of Birth."

Gwyn couldn't help but giggle. "It's *happy birthday*, Ilyana!"

The oldest of her ladies-in-waiting smiled. "Ah, my apologies, Your Highness. I am positive I will get a *hang* of your world's colloquialisms soon." She shot a triumphant glance at Nora, who responded with a scowl. The three of them chatted about the day ahead, waiting for the last member of their group.

Suddenly, another door slammed open, and Lorrena nearly stumbled out. Her eyes widened in surprise when she saw the three of them waiting. She quickly lowered her head in a curtsy. "I am sorry, Your Highness. I overslept."

Gwyn snorted and patted Lorrena's back. "It's quite alright, Lore. Here, let me tell you a secret." She leaned in close, whispering into her ear, "I used to get up late all the time and had to rush to get ready. My mom was always waiting for me. Every time, she'd be tapping her foot and had the eyebrow of doom locked and loaded. Then, she'd just smile, and we'd leave to go to school."

Lorrena smiled. "Thank you, Your Highness," she said quietly.

Gwyn chatted up the crew as they rushed to get breakfast and start the day. After all, it was her birthday!

After a hearty breakfast, Gwyn, her handmaiden Emma, and the three ladies-in-waiting set out on their shopping expedition. Taenya led the way. They were accompanied by a group of four guards, who scanned the surroundings with a protective vigilance that was both comforting and slightly intimidating.

Gwyn had asked if Sabina wanted to come, but the knight had things to do back at the manor. Even Theran and Keston were busy, so Taenya had suggested they just turn it into a girls' day.

After perusing the market for a while, they found themselves in front of a bookstore. It was a charming little place, nestled between two larger buildings. The wooden face of the structure was weathered and worn, but it had a welcoming aura that drew Gwyn in. As she stepped inside, the scent of old parchment and ink filled her nostrils, a comforting aroma that made her feel at home. The interior went farther back than the outside would have one believe and was a maze of towering bookshelves, each one filled to the brim with books of all shapes and sizes.

Behind a wooden counter stood a kind-looking dwarf, who looked up from his book as they entered, his eyes twinkling behind a pair of spectacles perched on his nose. She hadn't seen anyone else with glasses since she'd arrived on Eona. His beard was snowy white, contrasting with his ruddy complexion. He gave them a warm smile.

"Ah, customers! Welcome, welcome!" he greeted them, his voice a deep rumble that echoed around the room.

Gwyn took in her surroundings wide-eyed and slack-jawed.

Mom would love *this place!*

Gwyn, an avid reader, was like a kid in a candy store. "Look at all these books!" she cried, her eyes wide with delight. She glanced back at Taenya, who had an amused expression on her face, and that was all the young princess needed as she turned to the nearest bookcase.

The dwarf chuckled as she darted from shelf to shelf. "You seem to have quite the appetite for books, young lady," he commented, his eyes twinkling with amusement.

Gwyn grinned at him, her hands full of books she had picked out. "I just love reading! But I don't really know what I'm looking for. It's my first time in a bookstore in this world."

The dwarf's eyebrows rose in surprise. "Ah, you're a terran. What type of books did you read back home?"

Gwyn's smile turned wistful. "Oh, man. Magic and fantasy mostly! Or books about kids going through school. I love everything. I was reading this really good book before I left. It was about an undercover princess."

"An undercover princess, you say? Well, we have plenty of books about princesses here, though I'm not sure about the undercover part." He led her around the store, pointing out various books he thought she might enjoy.

Gwyn's eyes sparkled with excitement as she moved through the aisles of the bookstore, her fingers lightly brushing the spines of the books. Her gaze landed on a series of books with vibrant covers depicting a group of adventurers in a lush forest. The title read *The Search for the Val Treasure*. Intrigued, she pulled the first book from the shelf and skimmed the first couple of pages. The shopkeeper chuckled and explained that the series promised a tale of thrilling adventure, cunning riddles, and hidden treasures. Gwyn's heart fluttered. She had loved stories like these back on Earth. Without a second thought, she picked up the entire series and handed them to Emma.

Meanwhile, Ilyana had found a book about a woman who fought barbarians. Nora, ever the practical one, chose a book about etiquette and manners. Lorrena seemed out of her element, her eyes darting around the store as she looked for something that interested her, but Gwyn knew the girl wasn't a big fan of reading stories. With Taenya's gentle guidance, Lorrena looked for books that would help with her studies.

As Gwyn continued to explore the bookstore, she discovered several other books that piqued her interest. There was one about a young woman who was given powers by the gods, a historical novel set in the Queendom of Lehelia, and even a book about a group of friends navigating their year through an academy, which she hastily grabbed . . . as research, of course. Each time she found a book she liked, she handed it over to Emma, who was now struggling to balance the growing stack in her arms. Emma chuckled, her eyes filled with amusement. "At this rate, we'll need a cart to carry all these books."

Gwyn laughed, her heart light. "Don't worry! I'll help, and Taenya is super-strong."

Taenya laughed. "Just because I'm strong doesn't mean I'm carrying them all. We have plenty of strong guards just outside who would *love* to shoulder your burdens."

Shaking her head, Gwyn returned to her perusal. She loved the feeling of being surrounded by books, each one a gateway to a different world. She loved the smell of the pages, the feel of the covers under her fingers, and the anticipation of a new story waiting to be discovered. As she handed over another book to Emma, she couldn't help but feel a sense of contentment. Despite being in a different world, some things remained the same.

When it was time to pay, Taenya pulled out Gwyn's House Banking Guild badge, a yellow diamond set inside it. The dwarf sucked in a breath as he recognized the symbol.

"I can see how that story about an undercover princess would appeal to a young royal like you, Your Highness."

Gwyn blushed slightly, her fingers tracing the cover of one of her new books. "Yeah . . ."

Just as Taenya was about to pay, Gwyn turned back to the shopkeeper. "Do you have any pretty journals or notebooks?" she asked in a hopeful tone.

The dwarf's brows rose in curiosity. "A journal, you say? Is this for you, Your Highness?"

Gwyn gave him a soft smile. "It's for my mom. She loves notebooks, planners, and journals. She uses them to keep notes on all of her work and stuff. Everything goes into them."

The dwarf glanced at Taenya, who merely shrugged in response. He took a deep breath, his eyes thoughtful. "A journal fit for a queen," he murmured, stroking his beard. "Yes, yes. I think I may have something."

He disappeared into the back of the store, leaving Gwyn to wait with bated breath. When he returned, he was holding a beautiful leatherbound journal, its cover embossed with intricate designs. The pages were thick and creamy, perfect for writing on.

Gwyn's eyes lit up as she took the journal, running her fingers over the cover. "It's perfect," she breathed, her heart swelling with gratitude. "Thank you."

The dwarf merely chuckled, his eyes twinkling. "It's my pleasure, Your Highness. I hope your mother likes it."

As they left the bookstore, Gwyn couldn't help but feel a sense of contentment. The guards had happily offered to carry her bags full of new books to explore. She smiled as she reflected on how she had spent the day with people who cared about her, and they had so much more to do.

It was turning out to be a pretty good birthday after all.

Gwyn was a bundle of nerves. While out shopping with Taenya, Emma, and her ladies-in-waiting, they had collected their newly tailored dresses, each requiring a final fitting to ensure perfection.

Lorrena's dress needed a minor adjustment, which added an extra half-hour to their schedule, much to Emma's apparent frustration. Once the shopping was done, they returned home to prepare for the evening.

Getting ready was a lengthy process, involving meticulous attention to hair and makeup, the latter of which Gwyn was fortunate enough to avoid. She found herself growing restless as Emma helped her into her dress and styled her hair, while the other girls stood around, chattering and gossiping.

I hate it. Why are they so annoying?

It took everything she had to not just groan and walk away.

Eventually, Taenya and Sabina arrived to escort them, both in their ceremonial armor. The silver metal, adorned with blue and black accents, was a sight to behold. The intricate dragons etched into Taenya's armor were particularly captivating. As the knights inspected their outfits and hairstyles, Gwyn couldn't help but scrutinize them in return. She noticed a distinct lack of Sabina's usual stern demeanor, replaced by an uncharacteristic somberness.

As they were guided out of the suite, Gwyn spotted Ser Theran and Sir Friedrich across the hall. "Hi, Theran! You're home! Hi, Friedrich. How are you two?" she greeted them cheerfully.

Theran bowed in response. "I am well, Your Highness. Ser Siveril has kept me busy, as usual. I managed to add another location to our holdings."

Gwyn beamed at him. "Oh, that's fantastic. I can't wait until you can tell me all about it." She turned her attention to Friedrich. "Sir Friedrich, you're looking snazzy in your new armor."

Gwyn watched as Friedrich's smile caused his handlebar mustache to curl upward, a sight that never failed to make her giggle. "*Danke*, Your Highness. My Common is getting better, yes?"

"Absolutely, Sir Friedrich," she replied, her eyes twinkling with amusement.

As they left the room, she turned to Taenya, her curiosity piqued. "So, what's the plan?"

"This is a small event," Taenya began, her voice steady and informative. "The attendees include the families of your ladies-in-waiting, Guildmistress Batteux and a few guildmasters, Onas and his family, some merchants we have dealings with, a handful of nobles interested in establishing relations, and a representative from the Duke of Tiloral. You will be introduced to them as you sit upon the Seat of the House. They will also be presenting gifts at that time."

Ser Theran, walking ahead of them, turned slightly. "It's about appearance. They will each be competing to see who can provide the best, most expensive gift." He glanced at Taenya. "Lord Iemes is also sending a representative."

Gwyn barely registered Theran's words, her attention focused on Taenya. "The duke sent someone?" she asked, her voice filled with surprise.

Both Taenya and Sabina smiled at her reaction. "Yes, Lady Roslyn will be attending," Sabina confirmed, noticing the confusion on Gwyn's face. "The duke's granddaughter that you asked to meet."

Gwyn's eyes went wide. *She's coming! Please be nice. Please be nice.*

As they made their way to the hall, the knights took the time to coach Gwyn and her ladies-in-waiting, slowing their pace to ensure the girls understood their roles. After the formalities with the external guests, there would be a more intimate gathering with just the members of the house.

The grand entrance into the hall was a spectacle in itself. Gwyn had to stand quietly, her face adorned with a practiced smile, as Ser Siveril, in his role as majordomo, announced her and each of her knights and ladies-in-waiting.

Ugh! This is going to take forever!

CHAPTER TWENTY-FOUR

IN NEED OF A FRIEND

Gwyn found herself perched on an ornate chair that Siveril had procured, its design reflecting the colors of her house: blue, black, and silver. The chair, dubbed the "Seat of the House," was where she was to carry out ceremonial duties, according to Siveril's explanation. From this elevated position, she watched as a procession of individuals and families paid their respects.

Siveril, standing by her side, served as the announcer, introducing the notable guests and their roles in society. The guests, in turn, introduced their accompanying family members. Each visitor offered a brief speech, filled with diplomatic phrases about "relations" and "well wishes," before presenting their gifts. These tokens of goodwill were swiftly whisked away by servants, to be examined later at Gwyn's leisure.

Most of the gifts seemed like decorative items, the kind her mother would display on a shelf or tuck away in a box she kept in a closet.

The crowd was larger than Gwyn had anticipated, considering Taenya's description of a "small party." Among the familiar faces were Mister Onas and his family, including his jerk son, Kalen. They had gifted her a set of high-quality painting supplies and canvases, a present she genuinely appreciated.

Something practical, something I can actually use.

Following the Fenren family were seven merchants and their families, Guildmistress Batteux, and several guildmasters. Lady Batteux, a noblewoman in addition to her guildmistress status, presented Gwyn with a set of elaborate chalices and a new golden guild badge. The badge, adorned with a large yellow diamond, symbolized the tier of her house account. Both the badge and the chalices bore the carefully crafted crest of House Reinhart, a design painstakingly created by her with the help of Siveril, Taenya, and Mister Branigan.

I'm proud of that!

After the merchants and guildmasters, a handful of unfamiliar nobles wished her "a pleasant and many returns on her birth day." Despite the peculiar phrasing, their sentiments appeared genuine at first glance, and their demeanor was cordial.

But Gwyn would not be swayed by flowery words.

I still remember what you told me, Raafe.

The evening was turning out to be quite an interesting mix of ceremony, diplomacy, and subtle power plays.

Among the guests was a telv knight named Ser Oberin, representing Lord Iemes. He had been Theran's teacher in his younger years, a fact that intrigued Gwyn. Ser Oberin was a congenial man who presented her with a formal invitation to the Royal Academy of Avira, accompanied by a chest filled with school supplies and other useful items.

Next was Lord Camus of House Trenlore and his family. Gwyn noted Siveril's scowl during their interactions, which puzzled her, given his insistence on their inclusion in her house's service. The baron seemed oblivious to Siveril's disdain, even appearing to believe he was doing her a favor.

I'm not fond of him, but for Ilyana's sake, I'll hold my tongue.

Her oldest lady-in-waiting was quite nice to her, and seemed so . . . *different* compared with the rest of her family.

Lord Trenlore's family was large, including Ilyana's eight siblings. The thought of having so many brothers and sisters made Gwyn shudder.

I'd lose my mind if I had that many siblings. I'm grateful to be an only child. Grazie mille, mamma.

Lord Hagen of House Urileth, a widower with a sunny disposition, was next. He brought his children, including Lorrena, the youngest of his three daughters.

Lady Olacyne, the viscountess, was the head of the last of the three houses closest to her own. She arrived with her husband and their two sons, Nora's brothers. The viscountess was a charming woman who seemed to get along well with Siveril and Taenya.

She's pretty cheeky, too.

As the introductions and gift presentations continued, Gwyn found her thoughts drifting to one person. And then, finally, that moment arrived.

Siveril bowed, then straightened, his voice echoing through the hall. "It is my honor to present, acting in the stead of Dasron Tiloral, the Duke of Tiloral, and as the representative of the ducal house: Lady Roslyn."

Gwyn's breath hitched. *Roslyn. Such a pretty name.*

She nearly missed the start of the girl's greeting. She snapped back to the present.

"Your Highness, Princess Gwyneth of House Reinhart. I am honored to have been personally invited on the occasion of the eleventh anniversary of your birth. In celebration of this momentous day, House Tiloral would like to welcome you fully not only to the duchy and the kingdom, but to our world. To be torn from one's world must be such a difficult and trying experience, and I personally grieve for all that you have lost.

"However, this is a day of joy. While nothing I give can replace what you have lost, I hope this small token from our house will allow you to see that you can at least forge lasting relationships with our people. Relationships that will not all be negative."

Her words were thoughtful and considerate, acknowledging Gwyn's unique circumstances and expressing sympathy for her losses. Gwyn found herself impressed by Roslyn's maturity and eloquence.

Either she practiced what to say, as I do with Siveril and Taenya, or she's really mature. Hopefully mature! Wait . . . I think I just dissed myself.

Roslyn's knight companion, clad in striking red armor, handed her a glossy wooden box. The knight's attire, particularly his white tabard adorned with a golden sun, drew murmurs from the crowd. Gwyn found herself admiring the design, though she found the single-shoulder cape a tad peculiar.

It looks really pretty, but it's a bit silly.

Roslyn turned back to Gwyn, her hand resting on the lid of the box. "As befitting a princess, no matter her origins, I present to you a tiara," she announced, lifting the lid to reveal a stunning headpiece.

"We had it commissioned of silver, with sapphires, onyxes, and diamonds, to match the colors of your house. The center stone is also a diamond—one from our personal vaults, a treasure of the duchy. We hope that you will wear it with pride and see that you are welcome. I look forward to getting to know you better, both here and at the Royal Academy next year. Thank you."

Gwyn was so moved by the gift that she momentarily forgot protocol. She rose from her seat, her heart swelling with gratitude. Catching herself just in time, she bowed her head respectfully and thanked Roslyn. "This gift is beautiful. I appreciate your kindness and well wishes," she said, her voice filled with genuine warmth.

As Roslyn stepped away to let the members of Princess Gwyn's household to present their gifts, she took a deep breath.

She's unlike any royal I've ever seen.

"That went well," Evocati Khalan said quietly, and Roslyn couldn't help but agree with the paladin the Church had assigned to protect her.

She hadn't expected the terran girl to actually get up and address her like that. In fact, it appeared the princess had almost left the dais to approach her. That would have been an awkward breach of etiquette. But then she didn't. She recovered quickly, as befitting one of such rank, and showed respect uncharacteristic of what Roslyn knew of royals.

I should reserve my judgment. Not all royals are like those we must abide here in Avira.

Ser Janine, her knight and personal assistant, brought her a glass of water that she gratefully accepted. Roslyn drank from it quickly before having to lower it. She smiled at the two approaching ladies-in-waiting.

Lady Ilyana, the fifteen-year-old third daughter of House Trenlore, a small barony not far from Strathmore, was a tall and slender girl with a serious demeanor that belied her age. Beside her was Lady Aleanora, the thirteen-year-old only daughter of Lady Olacyne, an influential woman in Roslyn's grandfather's court. Aleanora's youthful face was bright and open, but there was a shrewdness in her eyes that suggested she was more than just a pretty face.

Both girls were dressed in the finest silks, their hair intricately braided and adorned with delicate flowers. Their eyes, however, held a maturity that belied their tender years. They were here on a mission, and Roslyn could guess what it was.

"Good evening, Lady Roslyn," Aleanora greeted softly. "We hope you are enjoying the celebration."

Roslyn smiled, nodding in acknowledgment. "Indeed, it's a lovely event. I am glad to have met the princess."

"Lady Roslyn," Ilyana began, her voice steady and her gaze unwavering. "You seem . . . interested in our princess."

Aleanora picked up where Ilyana left off, her tone equally measured. "Princess Gwyn is a very kind girl, who unfortunately does not know the depths of what Aviran society means."

Roslyn smiled, her eyes twinkling with amusement. "I know all too well what it means. After all, I am the heiress of a duchy. It is my duty to know. I trust you will guide Her Highness well in these matters, for she will need people close to her to protect her from the dangers of our world."

The two girls glanced at each other, a silent conversation passing between them. A subtle shift occurred, and Aleanora took the lead.

"With respect, my lady, we understand this. In the short time we've come to know her, we have learned that many will try to take advantage of her. Please do not count yourself among that number."

Roslyn's smile didn't waver, but her eyes hardened slightly. She was not a people person, but she was very political and knew her status as a future duchess meant she must be mindful of the way she spoke.

"It is admirable that you have dedicated yourselves to her after such a short time, but I assure you, ladies, I have no intention of taking advantage of Princess

Gwyn. I am here to offer my support and that of my house, should she need it. I hope you both understand that."

The girls nodded, their expressions softening. "We do, Lady Roslyn," Ilyana said. "We just want what's best for her."

"And so do I, Lady Ilyana," Roslyn replied, her gaze steady. "So do I."

She really didn't want to take advantage of the princess. It was against not only her grandfather's desires but also her own.

Roslyn maintained her composed smile, even as her mind began to churn. She was not one for idle chatter or needless socializing, but she understood the importance of maintaining appearances. As the future duchess, every word she spoke, every action she took, was under scrutiny.

The two young ladies before her were no different. They were part of the intricate dance of politics and power that was the Aviran Great Game. And yet, they were also fiercely protective of the princess, which seemed to take precedence over a clear rivalry the two shared, a trait Roslyn admired.

As she listened to their concerns, a thought struck her. The princess, the second person in the Church's Seeing, was someone with whom she could potentially form a genuine connection. A friend, not a political ally or a pawn in the grand scheme of things, but a true friend.

It was a foreign concept to her. Her life had always been about duty, about fulfilling the expectations that came with her title. Roslyn was surrounded by people, yet she was always alone. Not that she minded—while she could put up appearances, she was *not* a so-called people person. She would much prefer to spend her time with herself, doing something she enjoyed. Like reading—or literally anything else that meant she could just *be* herself, without having to put up this face that duty demanded, and interact with people who didn't truly care about her.

But perhaps, just perhaps, this could change.

She remembered her grandfather's words, his wise eyes looking into hers as he spoke of the importance of forming alliances, not just for political gain, but for personal growth as well. True *friendship*. At the time, she'd dismissed it as her grandfather simply doting on his granddaughter. A concern that she wouldn't truly follow because it didn't appeal to her.

But now, as she stood before these two young ladies, Roslyn couldn't help but hope—that the princess could be the friend she never knew she needed; that she could navigate the treacherous waters of their society not just as a future duchess, but as simply Roslyn, with a friend by her side.

For the first time in a long time, Roslyn found herself looking forward to what the future held. Perhaps her grandfather was right. Perhaps this was the beginning of something new.

* * *

The rest of the evening seemed to pass in a whirlwind of introductions, polite conversation, and formalities. Gwyn found herself being guided from one group to another by Siveril, seemingly countless people and their children. Few were her age, and those who were seemed as reserved and cautious as Lorrena.

Perhaps their parents warned them about speaking to a princess. I should ask Lorrena about that.

Dinner was a grand affair, with Gwyn seated at the head of the table. Roslyn was a few seats away. Despite Gwyn's desire to strike up a conversation with the older girl, nerves kept her silent. Instead, she found herself stealing glances at Roslyn throughout the meal, quickly averting her gaze whenever their eyes threatened to meet.

The speeches and toasts that followed were a blur, the well-wishes and formalities blending into a monotonous drone. It was, without a doubt, the most boring birthday party Gwyn had ever had.

Finally, after dinner, there was music and dancing. The evening's entertainment brought a welcome change of pace. Music filled the hall, and the floor was soon filled with dancing couples. Gwyn used the opportunity to slip away from Siveril and Taenya, leaving them engrossed in conversation with various dignitaries.

She was finally able to do her own thing, with only Sabina close behind her. While Gwyn was sure no one would attempt what had happened at the duke's court, she still felt safer knowing Sabina was there. Especially since she was pretty sure the knight wouldn't let anyone try to distract her the same way again.

As she navigated the crowd, Gwyn scanned the room for a familiar face. She was so engrossed in her search that she didn't notice the person crossing her path until Sabina pulled her back, preventing a collision.

Gwyn's eyes went wide as she realized she had nearly walked right into Roslyn.

"Oh, sorry. I didn't see . . ." Gwyn trailed off, her mind racing to find the right words.

The girl's soft giggle did nothing to ease her embarrassment. "It's quite alright, Your Highness. How are you enjoying an Aviran celebration of birth?"

"Oh . . . uh . . ." Gwyn froze. She didn't know what to say. *Do I tell her it's nice? Will she get offended if I tell her it's the most boring thing since plain toast?*

She felt her mouth opening and closing, but no words came out. It only made Roslyn chuckle more.

As if sensing her internal struggle, Roslyn leaned in, her lips brushing against Gwyn's ear in a way that sent shivers down her spine as she whispered, "It's dreadfully boring, isn't it? I absolutely loathe these."

Gwyn's eyes widened in surprise. Her heart pounded in her chest. She turned to look at Roslyn, who had stepped back and was now winking at her. The playful sparkle in her violet eyes was infectious as the elf's smile reached them.

Gwyn finally found her voice and replied, "Purple!"

What the heck! Get it together!

Roslyn's giggle was like music to her ears. "Purple?"

Gwyn felt her cheeks flush with embarrassment. "Your eyes, they're purple. People in my world don't have purple eyes," she tried to explain, definitely not covering up her blunder.

Roslyn's smile widened, her head tilting slightly in curiosity. "That's so strange. Many people do here. However, your blue eyes are certainly striking, Your Highness."

Gwyn's brain stopped working for a moment.

Whaa? Did she just compliment me?

"Th-thank you. Please call me Gwyn . . .?" she managed to stammer out.

The blond nodded in agreement. "Only if you call me Roslyn."

Gwyn raised an eyebrow, her courage rebooted, and she puffed out her chest with a sly smirk playing on her lips. She pointed a thumb over her shoulder and said, "But of course, Roz. What do you say we bust this joint?"

Ugh, crap. That was bad.

Roslyn's giggles filled the air once more. "I have no idea what that means!"

Sabina's chuckle from behind brought her a sense of relief. "What Her Highness means is, why don't the two of you go see the gardens? It's much less stuffy than in here."

Gwyn gestured over her shoulder, a playful grin spreading across her face. "What she said." The response sent Roslyn into another fit of giggles.

"You are funny. Let's bust this joint, Gwyn," Roslyn agreed, her laughter still lingering in the air.

Finally!

They slipped away from the crowd, making their way to one of the garden doors. The guard stationed there gave them a knowing wink as he quietly opened the door, allowing them to escape into the tranquility of the garden.

Good looking out, bud.

They found themselves strolling leisurely through the garden, Gwyn subtly guiding them toward the gazebo. They paused to admire the flowers, and Roslyn expressed a particular fondness for the yellow ones. Gwyn made a mental note to ask Emma about them later. Her handmaiden was bound to know their name, or at least how to find out.

Gwyn glanced back and saw the red-armored knight following discreetly alongside Sabina.

"Your garden is really beautiful, Gwyn," Roslyn remarked, bringing Gwyn's focus back. Gwyn smiled as she noticed Roslyn's eyes reflecting the vibrant colors around them in the flickering glow of the oil lamps and the bright light of the moons.

"Thank you! They certainly keep up with it well, don't they?" Gwyn responded, her gaze sweeping over the meticulously maintained landscape.

Roslyn's smile was warm and genuine. "They do. Thank you for getting us out of there. I always wish I could skip my own, as they are such a chore. All the meeting people and pretending to like their gifts . . . I really hope you like my—I mean ours!"

Gwyn's laughter bubbled up. "I *loved* your gift, Roslyn. It's so beautiful. Are parties like this common? It's much different back home."

"Oh, we have balls and events like this *all the time.* They are always for one house to show off to others. Then the others come and try to use that time to compete with everyone. It is so tiring, but it is the life Eona chose for us."

Upon reaching the gazebo, Gwyn invited Roslyn to sit with her. Their knights maintained a respectful distance, providing them with a sense of privacy while still keeping them within sight. The conversation flowed easily between them, and the two girls lost track of time as they discussed their hobbies and daily lives. They spoke of Gwyn's love of drawing and painting, and Roslyn's passion for reading, singing, and horse riding. They delved into Roslyn's responsibilities as the heiress of a duchy and her anticipation for attending the Royal Academy to escape them.

Gwyn wasn't quite sure how she felt about that, and told her so. "It just seems like so much. Is the Academy that good? Do you mind leaving your family for that long?"

Roslyn nodded, her gaze distant. "It is a lot, but it is the life of people like us here—those who will one day take the place of our parents and grandparents. I am luckily in line for the duchy. My siblings will be either married off or offered to the other duchies in return for closer connections. Does such a thing not occur in your world?"

Gwyn shook her head. "Not anymore, that I know of. At least not where I am from. My mom always tells me that I will choose my own future. No one else will do it for me, but she will be there to assist every step of the way."

A soft smile graced Roslyn's lips. "Your mother sounds wonderful. I wish I could determine my own future."

Gwyn's brow furrowed, her gaze searching Roslyn's. "Why don't you?"

Roslyn's smile faded, her gaze shifting to the ceiling. "Our ways aren't the same, Gwyn. I have a duty. Perhaps your mother simply had the ability and authority to allow you such freedom. I long for such freedom, but I cannot have it. Not truly. I have people who will one day count on me."

"I'm sorry if I upset you," Gwyn said quietly, her heart sinking at the thought of having already made a misstep.

Roslyn's gaze snapped back to Gwyn. "You did not offend me. I am just thinking about how different our people are. Could you tell me about where you are from?"

Gwyn's smile returned, brighter than before. "Sure."

She began to tell Roslyn about her home, life, and all the things she loved. But with each new detail, more questions arose. Eventually, Gwyn decided to avoid going into too much detail, as she found herself spending more time explaining what things were, like Netflix, YouTube, and *Super Smash Bros.* She realized it was futile trying to convince people how amazing these things were when they didn't even know what a television, computer, or video game was.

And I can't explain how a TV works. Mom could, though . . . Wait . . .

Gwyn fell silent, her mind suddenly awash with the realization that her mother had missed her birthday. The weight of this fact hit her like a tidal wave, and before she could stop it, a tear slipped down her cheek. Hastily, she wiped it away.

A gentle hand landed on her shoulder, and she followed it to meet Roslyn's concerned but pretty violet eyes. "Gwyn? Are you upset? Did I say something wrong? I am sorry that I do not understand what a bicycle is."

Gwyn let out a small, choked laugh. "No, sorry. It's not that. I-I just . . . My mom isn't here. She's never missed my birthday before. I guess it didn't really hit me until now." Her gaze drifted to Sabina, who was looking straight at her with a sad expression and glistening eyes.

She knows what I'm feeling, doesn't she? I hope I don't make her too sad. This is my pain to bear.

"It's been a long time since I've seen her, and I'm not sure how long it will be until I can again. Your world doesn't exactly make it easy to talk to people far away, like ours."

Roslyn's arm slid around her, offering comfort. "You seem to have good people here, Gwyn. They clearly care about you."

Gwyn smiled, thinking of all the people she had met since arriving. How quickly Taenya had decided to help her and fight for her. How Sabina had sworn to be by her side and protect her. Siveril did everything he could to build a home for her and protect her from bad nobles who wanted to take advantage of her. Keston always tried to make time to talk to her whenever he wasn't busy doing jobs for the house.

She thought about what Roslyn had said. She did have a lot of people who cared for her. But . . .

"You're right. There's one thing missing, though. Other than my mom, I mean."

Roslyn looked at her, concern etched on her face. "What is that, Gwyn?"

Gwyn took a deep breath, turning fully to face Roslyn, a mix of hope and desperation building up inside of her. "I don't have a friend, and I could really use one right now." She felt her eyes welling up again and quickly closed them.

How is it that someone can have so many people who care for them, but they still feel so lonely?

Her breath hitched as Roslyn pulled her close and crushed her in a hug. The blond elf leaned her head against Gwyn's, her voice a soft whisper in her ear. "Do not worry. I'll be your friend, Gwyn."

Gwyn felt much of her worry and sadness melt away. She wrapped her arms around Roslyn and gripped her shoulders as she cried tears of relief and joy. She had a friend, and it felt more than nice. It felt like home. Now all she had to do was get further settled into her new home within the city and start preparing to go back to school.

And avoid any other nobles who wanted to take advantage of her.

Her new friend squeezed her, and Gwyn couldn't help but smile.

Piece of cake.

CHAPTER TWENTY-FIVE

SMALL STEPS OF CHANGE

A knock echoed through the silence of Sloane's room, but she didn't stir from her seated position on the floor of her sitting area. She was like a sculpture, frozen in the moment, lost in a reverie that made her oblivious to the external world. The knocking intensified, growing louder and more insistent, yet she continued her silent vigil, her gaze firmly fastened on the door. When the cacophony of knocks finally ceased, she slowly pivoted her gaze back toward the small flame flickering in the fireplace. Leaning back against the wall, she exhaled a weary sigh that echoed the exhaustion cloaking her spirit.

Just let me sleep, she prayed silently, yearning for a momentary escape from the day. Her wish was abruptly disrupted by a sudden, vehement kick against the door. Startled, she jerked her head back, colliding with the wall. "Ow! Shit."

Frustration boiled over as she snapped at the door, her voice ringing out through the empty room. "Leave me alone!"

A muffled yet determined feminine voice retaliated from the other side. "Open this door, Sloane, or I swear to Alos, I'll get Deryk to knock it down!"

Sloane groaned. Heaving herself to her feet, she shuffled to the door and yanked it open to face a fiery mane of red hair. "What do you want, Maud?"

The red-haired knight bulldozed past her without ceremony, casting a quick appraisal around the room. With an assertive nod, Maud seized Sloane's arm, tugging her along toward her own room. Once they reached the bed, Maud placed a hand on her chest and . . . shoved.

"Maaauud!" Sloane's screech filled the air as she windmilled her arms in an exaggerated slow-motion fall, ultimately crashing onto the bed.

"Now. Tell me what is wrong," Maud said from above her.

Sloane threw a scowl at the woman. "For someone whose role is to heal people, you sure enjoy both inflicting and relishing my pain."

The telv merely raised an eyebrow and crossed her arms in a picture of defiance. "Sloane, spill it. What is wrong? You've holed up in here all day and haven't eaten a thing. Deryk's fetching your food as we speak. And when he brings it, you will eat and you will listen to him."

"I am not hungry. I'm fine," Sloane countered, her voice almost petulant.

Maud let out an exasperated sigh and sat next to her. She kept her gaze averted from Sloane, who was still sprawled where she'd fallen. In a softer voice, Maud ventured, "It's about Gwyn, isn't it?"

At the mention of her daughter, Sloane closed her eyes, knowing it would all but confirm her friend's intuition.

A tumultuous storm of emotions swirled within Sloane. *Of course it's about my daughter. Why the hell else would I be a mess up here? No leads. Nothing except business deals and politics. Nothing about finding Gwyn. We've been cooped up in this damn city for far too damn long, and I want to leave! I should be searching for her, not doing all this, and I hate that we have to do this shit. I hate that you are just going to leave me. Especially with two people I barely know, who are definitely not working for my interests. I hate that I want to beg you to stay. But most of all, I hate not knowing if she's safe!*

"I'm fine," Sloane muttered through gritted teeth, but a tear forced its way down her cheek anyway and betrayed her true feelings.

Maud's gaze lingered on her, the scrutiny as piercing as a surgeon's knife. "You're not fine. You're a ball of barely contained rage and tension." Her voice softened. "Talk to me, Sloane. I'd like to believe we've grown to be more than mere traveling companions. We're friends. I care about how you're feeling."

If we were friends, you all wouldn't be so ready to leave. The thought was a bitter pill, but she swallowed it down. That wasn't fair. They had shown her nothing but concern, and they had agreed to detour to Marketbol without hesitation. *I can't take my pain out on them,* she conceded.

Exhaling deeply, Sloane reopened her eyes, swiftly brushing away the tears that had pooled in them. "I was working, and I did the math. If there was no delay between leaving Earth and arriving here—which I have no concrete proof of either way—today would be Gwyn's eleventh birthday."

Maud replied with a simple, "Oh."

Sloane nodded. "Oh, indeed."

Maud sighed, her voice carrying a note of sympathy. "I'm sorry, Sloane. I didn't know. Listen, if you—"

A bang on the door caused them both to jump.

"Ugh. That would be Deryk, with the worst timing ever," Maud grumbled, her annoyance clear.

A feeble attempt at a smirk twisted Sloane's face into a grimace.

Rising to her feet, Maud shot one last glance at Sloane. "We're going to talk about this. Later."

Sloane nodded.

The door swung open, allowing the towering orkun man to enter, his hands laden with a hearty bowl of stew and a frothy mug of ale. The soft lighting of the room reflected off the enticing liquid, painting a comforting picture against the heavy air. "Stew and ale is perfect sad food. We need to talk," Deryk declared, placing the food on the table.

Sloane nodded, acknowledging the knight's concern. "Thank you, Deryk. Maud told me."

Maud nudged her with her shoulder. "Eat. He can talk while you get something in your stomach."

Sighing deeply, Sloane pushed herself up and trudged to the table. Picking up the spoon, she scooped a bit of the hot beef broth and brought it to her lips. The rich, savory flavor exploded in her mouth and she momentarily closed her eyes, savoring it. It was really good.

I hope Gwyn has good food.

The thought, rather than offering comfort, caused a lump to form in her throat. She fought back a sob and was momentarily startled by the gentle touch of a small hand rubbing her back and a larger one gripping her shoulder firmly.

Deryk's voice broke through the silence. "Sloane."

She took another spoonful of the stew, meeting the gaze of the knight. His eyes, usually stern, held a kindness she rarely saw. "I have a contact."

Sloane's eyes widened at his revelation. *Really?*

She quickly swallowed the mouthful of stew, and asked, "They're willing to meet with us?"

Deryk and Ernald had spent the better part of the past three weeks trying to make contact with the elusive Westari Order of Secrets. Their daily endeavors had been mostly fruitless, till now.

Deryk nodded, a faint smile crossing his lips. "Yes. It seems they attended the ball and witnessed . . . everything. They approached Ernald and me this morning. They knew we were trying to make contact, but your display at the ball swayed them."

The room swirled around Sloane as she tried to grasp the implications of this simple revelation. "When? When can we meet?"

"They will let us know. Soon."

A glimmer of hope sparked within Sloane. This was promising news. She might finally get a lead on Gwyn's whereabouts. If they knew anything. Hopefully, they weren't just meeting with her about magic.

That does seem the most likely circumstance, unfortunately. Don't get your hopes up, Sloane.

She drew in a deep breath, her gaze roaming over the familiar surroundings of her room.

"I have a lot to do before this meeting. Maud, I need to meet with the smith. He was done with the order yesterday, and I haven't even met the man yet."

"Deryk and I will accompany you," Maud offered.

Deryk echoed Maud's sentiment, curiosity twinkling in his eyes. "Yes, I'd like to see what you've been working on."

Sloane shoved her feelings back into their box and locked them up. She took another bite of stew before grabbing her mug and taking a long drink. She set down the mug with a little more force than necessary, and ale sloshed onto the polished wooden table.

Sloane narrowed her gaze, focusing on the pair of knights before her. The fire crackled softly in the background, casting long shadows across the room, flickering over her friends' faces. She leaned back in her chair, her hands flat on the table, fingers splayed.

"Alright," she declared, her voice resonating in the quiet room. "Here's the plan . . ."

Sloane walked with Deryk and Maud into the third district and, despite knowing what was coming, was instantly taken aback by what she saw. The district was a startling counterpoint to the posh central and bustling merchant areas, bearing closer resemblance to a dilapidated, third-world settlement.

Having been warned of the district's reputation by Deryk, the trio had made the prudent choice to suit up. Maud and Deryk, in their full regalia, stood in stark contrast to Sloane, who had simply donned her breastplate over her outfit, which also comprised billowing sleeves, sturdy boots, and a pair of sturdy pants, which all made her feel more like a swashbuckler in a fantasy than someone who fit in with the armored knights. The shortsword hanging off her left hip completed the look.

A rapier. Now, that would have been perfect. Maybe I'll have Elodie buy one. And why stop there? With a ship, I could become the Dread Pirate Sloane . . . or better yet, with a flying ship, a sky pirate! A fleeting smile danced on her lips at the thought. *Hashtag goals.*

"Arrr!" she murmured to herself, amused by the thought.

Maud turned to her, a hint of confusion in her eyes. "What was that, Sloane?"

Quickly, she brushed it off. "Uh . . . nothing?" *Smooth, Sloane. Very smooth.*

They continued through the district, and the scenery seemed to get worse. Sloane would not bet against the chance someone would try to rob them. Deryk's calm demeanor in the face of their bleak surroundings sparked a question. She leaned in and whispered, "Deryk, are you sure we're going the right way?"

He nodded. "Yes. We will arrive shortly."

Not completely assured but ready for any challenge, she followed along, her eyes trained on the path ahead, ready for a gang or something to jump out and mug them.

The sight of smoke wafting from a chimney in the distance piqued her interest. As they approached, the source of the smoke became clear: a blacksmith's workshop, housed in a worn-out building that had seen better days.

Well, I think I can figure out why he was so keen to join me.

Sloane and Maud followed Deryk inside the dilapidated building, uncertainty giving way to a sense of purpose. They stepped into a modest reception area that was as threadbare as the building's exterior. Crude shelves laden with all manner of items adorned the walls. Assorted bags of nails, horseshoes, and a variety of tools lay interspersed among other typical blacksmith merchandise. Sloane's mind drifted back to Valesbeck, to Tobin and his ceaseless efforts to forge weaponry and armor to fend off the wolves and other creatures.

She realized she had been so engulfed in the unfolding events back then that she had failed to ponder the significance of his work. In retrospect, it all made sense: the hurried construction of the wall, the arming of the militia, the lingering evidence of previous attacks.

I hope Tobin and his son made it out alive, she thought again.

Her gaze fell on Maud's waist, the mace swinging with each step. *Tobin probably thought we were there to assist them, and that's why he prioritized crafting the mace. But we left them . . . we ran . . .*

Sloane knew she shouldn't feel that way. They had no way of knowing the town would fall to beasts. Their mission was elsewhere, after all. Yes. But rationalization did little to assuage the gnawing guilt she felt for abandoning the villagers to their fate.

I wasn't cut out for this, it seems. I need to get my shit together, emotionally.

A tall, robust orkun emerged from a doorway nestled between two wobbly bookshelves, interrupting her thoughts. His pale, faintly green-tinted skin contrasted with his emerald-like eyes, which sparkled with intensity. Wearing a worn leather apron and heavy gloves slung on his belt, he looked every bit the part of a blacksmith. He wiped his hands on a rag dangling from his belt and surveyed his guests, his gaze lingering the longest on Deryk before shifting to Sloane.

His lips curled into a slight smirk. "You must be the Lady Reinhart I am to work for," he said.

Caught off guard by his tone, Sloane arched an eyebrow. "Were you coerced in any way?" she queried.

The blacksmith's hearty laughter echoed through the room. "No. No, I can't say that I was. You're one of them terrans I been hearing about, yeah?"

"I am."

"Hmph. Bigger than a telv, at least," the blacksmith replied, his eyes drifting over to Maud.

Maud huffed lightly. "I am quite capable, despite my size."

The man chuckled again. "Didn't say you weren't, Lady Knight. Just making an observation."

Sloane wasn't quite sure what to make of the man, but it was leaning negative. "Instead of examining my body proportions, can we get to why we're here?"

His eyes widened in surprise, and he held up his hands in a gesture of surrender. "Whoa, now. I didn't mean anything by that. My apologies, ser," he said, nodding respectfully at Maud.

Deryk smirked. "It is common among orkun communities to view the other races as diminutive. Given her height and build, Sloane bears a closer resemblance to orkun stature. There are communities of telv from the regions north of us who are similar, but they are not common among their people. I believe our smith was merely commenting on that."

Sloane's apprehension faded. "Oh. Then my apologies as well for my assumption."

The smith scratched the back of his head awkwardly. "Probably not the best first impression for your future employer."

Sloane smiled. "If it helps, I am a bit taller than the average terran woman. I'm sure orkun communities will add us to a list of people to make short jokes about . . ." She hesitated, trying to think. "I'm sorry. I didn't get your name from the Guild when they told me they had someone who volunteered."

"Ah, Koren Moore at your service. Welcome to my humble shop," he introduced himself.

Sloane extended her hand. "Pleased to meet you, Koren. I am Sloane."

Koren's smile was warm as he took her hand. She barely suppressed a chuckle at the firm grip, squeezing back just as tightly. He raised his brow in surprise and gave her a subtle nod of approval.

Withdrawing her hand, she quickly redirected the conversation. "I understand you have completed my order?"

He nodded enthusiastically. "Yes, I have! My shop may not be much to look at, but when it comes to small-scale work, my forges are unrivaled. It took thirty-one tries and failures of various combinations from your notes, but I was able to figure out one combination that worked out well. I believe I will need a more equipped forge in the future to maintain the temperatures needed."

As Sloane listened attentively to his explanation about forging the stainless steel, the blacksmith's enthusiasm became increasingly evident. Her own knowledge was rudimentary, gleaned from a late-night Wikipedia rabbit hole.

Hours . . . hours I'll never get back. It happens to the best of us.

The orkun led them to the back, where his forge and small foundry were. The man wasn't kidding when he mentioned that he had a small operation.

Koren caught her appraising glance and offered a bashful explanation. "I mostly focus on everyday items for the district. Nails, tools, that sort of thing. This project you brought in . . . it was a breath of fresh air."

Lifting a worn blanket from a table, Koren revealed an array of shiny stainless steel plates and meticulously crafted joints, per Sloane's specifications.

"Oh! You were able to do the joints as well!" She rushed over and started looking at it all. It was everything she needed to complete her falcon.

Cradling a piece of stainless steel in her hands, Sloane pushed her mana into it, delving into its structure. The rest of the world seemed to fade into the background as she did so, Koren's excited rambling drowned out by her concentration. Thankfully, Deryk and Maud filled in, explaining her preoccupation.

Satisfied with the consistency of the steel across the plates, she was about to express her approval when she noticed an anomaly on the second to last one. "This one has a minute fracture," she pointed out. Koren was quick to apologize, offering to remedy the error immediately, but Sloane shook her head.

She shook her head without looking away. She pushed more mana into the steel and Altered the material to repair the crack.

"It is no bother. I fixed it," she said simply, setting the plate down.

Koren stammered in confusion. "I'm . . . I'm sorry? What? What does that mean?"

Deryk was quick to step in, gently patting the other orkun's shoulder. "It is a long story, friend. We'll have time to explain on the way to Marketbol."

Sloane nodded in agreement, her blue eyes betraying her eagerness as they danced over the crafted components strewn across the blackened wooden table. "Yes, we certainly will. Koren, I have to tell you, your passion for your craft gives me a lot of confidence in our future endeavors."

A humble smile spread across Koren's weathered features. "I was also able to create the other item that was part of the commission."

A flicker of confusion crossed her face, her brow furrowing subtly. "Other item?"

With an affirmative nod, Koren turned, disappearing momentarily behind a partition. He returned bearing a set of documents and handed them to her. As she flipped through them, her initial puzzlement gave way to understanding. She recognized the work request that she and Elodie had drawn up specifically for the smith who volunteered to join her. It also included Sloane's sketches and notes on the engraving pen.

That sly woman.

Caught off guard, her eyes shot up to find Koren holding out a rather unassuming wooden box. A flicker of amusement danced across his face as he lifted the lid, revealing a creation that took her breath away: her engraving pen.

Koren's voice cut through her reverie, humbly explaining the complexities of shaping the nib from steel and the challenges of engineering an internal ink reservoir. The sketches she had painstakingly detailed came to life through his words. His final concern, that of the pen's simple aesthetics, hung in the air. It wasn't adorned with gems or filigree, unlike the usual tools of the nobility.

The pen was perfect in its simplicity. A sturdy wooden barrel complemented by the gleam of a stainless steel grip and a broad nib designed for her runic work and the nature of the ink. The craftsmanship was impeccable. It was unadorned, a tool made for purpose, not ostentation.

Sloane was quick to allay the smith's doubts. "Koren," she began, her voice resonating with sincerity, "it's perfect." Cradling the pen, she took a moment to appreciate its form, its feel, the flawless integration of her vision. "Everything, from its measurements to its balance, aligns with my vision. This . . . this is exactly what I needed."

Allowing her gaze to wander back to the pen, Sloane gently channeled her blue mana into the instrument. An immediate response followed: the instrument hummed, alive in her grasp. It was like a dance, the way her mana coursed through the metal, thrumming harmoniously with an energy that resonated deep within her. A thrill of delight sparked in her chest, radiating outward until her lips curled into a satisfied smile.

She almost purred.

Sloane couldn't help but think about all she'd be able to accomplish now. With it, she could carve out new paths, define new possibilities, and perhaps even rewrite the rules of this new world.

"I need to get going. I have . . ." Her words trailed off as she rose, intent on leaving. Her gaze met Maud's mischievous grin and Deryk's knowing glance.

He's going to find out anyway if he joins us on our trip.

Sighing, she admitted, "Fine, I really want to get back to my own project. I can't wait to take all this metal and bring my creation to life."

Koren laughed, a warm, hearty sound. "I can't wait to see what you create, Lady Reinhart. The metal you've given me . . . let's just say it's important."

Sloane shot him a knowing smile. "Trust me, Koren, I'm well aware of how beneficial this metal can be. Come see us at our inn when you're ready."

As they took their leave, Sloane could hear Deryk instructing the orkun blacksmith to prepare for travel. It was music to her ears. *Finally*, she thought, a bright, anticipatory grin spreading across her face.

As the red sun began its descent, painting the sky in hues of gold and purple, the group journeyed back toward the comfort of their inn. The bustling day was winding down, and shopkeepers were beginning to shutter their establishments. Moving briskly through the third district, they caused a stir, and curious glances following them as they progressed toward the merchant district. The guards at the entrance were initially suspicious, scrutinizing their presence in such an impoverished region, but a swift examination of their documents and they were through.

As they approached the central district, something unusual caught Sloane's eye. An elderly wagon merchant was packing up his wares, among them a singular plant casting an ethereal glow in the descending darkness. Drawn in by the strange luminescence, she ventured closer. It looked like a tea plant, but its leaves shimmered with an intriguing glow.

"Is this plant bioluminescent? What exactly is it?" she asked, startling the merchant who hadn't noticed her approach.

"Oh! You gave me quite the scare, my lady!" he exclaimed, catching his breath. "That there is a *tè luminoso* plant. It makes the most exquisite tea. A terran merchant sold them to me."

Sloane's head jerked in surprise. *Wait. What?!*

"A terran merchant?" Then his previous words fully registered, and her heart skipped a beat. "What did you call that plant?"

"Oh, sorry. It's from a language of the terrans. He called it a *tè luminoso*," he replied.

Luminous tea? That's Italian. Where? How?

She suddenly realized she hadn't even attempted to speak Italian since her arrival. She was in shock.

Gwyn always was the one more likely to speak it regularly.

"Is he still here? When did you last see him?" she asked, her mind racing.

The merchant, oblivious to her anxious curiosity, continued enthusiastically, "It was a couple of weeks ago, I believe. Would you like to purchase some? This tea, it helps you focus like nothing else, and just one magical cup can—"

"Yes, yes," she cut him off impatiently. "The terran, is he still around?"

Shaking his head while packing some of the tea, he responded, "No, I think he left shortly after his visit. I'm unsure where he headed next. I'm sorry, is one package enough?"

Sloane found her frustration rising, her thoughts in a whirl. *Stop worrying about your tea, man!*

"Yes. One is enough," she said, doing her best to keep her tone level. "Did he sell anything to anyone else who might know where he went?"

Maud advanced gracefully and placed several coins in the merchant's extended palm to procure the tea. The man, tracing an absent-minded pattern on his bearded chin, returned his gaze to Sloane.

"Can't say I recall anyone else, my lady. I simply mind my own wares," he confessed with a shrug.

The disappointing response triggered a wave of frustration, and Sloane couldn't stifle an exasperated groan. Maud, recognizing her friend's distress, laid a comforting hand on her shoulder.

"Sloane, we mustn't lose hope," she assured. "We'll find a way."

Sloane drew in a deep breath, letting the tension flow out with her exhalation.

"Thank you for the tea," she said, forcing a smile. "And your information is still appreciated." Extracting a small silver coin from her pouch, she pressed it into the merchant's hand and then pivoted on her heel, following the retreating forms of her companions. With a bag of tea that she didn't really want.

What the hell will it take to find one damn lead? She looked at Deryk as he led the way.

Hopefully, his contact pans out.

CHAPTER TWENTY-SIX

I NEED A DRINK

S loane sat at her desk in her room, her workspace arranged to her liking, dedicated to the task of giving life to her envisioned falcon. Ernald had assisted her earlier in the day, hauling up what she required from her workbench in the wagon to spare her the burden of trudging up and down the stairs.

Now, though, it was getting late in the evening and she was laser-focused as she engraved the feathered wings made from stainless steel. Her new engraving pen, crafted by Koren with exquisite precision, was cradled in her grip, dancing under her meticulous guidance. Its stainless steel nib glided with a grace borne from careful engineering and her own mana-infused touch.

Her vision was locked on the falcon's wings, shimmering segments of stainless steel awaiting the caress of her new tool. The lines she etched were minute, intricate, yet they held the potential to dictate the movement and thus flight of the mechanical creature.

Channeling her mana, Sloane surrendered herself to the arduous task, becoming one with her Artifice domain as she put the finishing touch on the |Lighten| rune. As it started to glow, she immediately felt the weight of all the steel lessen, satisfied that the rune worked as designed and would grant the weighty mechanical bird with the grace and lightness of a real falcon.

As her proficiency with runes continually improved, her ability to decipher or even *know* the runic language increased. It was almost as if Mana—big "M"— was helping her with the knowledge itself, making it seem as if it had always been an innate part of her.

She placed the wing and her pen down before examining her project. She *needed* to [Focus] on the work, but between her continued steady enchanting and its accompanying mana use, Sloane felt nothing but drained. The thought of adding more magic to the list made her hesitate. [**Runic Knowledge**] along with the manipulation of her domains and mana without spells seemed to strain her mind faster than spam casting [**Mana Bolt**].

Sloane leaned back in her chair, thinking. *Maybe a snack? No. Wait . . .*

With a spark of realization, she rose from her chair and ventured into the adjoining room. There, on the table, was the container of the *tè luminoso* she'd purchased earlier. Shrugging lightly, she filled the kettle with water and hung it over the fire, letting anticipation for the brew dance with her fatigue.

The merchant did say it would help with my focus. Maybe it will give the same effects as the spell, without the strain.

As the kettle slowly heated up, Sloane found herself sinking into a reflective silence. The last two bells had been filled with working on the feathers. They were hard, but she got it done. The most complex part of the puzzle was setting up the pathways through which mana would circulate. She concluded that mana flowed through stainless steel with sufficient effectiveness, which was good, because silver and steel did *not* mix. It definitely worked better than carbon steel, which was another benefit to doing the outer shell in the stainless variety.

Before that, Sloane had been working on the runic chains for the falcon in her notebook for another two bells. She sat and reviewed her work while waiting on the water, marking several changes she could make. The bird had multiple black diamonds arranged inside that would act as data storage. |**Store: (Intent: Knowledge)**| seemed like such a simple and broad runic chain, but that was the point. It was open-ended, and combined with the sapphires and blue core, it would allow the falcon to draw on the underlying mana to heavy-lift a lot of its functionality. Essentially, it allowed her to distribute most of the bird's cerebral processing to mana itself. The only problem was that it would increase the upkeep and maintenance of the bird. The rune would degrade faster, as there would be a constant channel requirement. Practically, however, that simply meant she would need to renew the runes once a year, rather than every five to ten.

Once the water had finally boiled, Sloane started the careful process of brewing her tea. She allowed the luminous leaves to steep for a solid five minutes before pouring herself a cup. Green tea wasn't her preference, but she could make do. A generous dollop of honey, which reminded her of the wildflower variant she and Gwyn were fond of, sweetened the otherwise bitter brew.

She noticed the lack of the plant's glow in her tea and silently thanked the heavens. After all, she knew that bioluminescent algae were toxic to humans. With a hesitant sip, she hoped it wasn't going to kill her or something.

Stop being a wuss. He was selling it to all kinds of people.

The taste . . . wasn't bad. The tea was predictably bitter and tasted like two shots of espresso's worth of caffeine, but the honey did manage to soften the blow. "Well," she murmured to the empty room. "I've tasted better."

Roughly half an hour later, Sloane found herself reinvigorated and her teapot almost empty. She felt *focused*. The tea had her all hyped up, and she had to get herself a snack of some nuts and dried fruits so her heart wouldn't explode. She was sure there would be no sleep for her anytime soon.

Her focus was now pinned on the bird. With newfound vigor, she grabbed the wing, aligning it with the torso's shoulder joint. After securing it in place with Alter, she swiveled the bird, preparing to attach the second wing. A frown creased her forehead as she noticed the opposite joint on the torso was margin-ally too large.

Damn it!

After channeling and using her mana to manipulate the structure of the torso to accommodate the joint properly, she then realigned the slot for the wing. Slowly pushing the wing into the torso, Sloane completed the connection and was satisfied that both wings were serviceable and able to articulate as designed.

Next, she reached for the mechanical bird's first leg, and her hand twitched involuntarily. She suddenly felt really . . . weird. Her head was feeling a bit loopy, so she took a moment to gather herself. After a few slow, measured breaths and a brief shake of her head, she felt stable enough to proceed.

The legs, unlike the wings, held a simpler structure, and attaching them was a less strenuous task. She shifted her attention back to the torso. A new idea had taken root in her mind, a small detail that could enhance the falcon's self-awareness. Drawing upon her mana and focusing on her **[Runic Knowledge]**, she searched for what was required and began to outline the plans for the bird's self-repair system.

It took her a while, but once she knew what she needed, she slowly etched the key runic chain. The sequence of runes would grant the bird the ability to sense any damage done to itself. However, sensing wasn't enough. The falcon had to act upon this knowledge.

The mechanical creature held three mana crystals within its structure, each associated with a pink sapphire. These precious stones were responsible for man-aging the energy of their respective crystals and distributing it as needed. The reason she had installed so many of the gems was due to the next runic chain.

Just as the engraver was about to make contact with the metal, Sloane stopped, her head spinning. The rush of caffeine seemed to rise like a tidal wave, threatening to drown her focus. She had certainly overestimated her tolerance for the potent brew.

Too much, too quickly, she chided herself, taking slow, deep breaths to regain her equilibrium. The feeling was worse than the first time, and the pressure on her head was intense. The focus she had felt before was gone. She took a few deep breaths to try to relax.

I'll just do this last chain for the night.

Fortifying herself with one last intake of air, she set about crafting the final sequence. This runic chain had a dual function. It had a basic |Repair| element, designed for minor fixes. For more extensive damage, equivalent to a quarter of the falcon's structure, the instruction would trigger a more mana-intensive repair mode, rooted in an amplified |Alter|. The distinction between the two was clear: while the repair function would attempt to reconnect and rearrange, the alter rune would . . . would manipulate the metal as if it . . . it was . . .

A sudden jolt brought Sloane back to the present, her heart beating erratically against her chest.

Shit. What the hell?

Blinking away the last vestiges of drowsiness, her gaze quickly fell on the runic chain she'd been working on. A twinge of paranoia prompted her to meticulously inspect the chain, scrutinizing each rune to make sure she hadn't botched anything in her semiconscious state.

With a sigh of relief, she confirmed everything was as it should be. As she began gathering her tools to call it a night, her hand swept an empty spot where her engraving pen should have been. A mild frown tugged at the corners of her lips.

Hmm. That's . . . weird. I must be more worn out than I thought. She rubbed her temples, trying to dispel the inexplicable confusion clouding her mind. Her eyes felt heavy as they fell upon the teacup, its contents long since drained. She tried **[Focusing]** . . . but then . . .

Okay, I don't feel well. What the hell was wrong with that tea? She shook her head a bit more forcefully and placed her hands on the table to stand . . . but . . .

Something isn't right. I'm just going to—

Sloane's breath hitched as an unexpected pressure descended upon her chest, something grazing the edge of her right breast. Recoiling, she came into contact with an unfamiliar chill, jerking herself awake at the sensation. As she opened her eyes, a beak abruptly filled her vision, bobbing curiously at her sudden movements. The bird's head tilted, opening its beak to squawk a peculiar sound.

"*Wryaat? Wryyyaat!*"

"Aaah!" Panicked, Sloane swiped at her chest, pushing herself backward in a frantic attempt to distance herself from the foreign creature. The bird, equally startled, flapped its wings and took off from its perch on her chest. Sloane's retreat was halted by the headboard, her breath ragged and uneven as she surveyed the room, eyes wide in search of whatever the hell was in her room.

"*Wryaat!*"

At the unexpected shriek on her right, Sloane yelped, hurling herself sideways off the bed and onto the floor. She scrambled backward, pressing against the wall as her looked about the room, searching for her sword. Spotting it across the room near her desk, she shook her head, resorting to magic instead.

With a swift motion, she conjured a [**Mana Bolt**], letting it hover threateningly before her.

A soft chirp drew her attention back to the creature on her bed, now hopping about curiously. As it hopped closer, her eyes widened in recognition.

Holy shit. It's my falcon. What? The? Hell?

With an awkward flutter of its wings, the mechanical bird hopped off the bed and made its way toward her. It paused next to her, tilting its head and squawking once more.

How are you alive?

Her eyes fell upon the chest of the bird, where a vibrant blue glow emanated from its core. The light flickered rhythmically, much like the indicator on a computer's hard drive during active use.

"How are you . . . finished?" she stammered, but the bird merely tilted its head inquisitively and, of course, did not respond.

Sloane sat at the table in her sitting room, locked in an intense, silent duel of stares with the mechanical falcon. The bird sat there, judging her—because of course it was. She had no idea what had happened or how she had finished the thing. She remembered only that before falling asleep, just the head and wings had an external covering. The entire torso had been exposed, and the core hadn't even been fully seated, let alone finished.

As if sensing her thoughts, the falcon tilted its head to the side, opening its beak slightly to emit a peculiar noise. *"Brrpt?"*

Sloane's eyebrows knitted together as she regarded the creature critically. "No. That is not a sound you make. You're a fierce predator, not a cute little hummingbird."

Upon hearing her admonition, the bird's head tilted to the other side. *"Wryaat?"*

A nod of approval from Sloane was quickly followed by a furrowed brow. "Wait . . . how are you making sounds?" Her mind raced as she tried to reconcile her hazy memories with the falcon's present state. *I genuinely can't remember finishing this. What in the world . . . ?*

Feeling as though she'd been thrown into a surreal dream, she leaned forward, scrutinizing the mechanical bird. "How were you made?" The falcon seemed to ignore her question, choosing instead to take flight and soar into the adjacent room. Sloane could only blink, bewildered.

"Do I . . . uh . . . follow it?"

Within moments, the falcon returned, a teacup precariously clutched in its claw. With a couple of quick flaps, it hoisted the cup aloft and dropped it into her outstretched hand. Sloane looked down at the cup, noticing it was definitely the cup she had used. The bird landed beside her while she examined the remnants of the tea that remained at the bottom.

Actually . . .

A realization sparked in her mind, though it only added to the confusion. "Did I tell you it was the tea that caused all this?"

"Wrrryat!" the bird replied, as cryptic as ever.

"I have no idea what that means. I don't speak bird," she retorted, but the bird seemed undeterred, responding with a sassy chirp.

Sloane sighed. She needed a drink. It was late, but not late enough that the bar would be closed. "Fine. I have no idea at the moment, so we're just going to go for now."

She grabbed her cloak and slung it over her shoulders. The autumn weather was starting to get chilly and she definitely felt the urge to go out walking for some fresh air after her drink. Opening the door, she looked back at the falcon that was staring at her from where it perched on her desk.

"You coming?"

Answering with a keen screech, the falcon soared across the room and settled on her shoulder.

Good thing I engraved the |Lighten| rune.

With the falcon perched comfortably on her shoulder, Sloane descended the wooden staircase into the tavern. It was late, the usual clamor of patrons reduced to a dull silence. The chill in the air seeped through the cracks in the walls, prompting her to pull her cloak tighter around herself.

Glad I didn't leave this behind, she thought, appreciating the added warmth.

As she approached, the bartender gave her a side eye and scrutinized her unusual companion. He jutted his head at the falcon, his eyebrows furrowing. "Whatever that thing is, it better not cause any damage," he grumbled.

Really? That's it?

Sloane tilted her head, taken aback by his nonchalant attitude. "Just no damage? Nothing else to say?"

The bartender turned his back to her, reaching for a bottle of some potent-looking liquor. He filled two tall, slim shot glasses and slid one over to her. He picked up the other and raised it slightly. Puzzled but intrigued, she mimicked his action. They clinked their glasses together and downed the contents. Sloane placed the empty shot glass back on the bar, her confusion undiminished. "I . . . I have no idea what that was for."

His laughter rumbled across the vacant tavern. "Really, I just wanted a shot . . . Word gets around, you know. Especially when there's a . . . famous . . . or rather, infamous individual like yourself causing a stir. All those stories about your little metal balls that explode and the magic you can do. And now this metal bird . . . it just adds to the narrative."

"Wryaat!" the falcon interjected, breaking its earlier stillness.

The bartender, caught off guard, let out a startled yelp as he jerked back in surprise. "It's alive!?"

Sloane turned to her metallic companion, a reproachful look in her eyes. "That was mean. You tricked him. Apologize."

The falcon rotated its head toward the flustered bartender, letting out a softer, more placating sound. *"Wryatt, wryyyatt."*

Sloane shrugged, giving the bartender an encouraging smile. "I think he apologized. I really have no idea, but let's go with it."

The bartender didn't reply.

"You okay there, buddy?" she asked.

The bartender, still visibly shaken, simply nodded, his gaze fixed on the falcon. "Y-yes. T-thank you."

Noticing the man's continued discomfort, Sloane slid her empty shot glass toward him. "Can I get another one of those shots?"

Without a word, the bartender hastily grabbed the bottle and shoved it her way, mumbling about some urgent task in the back room. With that, he beat a hasty retreat, leaving Sloane and her newfound companion in relative solitude.

Sloane responded to the bartender's departure with a nonchalant shrug. She filled her shot glass again and quickly downed it, her gaze briefly clouded over by the heady rush of alcohol. As she reached out to pour herself a third shot, a voice intruded upon her solitude.

"Mind if I have one of those shots, my lady? I could use a drink."

Sloane and the falcon pivoted in unison toward the voice. A moon elf stood only a few paces away, his presence a sudden, startling contrast to the otherwise quiet tavern. His heterochromatic eyes—one a soft pink, the other an intense, almost inky black—were undeniably striking. He was dressed almost entirely in black, from his sleek coat to his polished leather boots, which lent him an air of enigmatic sophistication. The sole exception was his hat—a peculiar splash of yellow that clashed jarringly with his otherwise monochrome attire.

The man looked to be around her age of thirty-four, perhaps slightly older, and his light-gray skin bore a few minor blemishes. It added a hint of character to his otherwise refined appearance.

The falcon, seemingly agitated by the sudden intrusion, let out a threatening screech at the moon elf. Sloane flinched, her movement causing the bird to tighten its grip on her shoulder to maintain balance.

Her eyes flicked between the half-filled bottle on the bar and the moon elf. After a moment of consideration, she offered him a noncommittal shrug.

"Sure, why not," Sloane conceded.

The moon elf's lips curled into a gentle smile as he smoothly claimed the stool beside her. The predatory glare from the falcon perched on her shoulder seemed to do little to unsettle him, a fact that sparked a flicker of curiosity within her.

Oddly calm and sure of himself, isn't he?

His casual and unthreatening demeanor prompted her to lean over the deserted bar, her fingers brushing against the cool surface of an unused shot glass. It sat among a few empty mugs and a stained towel, remnants of the bartender's hurried retreat. She snatched it up, the clear glass catching the dim light of the room and casting a small shadow on the worn wooden counter.

With the newly acquired glass in hand, Sloane straightened, her cloak shifting softly around her. She deftly poured a generous amount of the liquor into the shot glass, the amber liquid shimmering in the low light, and slid it to the elf before filling her own.

As she set the bottle down between them, the elf nodded his gratitude, fingers wrapping around the slender shot glass. As though honoring some unspoken ritual, he raised the shot in a casual salute, an acknowledgment of shared resilience in the face of a hard day's labor.

Smoothly, Sloane lifted her glass, meeting the elf's silent toast. A brief pause followed, the stillness stretching out between them as they held their glasses aloft. Then, in unison, they tapped their shot glasses against the bar and drained them in one fluid swallow.

She let out a contented sigh as she set her shot glass down onto the bar.

"Thank you, my lady," the man next to her murmured, the words touched with a sincere gratitude that softened his features. He paused, setting the empty shot glass down, a thoughtful look entering his mismatched eyes. "It was a long day at the Academy."

CHAPTER TWENTY-SEVEN

THE WALLS HAVE EARS

The terrans that arrived in our world, no matter their true origin, seem to have a quote, saying, or proverb for everything. An interesting cultural tic that is not unique to their culture, but is of a pervasiveness that evidently was an important developmental tool for their societies and peoples. Many of these small quotes hold generalized snippets of wisdom, while others are complete nonsense, with even more seeming to conflict with another. Some of my colleagues contend that this practice even exacerbates the typical distrustful and paranoid inclinations indicative of the Displaced on average. However, the extent to which they seem to dictate everything they do is a key window into their cultural mind. Thus, study should be encouraged as to better understand their culture.

"All governments suffer a recurring problem: power attracts pathological personalities. It is not that power corrupts, but that it is magnetic to the corruptible."

"A prince should have a spy to observe what is necessary, and what is unnecessary, in his own as well as in his enemy's country. He is the king's eye; and he who hath him not is blind."

A Cultural Study of the Terran
Peoples, 22 SA., Q. Branigan

EARLIER

Deep in the bowels of Count Kayser's secret dungeon, Giallo stared down at the lifeless body of the traitor to his organization as one of the intoxicating, telltale signs of the kill filled him like a rush of adrenaline that never stopped.

He was injured—the traitor had slipped a dagger under his guard and stabbed him in the ribs and shoulder. Giallo knew he had to leave, but he needed more proof of the count's illicit activities. Things that the Order of Secrets should have known—*would have* known—were it not for the traitor.

The man once known as Green had been hiding information regarding the count since the Flash, but now, thanks to information from the two Blightwych knights he had met with, Giallo knew.

He grimaced, pressing a hand against his side to stifle the pulsing pain. His mind snapped back to the present when a desperate plea echoed from the next room.

"Hey! Hey! Help me!" the voice called out.

Stepping over the lifeless guards he had dispatched prior to the traitor's confrontation, Giallo moved through an archway into a larger chamber, its stone walls lined with four grim cells. A woman, the sole occupant of these cells, was the source of the plea. With a groan, he righted himself, muscles straining in protest from the unanticipated effort.

"Are you okay? Can you get me out of here? The other guards will be back soon!" she urged.

Casting a swift, assessing glance around the room, Giallo approached the woman. "Who are you?"

"My name is Adaega. Please, you need to get me out of here," she implored, her voice faltering with desperation.

A terran.

As Giallo stepped closer, distant shouts pierced the eerie silence of the dungeon. His eyes darted around, noting a door to his left. "Where does that door lead?"

The terran with a dark complexion similar to a sun elf drew in a shaky breath. "I don't know, but I know it's another hallway. Quick, get me out. We can check together."

Giallo swiftly scanned the room for something to release the woman before retracing his steps back to the entryway. He rummaged through the pockets of the fallen guards and the traitor in search of keys, only to meet disappointment. Heaving a sigh, he hobbled back to the imprisoned woman.

"The keys aren't here. I don't have time to find them. I'm sorry. But we will come back to get you out of here. I promise," Giallo assured her.

The prisoner's response was a desperate plea, her voice trembling amid sobs. "No, no no no. Don't leave me here with them. Please . . . please take me. Get me out of here."

His heart clenched at her distress. Time was not a luxury he had, but he felt an undeniable pang of sympathy. "I need to get out of here, or no one will know where to find you. I'm sorry."

Giallo quickly turned and picked up the traitor's dagger and stuffed it into one of the man's pockets. He dragged the man through the door into the room where the first man lay and set the two bodies up so it looked as if they had killed each other. Grabbing the knife, he placed it into the man's hand and closed his fingers around it, thankfully still able to do so. With one last glance to ensure everything looked believable, he quickly made his way back to the cell room.

Opening the alternate door in the cell room revealed another hallway. He hoped it would guide him to an exit. Casting a glance over his shoulder at the sobbing prisoner, he reaffirmed his promise. "We'll be back, Adaega. When the rescuer comes, they will say, 'Giallo is the color of the terran sun.' Repeat it back to me."

The woman blinked up at him, confusion clear in her tear-streaked face. "Giallo is the color of the terran sun?"

He nodded in approval. "Good. Do not utter this phrase to anyone else. Stay strong, Adaega. Help will arrive soon."

She nodded, sniffling. Encouraged, Giallo pivoted on his heels and bolted down the hallway.

Several bells later, Giallo was sitting with his legs out in front of him on the ground in a barn. An animal doctor knelt behind him, patching up his shoulder. His handler stood in front of him as they discussed his infiltration into the count's manor.

"Giallo, Scarlet was able to find more information about what the traitor had been doing. Evidently, he had been selling the order's secrets to the count for almost a year. After the Flash and, subsequently, when the count learned of the terrans, Kayser ordered him closer. This caused him to get sloppier, which led to Scarlet finding out about him, even if she wasn't aware that he was another agent," the man said.

Giallo nodded. "That makes sense. Has there been any indication that the count knows I was there?"

A shake of the head. "No. Scarlet was able to deflect, and the count now believes the guard and the traitor simply fought over something else, killing each other in the end over some disagreement."

"Good. We need to get the terran woman out of there," Giallo said.

"That isn't going to be possible, Giallo. We are pulling out. We are leaving a team behind to deal with the count when the beasts hit the city, but then they will also evacuate. We do not have the bodies available to help," he said.

"We need to do something, Five," Giallo said. Unlike the more color-focused code names the senior agents held, the inner circle and leaders of the order used numbers. The lower the number, the more authority they held. Five was in command of the entire Ghyll region.

"I am sorry, Giallo. It's not possible. You get stitched up. Then you will join the group leaving just before the swarm hits. You'll be heading out the East Gate, then north. You are to establish yourself in Vilstaf," Five said. He looked down at Giallo, and when he didn't respond, he said one last thing before leaving. "Do not be late."

Giallo said nothing as Five walked out.

He winced as the raithe working on his shoulder pulled tightly, then wrapped some fabric over the wound. When he was done, he tapped Giallo's other shoulder. "You're all set. Take it easy on those ribs, shoulder, and arm."

Giallo stood. "Thank you." Then he turned and walked out of the barn.

It was about time he met Lady Reinhart. And he really needed a drink.

PRESENT

Sloane kept an eye on the elf beside her, scrutinizing his every move as he downed another shot of liquor, which she'd poured for him. His yellow cap sat in front of him on the bar top, an odd piece of headwear that piqued her interest. Its design had a Tudor-era vibe, a kind of flat cap with slight modifications to accommodate his elongated ears. The hat bore a fine black braid looping around the crown, an eye-catching detail.

Without warning, the falcon had hopped from her shoulder to the counter and was perched in such a way as to keep its focus on the man. It gave Sloane a bit of comfort.

The man seemed exceptionally fit, which seemed almost odd to Sloane. He looked more like a modern soldier than those she had seen around—even the knights. He had an almost aloof demeanor, for despite having asked for shots, he hadn't really said much else. His every movement felt carefully calculated, each action playing out as if he knew exactly the reaction it would provoke.

After another shot, the elf placed his empty glass upside down on the counter and locked eyes with her. "I have been told that you wished to meet us," he stated calmly.

Sloane quickly scanned the area, only now realizing the distinct lack of other patrons. She couldn't even recall seeing anyone other than the bartender when she first arrived. Uncertain who "us" referred to, she instinctively defaulted to caution, acutely aware of the spy threat looming over her group.

"And who is 'us'? Who are *you*, for that matter?" she challenged, maintaining a poker face.

"You may call me . . . *Giallo*," he replied in a steady tone.

Taken aback, Sloane raised her eyebrows. "Do you know what that means?"

"A fine man told me it is the color of my hat in his language. A tongue I believe you speak as well."

"That still doesn't tell me who you are," she countered, struggling to keep her surprise under control at the mention of another Italian speaker.

"I've already mentioned. I work at the Ghyll Academy," he said.

Sloane nearly sighed out loud. She had zero patience for such deliberate ambiguousness. Recalling her discussions with Deryk and Ernald, she started to form a theory about the elf's origins, but lacked solid proof.

Those two did say the Order of Secrets had agreed to meet with me.

"How do I know you are what you say you are? Anyone can just claim they work for your . . . organization."

Giallo's lips curved into a knowing smirk. "A tidbit of free information for you. Mister Rowe won't be a concern for you any longer. However, we were able to learn that he meant no *physical* harm to you. He simply wished to extort you for his own gain. His true goal was to wrest control of the central district from the count. That is now irrelevant, though."

Sloane considered what he had said. She had been wondering about Mister Rowe ever since the altercation in the alley, but there had been no way to investigate it. At least not without drawing unnecessary attention. She took a moment to think about how to phrase her next questions.

"What about the humans he took? His people tried to harm or kill me."

Her falcon screeched a sharp, disapproving *"Wryaat,"* echoing her sentiment.

Giallo's eyes flickered briefly to the counter-perched falcon before meeting hers again. "His people appear to have been overzealous with their instructions. They were told to bring you to him, alive. You *did* manage to ensure they paid for that mistake. Luckily for you, the guildmaster has taken a liking to you, enough to clear up your alleyway mess before sundown.

"The other man met the end of a Blade not long after leaving the scene. As for the terrans, he was only able to coerce two into working with him. Both adults."

The guildmaster *had* alluded to fixing the mess she had made in that alley. She wondered if Lanthil knew how closely these people were watching him. But with so many different entities spying on each other and enacting some sort of shadow war, she couldn't take too many chances.

Sloane picked up and swirled the bottle of liquor, thinking. Casting a sidelong glance at Giallo, who patiently awaited her next words, she voiced her concerns. "I am unsure whether we should speak further here. The walls have ears."

Giallo inclined his head thoughtfully. "I like that saying. Very *terran*. However, in this case, *we* are the ears in the walls. No one in this country, let alone the very city we call home, will listen in on what we do not wish to be heard. What we discuss here will only be heard by you and me. That said, I will, of course, inform my superiors."

Sloane offered a noncommittal nod, already anticipating he'd share details with others. His level of confidence, however, was unexpected, leaving her to ponder whether it was borne out of arrogance or fact. She poured a measure of the amber liquid into her glass and took a small sip, wincing at the burn. "What of other terrans? You clearly know a lot. Why didn't you help the terrans the count had?"

A deep inhalation filled Giallo's chest, which he released slowly, his expression turning grave. "That was our failing. A member of ours sought wealth and sold himself to the count."

Sloane nodded in understanding. It reminded her of another old saying, which she spoke aloud: "It's not the water around the boat that sinks it, but that within."

This guy isn't exactly inspiring confidence. She sighed. *Easy, Sloane. You just need his information.*

At her proverb, Giallo's eyebrow quirked in interest. "Indeed. That leak was swiftly plugged once discovered. Regrettably, we're unable to move directly against the count. However, a situation is on the horizon that may provide us an opportunity to rectify that."

"A situation?" She swiveled, pinning Giallo with a pointed stare. "And what about the terrans?"

He nodded. "Yes, a situation. I strongly recommend that you and your knights depart the city within a week." He shook his head slightly. "As for the terrans, eighty-seven are accounted for within the kingdom. Twenty-seven of them are children. Apart from you and Lord Bolton, there are six other nobles, including four children. None fit the description of your daughter. Only three of the children fall within the age range of six to eleven years."

Sloane's heart dropped. She opened her mouth to ask another question, but then closed it.

If Gwyn isn't in Westaren, where could she be?

She took a deep breath and gathered herself. "Among these terrans, how many arrived with someone they recognized?" she asked.

"Fourteen pairs in total. At the time of transportation, were you in physical contact with your daughter?" Giallo asked.

"No," Sloane shook her head, her brow furrowing at his line of questioning. "We were close though. She had just jerked away out of surprise."

Nodding pensively, Giallo said, "This gives us valuable insight. Among the pairs, eight were in a close embrace during the Flash. The others were merely touching to varying degrees. The most recent pair was barely touching fingers when they transported, only to land on opposing ends of the country."

A sharp intake of breath escaped Sloane's lips. Giallo looked at her sympathetically. "Your daughter is probably out there somewhere, but it's unlikely she's in Westaren."

"Why are you giving me all of this information?"

Giallo glanced at the bottle she was still cradling, seemingly pondering whether another shot was in order. Drawing a deep breath, he seemed to reach a resolution. "The war between the Empire of Vlaredia and the Sovereign Cities is not going well. In fact, it is only getting worse. We strive to remain neutral—as you can see, we have our own battles to fight. Westaren isn't the only place dealing with an influx of . . . monsters. We would like for you to deliver a message to Goosebourne, Marketbol, and Swanbrook."

She narrowed her eyes, though she was unsurprised by his precise knowledge of her destinations. The news about the war, however, was disconcerting. She would need to traverse the Sovereign Cities to reach Avira. Nevertheless, leaving this city and even the country, seemed appealing now that she had a solid hint that Gwyn wasn't in Westaren. "What's the message?"

"Vlaredia moves for the Malduhr Pass," he declared.

"Just that? Who do I even tell it to?"

With a nod, Giallo confirmed, "Yes, just that. Deliver the message to . . ." He leaned in close, his whisper delicately articulating three names and their respective locations.

Incredulous, Sloane recoiled slightly. "Wait . . . are you serious? You guys really have a muffin man living on Drury Lane?"

Giallo looked at her, a puzzled expression creasing his brow. "What are you talking about?"

"You said to find the baker on Drury."

Giallo's expression transformed into a stark, serious countenance. "Yes, the *Baker*. I do not know what a muffin is, but do not test him. Even I would fear crossing him."

Well . . . that's ominous. She made a mental note to jot down the names and locations as soon as she got back to her room.

Reclining in his seat, Giallo retrieved a small scroll from his pocket. "Give this to Ser Deryk. It contains information on the last terran the count has imprisoned in the city. We are incapable of freeing her ourselves. We ask that your knights assist her, and then take her along when you leave."

Sloane looked down. She remembered what Stefan had said about the terrans being held. She was sure the knights would attempt an extraction, but there was something that still bothered her. "What is the situation?"

Giallo tilted his head thoughtfully. "The same occurrence that befell Valesbeck will soon transpire here. My organization intends to capitalize on the . . . chaos . . . to confront the count."

A chill ran down Sloane's spine. *They plan to sacrifice the city to the beasts without warning, just to assassinate the count?*

"What of the men the count sent out?"

"They're dead. He sent far too few. Even now, the Crown's forces are en route to Thirdghyll, but they won't reach in time to prevent the city's fall."

Sloane's voice faltered. "B-but . . . what about all the people?"

Her falcon, sensing her distress, chimed in with a questioning, *"Wrrryat?"*

His gaze hardened. "This city is a breeding ground of dissent and corruption. You terrans seem to enjoy sayings with a facade of depth. Here is one for you: 'Sometimes, a town must be burned to save a nation from plague.'"

Her blood boiled, anger cresting like a wave. "You're going to stand by and let innocent people die."

"It is too late to do anything. The swarm will arrive within the week. You must use that distraction to escape. Head to Goosebourne. Deliver our message. Do not worry yourself over our city. Nothing you can do will change its fate."

"Warn them! Give them a chance to evacuate or, at the very least, barricade their homes. Anything to give them a fighting chance." Her thoughts abruptly flashed to her friends Reanny and Mulinn. "And Vilstaf?"

"Lady Reinhart, please lower your hand. I bear no wish to engage in a fight, or to harm you," Giallo cautioned, his tone even.

Sloane glanced down, surprised to find a **[Mana Bolt]** shimmering above her outstretched hand. She didn't even remember channeling it. With a thought, she dismissed the spell, and the connection to mana dissipated.

She was still angry. *There has to be* something *I can do.*

He nodded when the orb disappeared, seemingly content that they would not have to fight. "If we issue a warning, it risks alerting the count and his forces. Mister Rowe's underlings would undoubtedly get wind of it as well. However, I will allow you to inform the guildmaster. We have no intention of provoking the guilds."

Gisele will know what to do. "Fine," Sloane ground out.

Giallo rose from his seat abruptly, gathering his hat from the bar top and setting it firmly atop his head. "With that settled, my lady, I wish you a pleasant night."

As he moved to depart, she called out to him, "Wait! You didn't tell me about Vilstaf."

Pausing, he turned back to her. "Vilstaf is safe. The creatures are moving south of the lake. Guildmaster Romaris would do well to conduct an inspection of the town." He headed for the exit.

Sloane finally set down the bottle she had been gripping all along and called out to Giallo again as he reached the door. "You're doing the wrong thing by condemning your people to die."

He halted, his shoulders heaving as he inhaled deeply. "Sometimes . . ." He looked upward, seeming to contemplate his words. "Sometimes, the leak is simply too vast, and all the warning in the world cannot rescue a doomed ship. The rats would escape, only to infest anew elsewhere. I . . . we cannot allow the corruption and crime here to seep out and drag down the rest of the kingdom. It's a heavy burden to shield the many at the expense of a few."

"I hope you can bear that cost, Giallo," Sloane said.

"As do I, Lady Reinhart. As do I." With one last glance in her direction, the elf stepped out, disappearing into the folds of the night.

Sloane looked through the empty room at the stairwell. She needed to speak to Gisele immediately, then pass the small scroll to Deryk. Everything was going to start moving quickly. She needed to talk to Stefan as well. Romaris would require a warning. She had to speak to Rel, Kemmy, and Koren. The three of them needed to be prepared to leave soon. Especially Koren. The two alchemists were definitely ready, what with being without a home or shop currently.

"Let's go . . . uhhh . . . yeah, you need a name." *I'll have to deal with that soon, but not right now. I need to talk to Gisele.*

"Wrryat!" the bird screeched, as if in agreement.

Committed to a plan of action, she got up and headed for Gisele's room.

The falcon took off from the counter and circled around her before finally settling on her left shoulder.

Arriving at Gisele's door, Sloane rapped her knuckles against the solid wood. It was late into the night, and the banging and shuffling from inside led her to assume she had woken the woman up. But then the distinct utterances of colorful curses from two voices, one unmistakably Gisele's, the other deeply masculine, made Sloane realize it was likely an inopportune time.

It was too bad for Gisele that her news was important. *It's not the first time I've seen a friend in such a state, and it probably won't be the last.*

The sound of a latch being undone echoed from behind the door, which then creaked open to reveal Gisele's messed up hair and what looked like a man's tunic. The knight tried to keep a serious face but winced slightly when she focused on Sloane.

Sloane found it hard to suppress a smile at Gisele's flustered state.

"What is it, Sloane?"

"We have a problem," she replied.

Gisele groaned. "Can this wait until the morning? I was . . . sleeping."

Sloane arched an eyebrow at that. "No, I am sorry to interrupt you, but this cannot wait." She leaned closer to the door and lowered her voice. "I just met with someone who said he was from the Ghyll Academy but was clearly from the Order of Secrets."

At her words, the door swung open fully, revealing Cristole, shirtless.

"Where? Alone? What did they say?" he asked.

The look on Gisele's face was priceless, and if the news Sloane had wasn't as serious as it was, she would have taken advantage of the moment.

Gisele and Cristole? Nice.

The elf had a no-nonsense look on his face, while Gisele's expression was one of utter defeat. Sloane wouldn't be surprised if the others knew too, even if they'd been trying to hide it. Still, she was a good friend, and thus she very deliberately stared at Cristole's face, avoiding even a single glance at the elf's bare and very chiseled chest.

"Downstairs, just before I came up here. May I come in?"

Gisele looked at Cristole's bare torso, then down at her own lack of clothes below the waist. The situation was awkwardly comedic.

Huh. I wonder where she gets waxed. Sloane shook her head. *Damn errant thoughts.* "Perhaps you two should get dressed," she suggested, her cheeks tinged with a blush. "Then, meet me in my room. I'll gather the others."

Cristole appeared to be perplexed. "Why?" His question hung in the air until he glanced at Gisele and acknowledged her scantily clad form. "Oh. Oh . . ."

Gisele facepalmed. "We will be there shortly. Then you can tell us what that thing on your shoulder is."

Sloane couldn't help but steal a second peek at Gisele before turning on her heel as the door closed behind her. With her message delivered, she glanced at the bird perched on her shoulder, its head cocked in bird-like curiosity.

I really need to name it.

CHAPTER TWENTY-EIGHT

ESCALATION

The urgency to relay everything she had learned from Giallo was almost overwhelming for Sloane. But the first part of her impromptu meeting had been hijacked by the fascination her falcon commanded, with Maud fawning over the metallic creature as it chirped and fidgeted. Cristole seemed particularly intrigued by the small golem-like creation, already expressing an eagerness for her to explain how it was made when they had a chance.

Great idea, Cristole. Let me just figure out what the heck I did myself.

Only after the initial excitement died down did Sloane manage to steer the conversation back to her meeting with Giallo. As she unloaded the information, a flurry of questions erupted from her companions, requiring Knight-Captain Gisele's stern intervention to restore some semblance of order.

Ernald, his eyes revealing a veil of concern, was the first to restart the questioning. "Giallo said that we have one week before the same swarm of beasts that destroyed Valesbeck arrives here?"

She confirmed with a somber nod. "He said we needed to leave within the week, so I presume that's what he meant."

Deryk, meanwhile, had his attention fixed on the scroll she had handed him. "And the terran woman we learned about is being held on the count's estate. The order wishes for us to rescue her."

As she turned her attention toward Deryk, she began to reply, "Yes, and bring her w—"

Elodie, however, couldn't contain her interruption. "Hold on. Why are we ignoring the most pressing concern? The Order of Secrets is condemning the entire city."

"There is nothing we can do about that. To even try would likely just invite hostility toward us. We do need to warn the guildmaster, though. He can organize evacuations for those affiliated with the guilds," Stefan said.

"We need to come up with a plan. We cannot all go save the terran. There are Koren, Elodie, Rel, and Kemmy to think about. None of them are combatants," Ismeld pointed out.

Gisele rose, capturing the attention of everyone in the room. "Both Stefan and Ismeld make valid points." She swiveled to face Deryk, a serious look in her eyes. "Are we sure we can extract the terran without mishap?"

Deryk affirmed with a firm nod. "It should be straightforward. Distractions will be everywhere already."

Sloane blinked in confusion. "What?"

Cristole offered a casual shrug. "He's implying that during the attack, the city's guards will have more pressing concerns than us."

Gisele's finger tapped rhythmically against her chin as she considered their predicament. Finally, she nodded her approval. "Sloane, can you take Stefan and Elodie to discreetly warn the guildmaster tomorrow morning?"

Sloane nodded.

The orkun woman surveyed the room, her gaze thoughtful. "As the swarm nears the city, we will split into two groups. Ismeld, you will lead Sloane, Stefan, and our noncombatants out of the city through the East Gate toward Goosebourne. The rest of us will undertake the mission to retrieve the terran. We'll rendezvous at the second traveler's rest. We were planning to pass through that town anyway, so Sloane can deliver her message when we arrive."

Ernald turned to Cristole. "Can you lend a hand in preparing the wagons within the next couple of days?"

"I'll have the smith and alchemists assist as well," Elodie interjected. "I'll also accompany you to procure the supplies."

Sloane and Elodie had recently acquired two additional wagons for their travels. One had been kitted out with Sloane's workbench, while the other was designated for Koren's and the alchemists' materials. Given the increasing load of supplies and personal belongings, both wagons were a necessity. Stefan and Elodie had devised a seating arrangement ensuring everyone a place or duty. It meant that Rel and Koren would drive the two wagons, while Sloane and Stefan rode with them. This left Elodie and Kemmy to travel in the knights' wagon.

Sloane considered the size of the caravan. Her house now consisted of six people in total. The knights had their horses in addition to their one wagon. Sloane had two wagons and four horses to pull the wagons. When she was initially hesitant to invest in the animals and vehicles, Elodie had assured her that they could be sold upon reaching Swanbrook.

She had officially burned through the initial money the deal with the dwarves had given her. Anytime either of the Farum siblings accepted payment and deposited it with the Banking Guild, the organization would then pay out her percentage, as filed in the contract. Her payments would then come periodically as the branch in Thirdghyll was updated. She had already received two such payments, both surprisingly hefty. It seemed her partners in Vilstaf were making a fortune on the profitable trade route.

After another hour of meticulous planning, the group dispersed, each member retreating for a night's rest. Ismeld and Gisele lingered to accompany Sloane to her quarters. Collapsing onto her bed with a groan, Sloane lamented, "Why is it one thing after another here?"

Gisele empathized. "Things were not always this chaotic before the Flash."

The words slipped from Sloane's lips before she could reel them back in. "We really need to warn someone else."

Ismeld expelled a sigh of resignation, shaking her head. "That is not a good idea, Sloane."

But Gisele seemed to disagree. "I believe we might be able to get away with it. That guard captain, Ismeld, what was his name?"

A look of contemplation crossed Ismeld's face, her eyes narrowing as she fished for the elusive memory. "Captain . . . Fars, was it?"

Sloane's hand shot up, her fingers snapping in recognition. "No, Captain Jorin! He was present at the ball. Lars was the count's lackey."

Ismeld's eyes lit up with recognition. "Oh, yes. I remember now. Thanks, Sloane."

Sloane turned her attention to Gisele. "What about him?" she asked.

"We tell him."

Skepticism clouded Sloane's face. "Would he even believe us?"

Gisele's countenance grew somber. "He must. Otherwise, the city stands no chance."

The doors of the Banking Guild swung open as Sloane, flanked by Elodie and Stefan, confidently strode in. They maneuvered through the building with an air of practiced familiarity, undeterred by the hum of activity around them. Elodie took a moment to lean over the counter and exchange a few quiet words with Aimon, the clerk on duty.

His eyebrows rose in surprise, but after a quick nod of understanding, he dispatched a swift command to a runner, effectively clearing the guildmaster's schedule for the day.

Continuing their march, they ascended a grand staircase leading to the upper level. Reji, the guildmaster's orkun guard, opened the door to the executive suite with a sweep of his arm. They stepped inside, with Reji shadowing them.

Guildmaster Romaris jumped to his feet at their entrance, quill tumbling from his grasp and spilling ink across his neatly piled documents. His eyes were wide with surprise. "E-Elodie? What's going on?"

Elodie stepped aside, making room for Sloane to step forward. Sloane met Romaris's confused gaze with a calm, steady one.

"We've stumbled upon a rather pressing issue and I've been given . . . permission to warn you."

Romaris's eyes narrowed. "Permission? What are you talking about?"

Sloane simply nodded. "The Order of Secrets met with me last night. The beast swarm that annihilated Valesbeck will arrive here within the week. The order has condemned the city. Any attempt to alert the populace will be met with deadly repercussions."

The guildmaster inhaled sharply, color draining from his face.

Elodie stepped in, adding, "Their intent is to wipe out the count and anyone else with him."

"Fucking shit spies, always overdoing everything because they can't do their damn jobs. May Relena curse them all." Romaris glanced at his guard, a grim determination settled in his eyes. "Reji, initiate calamity protocols. Now. Have Aimon get up here and dispatch couriers to each guildmaster; they need to convene here within the hour. Every guild member must be ready for a discreet evacuation. And we're . . ."

He pivoted back to Sloane, curiosity etched in his features. "Which direction is the swarm headed from Valesbeck?"

"Vilstaf will be safe," Sloane assured.

Romaris nodded, sighing heavily. "Good," he said before turning back to Reji. "All guilds will be conducting a joint inspection in Vilstaf, courtesy of its rapid expansion and need for greater services. We need personnel from every guild to join. That's the official story, at least. The mercenaries and Blades will oversee security, and no word of this is to be spoken outside of those affiliated with the guilds. We take only what we can carry, and leave under cover of night. We'll have to bribe some gate guards . . ."

"I am meeting with Captain Jorin at the east fort tonight," Sloane interjected. "I could propose that he lets you leave from there in return for the information."

Romaris contemplated this for a moment before conceding with a nod. "That could work. Make sure to warn him about the order." He nodded to the orkun guard, and the man spun on his heel and departed the room with haste. Sloane could hear the pounding of his footsteps before the door even closed.

Guildmaster Romaris's gaze became piercing. "Are you absolutely certain about this? This is going to be . . . a massive undertaking. I'm not even sure how secret we can keep it. Lady Reinhart, if . . ."

Sloane cut in. "We're sure. For ourselves, we're planning to leave on the night of the attack."

Suddenly, Romaris swung his attention to his niece, concern creeping into his eyes. "Wait. If the attack is coming, why not leave sooner?"

"Kayser has people observing us," said Stefan. "The knights fear that if he sees us preparing to leave, he'll launch an attack. They're trying to prepare covertly, but that's only so practical. We're playing a game of chance of who attacks first—it's a toss-up: Kayser's men or the beast swarm."

Sloane whipped around to face Stefan, eyes wide with newfound concern. Stefan merely shrugged, as if the information was commonplace. Well, that certainly explained Gisele's sense of urgency.

Exhaling a defeated sigh, Romaris muttered, "Damn that man. I'd end him myself, if I could. Is this truly all just to kill Kayser?"

"And the corrupt officials, the compromised guards, Rowe's underworld organization, and other criminal elements," Sloane added.

"That makes up half the city!" the guildmaster exclaimed, the magnitude of the situation sinking in.

She gave him a moment to collect himself. The moment passed, and she knew it was time to go. They still had much to do. But there was one task he could do for her. Sloane pulled out a small, bound notebook from her satchel and stepped forward to place it in his hands.

"Please give this to the Farum siblings in Vilstaf. I trust you'll keep it confidential and ensure only they lay eyes on its contents," Sloane requested with a steady voice.

She was taking a chance on him, but she believed he wouldn't take advantage of her trust. He had too much to lose and everything to gain. Elodie was in House Reinhart.

The notebook contained everything she'd learned thus far about runes and enchantments along with information regarding the silden ink. It would allow Reanny and Mulinn to expand the business further and create even stronger items. Sloane needed their business to flourish. They were quite possibly the first truly magical goods–focused business in the world. If she was right in that assumption, that would net Sloane significant profits—funding that would support her search for Gwyn.

Romaris gave a slow nod. "Consider it done. We're partners after all," he affirmed, before his gaze softened, lingering on Elodie. "Promise me you'll look after my niece?"

Elodie blushed, a hint of irritation flashing across her face. "Uncle Lanthil, I'm more than capable of taking care of myself," she objected.

Sloane shared a knowing look with Elodie, then turned back to Romaris. "I promise," she reassured him.

Lanthil Romaris extended his hand, an offering of respect and trust. "Good luck, Lady Reinhart. May your ventures prove fruitful."

Sloane returned the gesture with a firm handshake and sincere smile. "Please, stay safe, Guildmaster Romaris. Fortify the town, even if it means seizing control until the royal army arrives."

He chuckled, a bitter edge undercutting his mirth. "I'll manage. Don't you worry about that." He turned his attention back to his niece. "Now, come here, Elodie."

Sloane stepped aside as Elodie and Romaris embraced, their hushed conversation barely audible. The room was steeped in a profound sense of understanding, acceptance, and parting. When Elodie finally pulled away and rejoined them, her eyes shimmered with unshed tears, reflecting the gravity of their farewell.

Sloane could only hope the warning would be enough.

There was very little time.

In the declining glow of the late afternoon, Sloane and Gisele strode up the stone-paved path to the imposing fort of the eastern garrison. As they neared the gate, a uniformed guard approached them, halting their progression.

Gisele was the first to break the silence as she spoke with urgency. "We require a meeting with Captain Jorin. He will know who we are."

The guard studied them for a moment, his gaze flitting between the two before he finally nodded. "Wait here." He turned on his heel and disappeared through a small side door nestled within the portcullis that led into the main body of the tower.

A few moments of tense silence passed before the door opened again, revealing a tall telv woman—Nemura. Her exasperated sigh at the sight of Sloane and Gisele echoed in the quiet courtyard. "Now what's the issue?"

Gisele barely gave Sloane a sideways glance before looking at Nemura. "We need to speak with Captain Jorin. It's both important and time-sensitive."

Skepticism flickered in Nemura's eyes as she examined them, but after a moment, she gestured for them to follow, turning to address the guards at the gate. "I'll handle this. You lot, stay at your posts."

"Yes, Senior Guardswoman!" one of the guards affirmed.

Nemura's response was an audible mutter, an inscrutable comment that sounded like "Nothing but lambs."

"Why do I feel like it's always something with you, Lady Reinhart?" Nemura quipped as they followed her through the fort's courtyard.

Sloane smiled. "I dunno, but I can just tell we're going to be the best of friends, Nemura."

The woman huffed but said nothing else.

They soon found themselves ascending the keep's stairway to the uppermost floor where an office lay. Inside, Captain Jorin was huddled over a map with two other guards. As Sloane drew closer, she could discern snippets of their hushed conversation about missing scouts.

Spotting their arrival, the moon elf captain held up his hand, effectively silencing his subordinates. "Yes, Senior Guardswoman Kho'lin?"

"Captain Jorin," Nemura began, her voice rigid with formality, "The terran and the Blightwych knight are here to speak with you. They claim it's 'important and time-sensitive.'"

Jorin simply nodded, subtly dismissing the other two with a terse order to investigate the missing scouts discreetly. As they departed, Nemura assumed a vigilant post by the door, her gaze alert and watchful.

"Lady Reinhart. Ser Gisele," Captain Jorin began, his gaze shifting between them. "To what do I owe the pleasure of this unexpected visit?"

Gisele took the lead. "You have less than a week before the city is attacked by the beast swarm. Further, and more important, is that any attempt to warn . . . anyone else will be met with lethal force by the Order of Secrets."

A sharp intake of breath echoed through the room as Jorin turned to Nemura, who seemed to be barely managing to suppress a string of curses. He returned his gaze to Sloane and Gisele, his eyes hardening with resolve.

"Alright," he finally said, "you've got my attention. How about we start at the beginning, yes?"

It seemed that no one wanted to piss off that order.

Sloane cast a brief glance at Gisele. "It all started when an agent of the Order of Secrets approached me . . ." she began.

The next week passed in a blur for Sloane, and the group was ready to leave at a moment's notice, as they expected the attack to happen soon. They had a plan, and unfortunately, it required the beast swarm to appear before they could enact it. Sloane would have preferred to simply leave days earlier, but she and the knights wouldn't leave the imprisoned woman behind.

In the meantime, Cristole was out with Ernald, gathering an order Elodie had arranged two days prior.

Captain Jorin was quietly positioning guards in key locations as a sort of quick reaction force. It surprised Sloane that the man had so readily accepted their information, as well as the warning to keep it quiet—although it was clear that he simply wanted to protect as many people as possible and knew subtlety would help with that.

The guilds had moved significant personnel over the past week, and the last of their people had left the night before. Only a few teams of Blades remained, which Stefan mentioned were there to assist Captain Jorin in return for his help in smuggling the guilds out of the city.

Sloane's thoughts were interrupted as her manatech falcon swooped ahead and down the staircase. Its gleaming form landed on an empty table. The inn's staff had grown used to the metallic bird's antics, but for patrons, it still seemed to stir an odd mix of fascination and occasional alarm.

Sloane had begun the week with two potential names for her steel-feathered friend. Now, with Ernald's assistance, she'd decided.

"Tiberius, is that where we're sitting?" she addressed the falcon, which cocked its head at her in response.

The bird let out an eerie screech.

"Yup, still have no idea what you're saying. There really needs to be a way to bridge the gap. You seem to understand what I'm saying, but I don't get anything back. Something for us to work on, I guess," Sloane mused. She dropped her pack beside her chair and seated herself at the table to which Tiberius had staked claim. The area was lightly populated, with only a few familiar faces from the inn scattered about.

Gisele's insistence on readiness had her fully outfitted, prepared for the unknown. They wouldn't get any notice when the beast swarm would hit, especially at such a late hour.

"Lady Reinhart."

The voice pulled Sloane from her thoughts, and she swiveled to find Stefan striding toward her. "Stefan."

He gestured at one of the free chairs. "May I?"

Tiberius let out a small chirp and hopped closer to Sloane.

"I guess he says it's okay," she said with a chuckle.

Tiberius turned its head, peering past Sloane. *"Wryyat."*

Sloane rose from her chair as Ismeld, with her usual stoic demeanor, appeared at the stairwell. Her sharp gaze skimmed over the room before landing on Sloane, standing somewhat awkwardly by the table, Stefan hovering in her wake.

"Sloane," Ismeld greeted, her eyes narrowing subtly at Stefan's presence. "Stefan."

"Ismeld! Please, join us," Sloane offered with a warm smile.

Ismeld seemed to consider before assenting with a brief nod, and they all sat.

"Any news?" Sloane asked, her voice dropping to a conspiratorial hush.

"Some. Captain Jorin doesn't have authority over the dispatched scouts. Still, he relayed that none have reported back. The count remains in obstinate denial," Ismeld revealed.

"The guilds' withdrawal has also meant a lack of intelligence. We're in the dark," Stefan supplemented.

Sloane released a heavy sigh, her fingers idly drumming on the tabletop. "I hate waiting for something horrible and potentially life-threatening to happen." Her gaze flicked toward the entrance across the spacious hall, just as the main doors were flung open and a large group of armed men barged in.

Stefan's eyes narrowed. "The count's men. Damn it, I lost that bet . . ."

"Shh!" Ismeld cut him off sharply.

Sloane slouched slightly in her seat, observing as the men confronted the woman at the front counter. They were too far to hear, but the sight of them, clad in armor, weapons and shields in hand, suggested they were expecting trouble and had thought of ways to mitigate her magic.

"Guys, this isn't good," she murmured urgently.

Ismeld was in her full armor, but Stefan wore only leather gear over chainmail that favored greater mobility. Ismeld's shield was inconveniently stashed away in the wagon, a mistake that Sloane now thought could come to haunt them.

The armed men raised their voices at the woman, and the innkeeper emerged, only to be quickly placed on the receiving end of their ire. The innkeeper cast a glance at Sloane's party, which unfortunately didn't go unnoticed by one of the guards.

"You!" the man yelled, brandishing his sword and pointing it directly at their table as he strode forward.

"Shit," Ismeld uttered under her breath. As all three rose from their seats, Ismeld swiftly drew her sword. "Stefan, alert the others upstairs. We are moving up our time frame."

"Understood," the raithe said and started toward the stairwell.

By then, the attention of the entire group of guards was fixated on them, several already hefting their shields and unsheathing their weapons. One guard, evidently the leader, shoved the innkeeper aside with little regard, sending him sprawling, before drawing his blade. "Stop right there! You are all under arrest by order of Count Kayser, the liege of Thirdghyll. You, raithe! Do not move. Everyone else needs to leave." He swept his gaze around the room. *"Now."*

Patrons hurriedly scurried off. Sloane noted several darting out the back door, while a couple dashed past Stefan up the stairs.

Repositioning herself slightly behind Ismeld, Sloane summoned several hovering [**Mana Bolts**] over her left hand. Her sword was a tempting option, but her magic would pack a bigger punch. Her amateurish swordsmanship wouldn't make a significant enough difference.

"Stefan, go. We can handle this. Sloane, stay back. Make full use of your magic," Ismeld instructed.

"Do not resist and you will be unharmed. Drop your weapon and cease your witchery!" the leading guard demanded.

Damn it, Bolton. I know it was you.

"It's not witchery!" she complained with exasperation.

Casting one final glance over his shoulder, Stefan sprinted toward the stairs.

"Damn it. You two, go get him!" The guard leader gestured to his men.

Keeping her [**Mana Bolts**] suspended over her left hand, Sloane channeled deeper, **[Focusing]** on drawing more mana into her right hand. A sense of strain was creeping up on her, but she understood the importance of her role. They couldn't afford to be taken by the guards.

There was too much at stake.

This is going to be rough.

CHAPTER TWENTY-NINE

TARGETED

S tefan darted toward the stairs to alert their companions above while Sloane and Ismeld moved to hold off the count's lackeys.

As the first pair of guards rushed to intercept Stefan, Sloane cast her [Flashbang] spell. A coruscating orb of light sprang from her hand, careening toward the two guards. The spell detonated with a brilliant burst, bathing the inn in blinding light and a thunderous roar, effectively halting the guards' pursuit as they cried out in surprise.

Tiberius screeched as he shot up toward the rafters with a strong flap of his wings.

Good, stay safe little buddy.

Brandishing her longsword, Ismeld barreled into the disoriented guards. The resonance of steel against steel filled the taproom as her sword clashed against their hastily drawn weapons.

"Watch for the witch's blinding magic! Shields up!" the group's leader bellowed, his command cutting through the pandemonium.

Heeding their leader's command, the rest of the guards hunkered down, their shields forming a formidable barrier.

Undeterred, Sloane released another [Flashbang] at the shielded phalanx. Though protected from the flash behind the row of shields, the guards still flinched with the spell's deafening boom.

Next, Sloane focused on her [Mana Bolts]. With a swift thrust of her hand, she launched one bolt after another at the guards.

One guard, his shield of simple wood, bore the brunt of her attack. The impact was cataclysmic, the shield splintering into a spray of wooden shrapnel. A strangled cry escaped the guard's lips he stumbled backward.

The other three guards held steel-reinforced shields, however, and weathered the barrage. Their shields vibrated under the force of impact, but remained firm. Yet Sloane could tell the blasts had taken their toll—the guards staggered back, their formation momentarily crumbling.

The taproom was now a battlefield, its peace shattered by the symphony of clashing swords and detonating spells. As the initial chaos subsided, Sloane assessed the situation. The guards were resilient, their defenses formidable. But they were still just men. Men who could tire, who could falter. She and Ismeld had held their ground thus far, but the real fight was just beginning.

Sloane took the chance to cast another **[Mana Bolt]**. Energy swirled and coalesced in her palm, forming into a pulsating orb of arcane power that launched forward at the unshielded guard, but another shoved him behind them and brought a shield up in time for protection, grunting at the force of the impact.

Ismeld, undeterred by the larger numbers, fought with a ferocity Sloane had come to admire. Her longsword was a whirlwind of lethal precision, dispatching one of the two guards she fought with swift, brutal efficiency.

But then she misstepped and stumbled. The man she was fighting used the distraction to bash her face with his shield. A spray of blood erupted from the blond high elf's nose and her head jerked backward, but even through that, she managed to dodge the swing of the man's sword.

As the man followed through with his swing, Ismeld spit blood in his face, making him flinch. She shoved him to create distance and then slashed her sword through his throat.

Another of the guards rushed at her, his shield up, his warhammer swinging in heavy arcs as he surged forward and sought to land a blow.

The sound of clashing metal echoed in Sloane's ears as she surveyed the chaotic fight. Her breaths came in shallow, rapid gasps, her chest heaving with the strain. The scent of sweat and blood hung heavy in the air.

But there was no time to linger on such thoughts; her sapphire-blue eyes narrowed, taking in the scene with a swift, practiced glance.

"Okay, Sloane," she muttered to herself, summoning a reservoir of mana to her palms. A vibrant, violet orb appeared, spinning in place like a miniature nebula. "Breathe."

She drew a deep breath, the cool air cutting through the acrid scent of battle. Sloane remembered her training with the knights, the rhythm of inhaling and exhaling, steady and certain. She assessed the room, her instincts guiding her focus to Ismeld, injured but still standing. Her friend.

She was a beacon in the storm, resolute and fierce. The sight of her was a balm to Sloane's frayed nerves, a flicker of hope amid the despair. "Hang in there, Ismeld," she tried to call out, but the words left her lips only as a fervent whisper.

With firm resolve, Sloane extended her hand, her fingers trembling slightly as she directed a [Mana Bolt] toward the unshielded man.

The orb whizzed through the air, hurtling toward its target with lethal precision. It collided with a jarring crunch and the man collapsed, this time for good.

But the feeling of triumph was fleeting. There were more guards, more enemies to deal with. Sloane looked over the room once more, her mind cataloging potential threats, analyzing vulnerabilities.

Which was when a guard advanced on Sloane, his eyes a mask of grim determination. Through it all, she clung to a singular thought, an echoing mantra in her mind.

I will protect Ismeld and the others. I will survive.

And with that thought fueling her own determination, Sloane launched herself into the fray, the violet glow of her magic painting the room in an eerie light. She was a mage in the heart of a storm, a radiant figure amid the tumult.

As her spell slammed into the guard's chest, a shower of mana illuminated the inn. He staggered, but continued his approach undaunted. Fear was a distant whisper, drowned out by the pulse of Sloane's heartbeat, the surge of her mana. She barely sidestepped a swing from his warhammer, the momentum of his missed strike carrying him forward.

We could win this. We have to.

She retaliated with a point-blank [Mana Bolt] that slammed into his throat, burning skin and armor alike. He collapsed to the ground, gasping and burned across his neck and face.

In the heat of the battle, Sloane found a strange sort of peace. She didn't even get a moment to spare as another guard charged her. Quickly, she flung a chair his way, hindering his advance for only a moment. But it gave her all the time she needed.

The doubts, the worries, the fears . . . they all faded away, replaced by a single, unwavering focus.

As he stumbled, Sloane cast a [Flashbang]. His shield rose in time to block the spell's blinding light, but as it fell to attack, she unleashed a second.

Today, she was a warrior, a protector.

The man was caught off guard, the explosion leaving him disoriented. Sensing an opportunity, Sloane rapidly fired a volley of [Mana Bolts] at him. The impacts jarred him and the successive blasts knocked him off his feet and onto the ground, where he stopped moving.

"Let's do this, Ismeld," Sloane whispered, her words drowned out by the clamor of the fight, but echoed within her heart.

They would fight, and they would survive. Together.

But then something in Sloane's peripheral vision alerted her to a new danger. One of the remaining guards held a crossbow and was leveling it at Ismeld.

When did he have time to load and cock that?! Instinctively, she sent a [**Mana Bolt**] hurtling his way.

But the guard leader was swift to intercept it with his shield. The force of the impact sent him reeling backward, and his helmeted head smacked into his own shield.

Sloane's eyes widened in panic and a warning cry caught in her throat as the other guard's hand squeezed the crossbow's lever.

Ismeld looked up and tried to twist and duck behind the man she was fighting but wasn't quick enough. The moon elf fired the bolt past the raithe and into Ismeld's armor, which deflected it downward at just the wrong angle. The bolt shattered and its head caught a gap in Ismeld's armor, slicing through her skin before it continued to the ground.

The knight looked at the wound and put her hand over the area instinctively, wincing in pain.

Capitalizing on her momentary distraction, the guard fighting her bashed her sword aside with his shield. He quickly followed it up with a powerful swing of his warhammer, striking her abdomen hard enough to lift her off her feet.

Ismeld's guttural grunt of pain reverberated through the room, her body folding over the impact.

Before anyone had a moment to respond, the guard flipped the hammer and drove the spiked end into her stomach. The stoic elf knight somehow managed to stay on her feet as they crashed back onto the ground. She staggered back, gasping for air, as she clutched at her stomach.

"Ismeld!" Sloane's cry echoed through the room. It was then that she knew she needed something more potent, more devastating. Her [**Mana Bolts**] were too slow and weak to do what needed doing. She needed a torrent of magical energy, a storm to bring down upon her enemies. She drew deeper on the mana through her core, pushing past the usual bounds of her magic, willing this new spell into existence.

And then, something *clicked* into place. She reached out toward the man before he could end Ismeld's life. Her outstretched hand pulsed with surging power.

"Havien, dodge!" the lead guard yelled out, his ability to gauge her actions damn near prescient at this point.

An [**Arcane Barrage**] erupted from her fingertips. A surge of energy swept across the room like a tidal wave, the crackling bolts of arcane magic darting toward their target with unerring precision and raining down on him. The air crackled with raw power as Sloane fought to protect Ismeld and turn the tide of the conflict.

The guard standing over Ismeld was taken by surprise. His eyes widened in alarm as he turned toward the source of the attack, but it was too late. The second and third bolts hit him in quick succession, their impact throwing him off balance. A hiss of steam erupted from the points of impact while the superheated steel of his armor glowed red and white.

Then the last two bolts of arcane energy, potent and raw, penetrated his weakened armor and seared into his flesh, silencing his screams of pain as he crashed onto the inn floor and the smell of burning flesh filled the room. The remaining two guards flinched.

But before Sloane could direct her magical onslaught toward anyone else, the guard leader lunged at her. The force of his collision sent her sprawling, her momentum halted by the hard floor. Scrambling up, her vision swam just as the guard's shield slammed into her face, catapulting her into a nearby table.

Without thinking, she reached backward and launched a [**Mana Bolt**], but the guard twisted aside and avoided it. She didn't get a chance to cast another before he was there.

His sword swooped down toward her and she rolled away, the edge of the blade barely missing her. She hit the ground, and immediately rolled away again as the guard tried to stomp on her.

Desperate, she cast a [**Flashbang**] as she tried to scramble backward. The explosion echoed around the room. The moon elf recoiled in surprise and shouted out in anger.

Through her blurry vision, Sloane saw the crossbowman training his weapon on her. She dove forward, narrowly avoiding a bolt as she tried to gain space between her and the guard leader. As it whizzed past her, she seized a piece of burning wood and hurled it as hard as she could across the taproom at the crossbowman, then grabbed another and flung it at the guard leader, who was once again advancing on her.

He swatted the flaming projectile away with his shield, undeterred. Spotting a fire poker within reach, Sloane snatched it up, using it to parry the captain's sword swing. Her grip on the poker weakened under the blow's impact, and the heavy iron tool spiraled out of her hands.

Without hesitating, she lifted her opposite hand and cast another [**Mana Bolt**]. The man tried to duck but the arcane spell blasted against his helmet in a crash of purple energy.

With a cry, he yanked off the charred helmet and tossed it aside, recoiling with pain from the burns on his face. In that moment, Sloane scrambled away, attempting to create distance from the man with a sword.

Sloane drew mana through her core as she kept moving away, building up a surge of power and arcane energy, then swung around in time to see the man striding toward her, his eyes full of venomous determination.

Her arm raised.

His shield followed.

She fired [**Mana Bolt**] after [**Mana Bolt**], and one after another, the bolts exploded against his shield in their arcane fury, each blast tearing at his sole defense more than the last. He managed to stop four bolts, but then something everyone had forgotten about cried out.

A piercing *"Wryaaat!"* echoed around the room. Sloane's concentration wavered.

Tiberius swooped down, dagger-like steel talons slashing at the guard captain's face. The man shrank back, his cries of surprise and pain muffled by the flapping of steel wings.

Seeing her opportunity, Sloane quickly pivoted toward the reloading crossbowman. Drawing upon her mana, she unleashed her newfound [**Arcane Barrage**]. A volley of five bolts of arcane fury streaked unerringly toward the man, burst against him, and sent him crashing to the ground.

As the man collapsed, Sloane's heart wrenched. "Ismeld!" she cried, her voice echoing in the now eerily quiet inn.

She rushed to her fallen comrade, the sight of the knight lying still with a steady stream of blood pooling from her abdomen sending cold dread through her. Her breath hitched as she fell to her knees beside Ismeld, her mind reeling.

She heard shouting and turned. The side door that led to the stables and wagons crashed open, and Gisele rushed in, sword drawn. Deryk was right behind her with a sword and shield, and Maud followed, her mace and shield at the ready.

The lead guard tried to get up from the floor, at the same time dragging his sword in an attempt to raise it. Gisele brought her massive *Zweihänder* down on the man's neck.

Sloane turned back to her friend. "Ismeld?"

The high elf was on her back, breathing erratically as she pressed on the hole in her breastplate with both hands, ineffectively trying to stop the blood from pooling under the armor.

"Maud, come here!" Sloane cried out.

Maud slid in next to Ismeld and gingerly looked over the puncture point. She winced, noticing the way the knight's breastplate was pushed into the wound.

Maud looked her fellow knight in the eye. "Ismeld, look at me. This is going to hurt. A lot. I need to take off your breastplate. Do you understand?"

Ismeld nodded jerkily, her eyes unfocused.

Maud glanced at Sloane. "Move to the other side and hold her as I undo her armor," she said. She glanced behind her. "Gisele! Get over here and pull this off her while I hold it away from the wound."

Sloane quickly shifted to Ismeld's right side and tried to hold her in place. She gripped her friend's hand in one of her own, and almost cried at the lack of strength the woman squeezed back with.

Maud undid the straps and clasps that kept the armor in place, counted to three, then slowly but deliberately pulled the breastplate away from the wound as Gisele rotated it away from Ismeld's torso.

As soon as the armor was away, Maud cut Ismeld's clothing to expose her stomach and the puncture wound. Sloane watched Maud place her hands over the wound and press firmly.

Ismeld cried out in pain, her back arching.

"Sloane, hold her!"

Sloane grasped Ismeld's shoulders and held her down, watching the telltale green glow of Maud's magic pushing into her.

Gisele and Deryk stood guard, coming over occasionally to check on them.

Even after the wound closed, Maud kept going, healing what Sloane figured were internal injuries. The process took far longer than Sloane would have suspected, and it was clearly draining the healer. Several times, she saw Maud jerk slightly as she strained to continue, but the look of determination to save her friend never left her.

A full bell later, when the healing was finally finished, Sloane saw the redhead wobble slightly. She opened her mouth to say something, but Gisele reached down and caught the healer before she fell over from exhaustion.

Ismeld had fallen asleep during the healing, and Sloane gingerly lowered the woman's head down onto a pack.

Gisele and Deryk had looted the bodies of the guards, and a pile of spoils lay next to the back door. The crossbow, especially, had been positioned almost gently, to ensure it wasn't damaged.

Sloane looked up at Gisele from where she sat next to Ismeld. "Where are Ernald and Cristole?"

Gisele shook her head. "I do not know. A group of guards attacked us as well in the back. We knew the count had us watched but we weren't expecting them to do anything tonight. We need to move up our timeline but—"

"I . . . I am ready to go," Maud said tiredly, yawning, as she slowly rolled onto her side and pushed herself up to a sitting position.

Deryk walked over to her, crouched, and put his hands on the telv's shoulders. "Easy. Be careful, you've exerted yourself a lot. First me, then Ismeld."

Sloane caught what the orkun said and quickly scanned him. There was a hole in his chainmail over his shoulder. "You got hit too!"

Deryk looked at her and nodded. "Crossbow. Close range. That's what took us so long. My injury was not nearly as bad as Ismeld's, though." He looked back down at the redhead. "Are you certain you can complete the mission?"

Maud sat up straighter and patted the hand on her shoulder. "I'm good. Just took a lot out of me. Ismeld's injury below the puncture was not good, it took time to fix everything. Those are more difficult."

"Sloane, you will take charge of your group now. Keep an eye on Ismeld—no matter what she says, the exhaustion alone may get to her. Get everyone to the East Gate," Gisele ordered. "We'll get Cristole and Ernald, then move to the estates to retrieve the terran."

"Wryaat." Tiberius flew down from the rafters and landed gently on Sloane's shoulder. She regarded the falcon with one eye. "Thank you for your help, little guy," she said, patting his head.

She looked back at the knight-captain. "We've got this. Do you think the other two were attacked?"

Gisele glanced at Ismeld, then Sloane. "Seeing as they attacked both of our groups, I think it is safe to assume they hit the men too. Don't worry. They will be alright."

"I hope so."

The orkun woman sighed. "We left equipment from the guards outside. It would be best if we took it along with us. Could you get the others to help load it into the wagons? Please."

Sloane nodded. Gisele thanked her and rejoined Deryk and Maud.

From the stairwell came the sound of footsteps, and Sloane turned to see Stefan first, holding out his sword, followed by Koren with two hammers, Rel with a large crossbow, and then Kemmy and Elodie, who were both carrying everyone's packs.

Stefan scanned the destruction around the room and whistled. "You two do not do half measures, do you?"

Sloane shook her head and walked over to the five members of her house. "We couldn't."

Elodie gasped at the sight of the still bloodied Ismeld propped up, sleeping. "Is she alright?" she asked Sloane.

Sloane nodded. "She is just resting now. Maud was able to heal her."

"That's good. We are going to need her if we're to make it to the East Gate as planned. The plan has already changed significantly, and we need to be ready for more things to go wrong," Stefan said.

"We will. That said, we need to prepare. Can you all please help me store the equipment piled by the door? There's also more outside. Keep your packs close to you, just in case something else happens. We're waiting on Gisele to make a decision about Cristole and Ernald," Sloane explained.

Stefan narrowed his eyes. "They're still not back yet?"

"No, and we're not sure where they are. Gisele and the others were attacked also, though."

"Then they were probably a target as well," Stefan said.

"That was our thought," she replied.

I just hope they're okay.

CHAPTER THIRTY

THE POLITE WAR

A gain!"

With a grunt of exertion, Gwyn lashed out at the wooden training dummy, her sword slicing through the air for what felt like the hundredth time. She pivoted on her heel, raising her blade just in time to parry the pole that swung toward her, thankfully slower than the first fifty million times her knight had already done it this session. Despite the slowed pace of the attack, the impact jolted her, causing her to grit her teeth.

He's so strong!

"Good. That is enough for today, Your Highness," Ser Theran announced, plucking a towel from a nearby rack and tossing it her way.

Catching the towel midair, Gwyn used it to mop the sweat from her face. She felt gross. They'd been at this all day, and her muscles ached from the rigorous training. And now, she had to switch gears to practice magic.

And what passes as deo for my B-O is horrible in this world.

"You managed to keep at it for an hour today, Princess. You are improving markedly. Tomorrow, we will start with a run around the training grounds."

Okay, maybe not s day.

She let out a theatrical groan, playing up the part of the beleaguered trainee. After all, it was only fitting that the student should act as if the work was grueling and overwhelming.

Showing him I enjoy it will just cause more work!

Her gaze swept over the training grounds that Theran had secured from the city guard. The space was expansive, roughly the size of a basketball court. It lacked stadium seating, but was lined with benches, tables, and equipment racks. Beyond that, walls and gates on all four sides led to different areas, primarily storage spaces for the guard that were strictly off-limits. Houses could rent the grounds for their people to work out or train large groups. Her house utilized it as a safe, private space to practice magic. The city boasted four such facilities near the different garrisons.

Theran's smirk caught her attention as she handed him the damp towel, a sheepish smile playing on her lips. "So, magic time?"

The knight chuckled, his eyes twinkling with amusement. "Magic time. Do you mind if I sit and observe? I am curious as to whether we can incorporate your magic into a fighting style for you."

Gwyn let out a genuine groan this time. "Of course you can watch, Theran."

"Ser Theran! You can sit with Lady Lorrena and me," Roz called out, her voice ringing clear across the training ground. "You are doing fantastic, Princess Gwyneth. Show us some magic!"

Turning to face her audience, Gwyn waved at Roslyn, who was proving to be the best hype girl she could have asked for. She took a moment to appreciate the elf girl's attire. Roslyn was clad in a black wool coat, buttoned up against the chill, and tall riding boots. Her red dress flowed down under her coat, and seemed made for movement, unlike the stiff things Gwyn was *forced* to wear. Black, silky gloves completed Roz's ensemble.

I like her outfit. Her gaze lingered on Roslyn's golden hair. *She's so pretty . . . she looks more like a princess than I do . . .*

Suppressing a sigh, Gwyn redirected her attention to Lorrena, who sat next to Roslyn. The girl was a bundle of timid excitement, her usual reticence momentarily forgotten. Gwyn wasn't sure what Lorrena's father had told her, but whatever it was, it kept the girl from doing anything she thought would make him scold her.

Probably a good thing Roslyn has been trying to include her.

The sound of the gate creaking open drew Gwyn's attention to an elf woman entering the training ground.

Theran chuckled. "And here is Professor Rolfe. I look forward to your practice, Your Highness." The knight joined the two girls and Roslyn's own knights, the one in red armor observing with a keen interest.

"Princess, good morning. Are you ready to begin?" Professor Rolfe asked as she approached.

"I am, Miss Rolfe."

"Fantastic," the woman replied, pulling out a small board and notebook. "What did you wish to work on today?"

Gwyn tapped a finger against her lips, mulling over her options. *Something new. Yeah.*

"I want to work on a few new spells. Since we have all this space, I may try and make something new."

"What do you mean by 'make something new'?" Miss Rolfe asked, her brow furrowing with curiosity.

"Well, every time I create a spell that's significantly different from my others, it seems to take on a new name and just *feels* different. My magic responds to it differently," Gwyn explained, struggling to put her experiences into words.

The elf professor paused, her gaze distant as she processed Gwyn's words.

Gwyn worried she had explained poorly. "I-I'm sorry. I don't really know how else to describe it."

"Your Highness, there is no need to apologize," Miss Rolfe reassured her. "I was just considering how best to assist you. Why don't we just get started? I'll ask questions as we go."

Gwyn nodded in agreement, and Professor Maya stepped back, leaving a safe distance. Gwyn took a moment to ensure everyone else was also far enough away. "Ready?" she called out.

"Ready, Your Highness! What is this one called?" Miss Rolfe responded, her voice carrying across the training ground.

Gwyn thought about what she wanted. Something *flashy*, something more potent than a single **[Fireball]**. An *eruption* of fire, but still narrow in focus. She drew on her magic, focusing on the center of the dirt training field. She felt the red magic swirl inside her, building up like an inferno waiting to be unleashed. She knew exactly what she wanted: a swirling red circle as wide as she was tall formed where she was aiming.

Wait, she asked what it was called. Err. [Focus], Gwyn . . .

"Pillar of Flame!" she shouted as she released the magic. She didn't need to yell the name of the spell to cast it, but she was trying both to maintain her focus and to tell the professor what she was doing.

From the red ring, fire flashed into existence, rushing to the center of the circle before erupting into a towering pillar of fire nearly five meters tall. The pillar held its form for a few heartbeats before collapsing into nothing, leaving behind a patch of blackened ground.

A rush of magic filled her, just like every other time she created a new spell. She felt stronger, more focused as the magic settled into her chest. A second rush expanded from her chest, causing her to gasp. It was a familiar sensation, but this time it felt slightly different, as if she had forged a stronger connection to her magic. She shook her head as a wave of dizziness washed over her.

Gwyn closed her eyes for a moment, only for darkness to close in around her vision as she opened them, narrowing until it enveloped her completely.

I found myself standing on a verdant plain, the scent of fresh grass mingling with the metallic tang of . . .

. . .

. . .steel. I looked up to see soldiers encircling me, their gazes fixed on the field ahead. Across the expanse, an enemy army seethed with rage, their shouts and roars echoing through the air. My eyes scanned the hostile forces, recognizing them as threats to my people.

My family.

Beside me stood a knight, resplendent in armor adorned with pauldrons in the shape of dragons.

With a nod, I drew upon my magic, feeling the familiar warmth of it surge through me. Dozens of **[Fireballs]** sprang to life around me, their fiery glow illuminating the battlefield. With a flick of my wrist, I sent them hurtling across the field, where they exploded amid the enemy ranks, sending bodies flying and filling the air with the acrid smell of burned flesh and singed armor.

As the enemy surged forward with a wave of fury and desperation, my soldiers responded in kind. Their unified roar echoed across the battlefield, a defiant challenge to the oncoming onslaught. They raised their shields in anticipation, forming a formidable wall of steel and determination.

I lifted my hands, summoning a magnificent bird of flame. It burst into existence with the brilliance of the sun, its fiery wings casting dancing shadows across the field. The avian creation of my own magic soared toward the enemy, its beak spewing jets of flame that incinerated all in its path. The battlefield was illuminated by its fiery glow, which cast long, flickering shadows. It dawned on me then that I was the center of this battle.

My soldiers were not there to engage the enemy directly; they existed to shield me, to protect me as I spearheaded the assault.

In an instant, the battlefield dissolved, replaced by a room swirling with misty magic. A massive tome floated before me, its pages inscribed with cryptic runes that danced and shifted before my eyes. My magic, a vibrant red mist, weaved through the air, transforming into fire as I explored new ways to manipulate and control it. The room was filled with the crackling sound of flames and the scent of burning parchment.

Blue magic misted and crystallized on the walls, frosting the towering bookshelves filled with tomes of all sizes and hues. The frost spread, forming a fortress around me like a bastion of knowledge and power. Black magic gathered overhead, a potent weapon held in reserve for my most desperate moments. It hung there, a dark cloud of potential, waiting for my command.

My gaze shifted to the side, catching sight of another color.

A color that seemed to shimmer and shift, as elusive as a mirage. I reached out to it, curiosity piqued.

. . .

It was . . .

. . .

* * *

Gwyn blinked back into awareness, her vision clearing as the remnants of the daydream faded. Roslyn's red knight was at her side, his hand steadying her arm. Theran mirrored him on her other side, his face etched with concern.

Miss Rolfe stood before her, lips moving in a silent question. Gwyn cocked her head, confusion clouding her features. "What?" she asked, her voice sounding distant to her own ears.

The professor's mouth moved again, but the words were lost in the silence.

"What?" Gwyn repeated, trying a bit louder as her brow furrowed in confusion.

Miss Rolfe's eyes widened, and Gwyn instinctively pulled her hand away from Evocati Khalan to rub at her ears. A sharp ringing filled her head, causing her to wince. She rubbed harder, and as the ringing subsided, the sounds of the world around her gradually returned.

She looked back up at the professor, then at the two knights. Roslyn, who was approaching quickly, wore a worried look on her face. Lorrena, who was a step behind her, seemed as if she were about to cry.

"Gwyn?" Roslyn's voice broke through the lingering silence, her tone laced with worry.

"I can hear you. I'm okay. Sorry guys, that was really weird," Gwyn said, chuckling in an attempt to downplay the strange episode.

Roslyn nearly tackled Gwyn, crushing her in a hug. "I am happy you are alright!"

Gwyn nodded, enjoying the hug but knew she needed to talk to everyone, so she gently squirmed out of Roslyn's death grip. "I'm good. Sorry, I just had, like, a really weird feeling after I made that new spell. Then I had a strange daydream that kind of felt like déjà vu."

Theran interjected, his concern still evident. "Your Highness, I think that may be enough for today. Let us get you back to the manor. Then we discuss what you felt more in-depth?"

Gwyn nodded, not wanting to cause further worry. "Okay. I'm fine to walk, though."

"Are you certain, Princess? No lingering effects? What did you see?" Evocati Khalan asked. His gaze was intense, as if he were searching for something profound in her response.

"Evocati, let us escort the princess back to the manor. You are welcome to join us as she explains," Theran suggested, his tone firm.

Gwyn shook her head. "If it's really important, can we just sit on the benches? I can explain what I saw, at least. I might forget it if we wait." She hoped this compromise would ease the tension between the two men.

Theran's gaze flickered between her and the other man before he sighed in resignation. "Over here, then." As they walked to the benches, Gwyn caught Theran muttering under his breath, "Taenya is going to kill me."

With Roslyn's help, Gwyn settled onto a bench. The elf girl clung to her arm, as if afraid Gwyn might suddenly collapse. Once seated, Gwyn began to recount her strange daydream. Khalan, armed with a piece of paper from Miss Rolfe, diligently noted down her words.

"Can you describe the men in the army you saw? 'The enemy' that you mentioned," Khalan asked, his quill poised over the paper.

Gwyn caught Theran's glance at the paladin. He tilted his head as if considering something.

She tried to recall the details of the dream. "No. I can't remember what they looked like, just that they were there. I . . . I remember how they burned, though."

"What about the knight who was beside you, what did his armor look like?" Theran asked, his gaze still thoughtful.

Gwyn smiled at the memory. "Kind of like Taenya's, but his armor had dragons on both of his shoulders. He wore a helmet that covered his face. His armor was exactly like I always imagined."

Theran asked her what she meant, and everyone sat quietly as she described the perfect knight armor.

Gwyn couldn't help but beam as Theran took her seriously and smiled.

"Can you remember the writing you saw in the tome that was floating?" Miss Rolfe asked next.

Gwyn shook her head. "No. Sorry, but I am sure I would recognize it if I saw it!"

The barrage of questions gradually subsided, and Gwyn shared a comforting hug with Roslyn that she didn't want to end, before she, Theran, and Miss Rolfe made their way back to the house. Khalan seemed to consider joining them, but after hearing Gwyn's account of her daydream, decided against it. As she left, she overheard him telling one of Roslyn's knights that he would need to report to the temple and the archpriestess before the day was up.

Gwyn wasn't sure what to make of that.

Taenya listened attentively as Theran recounted the day's events involving the princess. She had missed the initial conversation when the group returned to the house, but the more she heard, the more her concern deepened.

Gwyn's magic was growing stronger, and it was clearly affecting the young girl. Taenya had a theory about that. She suspected that magic was a resource that could be tapped into only so much before it began to have an impact on the user. It seemed it was time for her to have a candid conversation with Gwyn about this, perhaps sharing some of her own recent . . . experiences.

She'd been . . . practicing, after all.

As Theran described Gwyn's **[Pillar of Flame]** spell, Taenya couldn't help but envision the potential power the girl could wield in battle as she matured. But she also knew the devastating effect killing could have on a child as young as ten. Just because Gwyn was now eleven and her magic was stronger didn't mean she should be thrust into combat.

Eona willing, there won't be a need for her to fight again.

Theran was wrapping up his report when a commotion from the hallway caught their attention. Taenya turned to him, her eyebrows raised in question. "What's going on?"

The other knight shrugged in response but rose to his feet. "I don't know, but they are being loud, aren't they? I'll check."

As he approached the door, it swung open abruptly, narrowly missing his face. "Whoa!" he shouted, jumping back in surprise.

Taenya stood.

Ser Siveril stood in the doorway, looking surprised to see them. "Theran, Taenya. Where is Sabina? She needs to—"

"I am right here, Ser Siveril," a voice interjected from behind him.

Of course, she's already here. She likely felt the emotions.

Siveril pivoted to acknowledge the elf, a grave expression on his face. "Good. We have a pressing issue for the House," he declared, extracting a scroll from his pocket.

Unfurling the document, the majordomo began to read aloud. "By order of His Majesty, Crown Prince Kerrell, the Royal Academy of Avira shall have oversight of any citizens displaying or utilizing magical phenomena. All individuals must register with the Academy's Representative of Magical Affairs in each city for testing and safety. These representatives are so named and appointed . . ." His eyes darted back and forth as he skimmed the document, searching for a specific passage. "For the City of Strathmore and the Duchy of Tiloral, Marquess Torrell Angwin."

With a swift roll, Siveril secured the scroll, gripping it tightly in his hand before hurling it against the wall in frustration. "That conniving son of a—"

"Siveril," Taenya interrupted.

The man spun around to face her, a scowl etched deeply into his features.

She maintained her composure. "What does this mean? For us?"

Siveril inhaled deeply, his chest visibly rising and falling with the effort. "It means that Marquess Angwin is trying to force the princess under his control. This couldn't have happened without his hand in it."

Taenya glanced at the other two knights. Theran's face was a blank mask, and she suspected it would take Sabina to read his thoughts. That woman, on the other hand, was a frozen statue of barely restrained fury.

The order applies to all citizens. That includes her.

Taenya placed a comforting hand on Sabina's shoulder. "Sabina. Calm. We will figure this out. No one knows about your magic yet."

At her words, both Theran's and Siveril's heads snapped toward Sabina. "You can use magic?" the majordomo asked.

Sabina clenched her jaw, her eyes narrowing at Taenya before shifting to Siveril. "I can."

Taenya winced inwardly. *Shit. Sorry, my friend.*

Siveril exhaled a weary sigh, his hand absentmindedly rubbing his leg as he lapsed into thought. "Sabina . . . I'm aware of your nighttime activities. Has your magic been . . . useful in these?"

"It has," she admitted.

Siveril nodded in approval. "Good. I want you to gather all the information you can on Marquess Angwin. Do not get caught. Especially not while using magic."

Sabina's expression morphed into one of predatory anticipation. "They won't even see me."

"Theran, ready the guards for any potential attack on the house. This is the time to be vigilant for assassins in the night. The princess is not to go anywhere without at least four guards and one of you three accompanying her," Siveril instructed.

The elven knight saluted crisply. "I will see to it."

Siveril seemed to retreat into his thoughts, his gaze distant as if he were done with the matter.

Taenya narrowed her eyes. "What about me?"

Siveril turned his gaze to her, his eyes probing. "First, you and I will meet with the archpriestess. Then Angwin will learn the cost of making an enemy of House Reinhart."

Taenya arched an eyebrow. "The archpriestess? Why are we involving the Church?"

"I'm sure you've noticed the paladin who shadows Lady Roslyn. There's more to the young heiress's situation and the Church's involvement than you're aware of. And Her Highness is part of it. It's time we explore whether that connection can be used to our advantage," he elaborated.

Taenya understood what Siveril was hinting at. She was aware of the paladin assigned to protect the young ducal heiress and had heard whispers of the Seeing concerning the girl. The Church's assistance could indeed offer an unexpected advantage, but it could also prove to be a double-edged sword, especially if it became exploitative. The idea of Gwyn having a minder like Lady Roslyn didn't sit well with her.

Siveril seemed to pick up on her hesitation. "If this doesn't work, your blade is the next step, and one that is guaranteed if we have officially entered the Polite War."

That brought a smile to Taenya's face. "My sword will be ready."

Siveril's smirk was positively sinister. "Good. It will be stained with blood before we're through."

CHAPTER THIRTY-ONE

CHURCH OF THE CELESTIALS

The Seat, the spiritual epicenter of the Celestial Church, was established by the Thirteenth Archpriest, Othorion the Unifier. This was a result of the Valen Compromise, a pivotal decision to relocate the Seat of the Church to its own city on Ikios, thereby centralizing its religious authority after the Loreni diaspora.

Othorion's instrumental role in this unification of lands and peoples under the Celestial Pantheon and a single religious institution led to his posthumous apotheosis as the first Empyrean, marking him as a member of the pantheon hierarchy below the minor gods but above the Astria.

The city itself was renamed Empyrea City following the apotheosis of Archpriestess Sorisana the Teacher, the tenth individual to achieve such divine status. Following Sorisana's ascendance, each subsequent Empyrean has been honored within the city with dedicated libraries and statues. These monuments line the pathway to the Holy Residence, serving as a memory to their holy contributions. This renaming further underscored the city's central role in the veneration of these divine figures.

Chronicles of the Church, 302 PD

T hey exited the carriage near the entrance of the gates to what appeared to be a massive plaza beyond. Gwyn trailed behind Siveril and Taenya while her guards fell into step behind her. On her right, Roslyn's knight Ser Roderick gallantly held the door open for Roslyn to alight from her own carriage.

Her friend waved and approached her, taking on a more formal tone now that they were in public. "Are you nervous, Your Highness?" she inquired.

Gwyn shook her head gently. "No, Lady Roslyn, not really. Maybe? Only a little bit," she confessed, her words trailing off into a nervous chuckle.

I was more nervous meeting you.

Roslyn's paladin was waiting for them as they stepped out. Gwyn couldn't believe it had taken so long for someone to finally tell her he was not, actually, a knight. *To be fair, he has armor and red* is *one of the colors for House Tiloral.*

Evocati Khalan stood with a professional air, his soft smile barely visible. "Your Highness, My Lady. Welcome to Empyrea City and the temple complex," he said. "Her Holiness is expecting you."

Gwyn echoed Roslyn's polite greetings, her attention drawn to the surroundings. The area was densely built, reminding her of the older parts of Italian cities she had visited.

What stood out to her, *literally*, was the massive tree peeking over the building in front of her. It looked like a weeping willow, but as tall as the trees she remembered seeing in California.

What was the name again?

She shrugged off the thought and continued to take in the sights. Large buildings adorned with columns and draped in vines and plants filled her view. The area was filled with people of all types, yet they seemed to consciously steer clear of their group, or more likely, the paladin accompanying them. Gwyn had initially overlooked the deference people showed toward paladins, but now it was glaringly apparent.

The crowd was reminiscent of popular tourist destinations she had visited, like the Louvre or the Roman Forum.

They walked into the main plaza and Gwyn remembered exactly why everything looked familiar. She paused, her gaze sweeping over the picturesque scene.

The group halted, and Roslyn turned to her. "Princess?"

Tears welled up in Gwyn's eyes. *I-It's . . .* "It looks almost exactly like home," she whispered.

Roslyn gently squeezed Gwyn's hand, her eyes wide with curiosity. "Your home has a place like this?"

Gwyn hastily brushed away a tear, her gaze still locked on the familiar yet alien vista. "A place back home that I went to with my mom. Saint Peter's Square in Rome. This looks bigger, and—" She chuckled, pointing at the towering tree that stood where an obelisk would have been back home. "That is different. Ours has a big stone obelisk from a really old kingdom called Egypt. That tree is *much* bigger. The big pool around it is different too. But the columns, the layout . . . it's eerily similar."

She stood there and just let the nostalgic feeling fill her up. It was so similar, but also so different. The absence of humans, the pervasive greenery, and the sheer *size* of everything.

"Evocati Khalan?" she ventured, turning to the paladin.

He inclined his head slightly. "Yes, Your Highness?"

"Why is everything so . . . *big?*" She gestured broadly at the sprawling cityscape. "It can't all be in use, can it?"

A chuckle rumbled from Khalan as he took in Gwyn's awestruck expression. "It is. Empyrea City is an independent entity within the Duchy of Tiloral or even the Kingdom of Avira. It is the spiritual heart of our faith, and the main temple complex of the Church, housing the Grand Temple of the Celestials, the only location with a dedicated temple for each member of the Celestial Family in one city. Additionally, we have the Temple of the Stars"—he pointed at a large domed structure nestled amid lush gardens behind them—"and numerous other temples dedicated to specific minor gods."

Gwyn turned and looked back, seeing a large domed temple near a bunch of gardens. She almost laughed. Right there was another near copy of a building from Rome, the Pantheon, only pristine white. *This can't be real. Why is it so similar?*

Khalan continued, indicating a formidable fortress perched on a distant hill. "That is Dawn's Redoubt, a fortress that serves as the Holy City's primary defensive military contingent. It's also a significant stronghold for the Paladins of Alos."

He swept his arm to encompass the surrounding buildings. "Beyond the religious structures, Empyrea City is also the administrative heart of the Celestial Church, housing the bureaucratic apparatus and branches of each of the main Holy Orders. It's a bustling hub, attracting countless devotees and pilgrims from across Ikios and Loren. And of course, all these people need places to live. The city's walls enclose not just temples and administrative buildings, but a vast array of residences. It's a city within a city, a unique fusion of the sacred and the mundane."

As Khalan concluded his explanation, Gwyn found herself simply standing there, drinking in the view. Lost in her thoughts, she barely noticed when Taenya leaned in, breaking her reverie with a gentle question. "Are you ready, Gwyn?"

Gwyn nodded, tearing her gaze away from everything. "Yes. Please lead the way, Evocati."

The group began to move again, following a path that skirted the pool where the colossal willow tree stood. Roslyn leaned in, her voice a soft whisper. "This is the Tree of Life. It's said that Eona herself planted and nurtured it. That's why it's so massive. No other tree of this type ever grows this large. The entire city was built *around* it."

Gwyn's eyes widened in awe. "That is so cool." As they rounded the pool and the tree, another structure caught her eye. "*That* is different too."

Khalan's smile was warm. "*That* is the Grand Temple of the Celestials."

Dominating the rear of the plaza, a monumental edifice of white stone rose, its four columns nearly as wide as the tree they had just passed.

Roslyn chimed in, her voice filled with reverence. "Each column represents one of the four domains of the Family: night, day, life, and death." She pointed out each one, and the enormous door nestled between the columns dedicated to Day and Life. "That is the Door of the Celestials. It will remain locked until Alos himself comes to open it, ushering in a new age."

As they walked, Roslyn launched into a detailed account of the temple and its history, her enthusiasm infectious. Gwyn found herself captivated, not just by the stories, but by Roslyn herself. The way her eyes lit up as she shared each fact, the way her hands moved to emphasize her words, the way her lips curved into a smile and her eyes crinkled when she thought of something particularly interesting.

Roslyn smiled and tipped her head down to cover her mouth as she giggled about a fact she found amusing. Caught up in the moment, Gwyn chuckled along and reached out to sweep a stray strand of hair behind Roslyn's ear.

Gwyn nearly tripped but caught herself at the last second. "Oh. Sorry." She could feel her cheeks heating up. *I-I didn't mean to do that.*

Roslyn looked up at her, her fingertips touching where the strand had been, before straightening her back and lacing her hands together. She smiled, but her eyes didn't crinkle like when she was happy. "It is perfectly fine. Thank you, Your Highness," she said, returning to her serious public self.

Oh. Gwyn felt a lump in her throat. *I shouldn't have done that.* She sighed and stared ahead, following the group as they made their way through the crowd and then some doors into the temple itself. Gwyn focused on following the paladin, ignoring the sights around her. Nothing that would distract Roslyn. She didn't want to mess up again. She struggled to hold back her tears. *I am eleven now. No crying. That's for kids.*

Roslyn could feel the tension radiating from Gwyn, and she knew she was the cause. She did not mean to, but she had just frozen when Gwyn moved the hair out of her face.

I let myself get too informal in public.

The fault was hers, not Gwyn's. The princess was unfamiliar with the political intricacies of their world. It fell upon Roslyn to be her unwavering beacon, just like a guiding lighthouse in a raging storm. She promised herself that she would explain it to Gwyn later.

They moved through the familiar corridors of the temple, heading toward the private wing of the main administrative area. The halls were quieter than the last time she had been here, with fewer paladins patrolling the area. She remembered her own visit, when Evocati Khalan had been personally assigned by the archpriestess to protect her.

As they walked, Roslyn found her gaze drifting toward Gwyn. Ser Taenya, too, seemed to be stealing glances at the young princess. Gwyn, however, remained silent, her gaze fixed straight ahead as she followed Khalan and Ser Siveril. *She's really upset*, Roslyn thought, a pang of guilt settling in her chest. *I hope she isn't mad at me.*

Soon, they reached the staircase leading up to the hill where the archpriestess resided. As they ascended, Roslyn leaned in closer to Gwyn. "The building up here is called the inner sanctum. It's where the archpriestess lives and works. It's beautiful," she whispered.

Gwyn merely nodded, her gaze still fixed ahead. But Roslyn noticed the slight hitch in her breath before it steadied again. *Oh no*, she thought, a sinking feeling in her stomach. *I really messed up, didn't I?* Her first friend, and she'd already messed everything up for herself.

She forced herself to remain composed; after all, it was expected of the heir. She couldn't be seen as weak. On the verge of tears that would shame her, Roslyn whispered a silent prayer for help to Eona or whoever else would listen.

Don't let her hate me.

I'm in the most holy place possible. They'll listen. I hope.

The building on top of the hill was indeed beautiful: white and red with green vines and plants surrounding it, and gold accents and trim everywhere. It was almost a palace all by itself. Such a massive place for a single person. *I would be so bored all of the time.* Gwyn couldn't imagine having a home so large just for herself.

She also couldn't figure out what was going on with Roslyn. The girl's behavior was puzzling. *Is she mad? Is she not?*

She couldn't focus on it now. The group moved into the building after a pair of paladins opened the door and let them in. Her guards were required to stay outside, which they did without question or word. That left her with Siveril and Taenya from her house and Roslyn with her two knights, along with Evocati Khalan.

Gwyn still wasn't exactly sure of his connection to Roslyn, but she knew that it was important. He seemed to listen to her, but rarely ever left her side. The only times she could recall him doing so had to do with herself somehow.

Inside the building were more paladins. These were holding big polearms with large, curved blades under a sharp point. Their armor was the same red tint with gold trim that the rest had, along with the white tabard with a golden sun on it that they had as an emblem. She remembered that Evocati Khalan had called his people the Paladins of Alos. They looked really neat, Gwyn thought, but Taenya looked a hundred times cooler in her dragon armor.

Her gaze shifted to Roslyn's knights, a pang of sympathy tugging at her heart.

They were professional and well-dressed, but they lacked *cool* factor that was definitely the most important part of being a knight.

Looking at armor is the perfect distraction.

One of the paladins stepped forward and bowed before speaking with Khalan. Then he stepped back next to the door that was ahead of them.

Khalan then turned to them, his voice echoing in the grand hall. "Her Holiness wishes to see Her Highness alone first."

Gwyn recoiled in surprise. "Without Ser Siveril and Taenya?"

Khalan nodded. "Yes."

Taenya's eyes narrowed. "But, we have pressing—"

"That can be done after Her Holiness speaks with your charge, Ser Taenya," Khalan interrupted. "The archpriestess has spoken. Please, wait with me over here."

Siveril looked taken aback. "You are not entering either?"

Khalan shook his head. "This conversation is for them alone." He turned to Gwyn. "Please, Your Highness. She is waiting for you."

Gwyn nodded, placing a comforting hand on Taenya's arm. "It's okay. We'll all talk to her after. I'll tell her how important it is."

Taenya offered a small smile, bowing her head in acquiescence. "Very well. We will remain out here, Your Highness."

Taking a deep breath, Gwyn approached the grand doors. As she neared, the guards swung them open just in time, allowing her to step into the unknown.

The doors closed with a resonant thud, causing Gwyn to startle slightly. She found herself in a cozy room, a warm fire crackling in the hearth. An elderly sun elf woman sat in a plush chair by the fireplace, sipping tea from a delicate cup. The woman didn't even turn to look, her attention seemingly absorbed by the dancing flames.

"Well? Are you going to sit, dear?" The woman's voice was soft, yet carried an undeniable authority.

Caught off guard, Gwyn stammered a quick, "Oh . . . uh, sure," and moved to occupy the chair opposite the woman.

The elf glanced at her, a small smirk playing on her lips as she set down her cup. "Would you like some tea?"

Gwyn hesitated. She wasn't particularly thirsty, but she didn't want to offend the woman either. *Can I say no? Would that be rude?*

A chuckle from the woman interrupted her internal debate. "Typically, in these situations, you would accept the tea, even if you do not want it. However, that often leads to waste, as those who do not want it simply take small sips until the conversation is over, leaving the rest untouched."

"That is good to know. Thank you."

The elf winked conspiratorially. "We can keep it our secret if you do not wish to drink any. Here, we will just do . . . this." She poured a minuscule amount of tea into Gwyn's cup, swirling it around to give the illusion of a partially consumed beverage.

Gwyn smiled, grateful for the woman's understanding. "Thank you. I'm just not really thirsty right now, to be honest." She sighed, feeling a bit more at ease.

"We do have a plethora of confusing rules, don't we?" The woman's tone was light, almost teasing.

"There are so many!" Gwyn agreed, her tension easing further.

The woman laughed, a warm, genuine sound. "Indeed, there are. Now, I suspect you're quite curious as to why I asked to meet with you alone."

Gwyn nodded. She couldn't help but feel a little nervous. Siveril and Taenya had emphasized the importance of this woman, not just in Avira, but in the entire world.

"Perhaps we should introduce ourselves first? I am Vania, Archpriestess of the Church of the Celestials. I have heard much about you, young Princess Gwyneth of House Reinhart."

"You have?"

The archpriestess's eyes twinkled as she smiled. Her graying hair was neatly arranged in a bun. Gwyn found herself studying the woman's headpiece, a radiant sunburst of gold, adorned with painted flowers and verdant sprigs. Yellow gems sparkled at the tips of the sun's rays, while black ones embellished the base.

"Indeed, Your Highness. It seems you've found yourself in a bit of a predicament. I believe I may be able to help. Has Lady Roslyn explained why she has a paladin for protection?" Vania inquired.

Gwyn furrowed her brow, trying to recall the details of Roslyn's explanations. The reason for Evocati Khalan's presence had never been discussed. "No, Archpriestess. She hasn't."

The head of the religion for the entire world smiled. "You see, your magic is quite amazing. Yet, it isn't entirely unique," she revealed, causing Gwyn's eyes to widen in surprise.

Archpriestess Vania continued, "The Church has members who have shown abilities as well. Fortunately, as members of the Church, they do not have to—and *will not*—abide by the order of the crown prince. One of these members, a Priestess of Eona, was blessed with a Seeing. Unlike its cousin, the Prophecy, a Seeing is just that: a vision of an important event. In this case, it was a series of flashes involving two young women. The events themselves were unclear, but one of the women was unmistakably Lady Roslyn, albeit older. The other, Evocati Khalan believes, could be you."

Gwyn gasped. "Me?"

The archpriestess nodded. "It's not certain. We've described you to the priestess, but she remains unsure. Your ability to conjure fire certainly suggests it could be you. However, recently, a Priest of Alos was also able to manipulate fire to an extent. His ability was not even close to what you could accomplish, but it does mean that you are not unique in capability, just in *capacity*.

"Now, on to your current predicament. The Church remains neutral in the affairs of nations. However, as the potential subject of a Seeing, your magic use is of interest to the Church. I can assign a paladin to your protection as well. This would cause political issues for you. As a foreign princess, aligning yourself with the Church would actually push you further away from any influence you may have in Aviran politics. I would also caution against seeking the duke's assistance. The order came from the Crown, and the duke's support could jeopardize his own position."

Gwyn closed her eyes and dug her fingers into the armrests of her chair. This was the exact reason Siveril and Taenya had sought the Church's help—to prevent the marquess from gaining control over her. "So, we came here for nothing?" she asked, her voice barely a whisper.

Vania reached out and gently laid her hand atop Gwyn's. "Not for nothing, dear. I offer a final recourse. If all else fails, you can rely on us, as Alos would wish. But remember, there are consequences that you, as an outsider, would face. It's a reality your knights might overlook, as *they* don't see you as an outsider."

Gwyn exhaled a heavy sigh. "I don't think this is going to end well."

Vania patted Gwyn's hand before rising from her seat. "These matters seldom do. If you find that your house cannot resolve this independently, send one of your knights to me. Perhaps the one who guards you from the darkness," she suggested, her eyes twinkling. "Just remind her that Alos casts a great shadow, and she need not stray too far from the light to find it."

Gwyn nodded silently, standing up. She needed to talk to Sabina, especially if the Church was aware of her magic.

It's time Sabina and I talked about it. She seems almost scared to .

"Remember, I'll have a paladin on standby. You needn't summon her if you don't wish to, but I pray you will before things spiral out of your control."

"Thank you, Archpriestess."

"You are most welcome, young princess."

Gwyn walked out of the office and a paladin stepped forward, taking off their helmet as they did, revealing a beautiful sun elf woman underneath. Her hair was shaved at the sides, and she had tight, dark curls atop her head. Her eyes were a fiery orange, and a scar traced a path from under her nose, through her lip, and almost to her chin. The woman leaned in, her voice a whisper meant only for Gwyn. "I am Evocati Amari. I will be here, should you need protection, Your Highness."

"Thank you."

The woman nodded once before turning and walking away. At that moment, Siveril and Taenya stepped forward.

"Your Highness, is everything alright?" Taenya asked.

Gwyn glanced at Roslyn, offering her friend a smile that broadened when it was returned. She shook her head. "Not really, but let's go home. We will have to figure this out on our own."

Siveril exchanged a glance with Taenya, who met his gaze and nodded. Siveril leaned in. "Don't worry, Your Highness. Taenya and I will handle this," he assured her.

One look at Taenya and Gwyn was certain of one thing: whatever was to come next, the marquess was not going to like the outcome.

CHAPTER THIRTY-TWO

DARK NECESSITIES

The chill of the night bit into Sabina as autumn steadily relinquished its hold to the impending winter. She remained a shadow, unnoticed, as the woman she trailed slipped into a rowhouse nestled on a corner adjacent to a small park.

Two solitary trees, a row of shrubs, and a lone bench. Some noble probably patted themselves on the back for this "contribution."

Sabina moved with the stealth of a whisper, trailing the woman as she entered her mother's home. The mother was conveniently absent, visiting a relative. Drawing on the magic coursing within her, Sabina attempted to [**Detect Emotions**] within her range.

<<*Contentment*>>
<<*Happiness, Love*>>
<<*Anger*>>
<<*Lust, Disgust*>>
<<*Peace.*>>

The emotional signatures served as a map, indicating the locations and proximity of those around. It had taken her considerable effort to erect a barrier between her own emotions and those she sensed from others. Initially, their emotions had bled into hers—their <<*Rage*>> had ignited her own, their <<*Sadness*>>, like Gwyn's, had become hers.

No longer. Her mind and thoughts were her own. Protected within her [**Mental Fortress**].

But tonight—tonight was the culmination of all of her work, all her practice with her magic. She was determined to protect Gwyn and prove to Taenya she could use her magic in service of the princess, and not for evil.

House Reinhart needed evidence of the marquess's machinations. She would gather it. Along with a means to thwart his interference with the princess.

He can harm her over my dead body.

She inhaled deeply, her senses alert. She felt a presence—two presences—approaching.

Sabina's gaze flicked to the side as two city guards rounded the corner, their boots echoing on the cobblestone street. She delved into their minds, applying **[Alter Perception]**. It was a subtle nudge, not the overt mind control Taenya had cautioned her against. She simply rendered herself invisible to their senses.

The magic surged within her, a demanding tide that strained her control. She gritted her teeth, sweat beading on her forehead from the exertion. The magic was draining, but being discovered at this stage was not an option. She maintained the illusion, sidestepping as the guards strolled past, oblivious to her presence. Only when they had crossed the street and disappeared into an alleyway did she release her hold on the spell. Sabina exhaled sharply through her nose, then inhaled slowly through her mouth to steady herself, allowing the magic within her to settle.

I'll need to do that a lot more tonight. But being invisible is always more difficult than not.

After a moment to regather her composure, she approached the door. Drawing on her magic once more, she took a deep breath and knocked. It didn't take long for her to sense a presence approaching. <<*Confusion*>> and a hint of <<*Irritation*>> washed over her.

The woman was confused wondering who could be visiting at this hour, and irritated that someone would be coming so late. A faint undercurrent of <<*Fear*>> stirred within her, a spark of <<*Worry*>> for a loved one. While the woman's emotions were an open book, her surface thoughts remained surprisingly guarded. Sabina extended her *presence* and mental reach to **[Hear Thoughts]**.

Did something happen to mother? Think. Who else could it be this late? I swear if it is those Jenkins boys again . . .

Sabina took a small step back, releasing her magic just as the door creaked open. A twenty-seven-year-old high elf woman, personal attendant to Marquess Angwin, stood in the doorway. The sight of her blue eyes and black hair brought a smile to Sabina's face.

Marinella.

The woman's <<*Confusion*>> deepened as she failed to recognize Sabina. *Good.*

"Miss Marinella?" Sabina began.

"Yes? May I help you?"

"Are you the daughter of a . . ." Sabina feigned a pause, as if searching her memory. "Velma?"

Marinella's eyes widened, and a surge of <<Panic>> rippled through her. "Yes, I am. What's happened? Is something wrong?"

"Miss, could we perhaps discuss this inside? I believe this would be best—"

"No, tell me what's happened!"

"Miss Marinella. Please. Let's move this conversation indoors before we draw unnecessary attention."

Sabina delved into Marinella's mind once more, channeling her magic to [Conjure Hallucinations]. Marinella glanced around, her eyes catching sight of several onlookers who weren't actually there. She quickly turned back to Sabina. "Yes, yes. Come in. Nosy neighbors, even at this time."

A smirk played on Sabina's lips as she followed Marinella inside.

Step one complete.

Now, all she needed to do was to [Pull Memories] and make her exit.

Marinella will [Sleep] it off, and be none the wiser tomorrow.

Sabina approached the gate of the Angwin estate in Marinella's clothes, her hair styled just like the attendant's, her face clean of facial paint. The lone guard at the gate was Rikard, precisely the telv she had hoped to encounter.

She let her magic surge, pulling from the swirling darkness within her. Rikard squinted in the dim light, the only illumination coming from a solitary torch mounted on the wall beside him. Sabina probed his feeble mind, then focused her magic on herself, using [Alter Perception] to make her appear and sound like Marinella to his senses.

With a friendly smile, she waved. "Sorry, Rikard! I'm back. I need to finish up for Lord Angwin."

"Marinella? Wha . . . I thought you had to watch your mother's home tonight?"

Sabina used [Pull Memories] and recalled what the woman had done on her way home. "I checked it out, and the house is fine. You know how it is. Lord Angwin always has something else that needs doing. In my rush to leave, I nearly forgot that he wanted me to return," she explained.

Rikard sighed. "Tell me about it. Ever since that new order, the lord had Ser Moreno extend our shifts. I'm nearly at my thirteenth bell now."

Sabina feigned shock. "That's awful. You must be exhausted, Rikky," she said, using the nickname from the [Pull Memories] spell.

The telv nodded. "I am, but I should be relieved in two more bells."

"Two bells? You are liable to fall over by then."

He chuckled. "I hope not. Otherwise, I'd be liable to be lashed!"

She covered her mouth and offered a polite giggle. "Well, I shouldn't keep the lord waiting. Stay strong and warm! It's getting quite chilly out!"

They exchanged farewells as Rikard opened the gate and allowed Sabina passage. As she moved away and heard the gate close behind her, she drew a deep breath.

So far so good.

Her mental illusion held up to more scrutiny as she made her way through the servants' entrance and into the estate itself. There were only two bells to get it done. She would need to hurry.

She smirked. *There's step two.*

Sabina navigated the estate's corridors, her magical presence permeating the halls as she maintained her **[Alter Perception]** spell, passing unnoticed by the few late-night servants she encountered.

The tapestries looked downright eerie in the dimly lit halls. She probed each room with her senses, using **[Detect Emotions]** to confirm their vacancy before daring to peek inside. She discovered various sitting areas, a guest room, and storage spaces.

The final room Sabina approached was not empty—she felt a slew of emotions from two people inside. The wide range of <<*Indifference, Love, Dissatisfaction, Impatience, Lust*>>, however, left her puzzled.

Maintaining her **[Alter Perception]** spell, she knocked softly. The rustling inside prompted her to focus her magical senses on the room's occupants. She felt a sudden surge of <<*Surprise, Panic*>> followed by <<*Fear, Distress*>>.

Sabina concentrated so that she could **[Hear Thoughts]**, trying to ascertain what was occurring inside, as she was unable to physically hear anything other than muffled sounds through the door.

Oh gods, I knew I shouldn't have done this! If we're caught . . .

Shit. Shit shit shit. Where are my pants? Oh. There.

Sabina's eyes widened in surprise as the emotions she had sensed suddenly made sense.

I'll . . . give them some privacy.

She shook her head, a hint of amusement playing on her lips as she moved toward the stairwell, opening and closing the door behind her before the receding presences finally exited from their rendezvous.

She felt several presences in the hallway as she made it to the second floor, straightening Marinella's dress and pulling in her *presence* to make the effect stronger.

Taking a deep breath, she stepped confidently into the hallway. She quickly scanned the area, taking in the two guards, the marquess's majordomo, and Lord Angwin himself. A wave of displeasure washed over her, but she kept her expression neutral.

The majordomo, Ser Wentham, was the first to notice her. His brow rose in surprise as he assessed her. Lord Angwin, however, seemed unfazed by her unexpected presence.

"Ah, Marinella. I thought you had other business to conduct this night," he remarked.

Sabina channeled more magic into her [**Alter Perception**] spell. She stepped forward, performing a deep curtsey, as she had seen in Marinella's memories. Rising, she kept her gaze lowered, a sign of deference, before responding, "I completed them earlier than expected, Your Lordship. I wished to return in case you had any other duties for me."

The majordomo gave her an appraising look, then turned back to the marquess. "My Lord, do you still wish to respond tonight?"

Maintaining her demure posture, Sabina silently probed the minds of the two men with her [**Hear Thoughts**] spell, focusing first on the marquess.

—*when the prince sends his forces. I can finally strike a blow against the Tilorals and raise my house by having that princess under my thumb. That is, if that cursed royal doesn't take her for his own plans . . . I just have to ensure that doesn't happen.*

Sabina shifted her perception to the majordomo, delving into his thoughts.

—*Telford. If that fool was not so incompetent with what the marquess demanded of him, we wouldn't be expected to focus on the princess while we are trying to usurp the Tilorals at the same time. Hopefully, Telford's son can redeem their shame.*

So they're not just going after Gwyn, and Telford is working for the marquess.

"Yes, we should," the marquess agreed, turning his gaze to Sabina. "Marinella, come. You will write for me."

"As you wish, My Lord," Sabina responded, following the two men into the expansive office. She moved swiftly to the small scribe's desk, using Marinella's memories to select the appropriate stationery for a letter to the crown prince.

Angwin and Wentham conversed in hushed tones, a wave of <<*Irritation*>> radiating from the noble, while a sense of <<*Resignation*>> seeped from the majordomo. Eventually, the marquess heaved a dramatic sigh, and Sabina poised her quill, ready to transcribe.

I just need to write whatever he wants and then take this with me after obtaining his seal.

"Marinella, address the letter to the crown prince," the marquess instructed.

Sabina nodded and addressed the letter to Crown Prince Kerrell, with all of his appropriate titles. When she was done, she simply raised the quill, and Angwin continued.

"Your Royal Highness, I am deeply honored by your appointment of myself and House Angwin as the Representative for Magical Affairs within the Duchy of Tiloral. I pledge to uphold the responsibilities of the office . . ."

Sabina diligently recorded the marquess's grandiose claims and self-praise.

After enduring nearly a quarter-bell of his self-aggrandizement, he finally broached the topic that directly impacted House Reinhart.

"My first act in this position shall be to provide necessary oversight of the terran princess, as we previously discussed. As representative of your hand, House Angwin will proceed to seize all assets of House Reinhart and assume guardianship over the minor."

Sabina held her quill in suspension as the two men deliberated over the letter's content and the next course of action. At the majordomo's suggestion, the marquess resumed, "The child's egregious assault on a fellow Aviran noble with magic was not only defended by House Tiloral, but she was also granted restitution by the duchy. This is an unacceptable state of affairs, a disservice to the kingdom and the Crown, to have its highest-ranking nobles bow to a foreign royal.

"Given that House Tiloral is likely to obstruct the lawful decrees of my new office, House Angwin stands in solidarity with His Royal Highness and the Crown in condemning such actions. Upon your arrival in the duchy, House Angwin will demonstrate its commitment to your future reign by supporting any actions the Crown deems necessary to censure House Tiloral. I am confident that House Angwin can harness the magic demonstrated by the terran princess to further His Royal Highness's ambitions."

Sabina lifted her quill, her entire being straining to suppress the trembling fury coursing through her. The rage.

It would be so simple to— A surge of black mana pulsed through her core, coursing through her veins, pleading to be unleashed with a mere thought.

No. I cannot. I swore to Taenya.

"What do you think, Wentham?"

"It shall do, My Lord."

"Excellent. Marinella, please conclude the letter as is customary."

Sabina allowed a smirk to grace her features as she added flowery language that subtly committed House Angwin entirely to the crown prince's faction. She added subtle insinuations that when added together denounced House Tiloral, all the more to make Angwin an enemy of the duke.

The majordomo gave a nod of approval when she finished, then turned his attention to the aging marquess. "My Lord, I will ensure it is delivered first thing tomorrow," Wentham pledged.

"Nonsense, I require you tomorrow. We have court to attend. I've instructed Nicolas to accompany us as well."

Sabina felt the majordomo's surprise ripple through the room. "Your son— my apologies—Lord Nicolas is joining us?"

Angwin scoffed dismissively. "Of course. He is the heir to the house. This will be a significant session, he will represent the house in court while I am fulfilling the duties of this new royal office."

Wentham felt <<*Contemplative*>>, as if he wanted to voice more, but held back. "I will make arrangements for his attendance, My Lord," he said.

Lord Angwin ambled over to Sabina, picked up the letter, and scrutinized it. "Your calligraphy has improved, Marinella. I am impressed. Good. You will deliver this in my name. Dress in your finest when you present it to the royal courier's office. Here," he said, handing her his seal. "Seal it and leave it in the safe. You may retrieve it in the morning. Ensure you return to the manor before we return from court. Wentham, arrange for other servants to cover her duties at sunrise."

Both she and Wentham bowed their heads, acknowledging the marquess's directives.

It suits me perfectly.

She promptly sealed the letter with wax and walked to the safe behind the desk while Wentham and Angwin discussed their plans for court. She focused on another surge of magic to **[Conjure Hallucinations]**, creating a mental illusion of her placing the scroll into the safe, while in reality, she slipped it into her dress.

Sabina closed and locked the safe, neither man even flinching, instead continuing their conversation. She focused one last time on **[Hear Thoughts]**, trying to gain as much of an advantage as possible for the following day from the marquess.

—princess and her magic will soon be mine to control. With the prince's support, it is only a matter of time before I will be duke.'

Sabina gritted her teeth.

While she wanted to stay and get more information, she felt herself growing tired. The strain of using her magic to keep up the ruse for so long finally showed its hand. She reluctantly withdrew her mental intrusions, unable to sustain both **[Alter Perception]** and focus on the majordomo simultaneously.

With barely a glance in her direction, she slipped out of the office and made her way back to the gate. Her steps quickened the closer she got. Rickard, the guardsman, came into view as she approached. Another guard was making his way from the opposite side of the estate.

And there's the replacement.

She raised a hand and called out to the tired telv. "Rickard! I am off again for the night, and it looks like your replacement is finally here! I wish you a good night."

The telv looked at her and then over at the elf approaching in the distance, moving to open the gate. "Ah, finally! How did—"

"Rickard! It is time for turnover," Sabina heard from behind her.

"Sorry, Miss Marinella. Duty calls. Have a good night!"

"And you as well," she responded, slipping through the gate he held open for her and disappearing into the night beyond.

Step three . . . and a half. Complete.

* * *

Siveril strode into his office with the manor esquire, Niles Balfiel, at his side, with Ser Taenya and Ser Sabina trailing close behind. Sabina had roused them in the dead of night with her revelations about House Angwin. Her brazen act had quite possibly saved the young house and its royal head.

As the door closed behind them, Taenya broke the silence. "We must attend court this morning. We cannot let this pass unchallenged. Surely the duke will not remain passive in the face of such a threat to his house."

Siveril shook his head. "He won't. But that's not what will aid us, and we won't seek his help. The marquess has unwittingly provided us with what we need."

He wasn't sure if Sabina was reading his thoughts or simply sensing his emotions, but she looked almost puzzled as she studied him. He had to admit that her magic unnerved him, despite her assurances. However, she was doing everything in her power to prove her loyalty, and for that, he had to give her some credit.

"What did he give us?" Taenya asked.

"Grave Abuse of Authority."

The synchronized tilt of the two women's heads in opposite directions was almost comical. He elaborated, "Royal Decree of 896. Authority of Royal Appointments. By explicitly stating his intention to exploit the princess in an act against the duke, he is abusing the authority granted to him in his position overseeing magical affairs. This renders any decree against the princess unlawful."

Sabina nodded. "So, we are going to block his attempt to take over the house on legal grounds? Won't that just provoke him to seek other means to control her?"

The majordomo smiled. "Yes. It would. That is why we are not stopping there. His act is dishonorable in the highest degree and seeks to cause real damages against Her Highness's house and interests." Siveril shifted his gaze, locking eyes with Taenya. "We will not let this stand."

Balfiel chimed in. "House Reinhart will issue a formal notice of offense and demand satisfaction. Since he wishes to eliminate our house, our claim for damages will reflect that. I will write a notice now that we shall present in court. When he dismisses us—*and he will*, Ser Taenya, you will need to challenge his house to a duel. Since he wishes for the death of our house, you must challenge his house in a duel to the death."

Sabina gasped, her head snapping toward Balfiel. "To the death? There has not been a duel to the death in *centuries*. Is it even still legal?"

Siveril's smile remained. He and Balfiel had deliberated over this extensively. He took over the explanation. "Yes, it is. However, the offense must be so egregious as to warrant it. House Angwin seeks to dissolve House Reinhart, force the princess into servitude, and coerce her into hostile acts against a duchy. Our challenge is legal."

Taenya gave a curt nod. "I need to prepare."

Siveril surveyed the room's occupants. Balfiel was already moving to draft the notice. Taenya looked resolute—she would be ready. Sabina seemed slightly torn, as if duty were pulling her in two directions.

"Then do so. We must act swiftly. Sabina, you will remain here. You must protect Her Highness. Now is a prime time for the marquess's agents to strike."

Sabina straightened, steeling herself. "I will keep her safe."

"See that you do."

Taenya walked into the manor's entryway, wearing her full armor for the first time in several weeks. The dragons embossed on her armor gleamed, the dark-blue and silver fabric immaculate and vibrant. Her shortsword was secured at her left hip, and her new longsword hung from a frog on her right. Her left hand rested lightly on the hilt of her sword, the blade angled slightly for an easy draw.

Gwyn approached her, and Taenya dropped to one knee before the young girl.

"Taenya, I understand why you must do this, but I wish it weren't necessary." Gwyn fiddled with a piece of fabric in her hand. "I . . . I asked Emma to take me to a jeweler and had something made for you. I wanted to give it to you on your birthday, but now seems like the right time," the princess said, unrolling the fabric to reveal a large silver pin shaped like the sun and its rays.

Theran stepped forward to assist Gwyn in affixing the pin to Taenya's shoulder harness, positioning it over her collarbone and just above her heart, where it rested on her breastplate. Once it was secure, Theran retreated, leaving the two in a moment of privacy. Gwyn leaned in to hug Taenya, her hand resting over the pin. The princess whispered something in her ear, and Taenya felt the pin grow warm, even through her armor. She absorbed Gwyn's words, closing her eyes to etch them into her memory.

"Don't forget," the girl implored. Gwyn pulled back, and Taenya nodded in response.

"I will remember."

"Good. Now go kick their butts, my dragon-knight," Gwyn commanded, offering Taenya a surprisingly crisp salute.

Taenya smirked in response. "I'm not a dragon-knight yet, little princess. We don't even have a dragon."

I won't be able to call her that for much longer. She's sprouting like a weed.

Gwyn's face grew serious, and Taenya caught her mumbling under her breath. "One day we will."

The princess retreated as Taenya rose to her full height. She scanned the room, her gaze finally landing on Theran. "Ser Theran. We'll take four guards with us. Assemble the rest and secure the house. Anticipate trouble, even if it doesn't arrive today."

"Understood, Knight-Captain."

She looked at Sabina, who stood at a distance, awaiting Gwyn's instructions. Taenya locked eyes with her, offering a nod of understanding. Sabina returned the gesture, albeit with a hint of hesitation. Taenya tilted her head subtly, prompting a more confident nod from Sabina. Satisfied that they were on the same page, Taenya acknowledged the silent agreement they had reached earlier.

Turning on her heel, Taenya moved toward the open door and paused on the threshold. She cast a final glance over her shoulder, taking in the sight of Gwyn instructing her ladies-in-waiting to lock themselves in their rooms in the case of an emergency and open the door only for a house guard.

Emotion welled up in Taenya's eyes as she looked at Gwyn. *I will not fail her.*

Drawing a deep breath, she stepped out into the crisp mid-morning light. Siveril was waiting for her by the carriage

Taenya smiled. It was time.

CHAPTER THIRTY-THREE

POLITE ANTICIPATION

Gwyn navigated the corridors of her manor, Sabina shadowing her every move, while her three ladies-in-waiting and Emma trailed behind. Sir Friedrich and Keston approached, their faces etched with concern.

Keston exchanged a glance with Friedrich before turning his attention back to Gwyn. He began to bow, but Gwyn reached out to stop him. "Keston, none of that. Come on now."

The high elf paused, straightening up. "We heard about what's happening. How can we assist?"

Gwyn shared a look with Sabina, who furrowed her brow in thought, her gaze flickering to the three girls trailing behind them, their faces a mix of worry and uncertainty. "Senior Guardsman, I believe you'd be best suited to oversee the security of the ladies-in-waiting. Devise a plan of action and select four guards, then coordinate with Ser Theran."

Keston nodded in understanding. "Of course," he agreed, turning to offer the three girls a comforting smile. "We'll ensure your safety." He turned back to Gwyn. "And you? Are you holding up?"

Gwyn offered a small smile. "I'm good. Taenya's going to go kick some butt."

Keston chuckled. "That she is."

Gwyn stepped closer, rising on her tiptoes as Keston leaned down to hear her whispered words. "Things might get crazy around here, Keston. Be careful. But if you want to go . . ."

Her guard gently placed his hands on her shoulders, meeting her gaze with a firm resolve. "I've been training nonstop and will continue to do so. I'm not leaving you. It's what Raafe would have wanted, right? I'll do what's necessary, and hopefully, when that is complete, I can do more."

Gwyn nodded, her eyes welling up despite her best efforts. She quickly wiped them away. "I know you're training to be my royal chef, but why do you have to carry onions around? You know it attracts onion ninjas."

Keston smiled, giving her chin a light tap. "You're alright, kid. Don't worry about me. It's my job to worry. Now, Sir Friedrich is going to thrash me in our next training session if I don't let him talk. We'll talk soon, alright?"

Gwyn let out a soft laugh, turning her attention to the human knight as Keston walked away. "Hi, Sir Friedrich. How are you?"

The man returned her smile. "I am well, Princess. May I accompany you on your walk?"

She nodded. "Sure! I wanted to walk around the manor before taking a break for some tea."

"Then I will join you."

As Friedrich and Gwyn ambled through the manor, the knight shared his observations about Eona, comparing it to Earth. He noted the many similarities, but also the stark differences that became more apparent the more he learned about this world. He wondered aloud if there was anything he could do to bridge the gap.

Gwyn, in turn, asked about his family, a question that visibly caught him off guard.

He sighed heavily. "My Katherine . . ." He drew in a deep breath, his gaze distant. "It's not something . . . It's difficult to think about or speak of, Princess. With respect . . ."

Gwyn nodded understandingly. "I'm sorry, Friedrich. You don't have to talk about it. Are you going to be . . ."

Friedrich offered her a melancholic smile. "I have to be, don't I? All of us humans are in this together now. And it would dishonor the memory of my wife to leave you alone with none of your own people." His gaze shifted to Sabina. "No offense, ser."

Sabina shrugged nonchalantly. "None taken." She paused for a moment, and her eyes seemed to flash before she replied, "I believe . . . I believe I am uniquely qualified to say that I truly understand your feelings."

Friedrich stopped, as did Gwyn. The others stopped a respectful distance away as Friedrich studied Sabina with a long, searching look.

"You really would, wouldn't you?"

Sabina offered him a sad smile and stepped forward, her voice dropping to a whisper that Gwyn had to strain to hear. "I do. If you ever wish to discuss this in true privacy, I will do what I can to help. I swear upon my honor that what you say will be kept in confidence unless our princess orders otherwise."

Friedrich nodded. "Thank you. I . . . I should go assist . . ."

Sabina placed a comforting hand on his shoulder. "If you would, could you ensure that the house scholars are kept safe? Perhaps you can use that time to learn more about Aviran laws and customs, as well."

Friedrich straightened, placing a hand over his heart. "I will do so." He turned and performed a crisp bow. "Your Highness. I will speak to you soon."

Gwyn returned his smile. "Thanks, Friedrich."

After he walked away, she turned back to her ladies-in-waiting and asked, "What do you guys want to do?"

Aleanora glanced around, and when no one immediately responded, she said, "I wish to go over the relevant laws of the capital. We will be leaving soon, and I would like to be prepared to assist the house in whatever manner I can. I will brush up on the guilds, as well."

"That sounds like a great idea, Nora," Gwyn praised, earning a pleased smile from the elf.

Ilyana hummed with what appeared to be begrudging respect as she spoke next. "I will be studying as well, but in . . . other subject matters. I've also been doing some light workouts with Ser Theran ever since watching you train with your sword—nothing serious. But I have found myself interested."

Gwyn nodded enthusiastically. "Sounds like fun! He's really good at it. I think I'm getting better."

"You're doing amazing," Aleanora chimed in.

"You're alright," Sabina corrected, her tone teasing. "For a kid."

Gwyn's eyes widened in mock offense. "Sabina!" she exclaimed, but the woman merely huffed and looked at Lorrena expectantly.

Lorrena opened her mouth to speak, but was interrupted by the return of Keston, flanked by four guards.

"Apologies for the interruption, Your Highness," he said, his gaze shifting to Gwyn's knight. "Ser Sabina, Ser Theran is locking down the estate, and the guards are arming up."

Sabina nodded, her expression hardening. "Alright, ladies, please accompany the senior guardsman. Perhaps you three can go to the library for your studying?"

Aleanora and Ilyana both nodded in agreement. "We can. We'll help Lady Lorrena, as well," Ilyana said quickly, giving a comforting squeeze to the youngest's shoulder.

Sabina looked at Gwyn. "Alright, let's head to your suite, Gwyn. Emma, would you gather some tea for Her Highness?"

Emma acknowledged the knight and hurried away.

Gwyn looked up at Sabina, noticing the sudden shift in her demeanor. "You okay?"

Sabina nodded quickly, her eyes scanning their surroundings. "Yes. We need to keep you safe. Taenya and Siveril should be at the duke's court by now . . . yes. I will keep you safe, let's go."

Gwyn tilted her head in concern. Sabina's entire attitude had suddenly changed, and she wasn't sure why, but she trusted her knight. She joined Sabina as they made their way to Gwyn's rooms, the air around them growing tense with anticipation.

Gwyn observed as Emma placed the teapot on the table, her hands trembling slightly. The woman's eyes flickered nervously toward Sabina, who was standing by the window, her gaze fixed on the world outside. Gwyn found herself at a loss for words, the silence in the room growing heavy.

Sabina had been unusually quiet since receiving word that the estate was on full alert. After Theran had secured the estate and organized the guards, Sabina had remained close by, but her mind seemed miles away. Gwyn didn't need her magic to sense that something was wrong. She let out a sigh, noticing Sabina's slight flinch at the sound.

Gwyn's eyes narrowed, a spark of anger igniting within her. It wasn't Sabina's reaction that upset her, but the fact that the jerk marquess guy was doing all of this. His actions were putting her people—her family—under crazy stress.

Now, Taenya was forced to risk her life in order to protect Gwyn. Sabina was silent, likely channeling *her* magic to sense any potential threats.

I should be there to protect Taenya. I can . . . She took a deep breath, looking at Sabina. *I need to talk to her. It's time.*

Gwyn turned her attention to Emma, who looked worried and slightly shaky. But that was to be expected. Everyone was aware of what was going on. The danger they all faced was no secret.

"Emma?" Gwyn called out softly.

The elf perked up, her posture straightening as she prepared herself to cater to Gwyn's needs. Gwyn felt a pang of guilt, but she needed Emma to leave the room. While she was generally open about her magic, she wouldn't expose Sabina. The woman was incredibly private, almost as much as Taenya.

"Yes, Your Highness?"

"Could you please give Ser Sabina and me a moment to speak?" she asked, as politely as possible.

Emma curtsied gracefully. "Of course, Your Highness. I understand. I'll prepare a light meal for you."

Gwyn offered her a grateful smile. *That wasn't so bad.* "Thank you, Emma. I appreciate it."

Emma returned the smile, a flicker of relief passing over her features. Gwyn took a final sip of her tea, setting the cup aside for her to collect. She maintained a composed silence as Emma gathered the empty teacup and teapot onto the serving tray.

"If anything happens," Gwyn began before the woman walked way, "find a safe place. Don't worry about me. Sabina is here, and I have my magic."

Emma nodded slowly. "I will try, Your Highness."

Once Emma had exited the room, Gwyn took a deep breath, her gaze shifting to Sabina as the door closed behind her maid. She expected Sabina to break the silence, but the woman remained quiet, her eyes closed and her body still, seemingly lost in her own world.

She waited.

Sabina said nothing.

Gwyn waited some more, counting to one hundred in her head before her patience wore thin. "So . . . are we going to talk?" she asked, her voice echoing in the silent room.

Sabina didn't reply. Her eyes were closed and she remained still, oblivious to anything outside of what she was doing.

Gwyn closed her eyes and focused inward. The swirling orb of magic within her seemed to strain against its confines, the different colors churning within.

That's not right. My core doesn't hold magic, it calls for it. It's my connection to the magic, and its connection to me.

Gwyn concentrated on that connection, feeling the different types of magic inside her. Each had a unique rhythm, a distinct melody in the symphony of her magic. The blue magic was calm, like the soothing notes of a violin, methodical and purposeful. A song of logic and innovation. The red was righteousness and justice, a tempest of fury waiting to be unleashed. The black magic, however, sang the most demanding of songs. It whispered of change and vengeance, a potent force that could consume both her foes and her if she wasn't careful.

Yet another color, or rather, a lack of color, surrounded her. It was the most *confusing* song. Its melody was softer yet more pervasive. It was the magic in between, that connected to all others. The balance. It was space. It was . . . *time*. She knew that if she delved deeper into this magic, a whole universe of possibilities would unfold before her. It was a connection that could unify all her magic and empower her to protect her people.

Gwyn reached out to this colorless magic, feeling it respond willingly to her call. Yet, understanding it was a paradox—using it was both easier and more difficult at the same time. It was *everywhere*, but *understanding* it was so different than the other colors.

She pondered her earlier realization about how magic connected to her. Focusing on this connection, she traced it to its source, where it permeated everything around them. It was as if all of existence *was* magic—or rather, it was the substance that made magic possible.

Even though her eyes were shut, she had never seen more clearly.

A pulsing rush of that colorless magic flowed up from the ground and into her. Swelling in her core like blood pumping through her heart, before spreading throughout her body's magical veins. Every part of her it touched seemed to grow stronger. Her eyelids were tightly shut, yet a vibrant world of swirling colors and mists unfolded before her. While it wasn't perfect, she knew she could now walk or do anything blindfolded if she wanted.

Could I even do this without eyes? Would that make it stronger? She paused, recoiling at her own thought. *What a terrible idea . . . why would anyone intentionally blind themselves to try and see better?*

Her attention shifted toward Sabina. She gasped as she noticed the black mist emanating from the woman's head, drifting out of the window before dispersing thinly into the air. A quick pulse of concentrated black mist appeared, spinning in a large circle with Sabina at its center.

The sight reminded Gwyn of the radar screens she'd seen in movies, set in airports or military bases. The green screens that signaled incoming aircraft. As she studied the magic Sabina was manipulating, she noticed more pulses.

Her radar has four lines, not just one.

Gwyn opened her eyes, her regular vision seamlessly blending with the magical overlay. The magic flowing within her felt as if it tightened, and she started to feel more and more tired with the dual perception. Gwyn rubbed her eyes, feeling a strain similar to what happens after staring at a computer screen for too long.

Trying to [Focus] only helped a little bit before the onslaught of sensory input threatened to overwhelm her. It was definitely something she would need to practice before using for longer than short bursts.

Okay, that's enough of that.

She released the . . .

The . . .

. . . Sight

The magic itself felt like it was yearning for a name, something that it wanted to be called, but she couldn't figure it out. And her head was hurting. And it wasn't the time.

Focus, Me.

She sighed. Finally, Sabina turned to her, tilting her head as she studied Gwyn.

"What was that? I . . . felt something."

Gwyn smiled as she rubbed her temple. "I learned a new spell. Well, sort of. It's like the magic is teasing me because I don't quite have the right name or understanding. I am missing something."

Sabina nodded, opening her mouth to speak but Gwyn beat her to it.

"Sabina? We should talk. About your magic."

The elf seemed to freeze in place. "M-my magic?"

"We both know that I know, right? You're not exactly adept at keeping secrets. You didn't even react when I started getting angry. Why not? I know you can sense emotions."

Wait. Can she . . . Sabina? Can you hear me? Gwyn drew on her magic, channeling it into her thoughts. *Sabina! Can you hear me?!*

Sabina's nose crinkled, and her ear twitched as if she had physically heard her.

I know you can hear me. You're probably trying not to listen to my thoughts or feel what I'm feeling. That's how you knew about my nightmare, right? You sensed my pain and came running.

Sabina moved swiftly, dropping to one knee. "Your Highness. I swear. I swore. I-I-I . . ." The woman collapsed onto both knees, tears beginning to flow.

Gwyn stepped forward and grabbed her. She hugged her as tightly as she could, and rested her head against Sabina's. "I know. Keep this secret, Sabina. Share it only with those who need to know, but we'll figure out the rest. I trust you."

Sabina continued to cry. Gwyn released her and stood, placing her hands on either side of her knight's face before pressing her forehead to the elf's.

She whispered mentally, *You promised me that you'd keep the nightmares at bay. At first, I didn't realize how true you meant it. But you can't do that if you don't know my feelings. Teach me to keep my thoughts private when I want them to be, if that makes you feel better. I trust you.*

Sabina's shoulders sagged and she pulled Gwyn close, sobbing. She coughed as she tried to speak. "W-why?"

"Why what? Why do I trust you?" She felt the woman's head nod slightly. *Because you care. Because you would do anything to keep me safe and help me find Mom. You don't want to use me for your own plans.* She paused and then continued, *Because you worked so hard to control your magic, just to avoid betraying my trust. You're always there by my side when I need you. You're my last line of defense. My protector. My friend.*

"But I . . . I hurt someone," Sabina whispered.

Gwyn's eyes narrowed, her inner fire warming her. "And I've killed two people. You won't do that again to anyone who doesn't deserve it. Your magic is a weapon. From now on, you need to think about that if you're going to use it. It's taking away their free will. Even in our darkest moments, we should be able to trust our own thoughts. Remember that before you act."

"I will, Your Highness," Sabina whispered.

Gwyn smirked. "Sabina . . . it's just us."

Sabina looked up at her, raising an eyebrow.

Gwyn laughed. "And there's the eyebrow raise. You've got it down. You're going to make a great mom one day."

Sabina's eyes widened and she froze. "W-what?"

"I said, you're going to be a great mom one day. I can't wait to be an aunt. We need to find you a boyfriend."

The elf shook her head quickly. "No. What? Where is this coming from? An aunt? What are you talking about?"

"You're right. More of a cousin, since you're practically my aunt now. I'm going to be quite a bit older than your baby, though. So cousin seems weird."

"But I am not pregnant!"

"You're not pregnant, *yet*. We just gotta find you a boyfriend. You guys get married. Have a baby," Gwyn explained as if it were the simplest concept in the world.

"How do you even know how that works?"

Gwyn smirked. *Distraction. Got you.*

Sabina's eyebrow shot back up as she sat back and pointed at Gwyn. "You . . ."

Gwyn laughed, but her laughter faded into a sigh. "Sabina? Remember when I went to see the archpriestess?"

Sabina tilted her head. "I do. What does—"

"Well, she had a message for you. I'm not sure how she knows, but—" Gwyn stopped, switching to her thoughts in case Emma walked back in. *The archpriestess says that Alos casts a great shadow and that you don't need to stray too far from the light to find it.*

Sabina's eyes widened, her mouth falling open in surprise. "She said that?"

Gwyn nodded. "Yes. I got the feeling that she trusts you as well." *Your magic can be used for good too, Sabina. You've been doing it. Keep doing it. Just don't let it control you.*

"I will not allow it. I swear," Sabina vowed, her voice thick with emotion.

"Sabina?"

"Yes, Gwyn?"

Gwyn smiled, wrapping her arms around Sabina in a warm embrace, resting her head on her shoulder. It felt right.

Sabina and Taenya were like her quirky aunts, standing in for her mom until they could find her. And she was certain they would find her too. With Taenya and Sabina on the case, she had nothing to worry about. They meant the world to her, and she knew they cared for her just as deeply as she cared for them.

She lowered her voice, whispering, "Thank you for being great."

Sabina choked back a sob, returning the hug and holding Gwyn tight.

It felt perfect. Now all they needed was for her other aunt to return home safely.

Clad in her full armor, Taenya followed Siveril into the grandeur of the ducal palace. The guard at the entrance had recognized them, and with a respectful nod, had led them through the corridors toward the ducal hall. Behind them, Balfiel and their house guards trailed, their boots echoing in the marble corridors.

The four guards were ones she had personally selected and trained. They were a cohesive unit, their skills honed to work seamlessly together. Each time she glanced back at them, she felt a surge of pride. They were training to be a squad of trusted go-to guards for her to call upon, and they were ready.

As they walked, Siveril nudged her subtly, inclining his head toward a Loreni man striding purposefully through the hall. Taenya followed his gaze, her brow furrowing.

"Who's that?" she asked, her voice low.

"That's Lord Iemes's new representative to the court," Siveril murmured, his eyes never leaving the man. "Depending on how this goes, I might need to have a word with him, and the other houses. Except for the Trenlores. They're as useful as a broken horseshoe."

Taenya's eyes narrowed at his dismissive tone. "What?"

Siveril leaned closer, his voice dropping to a conspiratorial whisper. "Never rely on the Trenlores. They won't lift a finger to help us. House Olacyne, on the other hand, can muster a decent force of men-at-arms, and House Urileth, though smaller, is wealthy. They've recently been hiring from the Mercenary Guild. If push comes to shove, we'll call upon Olacyne first, then Iemes due to distance."

Taenya nodded, filing away the information. "But if Trenlore is unreliable, why did we—"

"Convince them to pledge themselves to us?" Siveril finished for her, a knowing smile playing on his lips.

Taenya nodded again, her mind racing.

"We already have the reason."

She fell silent, her mind working furiously. Then it clicked. "Ilyana."

Siveril's smile widened. "Exactly. Her Highness needs reliable retainers. If the Trenlores step out of line, they'll face the consequences. But for now, we'll see how it plays out."

As they entered the ducal hall, a buzz of conversation washed over them. Groups of nobles huddled together, their voices low and urgent. Siveril nudged her again, pointing to a quieter corner of the hall toward the front. They needed to keep a low profile.

For now.

As they moved through the crowd, Taenya caught snippets of conversation. The new royal decree was the topic on everyone's lips, its implications being dissected and debated. The tension in the room was palpable. There was a storm brewing beneath the surface of polite conversation.

One conversation caused her to pause and take note. A high elf woman, draped in a gown of shimmering silk, laughed dismissively.

"Magic? Surely you jest. Such things are the realm of the gods."

A telv man, his eyes twinkling with amusement, chuckled in response. "You've been out of the loop, haven't you? How did you miss all the whispers about the young terran princess?"

The woman's delicate eyebrows arched in surprise. "What are you talking about?"

The man leaned in, causing Taenya to strain to hear. "The girl caused quite the stir in court not too long ago. I'm surprised you weren't there."

She sighed, a look of annoyance crossing her face. "I just returned from Drakensburg. That trip is always so tedious. But really, magic is real? I've heard rumors, but I thought they were just silly."

Taenya couldn't help but smirk as she followed Siveril. *If only they knew.* The world was changing, and those who refused to believe would soon be left behind.

Taenya trailed behind Siveril, her eyes scanning the grandeur of the ducal court. They found a spot at the side, a strategic location that allowed them to observe the court without drawing too much attention, until they needed it.

Soon, the herald announced the arrival of the duke. The room fell silent as the man entered, his noble bearing commanding respect. He took his place on a high-backed seat, and once settled, he gestured for the proceedings to begin.

The first petitioner, a man of middling years with a nervous twitch, was called forward. His voice echoed through the hall as he presented his case. Taenya listened with half an ear, her mind wandering back to the manor.

I hope everything is going well, she thought, her fingers drumming a silent rhythm on her sword hilt while her other hand protectively covered the pouch, and the scroll that lay within, on her right.

The tension was palpable and a silent reminder of the high stakes they were playing. The Great Game was something the nobility played at, a Polite War among themselves for influence and power with deadly consequences.

It was not something Taenya had ever even considered would affect her, but now, as a knight-captain, she was about to enter it in a big way.

She took a deep breath, steeling herself for what was to come.

CHAPTER THIRTY-FOUR

A NOBLE RESPONSE

Taenya, Siveril, and Niles stood amid the throng of courtiers, quietly observing the proceedings. The house guards stood at attention along the wall behind them with those of the duchy, as expected. As they waited, Siveril was content to let everything proceed until it was time. They would let the marquess make the first move—after all, theirs was a reaction. As far as anyone knew, there was no way House Reinhart could have known what Angwin was doing.

Well, except for the convenient evidence we "intended" to present to the duke privately.

The court carried on in its usual rhythm, a dance of power and politics. Petitioners came and went, each presenting their case before the Seat of the Duchy, a throne that had been occupied by the Duke of Tiloral and his ancestors for three centuries. It was a position of power and prestige, coveted by many houses seeking to elevate their status.

The Duchy of Tiloral was once a kingdom, a proud and independent realm that had been conquered by the Kingdom of Avira after a grueling decade-long war. The Tiloral king of the time, weary of the conflict and wary of his rivals, had chosen to negotiate rather than continue the fight. In a move hailed by historians as a diplomatic triumph, the Tilorals had persuaded the Avirans to accept their kingdom as a duchy, with the king surrendering his crown to kneel before his Aviran counterpart.

In return, the Avirans, who held a grudging respect for the Tilorals, had integrated the new duchy into their kingdom without further conflict. It was an unprecedented arrangement, and the Duchy of Tiloral was one of only three in the vast kingdom that had never changed hands.

Rich in resources and trade, the Duchy of Tiloral was a prize many coveted. Even the Crown had cast envious eyes on it over the years. Some argued that this alone signified a long-term victory for the Tilorals. They had resisted a superior kingdom, transformed a potential defeat into a strategic advantage, and emerged as a powerhouse that even the Crown dared not antagonize.

Which made the move by the crown prince all the more . . . telling.

If the Crown felt confident enough to challenge the Tilorals, it must believe it had sufficient support and strength to weather the potential backlash of the historically neutral house aligning with the noble faction.

The game of power is shifting, Taenya mused, her gaze sweeping over the court. *And we are right in the middle of it.*

The political dance of the Kingdom of Avira was a delicate one, a balance of power between the Crown and nobility. This delicate equilibrium was maintained through a careful distribution of authority and influence, a balance that could easily tip if either side pushed too far. The Crown couldn't exert too much control without risking the ire of the nobility, and no single house could amass too much power without inviting the wrath of their peers or the Crown itself.

The real danger lay in the nobility banding together, a situation that had once nearly cost Avira a war when half the kingdom refused the king's levy.

The Tilorals had been the ones to resolve that crisis, earning them the kingdom's sole seaport as a spoil of war. Now, that seaport was the kingdom's largest income source, poised to elevate House Tiloral past the Crown as the wealthiest house and faction in the kingdom.

It was no surprise that the Crown felt threatened and compelled to act. Prince Kerrell *had* to try something. His status demanded it. The future king needed to solidify his own influence and ensure a smooth rise to power.

That didn't mean she had to accept it. A scoff escaped Taenya's lips, drawing Siveril's attention. The elder elf leaned in, his voice barely audible above the court's murmur. "What's on your mind, Ser Taenya?"

"The decree, and the reasoning behind it," she replied.

Siveril nodded, his gaze thoughtful. "I've been pondering it as well. Avira may have become more treacherous than we initially assumed for our young charge. The outcome of our next move will determine just how dangerous it truly is."

Taenya nodded in agreement, about to voice another thought when Siveril interrupted her. "Look. The marquess is making his move," he said, nodding subtly toward the center of the hall.

She exhaled a quiet sigh. "Here we go."

With that, Taenya fell silent, her eyes fixed on the unfolding drama. It was time to wait, to observe, and, when the moment was right, to act.

* * *

The marquess stood before the Seat with the duke peering down on him from the elevated dais.

"Lord Angwin," the duke began, his voice echoing through the hall, "I suspected you would speak. Proceed."

From her position, Taenya could just make out the marquess's features. A fleeting scowl seemed to cross his face before he offered the duke a perfunctory bow, barely more than a nod. He then turned to face the gathered nobility, his gaze sweeping over the assembly of aristocrats, wealthy merchants, and landowners. If he noticed Siveril among them, he gave no sign.

"All of you have, or should have, seen the decree from His Royal Highness, the crown prince," he began, his voice carrying through the hall. "I will not stand here and repeat what has already been ordered. What I am here to do today is lay out my own decree, as granted by my authority under His Royal Highness. As the representative overseeing the Office of Magical Affairs within the Duchy of Tiloral, I have been given the responsibility of managing the kingdom's response to this new phenomenon within the duchy specifically. As such, I have established my office within the grounds of the Royal Academy's branch in Strathmore."

He paused, letting his words sink in before continuing. "The exact decree will be made available to all within the duchy, starting today. However, I will inform you all now as to what is expected. One: due to the size of the duchy, my office orders the Duchy of Tiloral to enact a test of all citizens to ascertain the exact ability—"

"No."

Lord Angwin jerked in surprise, turning to face the duke, who had risen from his Seat. "Excuse me?" the marquess asked, a scowl marring his features.

"I do believe you heard me, Angwin," the duke replied, his voice firm. "Nowhere in the decree that was sent by the crown prince does it state that you may order me or my people to do your job for you. You will need to figure it out yourself. Perhaps the Crown can grant you a stipend to pay for personnel. If not, I am sure House Angwin has sufficient funds to support such an endeavor, but no, the Duchy of Tiloral will not spend a single coin in doing your duty." The duke's words rang out with finality as he sat back down, gesturing almost lazily for the marquess to continue.

"We will see about House Tiloral's dismissal of the intent of the decree at another time," the marquess retorted, his voice tight.

"We shall," the duke responded, almost tiredly.

Lord Angwin turned back to the crowd, his gaze sweeping over the assembly with an air of challenge, daring anyone to interrupt or contest his words. "Very well. Since the duchy *refuses*, any and all citizens within the duchy must register with my office if they have shown any level of magical ability. Nobles of sufficient standing will register with my house personally, and I will determine whether to personally provide oversight of the individual."

The duke cleared his throat, a subtle interruption that drew a scowl from the marquess, though he did not turn to face the duke. "Due to the small size of the Royal Academy's branch here," Angwin continued, "my house will invest in supporting their research and oversight of this new phenomenon and how it affects our citizens. The dean has already approved and welcomes this support." The marquess turned then, his gaze pointedly directed at the duke.

"As we have seen an incident recently, I have made the decision that any public disturbance or assault by someone with magic must be reported and assigned direct oversight of the individual by my office. Any noble will immediately be assigned oversight by me."

Siveril leaned close to Taenya. "That's our cue."

Taenya followed Siveril as they slowly made their way through the crowd, Balfiel trailing behind her with his documents at the ready. The marquess glanced at them as they moved, but he did not pause his speech.

"As such, I will immediately be providing direct oversight of the terran princess, Gwyneth of House Reinhart, for her magical assault of a member of the kingdom's nobility, even if the duchy chose to forgive it. Her actions prove the Crown's decision, as a child should not be trusted with such abilities without keen authority to guide them."

They emerged from the crowd, and Siveril addressed the duke. "Your Grace, with your permission?"

The marquess seethed as the duke waved Siveril on. "Of course, Ser Siveril. Address the court."

Siveril locked his gaze on the marquess, his eyes cool and calculating, as if taking the measure of the man. "With respect, Your Lordship, Her Highness does not fall under the purview of this decree. She is not a citizen of this kingdom. Her house was approved under the Recognition Act of 851. As a recognized noble-in-exile, she is granted the same status under our laws but is not, as I said, considered a citizen of the kingdom. Therefore, you may not provide direct oversight. To even suggest so is an affront, and House Reinhart takes offense."

The marquess sneered, and Taenya narrowed her eyes. "As expected from a knight with little mind to the nuance of high law," he said. "Unfortunately, your princess is a de facto citizen of the kingdom. She cannot claim to be in exile if the kingdom cannot even access her home nation. She is a girl displaced by the very phenomenon I have been tasked with overseeing. No law or decree governs her status, as such a thing was never envisioned. By granting her house status, and because of the fact that our kingdom is unable to communicate with her government, she is more a refugee than an exile. Therefore, the decree most certainly applies. I expect to see her—"

"Very well. Mister Balfiel?" Siveril's interruption was swift and decisive.

The esquire stepped forward. Lord Angwin tilted his head even as his hands formed into fists at being interrupted. The high elf cleared his throat as he unfurled the scroll he had written, his voice echoing throughout the hall. "House Reinhart takes grave offense to the presumptive and overreaching actions of the marquess for House Angwin. His Royal Highness's Decree of Magical Affairs does not state that the representative within may enact personal oversight and control over citizens, especially citizens that outrank him in status. It is House Reinhart's stance that Lord Angwin is seeking to cause irreparable damages to our house and thus the house cannot abide by his unlawful overstep of authority."

Balfiel paused, as discussed, waiting for the marquess to react.

It didn't take long. The marquess glanced at the duke, who had leaned forward in his Seat, listening intently but not intervening. When no response came, the marquess gestured exaggeratedly toward the three of them.

"House Reinhart openly admits to a willful disregard for the crown prince's decree and the lawful decree of the Royal Office of Magical Affairs. Your Head of House is not even present. Why? Because she is a child. A child who has shown a willingness to openly attack a noble. The office is well within its authority to provide oversight to the minor since it seems that mere knights are incapable of doing so. In fact, this situation exemplifies the very purpose for which the office was established: to ensure the safety and proper management of this phenomenon within the kingdom.

"If you wish to speak of law and legal standing, then note that the very laws you believe allow your house to ignore the order of the crown prince have provisions to protect the kingdom. They also state that any willful infringement of royal decrees and laws will result in a dissolution of the house, which the transgressor heads. As such, I demand the duchy follow through with upholding the law and dissolve House Reinhart."

Siveril stepped forward, his posture resolute, and turned toward the duke. "Your Grace, we would like to continue our statement."

The Duke of Tiloral rose. "You may continue, but you must address the marquess's very real concerns."

Siveril bowed. "We shall, Your Grace." The majordomo turned, his face hidden from the marquess, and shot Taenya a brief, confident smirk. "Mister Balfiel, please continue."

"Thank you, Ser Siveril." Balfiel bowed at the duke. "Your Grace. Now, House Reinhart recognizes that House Angwin wishes to utilize His Lordship's granted authority to further actions that would dissolve our house illegally. Additionally, House Reinhart formally accuses the marquess Lord Torrell Angwin of Grave Abuse of Authority as it pertains to the Royal Decree of 896."

Collective gasps and murmurs rippled through the crowd behind Taenya as the courtiers digested the bold accusation. The marquess jerked his head backward in surprise.

"How dare you."

The Duke of Tiloral nodded, his expression unreadable. "That is a bold statement, Ser Siveril. This is the stance of House Reinhart?"

"It is, Your Grace. We wish to submit proof that was given to our house by a concerned party," Siveril affirmed, turning to Taenya and giving a nod of approval.

Taenya responded with a curt nod, reaching into the satchel she wore at her side. She extracted the scroll that Sabina had penned and purloined, holding it with a firm grip. With measured steps, she advanced toward the dais and the duke. She offered a respectful bow, as was customary for a knight in armor, and handed the scroll to the guard who had stepped forward to receive it.

The guard passed it to an elven advisor, who scrutinized the seal before presenting it to the Duke of Tiloral. The two exchanged quiet words, after which the advisor broke the seal and unfurled the scroll. His eyes darted over the contents, widening as he absorbed the information within. Once he had finished, he handed the scroll to the duke and whispered into his ear. The duke's ear twitched as he listened, and he sat down to read the scroll, his expression hardening into a scowl.

Upon finishing his perusal, the duke rose from his Seat, holding up the letter. He paced back and forth on the dais, addressing both sides of the court. "It seems Lord Angwin covets this Seat," he declared, indicating his throne. The crowd gasped, but the duke continued undeterred. "It further appears that the marquess conspires with the crown prince to use the princess of House Reinhart as a weapon against our duchy."

He turned his gaze on the marquess, who stood in silent shock. "The crown prince is *not* king, yet. This letter, whose authenticity I do not doubt, provides clear evidence of the accusations levied by House Reinhart." The duke then addressed Ser Siveril. "Ser Siveril, do you have more to address?"

"We do, Your Grace."

"Continue."

Balfiel cleared his throat once more, his voice echoing through the hushed hall. "House Reinhart finds itself the target of a malicious scheme, orchestrated by House Angwin and its Head, who seeks to exploit the limited authority granted to him by the crown prince. The marquess's attempt to coerce Princess Gwyneth, a mere child of eleven years, into a state of de facto servitude, while simultaneously seeking the dissolution of her house, is a dishonorable act of the highest degree. As such, House Reinhart seeks reparation. Given House Angwin's intent to eliminate our house and enslave its Head, we believe the compensation should reflect the gravity of this transgression. Therefore, we request the transfer of all holdings of House Angwin in Strathmore and Maireharbora to House Reinhart. Furthermore, we demand a payment of one thousand gold coins per annum . . . for a decade."

The sum was staggering, enough to finance the entire duchy for a year. They had deliberated over the amount, settling on a figure that they knew the marquess could afford—though just barely—and one they were certain he would reject.

The marquess stood, seemingly petrified, the only plausible explanation for his silence and lack of reaction. Taenya observed him as he processed the enormity of the situation, his composure gradually returning. His fists clenched and unclenched, and he quickly shared a look with his majordomo, who promptly dispatched one of the guards, who rushed out of the hall.

Angwin swiveled on his heel to face Ser Siveril, his voice a low growl. "Did you harm my servant?"

Taenya was surprised that the first question was one of seeming concern for one of his people. Despite his numerous other flaws, this single act spoke volumes about how he treated those within his house. Even Sabina couldn't deny this when she recounted her observations and feelings within the Angwin estate.

Ser Siveril scoffed dismissively. "None of your people were harmed. Are you admitting that this letter is yours?"

With a dismissive shake of his head, Angwin allowed a smug smile to creep onto his face. "You've merely demonstrated that you've unlawfully pilfered privileged correspondence between the crown prince and my house." He pivoted to face the duke. "Your family has occupied that Seat, casting a haughty gaze upon the nobility of this duchy for far too long. Fortunately, no laws prohibit me from liaising with the Crown about royal matters. You've made an adversary of the Crown, Tiloral. Your purported neutrality will not shield you."

He waved his hand dismissively at Siveril. "House Angwin will not bow to some mere knight who deems himself significant because of a *child*. We *refuse* to yield to any demand made by such. The crown prince may not yet be king, but the reigning king has endowed him with extensive powers in anticipation of his ascension. This charade of a court will soon succumb to that authority."

The Duke of Tiloral responded with a hearty laugh, a reaction that took everyone, especially the marquess, by surprise. "Angwin, there have been countless pretenders like you throughout the centuries. Do you know what they all share in common? House Tiloral remains unscathed, irrespective of their petty schemes. If the crown prince seeks to antagonize Tiloral, I say let him."

He continued to chuckle, then turned to accept a goblet from a servant and took a generous gulp. He returned the goblet with a polite nod of thanks, and the servant bowed and retreated.

Angwin seethed in his spot, but had the sense not to interrupt the man who held dominion over the land he stood upon.

The duke swiveled back to face Angwin, his gaze piercing. "You may inform the crown prince that he has made his choice. I am certain at least one member of my family will be delighted to learn that House Tiloral is finally joining the Polite War." His last statement was accompanied by a sidelong glance and a smile directed to an area where Taenya noticed Roslyn, her two knights, and the paladin standing protectively by her as she observed the proceedings.

The fury etched on the young girl's face was not surprising. She had quickly formed a close bond with Gwyn.

Taenya's attention snapped back to the marquess when she heard him speak again.

"You will regret this, Tiloral," the man sneered as he took a step backward.

Quickly, Taenya stepped up, as it seemed the marquess was on the verge of storming out. "Lord Angwin," she said, demanding his attention. Then she turned to the duke. "Your Grace, I beg your pardon for the interruption, but House Reinhart has suffered harm and we demand resolution."

The duke nodded in agreement, gesturing for her to proceed.

The marquess turned to look at Taenya. "The commoner finally deigns to speak? Have you not learned when to hold your tongue in the presence of your superiors?"

"I am *Ser* Taenya Shavyre, Knight-Captain of House Reinhart and sworn protector of Her Royal Highness, Gwyneth Reinhart. You have sought to forcibly dissolve our house and exert control over my ward. You rejected our reasonable demands. You are a dishonorable blight upon our kingdom and unworthy of the status you hold."

Angwin scoffed dismissively. "That is not your decision to make, *commoner,*" he sneered.

"I am no longer a commoner, and you will accord me the respect due my title. However, you are correct that it is not my decision." She paused, allowing her words to permeate the tense air before continuing, "But this is."

With a swift motion, she removed her gauntlet and hurled it at the marquess, striking him squarely in the chest. His face registered shock as he grappled with the unexpected act.

Taenya held her ground. "For the heinous acts you conspired to commit against my charge, I challenge you to a duel. A duel that can only be resolved when one of us draws their last breath."

The sound of swords being unsheathed echoed from where the marquess's men stood.

Taenya paid them no mind.

"Have you lost your mind? I will see—"

"House Angwin accepts!"

Taenya's head snapped to the left, where the marquess's men stood. One of the high elves stepped forward, his sword sliding back into its sheath with a metallic whisper. The elf removed his own gauntlet and flung it to the ground, then spat at her feet in a clear sign of disrespect.

"I am Lord Nicolas Angwin, and on behalf of my father, I accept this challenge. I will mount your head on a pike, telv. And once I am done with that, your princess's will be next."

Taenya looked at the marquess, who seemed as if he were on the verge of exploding with rage. His features were twisted in a mask of fury. When he caught her looking at him, his scowl deepened.

She smiled—a cold, predatory grin. "It seems your heir is eager to fight your battles. A pity."

With a dismissive shake of her head, she strode forward and retrieved her discarded gauntlet. As she straightened, she spoke in a low voice, her words intended only for the marquess.

"I hope you have a spare."

CHAPTER THIRTY-FIVE

THROUGH BLOOD AND BLADE

The carriage with Taenya, Siveril, Balfiel, and their accompanying guards jerked to a halt in front of the manor. The horses snorted, their breath misting in the cool air, as the carriage door swung open. Taenya was the first to step out, her boots crunching on the gravel pathway.

Ser Theran was waiting for them, his posture rigid and his expression serious. His brown hair, usually neatly combed, was tousled by the wind, giving him a slightly disheveled look.

"Any complications?" Taenya asked, scanning the manor's exterior for any signs of disturbance.

Theran shook his head, his hair shifting with the movement. "All is well here. Should I stand everyone down?"

Taenya glanced at Siveril, who caught her eye and gave a subtle nod. "We need to be alert, but we do not need to be locked down," Siveril explained. "For the marquess to do anything right now would bring considerable backlash."

"Why is that?" Theran asked.

Taenya realized that they hadn't filled him in on the entire plan, only that they were going to confront the marquess.

Balfiel announced he was going to get to work, preparing other legal avenues. Siveril thanked the esquire for his help, and then also excused himself. The two headed into the manor together.

Taenya sighed at the expectant look that had settled into Theran's brown eyes. "I challenged Angwin to a duel," she said.

His face scrunched up. "That's all?"

"To the death."

"Oh."

"Yeah. His son accepted on his behalf. It will take place tomorrow."

Theran sucked in a breath, then nodded. "I'll prepare the House Guard."

"Thank you, Ser Theran."

"Of course, Knight-Captain," he said, snapping a perfect salute. She returned it, her mind already racing ahead to the duel that awaited her.

But first, she had a princess to explain everything to.

As Taenya approached the double doors leading to Gwyn's suite, the two guards present stood at attention. They were both telv, one a woman with tanned skin, and the other a man with a scar running down his cheek. Both wore the blue, black, and silver colors of House Reinhart, their armor polished to a shine.

"Ser Taenya," the woman greeted, her voice respectful. The man merely nodded, his gaze steady.

Taenya returned the greeting, her tone warm. Theran had personally trained these two guards, and she trusted them with Gwyn's safety. "Everything quiet?"

"Quieter than this guy's snoring, at least," the woman replied, her lips curving into a small smile. The man huffed but didn't take the bait, which made her purse her lips. "Well, I tried. He's more mum than an umbral monk."

Taenya raised an eyebrow. "Have you *met* an umbral monk?"

The woman nodded. "I *saw* some. Spent an entire three bells and they didn't utter a peep. But here you go, ser." She moved to open the door, but before her hand could touch the handle, the door swung open from the inside.

Sabina stood in the doorway, her face a mask of worry that instantly melted into relief upon seeing Taenya.

"Taenya," she breathed out, stepping aside to let her in.

As Taenya stepped into the room, a small figure hurtled toward her. "Taenya!" Gwyn's voice echoed in the large space. The girl slammed into her with a loud clang as her head hit her breastplate. Gwyn winced, pulling back.

"Ow. Armor."

Taenya chuckled, ruffling Gwyn's hair affectionately. "Yeah, silly girl."

Gwyn looked up at her, her eyes wide and full of concern as she rubbed her head. "I'm glad you're okay. What happened?"

Taenya sighed, glancing around the room. Sabina had closed the door behind them, and the guards were back at their posts outside.

They were alone, and it was time to explain. "Let's all sit down," she suggested, guiding Gwyn to a plush couch. "I'll explain what happened and what you both need to expect for tomorrow . . ."

"What's the consensus?"

Taenya waited, feeling the tendrils of magic emanating from the woman next to her. She wasn't sure when she had become so sensitive to it, but it was defi-nitely beneficial when working with magic users. *I need to get back to my training. I am so close. This week.*

"They're angry," Sabina responded. "Angwin is berating his son again for taking the decision away from him. However, they don't seem particularly con-cerned about your upcoming duel. Their main worry is the potential damage to their house's reputation."

Taenya let out a derisive snort. "How much do you think he's done since the Flash?"

Sabina turned to look at her, a single eyebrow arched in question. "Not much, I'd wager. You believe you've made more progress?"

"I have. I can feel the changes within me. I just wish we had a way to measure the progress of others."

"That would indeed be useful," Sabina agreed, her gaze drifting toward the side of the training grounds, where Gwyn sat on the newly installed stands. "I should join her. You'd better ensure you don't get injured. I don't want to see her reaction if you do."

Taenya snorted. "I am about to have a duel to the death, and we're more wor-ried about the reaction of an eleven-year-old."

"When said eleven-year-old has the power to reduce everyone here to ashes with a mere thought? Absolutely. I don't think Angwin fully considered his plan. She would never stand for it."

"No, she wouldn't," Taenya agreed. "Stay close to her, and keep an eye on that paladin. I'm still uncertain about the Church's interest in the girls. There must be something they're not telling us. Have you heard anything from the paladin assigned to Roslyn or the one on standby for Gwyn?"

"None. Gwyn has been told she can call upon her paladin if needed. As for the one shadowing Lady Roslyn, his thoughts are as tightly guarded as yours. He reveals nothing."

Taenya nodded sagely. "Don't rely solely on your magic. Watch his body lan-guage, feel for emotional leaks, and his reactions to different stimuli."

Sabina responded with a curt nod, her hand making a brief gesture of understanding.

Taenya took one more look at the young girl who, by all rights, should not have been present. The nature of the event was hardly suitable for an eleven-year-old, but Gwyn's status as the head of House Reinhart necessitated her atten-dance. She was, after all, the one wronged in this situation.

"Sabina, try to make sure she doesn't see the result."

Sabina glanced back at Gwyn before she reached out and clasped Taenya's wrist. "I will. Fight well, Taenya."

"Thank you, Sabina."

As Sabina walked away, Taenya turned her attention to her opponent. The heir to House Angwin, the marquess's only legitimate child, was fastening the straps of his gauntlets, a servant fussing over his armor.

He should have done that before arriving.

With a sigh, Taenya donned her helmet and took her position. She stood still, focusing on her breathing. Nervousness was a given in such circumstances. Anyone who claimed otherwise was either lying or fighting an opponent incapable of fighting back. Duels of Honor were a form of trial by combat, a contest between two representatives of their respective houses. Interference from others was strictly forbidden, punishable by death. Yet, even with such a severe penalty, vigilance was crucial.

Each side was allowed a semicircle of guards surrounding the combat field. These guards could act in defense of their house only if the opposing house violated the duel's rules first.

This gray area was wide open to interpretation and was the main reason for the Ducal Guard being present around the outer perimeter of the grounds. Even still, many duels had ended with the opposing side killed by a guard.

The duke was technically presiding over the duel, but as the two parties could not come to an agreement with words, once they were ready—which she was—the only permitted speech would come from the victor.

And I intend to be that person.

As Lord Nicolas finally completed his preparations, he turned and strode toward her, halting a few meters away. Taenya drew her longsword from its sheath.

His eyelid twitched at her readiness, and a smirk tugged at her lips.

She positioned her left foot forward, her right foot back and out. Lowering her blade and pointing it at the ground, Taenya settled into her sinister stance, ready for the duel to commence.

With an almost primal roar, the man lunged into action.

He swung his blade wide, arcing upward before crashing down in a powerful follow-through. Taenya parried the swing with ease, retaliating with a swift strike of her own that connected with the man's breastplate, the loud clash of steel reverberating through the air.

Nicolas rolled with the impact, his blade swinging in a counterattack as he moved. Taenya brought her sword up to block the attack, her mind whirling.

What is he doing?

Armor was truly a formidable defense, especially against swords, but it wasn't invincible. Purposefully taking hits could cause unseen injuries beneath the protective layer.

Their duel continued in a flurry of attacks, with Nicolas managing only a glancing blow against Taenya's bracer. In contrast, she struck him three more times on the thigh, stomach, and back.

Yet, he kept coming, seemingly unfazed by her strikes. She knew from experience that the only way to truly injure him was to target the weak points in his armor.

So, she bided her time, skillfully parrying and evading his swings. His attacks were almost comically telegraphed, as if he was announcing his intentions before each move.

Nicolas narrowly avoided a strike to his leg and managed to knock her sword away. He then brought his own blade up in an overhead strike that she dodged by moving under and toward him, a maneuver she had used countless times against overconfident opponents.

Taenya punched him in the throat, then grabbed her sword with both hands again and spun around, swinging hard. She pulled at the magic flowing through her and used her [**Empowered Strike**].

The blade caught the man in his gut hard. He folded over but still didn't fall. She pulled her blade and saw the long horizontal dent in the man's armor, then gasped in surprise as he grabbed her with one hand and yanked her forward. Her sword was at an awkward angle, and she shifted so she could shove him away, but then Nicolas did something that completely took her off guard. He slammed his helmeted head into her, causing her to wince in pain at both the sound and the shock as she staggered backward.

She was nearly too slow as he thrust his blade forward, directly at her chest, and she brought her sword up just in time to parry the blow.

Nicolas, seemingly unfazed by the hits he had taken, began to fight back with a wild, reckless abandon. His strength, greater than Taenya's, started to tip the scales in his favor. Their swords clashed, the metallic ring echoing around the field. They locked together in a test of strength, and Taenya felt herself starting to buckle under the pressure.

In that moment, she reached deep within herself, tapping into the fury that coursed through her veins. She was a knight. Her princess's protector. She would not falter here. Magic had already gifted her with enhanced abilities, augmenting her body beyond the limits of a normal telv woman. But now, she needed more. She needed to be *stronger*.

With a scream that echoed her fury and determination, she felt the magic surge within her. Red energy coursed through her body, a tangible manifestation of her will. A *click* resounded in her head as the [**Arcane Capability**] settled into her.

Suddenly, a rush of strength surged through her and the overwhelming pressure from Nicolas was no longer insurmountable. The scales had been balanced. No, more than balanced. She was stronger. She could feel it in the way her muscles responded, the way her grip on her sword tightened without strain.

Nicolas's eyes widened in shock as she pushed back against him, breaking their deadlock. She shoved him away, creating a gap between them. Without wasting a moment, she charged forward, her movements fueled by her newfound strength.

In two powerful bounds, she closed the distance and shoulder-checked him. The force of the impact catapulted him off his feet, and he landed on the ground with a resounding thud that sent dust clouds billowing. As much as the surprise registered on Nicolas's face, Taenya herself couldn't hide her astonishment at the successful use of her untested magical prowess.

The thrill of triumph, however, cost her precious seconds. Caught up in her unexpected feat, she momentarily froze, squandering the opportunity to press her advantage. In that brief respite, her opponent managed to regain his footing and reclaim his sword.

Stupid, she reprimanded herself.

Nicolas reassumed his fighting posture, chest rising and falling heavily as he gasped for breath, all the while maintaining unbroken eye contact with Taenya. There was something there, a flicker of surprise and . . . perhaps fear.

But it was gone as quickly as it had come, replaced by a hardened determination. His movements were slow and deliberate, resembling a cornered beast ready to lash out. Taenya realized his dangerous predicament, but it wasn't only him she had to worry about. The prying eyes of his guards were tracking her every move. She needed to finish this with care.

Nicolas tightened his grip around the hilt of his sword, his silence making the moment even more tense. He was waiting, she realized, for her to make the next move.

Nicolas shifted his weight, his muscles tensing as he prepared to face her. He was on the defensive now, she saw. He was waiting for her to attack, ready to counter whatever she threw at him.

But Taenya wasn't about to rush in blindly. She had the advantage now, and she wasn't about to throw it away. She took a deep breath, steadying herself. She needed to be smart about this, to use her newfound strength wisely.

She raised her sword, her grip firm but relaxed. She met Nicolas's gaze, her own eyes hard and determined. She was ready. She would not back down. She would not falter. And with that, she charged.

Nicolas braced himself, his sword raised in a defensive stance. His eyes were narrowed, focused solely on her. He thought he was ready for her, she knew, but she also knew that she had the upper hand.

As she closed the distance, she saw him shift his weight, preparing to counter her attack. His muscles tensed, his grip on his sword tightening.

Just as she was about to reach him, Nicolas moved. He swung his sword, aiming for her midsection. But Taenya was also ready. She twisted her body, narrowly avoiding his blade. At the same time, she swung her own sword, aiming for his exposed side.

Nicolas was quick, though. He managed to bring his sword around in time to block her attack. Their swords clashed, sparks flying from the impact. But Taenya didn't let up. She pushed against him, using her [Arcane Capability] to her advantage.

Nicolas grunted, struggling to hold her back. But Taenya was relentless. She pushed harder, her muscles straining with the effort. And then, with a final burst of strength, she managed to push him back.

He stumbled, barely managing to keep his footing. He didn't have time to recover. Taenya was already on him, her sword swinging down in a powerful arc. He raised his sword to block her, but it was too late.

With a resounding screech, Taenya's sword struck Nicolas's faceplate, the force of her blow sending him reeling. The metallic echo of the impact rang out across the silent field.

But Nicolas was not defeated yet. In a desperate move, he scooped up a handful of dirt from the ground and flung it at her. The dirt clouded her vision, some of it lodging in the slits of her helmet. She blinked, trying to clear her sight, but it was too late. Nicolas was already swinging his sword at her.

Reacting instinctively, Taenya spun forward, moving with a grace and speed that belied the weight of her armor. Nicolas's sword whistled through the air, missing her by mere inches. His momentum carried him forward, and he stumbled, his footing lost due to his overcompensation.

Taenya didn't waste the opportunity. She spun around, her sword raised. Nicolas was still trying to regain his balance, his back turned to her. She moved in, her sword swinging down in a swift, decisive arc with her [Empowered Strike].

The anguished cry of Nicolas echoed across the field as he was sent sprawling, his weapon skittering away in the dust.

Taenya wasted no time in capitalizing on his vulnerability, charging forward and delivering a powerful kick to his face. His head snapped back with the force, a weak groan escaping his lips as he rolled onto his side.

Her sword was already arcing down, poised to deliver the final blow to his exposed neck, when an unexpected sound made her halt. The rustle of movement behind her.

In a fluid motion, she spun around, her blade lashing out to meet the incoming attack. But it was blocked by one of House Angwin's guards. His counterattack was swift, his blade finding a gap in her armor and biting into her side.

A grunt of pain escaped her lips, but she had no time to react as the guard lunged, tackling her to the ground.

As they tumbled, she caught sight of her own guards rushing forward. The world spun as she hit the ground, the guard's weight pressing down on her. He was already pushing himself up, his blade glinting menacingly in the sunlight.

No!

The thought of Gwyn flashed through her mind, and she remembered what the girl had given her. Taenya slammed her hand against the pin, praying to all the gods it would be something that could help her.

The pin heated up, searing her skin through the layers of her armor. She screamed in pain, but held on, feeling a strange pull inside her. Then, a rush of magic flowed from her into the pin.

And then, the world was ablaze.

Fire erupted from her, engulfing everything around her. The guard atop her let out an inhuman scream, thrashing wildly as the flames consumed him. His armor, once solid and unyielding, seemed to melt under her touch as she pushed against him with all her might.

With a final, desperate shove, she managed to dislodge him. He fell away from her, his screams echoing in her ears as she lay there, surrounded by the flames of her own making.

Taenya rolled onto her side, her gaze sweeping across the field. All around her, guards from both houses stood frozen, their swords drawn but held in check by the spectacle before them. The world seemed to hold its breath as she pushed herself to her feet, drawing her shortsword.

Slowly, both House Angwin's guards and her own backed away. She caught sight of Lord Angwin yelling, but couldn't hear him. A high-pitched ringing filled her ears, drowning out the world around her. She opened and closed her mouth, trying to alleviate the discomfort, but the ringing only shifted in pitch.

Out of the corner of her eye, she caught sight of movement. Lord Nicolas was crawling to his sword. Ignoring the pain that flared with each step, she moved toward him, her skin raw and tender beneath her armor.

Seven agonizing steps later, she was standing over him. Drawing on her magic, she reached down and grabbed him, flipping him onto his back and yanking his head off the ground. She glanced around, ensuring no other guards were approaching, before setting her knee on his chest. She dropped her sword out of his reach and began to pummel his face, her gauntlet connecting with his helmet again and again. After five strikes, she yanked off his helmet, revealing a bloodied face and broken nose.

With a final shove, she forced Lord Nicolas back to the ground and resumed her assault, her fists raining down until he coughed up blood. Satisfied, she grabbed her blade and stood, her gaze sweeping over the resigned faces of Angwin's guards and the loathing expression of the marquess.

She looked down at Lord Nicolas, a question nagging at the back of her mind. Why had he been so eager to accept the challenge? He showed an amateurish skill with the blade and no foresight.

It's almost as if he wanted to die. Did he really think it would be that easy? She shook her head. Those thoughts were unnecessary. It was a question she would likely never have an answer to.

With a grunt, Taenya pulled Lord Nicolas to his knees. One last glance at the marquess confirmed that he was surrounded by his guards, as well as the Ducal Guard. Her attention narrowed to the man kneeling before her. She drew back her shortsword, the magic within her surging to the surface, and used her [Empowered Strike].

She really hoped Sabina had managed to shield Gwyn from what came next.

Her gaze flicked back to Lord Angwin, who was yelling incoherently. She shook her head, the ringing in her ears intensifying. She removed her helmet, rubbing her ears in an attempt to alleviate the discomfort. The ringing subsided slightly, enough for her to hear muffled sounds.

She stood tall, despite her injuries, and knew she needed to speak. Honor demanded it. And *her* honor was not besmirched. Her voice echoed across the silent field.

"House Reinhart's legitimacy has been proved today in the old ways, through *honorable* combat," Taenya declared, unable to keep the sarcasm from her tone.

Then her body felt like it was being stabbed all over by countless needles. *Ah, fuck. Keep it short.*

"We . . . demand that the parties accept the outcome . . . by ending all illegal actions against our princess, and that House Reinhart . . . is given its rightful dues."

She paused, catching her breath and taking the time to look over the crowd where the duke sat and then back to the marquess. She still couldn't really hear anything, and it was starting to get a bit concerning, but she continued, her voice struggling as her battle fervor ebbed.

"Any further disputes can be settled through civilized discourse or, if necessary, at the end of my righteous blade."

She turned and suddenly felt lightheaded, and closed her eyes for a moment. When she opened them, Sabina was rushing toward her, her mouth moving in a flurry of words. Taenya strained to hear her, but the ringing in her ears made it impossible. *I can't hear for shit.*

"Taenya!"

"What!?" she replied in what was definitely too loud of a volume.

Sabina spoke again as she arrived by her side. "Are you okay?"

Read the lips, Taenya. "Yes! Head is ringing!"

Sabina nodded and placed her hands on either side of Taenya's head, leaned close, and peered into her eyes. Taenya noted that Sabina's were pitch black.

I am only doing this so it looks like I am examining you. If you do not want me to speak this way, shake your head, Sabina said telepathically.

Taenya nodded, understanding, and tried to speak as quietly as possible. "It's a good idea. Keep doing it."

Speak in your mind. Focus on talking to me.

Taenya concentrated, directing her thoughts at Sabina. *It's a good idea. Keep—*

A sigh echoed in her mind. *I heard that, Taenya. Are you okay? You're bleeding from your side.*

That guard got me, and it hurts. So bad. Whatever Gwyn gave me saved my life, but it burned me and everything is muffled and ringing. I hurt everywhere. Keeping my magic swirling inside me is helping me keep moving. I know that as soon as it goes away, I'm passing out.

We need to get you home. Siveril is handling everything.

Angwin? Taenya questioned mentally.

*Has vowed revenge and stormed out, of course. The duke is already working on a suitable punishment for his guard's transgression. He warns that nothing will likely come of **that** because you burned him alive.*

Yeah . . . I didn't know it would do that.

Gwyn didn't either.

What?!

Don't tell her I told you. She's just happy it worked.

Taenya groaned. She was thankful for the girl's aid, but a little forewarning would have been nice. They really needed to practice together more.

Does this look weird? You staring at me?

Yes, Sabina confirmed. *One hundred percent. We should probably move.*

With Sabina's and a guard's assistance on either side, Taenya began to walk to the rest of their group. As they walked, Taenya turned to Sabina.

What's next?

We get you home. We get you healthy.

That sounds lovely, Taenya thought as her vision started to fade and she stumbled.

CHAPTER THIRTY-SIX

UNDER THE COVER OF DARKNESS

There is silence and then there is . . . absence.

An ominous harbinger of impending doom. You know something bad is about to happen when cats don't fight in the alleys, the birds don't flap a single wing, or when even the rats do not scurry in the night.

Senior Guardswoman Nemura Kho'lin knew it. When she navigated the city streets toward the fort that night, a skin-crawling stillness hung in the air. The city's denizens, blissfully ignorant, went about their routines, oblivious to the shroud of unease. A flicker of guilt touched Nemura as she passed by them, each seemingly engrossed in their own world. Despite knowing what loomed ahead, she hadn't even considered warning them.

The captain had been very clear in his orders, and Nemura knew that they were the sort that one simply did not disobey. She knew that despite the guilt, the choice to remain silent at least gave them a chance.

Upon reaching the East Fort's courtyard, the guardswoman found herself surrounded by the hushed whispers of the other troops, their voices barely piercing the silence. The comforting nightly hum of nature seemed to have abandoned them—even the persistent insects had surrendered to the silence. It was almost time. The anticipation curled in her gut, as palpable as the cool night breeze ruffling her copper hair.

Lady Reinhart and one of the Blightwych knights had come to warn of the beast swarm that was fast approaching the city. Initially, the grim warning brought by the terran baroness was met with skepticism. Yet, the mere mention of the Order of Secrets triggered anger within both her and the captain. While she personally wasn't worried about tangling with one of their agents in a one-on-one fight, she knew they didn't resort to such measures. They killed when you least expected it, and even for one with her background, there were always times when you would be vulnerable.

The situation was dire and she knew all they could do was prepare for what was coming.

An entire city condemned all for one noble.

The Sovereign Cities and the mighty Empire teetered on the brink of war while the Westari Crown, entangled in its own paranoia, was hunting dissidents within its realm.

"Senior Guardswoman," a voice infiltrated her brooding thoughts. Twisting around, she found Senior Guardsman Viktor Constine advancing toward her, his face etched with news of some import. "I bring updates."

"Join me," she beckoned, keeping her voice hushed and tone discreet. She led the way into the guardhouse and commandeered a room from a group of planners. She frowned when she saw a table scattered with tools of strategy and blueprints of their fort. Documents sketched with lines of attack and circles of defense lay spread out on the table.

If our enemy were anything other than beasts, this lack of discipline would be our doom.

She sighed and turned around. "Okay, what have you learned?"

The senior guardsman leaned in and spoke in a low voice, "Captain Lars has taken action. He and his men have moved against the terran baroness, Lady Reinhart."

She raised an eyebrow and met Viktor's serious gaze. A flicker of surprise rippled through her before she quickly schooled her features into a neutral expression.

"From what we saw," he continued, "Lady Reinhart and her knights have annihilated the first wave of Captain Lars's men. However, it seems the captain was not so easily deterred. He is amassing more forces with an evident intention of capturing the woman."

She cursed. "Damn that man, and damn the count. We're going to be attacked any moment, and he continues with his ridiculous fixation on the terrans."

Viktor nodded. "His mind is clearly addled. What should we do?"

"Nothing about that. I'll let the captain know. Join the rapid response squads and be ready to get into the city to rescue whoever you can."

"Understood."

He turned to leave, but then paused. The ash-colored raithe turned back and looked up at her, reaching out his hand. "Good luck, Nemura. It's been an honor. You're too good for us lowly city guards, but I can't say I regret being able to learn from you."

She smiled as she clasped his wrist. "You've all accepted me when you didn't have to. The honor has been mine, Viktor."

As she left the room, Nemura narrowed her eyes on the planners who were waiting. "Get in there and secure the room. Do not leave things that would be useful to an enemy lying around. That is intelligence that would get us all killed. That is information that should be discussed in the security of the keep. Now go!"

"Yes, senior guardswoman!"

Nemura quickly made her way through the fort and onto the battlements, where one of the guards pointed her to where Captain Jorin stood, overlooking the city.

"Captain."

The moon elf turned and looked up at her. "What is it, Nemura?" he asked, his voice quiet but full of authority.

She inclined her head slightly. It was what she respected about him. Unlike so many others, he was a true soldier, and knew that following through with what needed to be done was sometimes the hardest choice.

"Captain Lars and his men have moved against the terran. The knights and the baroness completely wiped out the first wave of men. Lars is moving more forces to capture the terran woman."

A heavy sigh escaped the captain. She knew what he was likely thinking. It was something he'd complained to her about many times. *"What a kingdom of short-sighted, power-hungry idiots we've become,"* he had said.

"This came from Senior Guardsman Constine?" was the only thing he vocalized.

Nemura nodded, keeping her movements precise. What could be done? There had to be something. She was no great strategist, though. Her focus had always been on small squad tactics and operations . . . even before.

"Has there been any word from Captain Gheata about the walls or his scouts?"

Nemura shook her head. "No, Captain. I haven't heard from anyone except our own garrison."

"What about our status?"

"East Fort is secure," she confirmed.

Captain Jorin nodded. His role within the Thirdghyll Guard gave him command of the Eastern Fortress, which protected the city from the lands outside the kingdom. The fortress was also likely where the remnants of the city's people would be required to shelter once things turned grim.

The captain was not nearly as confident in the city's ability to stand now that they knew the Academy *expected* them to fall. Based on what Nemura knew of the plan, he wanted to be sure the beginning of the end didn't come from their side of the city.

Captain Lars's role, on the other hand, placed him in command of the garrison within the central district. The garrison that was both *coincidentally* and *thankfully* filled with the most corruption.

"Nemura," Captain Jorin said, grabbing her attention. "Gather a squad. Head to the inn where the terran noble is staying. *Be careful.* If there's any hint of an assault, abort the mission and get your people back here immediately."

Ah. He wants to help extricate the terran. This is going to be . . . interesting.

It would also bring her in direct conflict with fellow members of the City Guard. A task fitting for one like her. After all, she had been assigned to his garrison due to her foreign origin.

She would see it done. "We'll bring them back safely to the fort, Captain," Nemura affirmed, her hand moving in a crisp salute. The captain returned the gesture, and she retreated toward the courtyard. She moved with a commanding presence, summoning a squad of guardsmen she knew would be best.

"What's the mission, Senior Guardswoman?" one of the men asked.

"Extraction. We're moving for the terran noble. Captain's orders. She's the reason we're going to survive the night, so we're going to return the favor."

There was an immediate sense of understanding that rippled through the squad. They nodded in unison, their determination unwavering. *Good.*

However, Nemura felt the need to share one more vital piece of information. "We may come face to face with Lars and his men," she added, her voice turning cold. It was not a command, but an offer, a chance for them to step away from this precarious undertaking. She would go with or without them.

As soon as the city was hit, everything would be shut down and locked. Squads would quickly rally at preplanned locations, including four squads—now five with Viktor's—whose purposes were to exit the fort and escort the families of everyone there back. Those families knew to immediately gather at the four points the squads would set out to. The squads knew that time would be of the essence. She only hoped it would be enough.

One of her men glanced at his comrades, shrugged nonchalantly, and then returned his gaze back to Nemura. "So? Is it finally time we show that self-important twit his place?"

A predatory grin spread across Nemura's face, her eyes glittering with a dark anticipation. "Arm yourselves. Aggressive negotiations might be necessary to ensure the baroness's safety. Remember, she will have noncombatants and knights with her."

With a nod, Nemura and her seasoned squad swiftly armed themselves with a medley of weaponry, their faces grimly set. Their hands, hardened from years of combat before retiring and joining Ghyll's City Guard, grasped the familiar leather handles of their weapons with practiced ease. Moments later, they swung themselves up onto their waiting horses, the well-trained steeds barely making a sound.

The cobbled city streets sprawled out before them, now bathed in an eerie glow from the dimmed street lamps. As they filed out of the East Fort's imposing iron gate, they spurred their horses into a gallop, their hooves clattering rhythmically on the stone.

Suddenly, the distant tolling of city bells reverberated through the night air, sending a cold shiver down Nemura's spine. The alarm was coming from the west district.

Pivoting in her saddle, she addressed her squad with a sharp tone, her eyes hardened with determination. "The bells are from the west. We need to move quickly. Stay vigilant for any beasts! Crossbowmen, watch our flanks."

Various colorful curses rang out from the squad in response, their anxiety thinly veiled by the vulgar humor. But Nemura's chest swelled with pride. They were men after her own heart, ready to face the unknown with a snarl and a curse.

"The fort is going to be locked down, we don't have much time before even we will not be permitted back in."

That spurred them on. She knew the plan. By now, most back in the fort would be grabbing spears, bows, and quivers of arrows. Others, supplies and the large bolts for the ballistae, which even now were surely being repositioned to target into the city. Barricades were to be moved into place at the two gates. They would not be caught off guard by an attack coming from inside the city.

Tenera willing, they would survive the night. Then Nemura would be ready to enact the longer term plan that the captain and she had come up with for the terran. A way to . . . thank her for saving what she could of the city.

She prayed to her people's patron goddess, Brysphine, Goddess of War, that it would be enough.

She had heard the bells sound, but as Rayka stood on the western wall, leaning over the parapet, there was nothing to see in the darkness below. She heard nothing except the bells, not even the sounds of fighting that one would expect. She kept peering into the darkness, hoping to see something . . . anything that would warrant the bells being rung.

After a while, Rayka sighed and pushed herself back up. She grabbed her spear, hefting it up as she was turning around. Her eyes narrowed once she noticed there was no one around.

She looked back and forth, then called out into the torchlit night, "Ander? Mila?"

There was no response.

Her breath quickened. "Imelan? Loran? Anyone?" she tried again.

There were supposed to be four others from her squad in this short section of the wall between two towers. She looked up at the tower closest to her. "Hey! Down here!" she yelled.

A head peaked over the edge of the tower. "What?! We're busy up here!"

"Is my squad in there?" Rayka called back.

The man from above yelled out, "What?"

"My squad! I'm alone!"

The head jerked away from the edge. Rayka tilted her head.

That's odd.

She cupped her hands around her mouth and yelled, "Hey!"

There was no reply.

Rayka walked to the door and banged on it. In the case of bells, all doors would be bolted shut and a drawbar put into place. She banged a few times, but no response came.

At least someone should be in there. What is going on?

She turned back and quickly moved toward the other tower. Rayka was on edge, panic was settling in.

Where is everyone?

Rayka was halfway there when she heard it. She gripped her spear tightly and slowly turned. There was nothing there, but then she stopped, held her breath, and listened.

A low growl cut through the silence.

She widened her eyes in the dark and fumbled to get her spear in front of herself. But she didn't see anything. *I need to get to the tower.*

She kept her eyes wide and searched for the source of the noise. As she got closer to the tower, it seemed to surround her. It didn't get quieter, nor did it grow louder. It was just a constant presence of terror. A reminder that she was prey.

She banged on the door. *Come on. Come on. Come on.*

There was no reply.

Rayka was shaking. She turned around, keeping her back to the door. The growl was still there. Taunting her. No one was responding. She was alone.

She steeled her nerves. "Well? Come on then! Come on, you beast!"

Nothing. She looked left and right. Suddenly, the deep rumbling got louder. Closer. "Where are you?!" Rayka yelled, her spear was firm in her grip. She was ready. Her head twitched as she felt a drop. She wiped it off her forehead.

Odd. It's red.

Rayka looked up into the eyes of a feline *monster*. Its fangs dripped with blood. Two appendages like tentacles with what looked like hooks on the end unfurled from its back and pointed down at her.

It leaped.

The walls were breached all across the west and south districts, the monsters spreading out as they entered the city. Then they started hunting. Screams and more bells rang across the walls as the roars of monsters could be heard throughout the city. Men and women called out as they were attacked.

Rayka did not respond.

* * *

Sloane was perched on a stool, watching as Gisele and the knights engaged in a heated discussion about going out and searching for Cristole and Ernald. The gruesome sight of bodies strewn around the area and the shrill scream of a server who had stumbled upon the horrific scene still echoed in her mind. The usual bustling atmosphere of the inn and its staff had come to an abrupt halt, replaced by a chilling silence.

They had managed to haul the equipment used in the battle in the inn, promptly loading it into the wagons. One of the knights had helpfully sorted the spent grenades, which offered Sloane the opportunity to recharge them later. The damaged items, though seemingly worthless, were salvaged—Koren believed he could make them reusable when they had time. When tallied up, the aftermath of both battles would yield an advantageous stockpile for the small caravan.

Stepping outside, Sloane was taken aback by the carnage the knights had left behind. Fifteen lifeless bodies lying in various states of disarray showed how lopsided the assault had been. Clearly, whoever had targeted the group had thought themselves prepared, but obviously underestimated their targets. Considering Gisele's shields and Maud's healing, she expected her group would have been able to handle even more.

Sloane's house members sat nearby, their gear packed, ready for the signal to head for the East Gate. Ismeld had finally awoken and had attempted to join in, only to be promptly silenced by a fiery redhead who insisted she rest.

Suddenly, a loud bang against the back door made Sloane snap to attention, three [**Mana Bolts**] forming above her outstretched hand, poised for attack. Another bang, and the door burst open to reveal Cristole, propping up a bloodied Ernald.

"Maud!" Cristole's call sliced through the tense atmosphere, and the telv woman wasted no time rushing over to the injured sun elf.

Sloane stayed out of the way, carefully observing as Maud worked her magic on the mostly superficial wounds. A deep one required the knight-medic's focus for five minutes, but in the end her magic was quick in enabling Ernald to be back on his feet with surprising ease.

The distant sound of urgently ringing bells suddenly reverberated through the still air. A knot tightened in her stomach.

They're here.

Her gaze locked with Gisele's. The other woman held her stare, offered a slight nod of understanding, then turned her attention back to the room.

"It's time. We need to move. All of us should have been gone already. We're behind schedule," Gisele commanded, her stern tone slicing through the tension-filled air.

Sloane's gaze swept across the faces of their small, determined group, each one marked by a grim acceptance of the imminent peril. "Okay, get to the wagons. We need to move, now. The bells are ringing," she echoed Gisele's urgency.

Ismeld rose to her feet, a pained groan slipping past her lips. "I am ready," she declared, her eyes flickering with steely determination.

Kemmy exchanged a quick glance with Rel before turning back to the rest. "Is there anything we can do?"

Gisele shook her head curtly. "Just get into the wagons, and stay calm. Keep the doors locked." She looked at Deryk. "You ready?"

With a firm hand on Cristole's shoulder and a nod of acknowledgment, Deryk responded, "We are ready."

Sloane swallowed the lump in her throat, feeling the prickling sting of tears welling up in her eyes. "Be careful. All of you," she managed.

A smile softened Maud's face. "Don't worry, Sloane. They have me. I'll bring them back in one piece."

"You'd better, or we shall have words, Ser Maud," Ismeld retorted, making her way over to her fellow knights.

Sloane watched the knights huddle, their camaraderie echoing in the tight embraces they exchanged with Ismeld before disappearing through the back door.

As the door closed behind them, Stefan stepped forward, addressing the remaining group. "As sentimental as that was, let's load up. We need to move."

Ismeld nodded in agreement. "He is right. Let us depart." There was no room for hesitation. The night had come, and with it, their fight for survival began.

The wagons trekked along in the night slowly, remaining as quiet as possible yet purposeful in their movement along the cobbled streets. Ismeld, sitting on Sloane's left, scrutinized the maze of side streets with an eagle-eyed gaze. She drove one of the wagons Elodie and Koren had purchased, while Sloane sat next to her with her senses on a hair trigger, ready to cast at a moment's notice.

Even though Sloane heard the bells, and the screams and sounds of fighting in the distance, the center of the city was calm. It almost seemed too good to be true, and she constantly glanced down at her watch as it also scanned their surroundings, but for mana use.

As Sloane had a moment to think about it, she wasn't even sure they would make it out of the gate from the central district. Surely it would be locked down by now due to the attack. If it was, they would need to open it. Which could prove difficult.

Rel held the reins of the knights' wagon, her frame garbed in a simple gambeson and an iron helm, a shield at her side for added protection. Elodie and Kemmy were tucked safely inside, with the wagon's doors bolted and reinforced with a wooden bar. Stefan and Koren were bringing up the rear with the last wagon.

The plan in case of attack was that Stefan would cover the rear, or, if there was nothing, he would move to support Ismeld and Sloane. Rel had her big crossbow with her, but seeing as how she was driving the wagon with the other two women inside, she was to remain there.

A sudden gust of wind, chilling to the bone, swept over Sloane, snatching her from her thoughts. A shiver ran down her spine. She tightened her cloak around her, securing the clasp, bracing against the piercing cold. The streets lay submerged in darkness, save the silver glow of the two moons adorning the sky. One, a full-bodied sphere of light, and the other, a slender crescent, hung high above them like twin sentinels guiding them over the treacherous path.

Sloane was surprised by the complete lack of people, even guards. It was a good thing that people remained indoors, but other than a dearth of activity, there was nothing to give the impression of a city under attack . . . that is, if one looked at the current district alone and ignored the distant sounds in other districts of Thirdghyll.

As they navigated their slow but determined path toward the city gate, signs of life started to emerge. Scattered guards, torches ablaze, patrolled the cobblestones with a resolute stride. The main street, tracing a gentle curve through an imposing arch between two towering structures, straightened into a direct stretch, culminating at the grand gatehouse. Its opulence was a beacon of the district it represented.

Sloane jerked her head in surprise. Leaning closer to Ismeld, an edge cut into her voice, she asked, "The gate is still open? Why?"

Ismeld frowned, her usual composure shadowed by perplexity. "I am unsure," she admitted, a hint of trepidation sneaking into her voice. "The gate should be sealed during an active attack on the city."

Sloane's unease heightened, her gut gnawing at her with a relentless sense of dread. "Something isn't right. I've had a bad feeling this whole time. It's too quiet."

Ismeld swiveled to face Sloane, her eyes wide with surprise and a touch of indignation. "And you are just telling me this now?"

CHAPTER THIRTY-SEVEN

BEING WITH YOU IS BAD LUCK

Ismeld drew back on the reins as they got closer, slowing the horses to a more cautious pace. They were met with the indifferent gazes of guards, all of whom continued their rounds as if it were just another unremarkable day. A moon elf in chainmail detached himself from the vicinity of the gate of the wall that surrounded the central district and lifted a commanding hand. "Halt! State your business," he demanded.

As Ismeld brought the horses to a standstill, she mimicked the guard's gesture in respectful acknowledgment with a gloved hand. "I am Ser Ismeld. We are bound for the east district on business." With a steady voice, she launched into their carefully constructed cover story. "We serve a client who has generously paid us for our services."

A condescending voice from the side questioned, "And who might that client be, high elf?" Sloane turned to locate the source and was met with the disdainful gaze of the guard captain they'd encountered at the ball.

Damn it.

As the moon elf captain advanced toward them, flanked by a sizable contingent of guards, his eyes darted from Ismeld and Sloane to the two wagons behind them. He scrutinized the caravan, his gaze keen and piercing. With a subtle nod of his head, he directed half of his men to blockade their path.

"Sloane Reinhart," the captain declared with cool authority, "you stand accused of assault and murder of this city's guardsmen. By order of Count Kayser of Thirdghyll, you and the Knights of Haven's Hope are now declared enemies of the Crown and condemned to death. All those known to associate with you share the same fate. Surrender now, and we assure a painless execution. Defy us, and the assurance is withdrawn."

Undeterred, Ismeld secured the reins to a wagon post and engaged the hand brake to immobilize the wheels. Rising from her seat, she seized her shield and vaulted nimbly from the wagon. With her longsword unsheathed, she advanced, a towering figure of determination. Sloane followed suit, clutching an additional shield and descending from the wagon to join Ismeld at the forefront.

As the moon elf captain unsheathed his sword, his men followed suit, creating a chilling symphony of metallic whispers in the quiet street.

The cobblestones echoed with the sound of approaching steps from behind. Sloane swiveled to see Stefan, equipped with a short spear and towering shield. Beneath his loose clothing, the telltale bulk of fitted chainmail hinted at preparedness. The raithe gave her a silent nod of solidarity as he moved to stand at her right, completing their defiant front against the imminent conflict.

"Where are the other knights?" the captain probed, steering the remaining troops to join the ranks already amassed in the street.

Ismeld retorted with a steely glare, her voice laced with contempt. "That is no concern of yours."

The captain chuckled mirthlessly. "We will find them, regardless. So, do the three of you actually plan to contend with our entire garrison?"

Sloane quickly surveyed the scene. She counted twenty guards on the ground level, supplemented by another ten scattered atop the gate's battlements and along the walls. All considered, it was a surprisingly paltry number for what was ostensibly one of the city's primary entrances.

Let's hope the West Gate is drawing the majority of their forces.

Sharing a fleeting glance with Ismeld, Sloane let a calculated smile play upon her lips. "Not the entire garrison, captain. There are a few of your men back at the inn who won't be able to join the party." Lifting her hand, she strained to channel her mana, generating five luminous, purple **[Mana Bolts]** that orbited her.

The guard scowled at them. "Men! Shields!"

In response, the guards shouted in unison, their shields snapping up to form a formidable shield wall. The formation curved slightly, creating a defensive arc that spanned the street before them.

Without breaking her focus, Ismeld shot a glance at Stefan. "Stay with me. Sloane, you remain behind us, casting as much as you can. Don't concentrate your attacks. Keep them guessing and exploit any openings they leave," she ordered, her voice firm yet calm.

"Understood," Stefan said.

Sloane mirrored his sentiment, nodding with determination. "Got it."

She looked down at the back of her shield, where two grenades were strapped.

One was a flashbang but the other had an experimental spell called [**Arcane Explosion**] channeled into it. She wasn't sure how it would do.

"Spears! Forward!" The captain's command rang out like a death knell, and the men's spears thrust forward as they advanced a step.

Shit. This isn't going to be easy.

The horses began to panic, skittishly attempting to retreat but finding their movement restrained. Stefan and Ismeld moved in synchrony, hoisting their shields defensively.

"Ismeld!" Sloane called out breathily, trying to be both loud and whispering at the same time.

"What?" the knight replied and tilted her head to listen.

"Do we attack first?"

"Yes! There are twenty of them! Of course, we do!"

Shit. Okay. Shock and awe.

Sloane zeroed in on five distinct targets dispersed along the shield wall, sending her [**Mana Bolts**] careening toward them. The bolts slammed into the guards' shields, the impact jolting them backward yet causing no visible injury.

Unfazed, she resumed her barrage, launching successive [**Mana Bolts**] at an array of targets. Their formation wavered as her spells sent men reeling, some even bashing themselves with their own shields, but their advance didn't halt.

"Stay together! The witch can't get through our shields!" a guard bellowed encouragingly.

"Sloane! You need to do something!" Stefan's voice pierced the escalating chaos.

Sloane took a deep breath. She channeled an [**Arcane Barrage**], unleashing it awkwardly while clutching her shield. Purple bolts of energy pummeled the shields, forcing the men to huddle closer together for mutual support. Some guards scrambled behind others whom they anticipated would need extra assistance.

Sloane honed in on a faltering raithe.

One. Two. Three bolts detonated against his shield in quick succession, each impact eliciting a pained grunt, culminating in a sickening crack as his shield warped unnaturally before clattering to the ground. The moment it began to fall, a crossbow bolt streaked through the air, striking him squarely in the collarbone, piercing the chainmail and felling the guard.

With a gasp, Sloane whipped her head toward the unexpected aid, eyes wide in surprise at the sight of Rel, the orkun alchemist, already reloading her hefty crossbow. Rel met her gaze with a resolute nod. "Keep going!" she shouted.

Spurred by the orkun's encouragement, Sloane threw herself back into the fray, channeling another surge of the [**Arcane Barrage**], pouring every ounce of her energy into staving off the impenetrable shield wall.

"Hold! Cover!" the captain's warning echoed, prompting the guards to hunker down just as her barrage crashed against their shields. Her gaze hardened as she swiftly reached for one of the grenades strapped to her belt. Timing would be everything.

"Up! Forward!"

The moment the command left the captain's lips, Sloane lobbed the grenade into the fray. It skittered beneath the momentarily raised shields before erupting into a blinding [Flashbang]. Cries of shock and pain resonated as three guards in the epicenter were stripped of their shields.

Sloane wasted no time, her [Mana Bolts] slamming into their exposed chests and sending them sprawling backward. Another guard, distracted by his fallen comrades, was swiftly silenced by a second crossbow bolt sprouting from his exposed neck.

"Re-form!"

"Stefan! Now!" Ismeld's command cut through the chaos.

With impeccable synchrony, the pair hurled themselves at the regrouping guards, driving their shoulders between a pair of shields on the right flank and shattering the formation. Ismeld ruthlessly bashed one man's head with her shield while slashing into another with her sword. Simultaneously, Stefan skewered a guard with his spear, promptly releasing the weapon only to unsheathe a shortsword and fend off another assailant attempting to retaliate.

Refocusing her attention, Sloane unleashed an [Arcane Barrage] at the other side of the shield wall, a desperate attempt to suppress their advance. She would have sworn she heard bones breaking in guards who had not braced themselves for the punch of the hard-hitting spells.

"Break! Break! Where are my archers?"

The shield wall collapsed, and it became every man for themselves. Another crossbow bolt appeared in a guard who lowered his shield, and Sloane fired a [Flashbang] at two guards on the wall who were trying to bring their bows to bear. Both men screamed, and one stumbled and fell over the wall, landing with a sickening crunch.

As the guards tried to recover, four maintained sight of Sloane and kept their shields together, but the rest started to spread out to focus on the two melee fighters taking apart their flank. Sloane countered by firing another [Flashbang] at the persistent quartet obstructing her view.

One guard reacted quickly. "Cover!"

They shielded their faces, unwittingly falling into her trap. While their senses were reeling from the blinding flash, Sloane swiftly reached for her second grenade, activating it before lobbing it into their midst. It skidded to a halt by one guard's foot. He let out an alarmed shout.

"Light contraption!"

A what?

In a desperate attempt, he swung his foot to kick it away, but the |**Arcane Explosion**| detonated prematurely. The explosion was pitifully small, a sphere of sizzling purple mana that barely grazed the others. But the unfortunate guard's foot vaporized in an instant.

Tucking away the memory of the grenade's disappointing performance for future analysis, Sloane quickly refocused, launching a [**Mana Bolt**] at a moon elf guard rushing to aid his fallen comrade. The spell hit the man just above his shoulder and burned through part of his skull. The kinetic force of the impact sent his lifeless body into another guard, who let out a horrified scream as he futilely tried to push the body away.

Just as Sloane was about to exploit the guard's distraction, a sudden movement in her periphery made her recoil, and she instinctively snapped up her shield. An arrow lodged itself in the shield with a resonating thud. Her breath hitched as the close call sank in.

That almost hit me.

Risking a peek around the edge of her shield, she spotted the archer nocking another arrow. But he was forced to take evasive action, ducking from a retaliating bolt that zipped past him. He repositioned, taking aim once more, but Sloane wouldn't grant him the opportunity to target Rel. She cast a full [**Arcane Barrage**], unleashing a shower of bolts at the archer.

Of the eight bolts, only two found their mark. Fortunately, only one was necessary.

"Guardsmen! Stand down!" a commanding shout echoed from the gate.

Through narrowed eyes, Sloane saw a squad of eight guards advancing, led by a formidable telv woman encased in battle-worn armor.

Nemura! I'd recognize that mountain anywhere.

Ismeld capitalized on the momentary confusion, driving her blade into a nearby guard before retreating, just as Rel's deadly bolt took out another archer. The lifeless guard plummeted from the wall, crumpling at Nemura's feet.

"Guardswoman Kho'lin! I am assuming command of your unit. Form up, we need to eliminate these foreigners," Captain Lars ordered with a hint of desperation in his voice.

Nemura scanned the scene of strewn bodies and chaos, shaking her head in disbelief. "Captain Lars, the city itself is under attack and your concern is this? Why is the gate open?"

"Do you not comprehend the damage they have inflicted?" he countered, seeming surprised that he had to. "I am your superior, not a mere guardsman. You will—"

"Enough!" Nemura's voice boomed, effectively silencing him. She pointed at a visibly anxious raithe guard. "Explain to me why this gate remains open while our city is under siege," she demanded. "The west district has already been breached."

"W-we were given orders to keep the gate open . . . to lure the terran here . . . to kill her on the count's orders," the raithe stammered.

"You are not obligated to answer to her! I am your commanding officer here," Lars snapped, turning his full attention to the towering telv.

Sloane sighed, watching the escalating argument unfold. *This isn't going to end well.*

"You will obey my orders, *telv*, or I will consider you a traitor and sentence you myself. Now, you and your unit—"

All within an instant, Sloane [**Focused**] and let the currents of her mana weave within her with an even deeper pull than normal that made her sweat with the effort. A concentrated, swirling torrent of energy coalesced at her fingertips, her intent driving the structure of the spell. She [**Altered**] the [**Mana Bolt**] to be more potent, more penetrating as it elongated and narrowed to a point.

Without a sound, she unleashed the modified [**Mana Bolt**], its trajectory unwavering as it shot toward the moon elf. The spell collided directly between his shoulder blades, piercing through the gaps in his armor. The modified spell didn't explode immediately upon impact, but continued its devastating journey, burrowing deeper into the elf's body.

Only then, when it had infiltrated past his defenses, did the [**Mana Bolt**] detonate. The arcane energy erupted from within, causing severe burns to his upper back and lower neck, radiating outward from the center. The powerful blast flung Captain Lars forward, his armored form tumbling awkwardly to the ground, an unsightly crumpled heap under the pale moonlight

Sloane mustered her mana again, the strain evident as she formed seven [**Mana Bolts**] in the air around her, each locking on to one of the captain's remaining men. "Does anyone else wish to postpone our departure? We are leaving," Sloane announced, her tone icy.

Nemura's frown deepened, but she shifted her attention to the guards, as Lars's form remained motionless. "Who is next in command?"

A moon elf guard, his gaze flitting between Sloane and the fallen captain, finally settled on Nemura. "I-I am, Guardswoman. L-Lieutenant T-Treen," he stuttered out.

"Assume command. We are departing. Close this gate and prepare for combat. Hold this point," Nemura commanded, her tone brooking no argument.

"That's it?" Sloane asked.

Nemura fixed Sloane with a stern gaze. "We do not have time for this. Get back on your wagons, and let's go. Captain Jorin is expecting you," the big telv said.

After they got back on the wagons and started to move, Sloane glanced one last time at the captain, wondering what why the count had gone to these lengths, even while his city was under attack.

Sloane looked at her watch, the display a flurry of green, red, and yellow mana pulsations, an ominous dance of colors signaling danger all around.

"Nemura! There are more around us!" she yelled out.

The telv, astride her horse at the vanguard of the caravan, swiveled her head to assess their predicament. Her squad of guards had formed a protective perimeter around the wagons, providing cover as they hastily navigated toward the fort. No sooner had the sturdy gate to the central district slammed shut behind them than they'd had their first nightmarish encounter with the monstrous creatures. The journey since had been a relentless, harrowing struggle.

Nemura looked around and then at Ismeld. "Hurry! We need to move!"

Sloane's attention snapped back to her watch, her heart pounding against her ribcage as she noticed a blotch of yellow mana darting toward her with alarming velocity.

A scream teetered on the tip of her tongue as an arrow whizzed past her, finding its mark in a large, panther-like beast. The guard responsible for the beast's demise sent her a curt nod before swiftly nocking another arrow and releasing it with lethal precision at a predatory wolf skulking down a parallel street.

They had barely breached the boundary of the merchant district when the predators had ambushed them—gigantic wolves and panthers, the size of full-grown horses, stalking and hunting their prey. Nemura's desperate strategy was a headlong, frenzied dash, simultaneously engaging in combat to fend off the beastly threats.

"Lady Reinhart! Use your noise magic!"

My noise—oh!

Sloane looked up, rapidly assembling a plan in her mind. "Ismeld! Try to keep the wagon stable," she urged the woman beside her.

"How in Relena's name do you expect me to do that?!" Ismeld shouted back, her voice strained with frustration.

"Damn it. I'll figure it out!" Sloane retorted and scrambled up onto the roof of the swaying wagon. She hooked her feet into the ropes securing their luggage.

Please don't let me fall. Please don't let me fall.

She brought her watch up and used it to help her aim, searching for the mana signatures. Seeing a green mass coming close from the next road over, she aimed, and sure enough, a side road opened up and a pack of wolves came at the group. With a swift gesture, she launched a [Flashbang] at them. The resonating blast and subsequent yelps of surprise confirmed the accuracy.

She scanned the surrounding rooftops, looked down at her watch, and sent another [Flashbang] sailing toward the summit of a nearby building, its bright flare illuminating an ominous, lizard-like silhouette. It looked almost like a small dragon, but without wings.

Seeing the creature, Nemura bellowed a warning. "Drakyyd!"

Sloane aimed and launched an [**Arcane Barrage**] at the thing as it leaped from the rooftop, catching one of the guards and its horse. Amid screams of terror, she swept her hand toward the beast, and the final pair of arcane bolts veered in its direction, detonating upon impact just as the monster eviscerated the horse's throat. Its enraged roar filled the night, and it fixed its gaze on Sloane. Chaos ensued, the caravan screeching to a halt as guards shouted and scrambled into action.

Arrows whistled through the air, but they seemed to shatter upon impact with the creature's hide rather than penetrate it. One guard lunged forward, jabbing at the drakyyd with his spear. With a swift, savage motion, the creature seized the weapon in its jaws, violently dismounting the guard before pouncing and sinking its teeth into him. Despite a rain of arrows, the beast appeared undeterred.

Sloane launched a salvo of three [**Mana Bolts**], each creating a burst of purple arcane energy upon impact. The drakyyd roared in pain, its attention now riveted on her. It roared and sprinted toward the wagon, crouching and then jumping up at her. She channeled her mana and threw everything she had into an [**Arcane Barrage**]. She aimed every bolt at its face.

Two bolts connected midleap, and then, just as the drakyyd was about to reach the roof, a sword thrust from below punctured its exposed underbelly. The remaining bolts detonated on its gaping maw, yet the beast's momentum carried it forward into the wagon. The impact unbalanced Sloane, sending her sprawling backward.

She cried out, her arms flailing desperately as she toppled over the side. The ground met her with brutal force, expelling all the air from her lungs. She emitted a guttural groan and arched her back as a wave of pain surged through her.

"Lady Reinhart!" Nemura cried out. She dismounted her horse with an urgency that set her armor clattering. Swiftly crossing the distance, the senior guardswoman reached Sloane just as she emitted a pained groan, curling onto her side.

"Are you alright?" Nemura's query was laced with concern, her hand sliding under Sloane's armpit to hoist her upright.

A groan, roughened by pain, escaped Sloane's lips as she found her footing, leaning heavily on Nemura for support. "I-I'm good. I need to get back on the wagon," she managed to say, squinting at the telv woman through the grimace of discomfort etched on her face. "Your men?" She forced the question out.

Shaking her head in grim resolution, Nemura replied, "We should go. I don't think there are any more monsters . . . yet. You did good."

Sloane nodded, allowing Nemura to help her slowly move back to the wagon.

* * *

"Are you certain you are well, Sloane?" Ismeld asked, as their caravan trudged into the east district.

"I'm fine, Ismeld. Really." Sloane tried to brush off her concerns. "That stab of yours saved me," she added, attempting a smile.

"You did amazing up there."

Sloane simply nodded in acknowledgment, too weary to respond.

A sudden interjection from Nemura, who was riding beside them, broke their exchange. "What is that?" Her voice was laced with uncertainty.

Sloane forced herself to straighten and stand, squinting through the dim light at a throng of people illuminated by torchlight. A *formation* of people. "Looks like soldiers?"

Nemura tilted her head. "They should be in the fort."

"How far are we from there?" Sloane questioned.

"About five streets."

Their caravan decelerated as they neared the looming crowd. A man, distinguished by his elaborate armor, dismounted his horse and advanced toward them.

His booming voice reverberated through the otherwise silent district. "Lady Reinhart, your witchcraft has unleashed these beasts upon our city," Count Kayser declared. "You will be burned at the stake for your crimes. Tenera willing, your death will cause the beasts to disperse."

Sloane caught sight of Lord Bolton on a horse behind the count, with a large number of the forces that should have been defending the city around them.

She couldn't suppress a groan. *I cannot catch a break, can I?*

"Nothing has gone according to plan! We were supposed to be out of the city and waiting for the others by now," Sloane bemoaned, frustration building up inside of her. She looked around, trying to find any way out of their current predicament.

Ismeld pivoted to face her, her hand instinctively reaching for her shield. "I am starting to think being with you is bad luck," she muttered.

Sloane flinched at her words. "I'm trying here, Ismeld," she said curtly. A feeling of helplessness began to snake its way up her spine as she took in the scene unfolding before them. *How do you fight that?*

Caught in a whirlwind of thoughts, Sloane latched on to the first thing that came naturally to her—using humor to deflect her spiraling negativity.

"On the bright side, the others will have a smoother journey, perhaps?" She sighed internally. *At least, I hope they are, because I have no idea what we're going to do.*

But Ismeld merely returned a scowl.

CHAPTER THIRTY-EIGHT

THE FALL OF THIRDGHYLL

T he amassed army was gearing up for an offensive. The sheer number of men, the soldiers and guards who were supposed to be protecting their city and its inhabitants, only managed to stoke Sloane's rising ire.

How delusional can they be? This mustache-twirling, pathetic man is dooming all of his people to die.

How many people could have been saved had these guards manned their posts properly? It infuriated her. It infuriated her that there was nothing she could do. The only option she had available now was to run the way she'd come. *Back* toward the monsters.

Wait . . . Oooh, this is dumb.

"Ismeld, I have a really idiotic idea. I don't know how well it's going to work . . . but we will need to move *very* quickly if it does," Sloane muttered, her voice hushed.

Ismeld sighed in exasperation. "I am going to hate this, aren't I?"

Sloane cocked her head, a teasing smile on her face. "Was that your first contraction?"

Ismeld shot her a withering glare but chose to ignore the jab. "What's your plan?"

"I . . . uh. I'm going to call the monsters to us," she confessed.

Ismeld's eyebrows soared upward, reaching for the twin moons in a manner that would have been comical under less dire circumstances. "Th-that is *not* a sound idea, Sloane."

Sloane pointed a finger at the formidable force amassing before them. "Does fighting this with eleven people seem sound to you?"

"What are you two murmuring about? What's the plan?" Nemura hissed from beside them.

"Aw, fuck it. I'm doing it. Nemura, get ready to run like hell," Sloane announced as she stood up.

Nemura darted her eyes back and forth between the two women, confusion etching her features. "What's she talking about, Ser Ismeld?"

Grabbing her shield, Ismeld readied herself for battle, tightening her grip on her horse's reins. "Prepare the others. We're about to have some unwanted company," she instructed, her voice grave. "Of the monster and beast variety."

Nemura's eyes widened in realization. "Thezmos's green, hairy, dust-puffing spear . . . Shit. Alright," she muttered before scrambling off to relay the alarming news.

The army seemed to be nearly ready, just awaiting word to attack. Sloane started channeling mana through her. Nemura rushed back next to them on her horse, nodding to Ismeld as she came to a stop.

Ismeld looked up at Sloane. "Now or never."

Sloane steeled her resolve and [**Focused**]. This time, she needed more than a basic [**Flashbang**]; she needed a spell powerful enough to distract and suppress an entire army. Drawing on a surge of blue mana, she channeled it through her core, forging and pushing her intent into the spell. A familiar shimmering rune floated into her consciousness, the symbol of the [**Flashbang**]. But she aspired for something stronger, something more impactful.

Delving into her [**Runic Knowledge**], she began to manipulate the existing rune, reshaping it with her Artifice until it transformed into something significantly more potent. The modified rune locked into place within her mind with a mental *click* before it raced toward a swirling sphere of blue, red, and yellow mists and settled into orbit alongside other runes, her existing arsenal of spells. Understanding of her new creation settled into her and she lifted a hand, then cast the spell.

A trinity of brilliant, crackling yellow orbs erupted from her outstretched palm, whirling around one another in a hypnotic ballet. They soared into the sky until, at the zenith of their ascent, the [**Starburst**] spell exploded above the sprawling forces. It discharged an overwhelming surge of sound and a blinding light that bathed the night-draped battlefield in an artificial daylight.

The soldiers' panicked cries as they tried to shield themselves did little to distract Sloane. She remained unflinchingly focused and held her ground amid the ensuing pandemonium, launching one [**Starburst**] after another over the disoriented army below. She lost count of the spells she loosed, each burst illuminating the night like a grimly majestic fireworks display. Except, of course, this spectacle was utterly devoid of any celebration or joy.

In a fortunate twist, the repeated [**Starbursts**] served an additional purpose—they suppressed the archers and created a communication breakdown within the enemy ranks.

Sloane didn't even pause when she heard the first monstrous roar. While it was doubtful anyone else heard it amid the chaos, Sloane knew it wasn't enough. A glance at her watch revealed multiple mana signatures converging from the side, hurtling toward the area she was targeting.

Despite her mental fatigue and the tunneling of her vision, she doubled down on her resolve. She peered down at the army and caught sight of the first monster emerging among the terrified troops. A grim sense of vindication washed over her.

The monsters were clearly more intelligent and belligerent than simple beasts, and reacting in this way solidified that fact even more. A beast would have been scared off by the noise, but the monsters specifically came hunting for the cause of discomfort.

This first monster looked like one of the panthers from before, except mutated. It was easily five meters long and around two or two and a half meters tall at the first set of shoulders. The head was much more ferocious looking, with two gargoyle-esque ears and a fierce short snout with massive teeth. The most terrifying part of the animal, though, were the two long appendages, like tentacles, that ended in a fan-like pad with hooks on them.

It crept along the roof of a building above the soldiers, wincing at each [Starburst] filling the sky. Sloane stopped casting when it started looking around, likely searching for the source.

This monster in particular was even more cunning than the others. There was a level of intelligence in it that terrified her.

Great, I lured it right here. But we're not the targets . . . It needs to be distracted by . . .

The idea struck Sloane like a lightning bolt, and her fingers almost twitched to snap, but she managed to restrain herself just in time. She plunged into the depths of her mana, shaping and aligning her intent with her spell. Glancing at Ismeld, she warned, "I may pass out from this. Please, keep an eye on me."

"Sloane—"

She redirected her [Focus] toward the army and felt a surge of connection to her mana. Such a simple spell, yet the goal was a monumental task to accomplish. She felt like her nose was running, and soon tasted copper on her lips, but she did not stop. Her control started to waver, but she kept at it. A rush of mana poured through her and into that small working.

Half a football field away, the army came into focus. Above them, she spotted it—a small orb taking shape amid the chaos. One man in the army, Lord Bolton, spotted it too—he was pointing at the bright white and gold sphere of crackling energy. The beast followed his gesture, its gaze sliding from the orb to the man who had drawn attention to it.

With a final surge of effort, Sloane catapulted the [Flashbang] upward, triggering its explosion. This burst was not as potent as her earlier spells, but it accomplished precisely what she intended.

And it changed *everything*.

The monster bellowed a thunderous roar that was echoed by the cries of other beasts leaping onto the rooftops of buildings and hemming in the army. These newcomers were similar to the first creature but smaller—only three meters in length.

Yeah . . . only.

Yet, for a lesser size, there were many of them. Sloane counted over twenty before she stopped, and then with one more roar from what she assumed to be the alpha of the pack, they attacked.

A wet trickle slid down from her nose. She lifted a hand to find it smeared with blood. Exhaustion clawed at her, sapping the strength from her body.

She was just so tired.

Just need . . . to close . . . my eyes for a moment.

Ismeld stared wide-eyed as the monsters charged the large company of house guards. Beasts did not typically approach large groups of people, never mind a force of around two hundred armed with spears and bows. That is what these monsters did, however. The first beast managed to crash through a dozen men, breaking spears as it decimated the cohesion of the front line before it was brought down.

In a surprising turn of events, the company held together, retaining a hint of order amid the chaos. They swiftly adapted their formation to respond to the continual onslaught of monsters charging from every direction. A group of archers, however, found themselves at a disadvantage when one of the creatures dropped from a rooftop straight onto them. Its gruesome appendages lashed out, slicing through the men and women around it while it shredded others with its powerful claws and ferocious teeth.

While she kept an eye on the alpha creature, Ismeld's focus was pulled away when Nemura spoke up, her voice trembling with fear. "Alos save us. We need to move."

Ismeld nodded in agreement. "Agreed. Guardswoman Nemura, lead the way."

Suddenly, a weight leaned against her. She turned to find Sloane slumped over, blood trailing from her nose. Ismeld pulled her close, quickly wiping away the blood staining her face.

"I have you, Sloane. We are leaving."

Sloane nodded weakly, her head resting against Ismeld's shoulder. "Just . . . just give me a moment."

Ismeld glanced back, looking for the alpha, only to find that it was nowhere to be seen.

* * *

Lord William Bolton found himself in the midst of chaos, his sword trembling in his grip. The fighting company Count Kayser had assembled was disintegrating around him. The witch had summoned hellish creatures to rain destruction upon them. Frantically, he searched for the count, hoping to implore him to retreat. Yet the man was nowhere in sight.

William seized the arm of the moon elf guard assigned to his protection, his voice strained with urgency over the cacophonous sounds of battle. "Where is the count?"

The guard, equally rattled, cast anxious glances around. "He must have withdrawn from the fight. Stay calm, the company—"

His words were cut short as his eyes bulged in shock. In a horrifying display reminiscent of the witch's magic, the man was suddenly lifted off the ground. Reaching out in a futile attempt for help, he was yanked sideways and hurled through the air. William gasped as he registered the monstrous figure now looming where his blue-skinned elven protector had once stood. The creature advanced on its four legs, closing the gap between them. Its head tilted down to examine him, its two writhing appendages cutting the air, poised for combat.

An icy dread snaked its way down William's spine as he found himself locked in a face-off with the beast. Its gaping maw, large enough to fit his head, released a waft of heated, foul breath. Its eyes, eerily intelligent, scrutinized him with unsettling patience, its monstrous restraint all too evident. The creature's gaze felt as though it could peer into the very depths of his soul, measuring him, awaiting his response. Its inky fur bristled menacingly. Its shoulders were hunched and tensed, ready to respond to any threat.

William raised his eyes, looking where the witch's spell had detonated. He remembered extending his hand, pointing at it. The realization of what the woman had done hit him with an overwhelming force.

"Oh. That damned witch." A sense of despair washed over him, and something within him shattered. His sword slipped from his grasp and clattered to the ground. The monster's eyes narrowed, its tentative hesitation replaced with a clear verdict. As the truth dawned on William, his body convulsed with fear. He was about to meet his end. The beast drew back, preparing for its lethal strike.

A whimper escaped the baron's lips, and Bolton squeezed his eyes shut, willing back the tears welling up. "May almighty God have mercy on us, forgive us our sins, and bring us to everlasting—"

He was cut short as a searing pain engulfed him, followed by the sensation of being yanked upward. Then, all he knew was darkness.

Sloane sat in silence, nursing a throbbing headache, her body teetering toward Ismeld with an involuntary rhythm. Her focus alternated between the time on her watch and a vigilant scan of the surroundings. Their caravan rumbled on toward their ultimate destination—the East Gate and the looming fort beyond. Sloane's spells seemed to have created a safe passage; they hadn't encountered any further monsters as they traversed the city's back alleys.

Emerging from a narrow side street onto the city's primary route, they finally caught sight of the fort. Its intimidating gate was securely shut, and, to her relief, no monstrous creatures were laying siege. Surveying the fort's walls, she spotted guards on duty. The sight of the manned fort elicited a sigh of relief she hadn't realized she'd been holding in.

Upon reaching the gate, their caravan was swiftly admitted. The substantial formation of soldiers who had been monitoring the entrance parted to let them pass. A moon elf, evidently in command, was busy directing other soldiers, who were escorting a group of civilians to an inner doorway of the fort. She hoped it led to safety.

They climbed off the wagons, Ismeld lending her a supportive arm that, despite the assistance, drew a grunt. Accompanied by Ismeld and Nemura, Sloane slowly made her way to the commanding officer.

"Captain Jorin!" Nemura hailed him.

The moon elf turned and his eyes narrowed as he took in the group. "Senior Guardswoman Nemura. You managed to get them out."

"We did. Lost two of my squad to the monsters, though. We need to discuss the situation in the city."

Captain Jorin nodded gravely. "Let us go inside, then." His attention shifted to Sloane and Ismeld. "I'm relieved that you and your people made it out. The rest of your knights are inside the barracks. The knight-captain anticipated you would wish to depart promptly. It's permissible, so long as we're not under siege. I advise you to leave soon. The city is no longer safe. If you'll excuse me now. Guardsman Yuro," he motioned to a raithe standing at a distance, "will assist you when you're ready to leave."

Ismeld acknowledged the young man with a nod, then turned back to the elf. "Thank you, Captain Jorin, for all your help. Senior Guardswoman Nemura saved our lives. Fight well, and may Alos be with you."

As he started to walk away, Sloane stopped him. "Wait. What's your next move?"

He glanced over his shoulder at her. "We'll survive the night. Then we'll consider retreating to Vilstaf. We're ill-equipped for a drawn-out siege, especially with the civilians in our care. Your warning saved thousands, Lady Reinhart. You have our gratitude."

She nodded, reaching into her satchel to produce two letters. "Could you ensure these reach Guildmaster Romaris? One is intended for Reanny Farum. He'll know to give it to her."

He took the proffered letters, briefly glancing at them before meeting her gaze. "I'll make sure they receive these."

"Thank you, Captain Jorin. For everything. Good luck."

"And to you as well."

Sloane looked at Ismeld and nodded. It was time to regroup with the remaining knights and evacuate the city.

Adaega Merbaker sat off to the side. She wouldn't consider it brooding, exactly, but she couldn't help but feel the weight of her circumstances crash upon her. The knights who had rescued her stood together speaking, the one named Ernald stealing glances her way. Before everything that had happened to her, and in her self-absorbed younger years, she would have assumed the man was checking her out. However, he was nothing if not a gentleman. His dark skin was smooth and so similar to her own, which, it shamed her to admit, was comforting.

She had never felt more *alien* than when she had been imprisoned by the blue, gray, and purple elves.

Adaega shivered as her mind started going down the path of remembering everything those people had done. She absently felt the scar on the back of her head, from when her braids had been forcibly cut off.

"Miss Adaega?"

She shook her head and looked up, seeing the concerned look on Ser Ernald's face. He knelt next to her and gently placed a gauntleted hand on her shoulder.

"You are safe now. We will be leaving the city soon. We are just awaiting the arrival of the rest of our group," the sun elf said, his fiery yellow eyes filled with a kindness that almost made her weep. She didn't feel like she deserved it; she'd known only hate since arriving.

She nodded, then took a sip of the water she had been given. Ernald hesitated but then patted her shoulders and stood, to return to the others. She watched him walk away, longing for the safety his presence made her feel.

Her hand slipped to her belt and pulled out the small dagger that Ser Ernald had given her. Finding a bit of comfort from it since it was from *him*.

Adaega observed as the knights spoke again. The redheaded one had healed her wounds, and she recalled the tears in the woman's eyes as the telv realized her magic wouldn't be able to heal the scars.

All that . . . She closed her eyes. *All to gain magic that was already usable by others from this world.* She'd seen the redhead's green magic heal wounds. *I felt it, even.*

Adaega had watched the large woman, whom she assumed was an orc, use magic to create *shields* of energy. It made Adaega so angry at how . . . *unnecessary* it had all been. How degrading and inhumane it had been to be treated as an abomination.

I can't even use magic.

As she contemplated, she absentmindedly played with the tip of the small dagger, drawing a small cut along her palm. She winced as she looked down. She flexed her hand and looked up at the knights as the door to the barracks opened.

Two women walked in. The first was a blond elf woman whose shoulders visibly dropped in what seemed like pure relief when she saw the knights. The second was a white woman, a *human*, who looked about Adaega's age. She looked tired, and dried blood sat under her nose, but as soon as the she saw the knights, she smiled.

"Gisele! Maud! Deryk! Cristole!" the human woman called out.

Adaega scowled. *What about . . .*

Ernald's mouth opened as if he was about to say something.

"And even you, Ernald," the woman said as she grabbed the sun elf and hugged him.

She let go of him and stepped back.

"It is good to see you too, Sloane. Ismeld. What took so long?" Ernald asked.

The blond elf looked at the human beside her and sighed. "We ran into the count's men before even leaving the noble district. Then the count himself on—"

"The count? Where is he? Is he coming here?" Adaega rapid-fired her questions without thinking.

The two women turned and looked at her, the human's eyes widening in shock.

The blond shook her head. "I did not see where the count went, but he managed to leave the area where we last saw him sometime during the fight."

"Ismeld, Sloane. Allow me to introduce Miss Adaega Merbaker," Ernald said, kindly.

She put the dagger away before she stood and walked over to them, reaching out to shake the human woman's hand, only to realize there was still blood on her own hand. She looked down and awkwardly kept her hand out, palm up.

"Adaega! Let me get that," Maud said as she pushed past the others and grabbed her hand.

A feeling of relief and power filled Adaega as she watched the small cut on her palm close. "Thank you, Ser Maud."

"It is nothing. Please, let me know if you are hurt. I can help," Maud said.

"I will. I promise."

The human, Sloane, reached out a hand. "I'm Sloane Reinhart. It's nice to meet you, Miss Merbaker."

Adaega grasped the woman's hand and shook. "Please, call me Adaega. I overheard you talking. Are you saying that the count could be coming here?"

"I do not think he will come here," said the knight Ismeld. "I suspect he is making his way back to the inner castle within the city. It is the most defensible location."

Sloane nodded. "I agree. Now, it is a pleasure to meet you, and I apologize for the terse greeting," she said, glancing around, "but Ismeld and I spoke to Captain Jorin, and we really should leave. As soon as possible. The captain says we can as long as the fort is not under attack. Judging by all we've been through, I don't think it will be long before the monsters attack here."

Gisele, the orc woman, stepped forward. "We will speak on the way. For now, let us depart. Are the others ready?"

Sloane nodded.

The green woman turned and faced the group. "Alright everyone, gather your things. It is time we left the city."

Adaega observed as the knights meticulously collected their gear and provisions. Having nothing, all she could do was wait.

I can only hope things get better.

Sloane stood on the hill and gazed into the distance as the morning light allowed her to see Thirdghyll. It had taken them the rest of the night, but they had finally stopped. They were far enough east and up into the hills to not have to immediately worry about monsters. The city was burning, and entire sections of buildings were already rubble. The central district appeared to have the most destruction. The fire there had raged harder through the night, and even now, a quarter of it was still on fire—including the castle.

Almost as if it were by design.

She could just make out the East Fort. Sloane hoped that—

"Captain Jorin will be fine," a voice said from beside her.

Sloane looked at Nemura as the guardswoman joined her. "I hope so."

"The fort still stands. They will evacuate either when things die down or if the fire starts to threaten them."

Sloane nodded.

Captain Jorin had sent Nemura with them, ostensibly as a messenger to the nearby cities. However, in a completely surprising turn of events, once they were clear of the city and in relative safety, the tall, muscular telv woman had pledged herself to Sloane and her house.

It made Sloane think that the captain had other ideas, and she could only accept the generous offer of support. *Although, I guess our warning really did help, and Nemura does seem awfully protective of me now.* Having a second guard, and one who had trained as an actual *guard*, would likely prove to be a godsend.

At least, with my *luck . . .*

"We should get back. It's going to be a long trip to Goosebourne, Lady Reinhart."

Sloane nodded. "Let's do that. With luck, things will go well this time."

One step closer to finding you, Gwyn. I hope you are okay.

CHAPTER THIRTY-NINE

THE ROAD AHEAD

Taenya's eyes fluttered open to the soft morning light seeping into her room. She sat up and stretched, feeling a twinge of soreness in her muscles and what had been clearly a dagger strike to her head.

Her injuries from the duel a few weeks prior had healed faster than anyone expected, but her hearing had taken its time to recover. Sabina and she speculated that magic might have played a part in her swift recuperation.

The memory of the duel still haunted her. The searing heat of the flames, the horrifying screams of a man burning atop her . . . Some days, the echoes of that day were louder than others.

Today was one of those days.

Her head pounded with a relentless rhythm, but she refused to let it keep her confined to the comfort of her bed. She had responsibilities, duties that couldn't be ignored. A knight couldn't afford to hide away . . . cocooned in the . . . soft embrace of her sheets . . .

With a sigh, she began her daily ritual by tidying up her room, straightening the sheets and arranging her belongings neatly, before moving to the washbasin and splashing cool water on her face.

She looked at her reflection in the mirror, tracing her fingers over the red scar on her side from the recent duel. That mark was now a badge of honor. What wasn't, however, was what her focus stayed on.

My hair looks like crap.

She grabbed her brush and sat down, working through the tangles, the rhythmic strokes providing a soothing distraction from her discomfort.

Next, she dressed, pulling on a tunic of soft, blue fabric and black pants that were a far cry from the simple attire she had worn before her knighthood. As she dressed, her thoughts drifted to Gwyn. The young princess had arrived with an array of unique clothing and undergarments, which she still possessed. But Gwyn was growing up like an Eona-cursed weed, and Taenya knew it wouldn't be long before she outgrew them.

And us.

She slipped into her leather boots, the sturdy material reaching up to her calves. As she laced them up, she pondered on the need to find a seamstress who could craft garments similar to those Gwyn was accustomed to.

Maybe when we get to the capital.

Next, she fastened her sword to her belt, the weight of the weapon a familiar comfort at her right side. Lastly, she pinned the small sunburst emblem to her tunic, Gwyn's gift, which had miraculously survived the duel.

Stepping out of her room, she was greeted by a servant.

"Good morning, ser. I was just coming to inform you that breakfast is being served."

"Thank you," Taenya replied, nodding her appreciation. She turned to the guards stationed outside her door and inquired about their well-being, then made her way to the manor's dining hall.

Siveril and Sabina were already seated at the table, deep in conversation. The sight of them brought a small smile to her face, a welcome distraction from the lingering pain of her injuries.

"Good morning," Taenya greeted them, her voice carrying a hint of fatigue as she took a seat at the table.

"Good morning, Taenya. Are you well?" Siveril asked, studying her for any signs of discomfort.

"I am. Thank you."

Sabina, sitting across from her, gave a nod of acknowledgment. *Good morning. Rough night?*

Yes. Headaches, still. Don't tell him though. I have things to do.

Your secret's safe with me. Sabina pinched her thumb and finger together, running them across her lips as Gwyn liked to do. Taenya chuckled when Sabina mimed locking and throwing away a key.

Siveril, oblivious to their silent exchange, shook his head in mild exasperation. "Taenya, it's time to start getting things in order."

She nodded. *Finally.*

"Liam is going to lead the guards going with Niles, correct?"

Taenya reached across the table to grab one of Sabina's rolls.

"Yes and I spoke with Niles last night. He's ready to go," Siveril confirmed.

"When should we expect to leave?" Sabina asked, casually trying to swat away Taenya's hand. Unsuccessfully. *Thief!*

Taenya smirked.

Siveril ignored their antics and replied, "Four weeks, eight at the absolute most. I spoke with Her Highness this morning to inform her of what to expect."

Taenya nodded, taking a bite of her stolen roll. "That reminds me—"

Their conversation was interrupted by the entrance of a servant. The sun elf bowed respectfully. "Sers, apologies for the interruption. Mister Fenren is here to see Ser Taenya. He said it was important."

Taenya raised an eyebrow. *Did he finally hear back?*

Taenya looked at fellow knights. "I'll handle that," she declared, her tone firm. "One more thing: I've been considering sending Friedrich with Niles. Having a knight with him would ensure his safety, and Friedrich's skill with the sword is commendable. Plus, his status would also make things go a bit more smoothly."

Sabina snorted at her words, a smirk playing on her lips.

I will not dignify that with a response.

Sabina's smirk widened.

Siveril, however, nodded in agreement. "That's a good idea. And do let me know if Onas has anything important to share."

Taenya offered him a playful smile. "Don't I always?"

Siveril merely shook his head in response, a hint of amusement in his eyes.

With the meeting concluded, Taenya followed the servant out of the hall to meet with Onas. As she walked, her mind began to wander, mulling over the current state of House Reinhart.

So many things are starting to come together, she mused, a sense of hope kindling within her. *The road ahead actually seems to have a reachable destination now.*

"So, Ser Siveril mentioned we'll be heading to the capital soon," Gwyn said, pulling her wool cloak tighter around herself to keep out the chilly air.

Seated alongside her, Ilyana, Aleanora, and Lorrena wore expressions of varying degrees of curiosity and concern. Their dresses, along with their warm cloaks and gloves, vibrant against the backdrop of the garden's muted tones, rustled softly as they shifted in their seats.

"Has it been decided who will accompany us?" Ilyana queried, looking at the others.

They were all gathered in the gazebo nestled within the estate's gardens. The structure, with its intricate latticework, stood starkly against the backdrop of the garden's autumn hues. A gentle breeze rustled the bare branches overhead, and the air was scented with the earthy aroma of fallen leaves.

"Yeah—"

"Ser Siveril was sharing some details about—oh, I beg your pardon, Your Highness. I didn't mean to interrupt," Nora interjected, her cheeks flushing a soft pink.

"It's quite alright, Nora. As I was saying, Taenya, Sabina, and a good number of the guards will be joining us. Maya and Quinn too. Keston was supposed to come, but I persuaded Siveril to let him stay back for knight training. He'll join us after the first year," she explained.

Emma, ever the dutiful handmaiden, stood a respectful distance away from Gwyn, her eyes alert and watchful. Her hands were clasped in front of her, her posture rigid yet poised.

Guarding the entrance to the gazebo were two of House Reinhart's guards, their vigilant gazes scanning the surrounding gardens. Their presence was a silent reminder of the constant threat that loomed over them, even in such peaceful surroundings.

"My mother is quite pleased that we're going. She's arranged for our accommodations along the route."

"Oh, yeah! Make sure to tell her thank you, Nora. Mister Balfiel leaves today with a group of guards as well. They're going to look for a house for us all there when they arrive. Have you two discussed what you will do when we arrive?" Gwyn asked, her gaze shifting between the two older elves.

Ilyana nodded. "I will be nearly sixteen at that point. The house tutors have agreed to finish my education. After that, I will apply for the Royal Academy. It . . . it will be something none in my family has accomplished, a point of pride for myself."

Nora looked taken aback by the revelation, and Gwyn tilted her head in confusion. "The Academy? I thought you could apply earlier. Isn't that why Lorrena and I are going?"

Ilyana shook her head, a patient smile on her lips. "It's a common misconception. Once someone turns sixteen, they're considered an adult and can make their own decisions—"

"To a certain extent, if you are a noble," Nora clarified, earning a conceding wave from Ilyana.

"Yes, yes. Well, after someone is sixteen, the Royal Academy has an entirely separate Upper School for education that is meant for nobles, professionals, and the like. It is meant to produce higher-quality citizenry for the kingdom."

"Oh! Like a college or university! I understand now. We have those too. I wanted to go to the University of Milan with my friend when we got old enough." Gwyn sighed. *Not that I will now . . .*

Gwyn's gaze shifted to Nora, who seemed somewhat perturbed. "What about you, Nora?"

"I . . . I'll be attending classes at one of the city schools until I turn sixteen as well. My mother hasn't mentioned anything about the Royal Academy."

Ilyana regarded Nora for a moment before reaching over and taking the other elf's hand in a surprising gesture of solidarity. "I can help you prepare. We'll get you in. That is . . . if it's what you truly want."

Nora looked up from their entwined hands to meet Ilyana's sincere gaze. "Please."

We're becoming a team—a family, even, Gwyn thought, her heart swelling with pride.

"I'm glad we're all supporting each other," she said, her voice soft. "We're going to face a lot of challenges, but I believe we can get through them together."

Ilyana squeezed Nora's hand gently before releasing it. "Indeed, Your Highness. We're stronger together."

The conversation flowed easily after that, and Lorrena joined in as they discussed their plans and aspirations. Gwyn shared more about her home, her friends, and her dreams, which seemed so silly now that she was in an entirely different world. Ilyana spoke of her desire to excel at the Upper School, and there was a fierceness there that left little doubt in her commitment.

Gwyn turned her attention to her handmaiden. "Emma," she began, her voice carrying a note of curiosity, "have you ever been to the capital before?"

Emma, taken aback by the sudden inclusion in the conversation, blinked in surprise. She quickly composed herself, and gave a polite smile. "No, Your Highness," she replied smoothly, with a hint of regret. "I've never had the privilege of visiting the capital."

Gwyn's eyes widened slightly, her curiosity piqued. "Really? I thought you might have been there before. You seem so well traveled."

Emma chuckled softly, a blush creeping up her cheeks. "I'm flattered, Your Highness, but my worldliness is limited to the books I've read and the stories I've heard. My family hails from a small village near Larton. We didn't have the means to travel much, and I managed to join House Iemes with my mother's help. Which eventually led me here."

"What was it like, growing up in a village? This world is so different from mine."

"It was simple, but fulfilling. We worked hard, but we were a close-knit community. Everyone knew everyone, and we looked out for each other. I'm excited to see the capital. I hear it's beautiful with its many canals and parks."

"You know, I've never been to the capital either," Ilyana added. "I'm actually quite excited to experience it. I think Mother has only been once, and I don't think Father has at all either. I know none of my siblings have."

"The capital is indeed grand, but it can also be overwhelming. It's a place of power and politics, where every word and action can have far-reaching consequences," Nora explained.

Gwyn sighed at Aleanora's words, her mind filled with images of the capital. "It sounds like here," she admitted, "but the canals sound really cool. I miss Venice—I always enjoyed going there. I can't wait to see if it's similar."

Aleanora smiled at Gwyn's enthusiasm. "Just remember, Gwyn, the capital is like a grand stage. And we must all play our parts."

"I've been twice. Once . . . once before my mother passed," Lorrena said quietly, a hint of melancholy seeping into her words. The others turned to her, their expressions sympathetic. "It was a grand affair during the Festival of Trade. The city was alive with music, laughter, and the scent of exotic spices. The canals were filled with boats, their lanterns reflecting off the water like a thousand stars. It was . . . magical."

Gwyn's eyes sparkled with curiosity. "That sounds wonderful, Lorrena. I'm sorry about your mother."

Lorrena offered a small, sad smile. "Thank you, Gwyn. She loved the capital, the vibrancy of it. I think you will too."

Emma, who had been quietly listening, chimed in. "I've heard stories of the grand balls held at the palace, the beautiful gowns, the music. It sounds like a dream."

Gwyn chuckled. "Don't let Roslyn hear you say that. You know how she is about . . ." she gave her best approximation of her best friend. "'Dastardly royals!'"

Everyone giggled.

Ilyana laughed lightly. "It does sound like a dream, doesn't it? But remember, every dream has its shadows. The capital is no different. None of us are really prepared—no offense, Nora."

"None taken," she replied. "But it's the shadows that make the light seem brighter. We'll navigate them together. Don't you worry, Your Highness. We've all got your back. I think your Lady Roslyn will be quite a beneficial ally in this regard."

My Roslyn?

Gwyn smiled. "I'm glad I won't be alone. I'm happy I have all of you with me."

Ilyana leaned back against her seat, looking out across the courtyard. "Ser Taenya is coming."

Gwyn's head whipped around, her eyes scanning the courtyard until they landed on the familiar figure of her knight. Beside Taenya walked Onas.

Oh! Haven't seen him in a while.

As they neared, Gwyn rose to her feet, a bright smile lighting up her face. "Onas! Hey, Taenya."

Taenya responded with a mock hurt expression, her hand dramatically clutching at her heart. "Why are you so excited to see him and not me?"

"I see you *every* day. Not him!"

Onas chuckled, then bowed to her. "How are you, Your Highness?" He nodded at the crew. "Ladies."

Gwyn closed the distance between them, wrapping Onas in a warm hug. "I'm doing well, thank you. But what brings you here today, Onas? You're usually so busy."

The elven merchant offered a wry smile as Gwyn stepped back. "I came for two reasons, Your Highness. One of them is quite serious. May we sit?"

Gwyn nodded, leading the way back to the group of benches. She took a seat next to Ilyana, while Taenya remained standing beside Onas, who occupied the bench opposite them. Lorrena and Aleanora shared the last bench, their expressions curious.

Onas took a deep breath, his gaze flicking to Taenya, who simply gestured for him to continue. He turned back to Gwyn, taking another breath, causing her to giggle.

"Onas, what is it?"

"I have news from the agents I sent out."

Gwyn's smile faltered as she processed what he said. "News? About what?"

"About your mother."

Gwyn gasped and jumped up. "You found her?! Is she okay? Where is she? Is she—"

"Gwyn. Gwyn! Please," Taenya interjected calmly, her voice an anchor in the storm of Gwyn's emotions.

The hopeful light in Gwyn's eyes dimmed as dread spread through her. She sank back onto the bench, her breath hitching in her throat, and crossed her legs. Her mind raced as she kept her gaze on the ground.

Onas allowed a moment of silence to pass before he continued. "Your mother, as far as we can tell, is not in Avira."

Gwyn heart sank. She opened her mouth to speak, but no words came out. She was at a loss, her mind a whirlwind of confusion and fear. She didn't even know what to say.

Onas reached out, his hand hovering in the air as if he wanted to offer comfort, but he hesitated and withdrew. "That is not all of it, though. Word is that terrans have been found all over the Sovereign Cities. I have contacts in the cities who will help us search further. We will find her, Gwyn. It may just take a while longer."

Gwyn nodded, her throat tight. "We'll find her. At least we have somewhere to look. These Sovereign Cities . . . Mister Branigan has talked about them a bit. There are a lot of them, right?"

"Yes. The cities make up a large portion of this region. It will take time, but we will figure this out. Most of the headquarters for the various guilds are within the Sovereign Cities. We will start with Pyrlan on the other side of Lehelia. It will also be a good place for me to place someone long term as almost all of the merchant shipping travels through the Arros Strait."

"Thank you, Onas."

Onas bowed his head, then offered a small smile. "I do have one other thing. This is just something I thought you would be interested in, because of your . . . *magic.*"

Gwyn smiled, but her heart wasn't in it after the news about her mom.

His smile faltered. "I can come back another time?"

She shook her head. "No, no. Please. What is it? I do enjoy magic."

He regarded her for a moment. "I heard rumors from some merchant sailors that I have connections with. There is apparently a small company in the west selling magical items. They're a bit inland, but some have made it to the coast. I wanted to see if you would be interested in any?"

Gwyn furrowed her brow. "Magical . . . items? What are those?"

Onas gave a noncommittal shrug. "Evidently, a pair of dwarven inventors found a way to make different magical objects: rings, necklaces, mugs, household goods, and the like. I am not sure how they work . . . *or if they work* . . . but I can attempt to obtain something. Maybe you can even figure out how it works and we can make more?"

Gwyn perked up slightly. "That *does* sound interesting. Hmm . . . you know, Mom really likes to make stuff. I think I told you she was making a watch."

"Perhaps you could acquire a magical item for your mother to experiment with? I imagine she would be thrilled to have such a novelty when you find her," Ilyana suggested, her voice soft but encouraging.

Gwyn turned to Ilyana, a genuine smile lighting up her face. "That is a great idea, Ilyana!" She turned her attention back to Onas. "Can you get something nice that I can give to Mom? She would love to try new things. Especially if they're magical things!"

Mom is going to absolutely love tinkering with something magical.

A while later, Gwyn was walking through the garden with Taenya. So much had happened, and everyone in the house was busy. The aftermath of Taenya's duel had only added to the chaos. Gwyn tried to push the memory of the duel to the back of her mind, the thought of Taenya's near-death experience still too raw.

Her knight was strong, she had proved that to everyone. Yet, Gwyn couldn't shake the fear that Taenya's display of strength had only painted a larger target on her back.

"Gwyn?"

"Yes, Taenya?

"Are you excited to leave for the Academy?"

"Honestly? I am not sure. I am worried more people will try and hurt us. What about the people we leave behind?"

Taenya halted in her tracks, scanning their surroundings. Gwyn followed suit, her eyes darting around the garden. But they were alone.

"Gwyn? We're going to be okay. Do you want to see how I know?" Taenya's voice was hushed, her eyes still darting around as if she were telling her the biggest secret.

What is so secret that she keeps making sure we're alone?

Gwyn nodded a few times, feeling slightly confused, but that was easily overwhelmed by a strong sense of curiosity.

A smirk tugged at the corners of Taenya's mouth as she lifted her hand slightly and closed her eyes. Gwyn watched her, head tilted in puzzlement. Then, an idea struck her and she looked at what Taenya was doing using her **[Mana Sight]**.

As her magic settled into her eyes, Gwyn saw a swirling red mist enveloping Taenya. After a few heartbeats, the mist surged from Taenya toward a spot on the ground next to them. A pulse of red energy erupted from the mist, and a blinding flash of light forced Gwyn to release her Sight spell and shield her eyes.

When the light faded, she squinted at the lingering cloud of red smoke next to Taenya. She leaned forward to get a better look.

The mist was melding together into something . . . that *moved*.

"Miss Levings, accompany me, if you would."

Turning, Amanda found the older telv noblewoman approaching, a knight trailing in her wake. The man's helmet was an odd sight, its sharp protrusions designed to accommodate an elf's elongated ears. She offered him a polite smile, only to be met with indifference. Her smile faltered, and she fell into step beside Lady Racine.

"What can I do for you?"

Lady Racine's eyes narrowed slightly, a hint of scrutiny in her gaze. "Has House Reinhart made any further overtures to you since you met with the princess?"

"They haven't."

"Have you heard of what occurred earlier this week?"

Amanda nodded, her mind flashing back to the news of the brutal duel to the *death*. "Yes, I heard. It's absolutely barbaric. I can't believe that poor child was forced to observe such a thing."

Lady Racine nodded her head slightly. "There is *something* . . . It seems that the Polite War is set to become even more . . . interesting. We will need to obtain more terrans."

Amanda looked at the woman in surprise. "We're going to find others?"

"Yes. While I have my agents do that, *you will attend to my grandson* while he is in the capital. I will return home to the Duchy of Nieth and join you after I attend to some . . . business. Until your departure, you will train with Ser Weylind to ensure you are prepared for your duties. *And continue them after arriving.*"

She felt like a wave of dizziness spread through her that made her head spin. "O-of course, My Lady."

As she turned to glance at the knight behind them, a shiver ran down her spine. His piercing green eyes seemed to bore into her through the narrow slit in his helmet, leaving her feeling uncomfortably exposed.

EPILOGUE

ARTIFICER

ONE MONTH AGO

The forges of Dheg Malduhr were some of the most extensive in the world and the source of the largest portion of its exports. However, trade in the region was now in jeopardy as the Empire of Vlaredia invaded the Sovereign Cities—a dispute that the city did not wish to get involved in. Even the Sovereigns would be tempted to take advantage of the fighting to pick at unaligned cities if the opportunity presented itself. Which is why the city was developing weapons that could defend it against the massive armies that either side was known to field.

Dheg Malduhr was in an ideal location. The dwarven fortress city sat nestled in the mountains overlooking the Malduhr Pass, a key trade route for Westaren, Vlaredia, and the Sovereign City of Sacksburn. This strategic location necessitated the city pouring large amounts of its resources into protecting its interests. The resulting fortress its forebearers had built was considered impenetrable. A bastion that had held against all enemies for centuries, allowing the city to turn into a flourishing city of trade.

At least, that was what Aedan Solla had been told when the dwarven council of Dheg Malduhr offered to trade with him for his knowledge. A relationship that he had thought was a partnership now had deadlines, demands, and overseers.

Aedan looked down at the last piece of the device he was constructing. It would act as the control panel for the Anti-Army Incursion Mine. He had learned much since arriving on Eona, and one thing was that the denizens were vastly outclassed by what he could bring to the table in terms of technology.

As a lieutenant in the Terran Interstellar Union Navy, his primary focus was on communications technologies, and this is what helped him decipher the Arcane Runic Language. Something about the arcane energy that permeated the air around them allowed the runes to draw upon the energy in various ways.

"Mister Solla. Is it done?"

Hearing his name jerked him out of his thoughts. He looked at the root of this rough and serious voice, a dwarf man to his right.

"Allow me to finish this . . . last . . . rune . . ." Aedan grabbed the conduit probe that had somehow arrived in the world with him. He then channeled energy through the device, and a teal beam emitted from the front aperture and etched the final line of the runic sequence. He had devised the sequence that would draw in the arcane energy of the surrounding area of the mine to strengthen the blast, similar to a thermobaric reaction.

"You are sure this will work?"

"Yes. I included a rune that is supposed to amplify the effect as well. Due to our other experiments, we know that beings can be even greater sources of the arcane energy of the planet. This will draw upon that to create a chain reaction in any army," Aedan explained.

"Good." The man nodded. "Then let us install it and prepare for the test."

"Hold on. I thought we were going to wait for that?"

"You said you are sure it will work. The Empire has moved more quickly than expected. We need to test the device in a controlled environment so that we may be sure it works when we have to rely upon one."

"Team three completed the test room sufficiently?"

"This is not a discussion, Mister Solla. We have orders to test the device. Now come."

Two guards stepped forward and Aedan tensed, but in the end, he simply nodded. He followed the man with the control panel through the halls of the research area of the city. Aedan had convinced them to prepare a site that was not directly in the city. The test area was a cavern that was dug out and reinforced with steel precisely for this reason.

When they walked into the cavern, Aedan took a deep breath. He couldn't deny that he was excited, and seeing his device there set up and prepared on a pedestal in the center washed away any hesitation.

"The chains were made to specifications?" he asked the dwarves working around the device.

"Yes, Mister Solla. Just waiting on the final piece."

"Aedan! Finally! The control panel was inscribed with the rune for distant triggering?"

Aedan smiled and turned to see the one reason he had put up with everything. Norie was his partner on the project, and her ability to learn everything he put in front of her made the dwarf woman indispensable. In fact, she had been the one to design a remote activation function of the mine.

"Norie, it's *remote activation*. Your name for it isn't going to catch on."

She waved him off. She had purposely come up with new terms for everything he explained to her. It had turned into a fun game for them.

"Yes, it's ready. You just need to mirror them together with the transmitter."

He handed her the control panel, and she went to work making the appropriate arcane connection. She clearly had been waiting for some time, because everything was prepared and she was soon installing the panel into the mine's housing.

When she finished, Norie cheered, which caused everyone to clap and yell. After a quick celebration, she called out for everyone to quiet and explained the test process. She reached out for Aedan's hand and asked if he was ready.

He nodded, a smile unable to leave his face as he grabbed her hand and walked with her to the reinforced bunker.

After the test area was locked down, and everyone was safely inside the bunker, they looked through the reinforced glass portholes that would allow them to observe the reaction. Men stood by levers that would slam shutters into place in case of any issues.

When everything was prepared, Norie held out the transmitter to him. "Would you like to do the honors?"

He smiled and shook his head, closing her hand around the device. "No. You believed in me. You should do it."

With a nod, she turned her head and looked at everyone. "For the glory of Dheg Malduhr!" she called out excitedly. She pressed the button.

They watched as the runes began to glow purple, and pulses of energy started running through the conduits they had created within the outer casing. He glanced at Norie. She was staring with rapt attention.

The pulses running through the conduits went faster and faster, until they moved at a speed that created the illusion of them glowing brightly with a solid color.

"It's beautiful," Norie said, awed.

"It is," he said, looking at the woman next to him, smiling as she squeezed his hand tightly.

The device began shaking, slowly at first, making him think it was nearly at the reaction stage, taking a bit longer than he had assumed it would. Then, the shaking intensified and a loud explosion of air came from the device, followed by a purple sphere of sparking energy that was just wider than the device.

He tilted his head in confusion. *That . . . shouldn't have happened.*

The sphere pulsed and grew massively in the span of a second to cover over half of the cavern.

"Aedan?"

"I don't know. Maybe we should—"

Another pulse of energy emitted from the device and suddenly the sphere of energy collapsed into what looked like . . .

No—

Another loud crack of deafening noise was emitted and Aedan felt a rush push through him. His eyes widened but Norie was ahead of him.

"Collapse the shutters! Now!"

The men slammed the levers into place and three of the four shutters crashed shut. The man at the one still open yelled even as he kept trying to reset and move the lever again. "It's stuck! I cannae get it!"

Aedan panicked and rushed to the porthole, looking out. The energy collapsed again and he looked at what seemed like . . . *How?! There weren't nearly enough crystals or cores in there.*

"Aedan! What is it?"

"A singularity! It's expanding! We need to evacuate!"

Norie shook her head. He knew she didn't know what that was, but surely—

He looked back. Realization hit him like a hammer. *The only exit leads back into the cavern. We'll never make it.*

"We need to get this shutter down! *Now!*"

Men rushed into action. Two men hammered on the shutter while Aedan looked around for something he could use. He grabbed a bar and hurried to the porthole. "Here!"

He shoved the bar under the lever and yelled with effort as he wrenched it upward, the latch finally catching and slamming the two-meter-thick shutter shut. He dropped the bar and took a deep breath. He looked at Norie. The lamps in the room flickered, a massive crash hit the wall, and what felt like an earthquake sent them all tumbling to the ground.

He looked up, and all the fire from the lamps seemed to rise into the air before just . . . disappearing into nothing. The room was plunged into darkness and people screamed out.

Aedan's teeth began to vibrate as he felt the energy in the room increase. He looked around in the dark, trying to see. *This is going to be enough. We're safe.*

"Aedan?!"

"Norie?"

He felt around, falling several times as more earthquakes hit, and then when he found her, he pulled her close. Another explosion made Norie grip him tighter.

"Aedan? I'm scared."

"It's going to be—"

The device rattled. Mana rushed in from all around, the steel and cavern offering minimal protection. The mine glowed purple and pulsed as the amplified loop built within the runic chain worked as designed and drew more and more mana. Fissures opened throughout the mountain as the chain reaction spell started by the device was overwhelmed as mana tore at spacetime and condensed gravity into that one location. A saturation point was reached within the manasphere of the world and the singularity collapsed, as it could no longer sustain its own nature. The resulting implosion ripped at the cavern walls, causing the mountain to crumble in on itself.

The city that was supposed to be safe was unprepared. Excess energy had nowhere to vent and was directed through the fissures of the falling mountain. It expanded throughout the tunnels and into Dheg Malduhr itself. The energy built up in the largest area it could expand in.

Ripples spread from the ground and into the pass, causing avalanches and uprooting trees. The entire surrounding mountain, in which the city lay, fell into a massive rubble-filled sinkhole. The air rushed back into the vacuum and caused a second explosion of pressure that blew out a crater half a kilometer wide, centered on the largest cavern within the city's network of tunnels. The same cavern that housed the city center.

It took a day for the dust to finally settle, but when it did, all that remained of Dheg Malduhr was the solitary tower that sat a kilometer south at the entrance to the pass. Its garrison worked tirelessly to search for survivors. Of the bastion and mountain north of the valley, only rubble and ruin remained. As the sun rose on the second day, an army appeared.

Dheg Malduhr was no more, but their legacy would live on. For the city had built an impenetrable fortress. Just not the one most would suspect.

PRESENT

"Kendel! Toss me a wrench!"

Alyce narrowed her eyes as the man rushed over and handed her what she had requested. *I coulda caught that.* She turned and looked at where one of the guys was working on precise machinery.

"Oi, look out. Let me get in there."

The man looked over his shoulder and nodded. "Yes, milady."

She crouched down as he moved, and got to work. "I'm not a 'milady'!"

The man laughed. The crew had all taken to calling her a lady after a minor spat with a noblewoman during one of the dinners in the palace. It wasn't her fault the lady was as stuck up as a steel rod.

Rust. I probably shouldn't have said that.

The lady had been all offended and flustered, after which she had called Alyce the "short-eared lady of hot air." Alyce couldn't help but laugh at the absolutely horrible attempt at an insult. She also probably shouldn't have told the lady she obviously had a few gears loose.

But the woman was positively daft!

The king had simply covered his face with his hand, and after that, it became a game during the dinners to come up with the poorest insults possible among the nobility.

She sighed as she tightened the bolt on the last gear. Closing up the panel, she handed over the wrench to the man and patted him on the shoulder. "There you go, Nev. This section is done and ready for the magic scribes."

She moved on and jumped in with another worker, fixing more gears and aligning the machinery that would make this big, monstrous, ugly, beautiful, wonderful steam engine purr.

Alyce walked up to a group of men and a woman who were next to the main boiler. "Hey, what's got you guys all clogged up?"

The woman turned and threw her hands up. "It's these glyphs! They are not performing as they should."

Alyce nodded. "Here let me take a look." She grabbed the inscribing pen from the woman and touched the tip, making sure the ink was flowing. *Very important, that.* "You have more palladium ink, right? This seems a bit low. It will start gunking up soon unless we fill it."

The sun elf nodded. "Yes, milady. We have eight more batches."

"Good." She turned back and looked at the glyphs the team had already inscribed. Everything *looked* fine. "Which glyph did you need next—oh, never mind. I see."

She pushed some magic through the pen and into etching the next glyph for |Heat|, then pushed magic into the rest of the glyphs, where it settled into the ink and lit up. Their ink wasn't perfect, but that would take a lot more trial and error than they had time for. The problem wasn't that the glyphs were bad, it's that they just took a little bit more love and *magic.*

Alyce gave the glyphs a moment to settle, then pushed more magic into them. They finally stabilized and held a solid purple glow. She smirked and stood up, handing the pen back to the sun elf magic scribe. "Let it settle, then push your magic into them a second time. Don't let the magic dissipate before you do."

The woman nodded. "Got it, Alyce. Thank you."

"No problem!"

Many of the sun elves had a hard time acclimating to proper technology, but that's why she was there. Alyce stepped in where she could and helped out those who were struggling. At the end of the day, she felt like they had managed to get a lot done, and she told her crew that as they trickled out, returning all of their tools and equipment under the watchful eyes of the palace guards.

Later, she stood overlooking the site from the terrace outside the palace.

They had converted the grounds where they rode horses into her project site. It allowed it to be hidden and protected from any who would spy on them.

"Miss Maxwell. I heard today went well," she heard from behind her.

It also brought direct oversight from the king.

She turned and smiled at the middle-aged sun elf who approached her. He wore a stylish tunic and pants, and unless you knew him, you wouldn't guess that he was the king of a nation. There was no crown on his head, no extravagant jewelry, and his clothes looked like something any wealthy person would wear. She liked that about him.

Alyce dipped her head respectfully, knowing he disliked formal bows or curtsies when in private. "It did, Your Majesty. I think we can proceed to stage two in as little as two months."

The King of Rosale smiled. "Miss Maxwell, that is just—oh, what was the word? *Rust* it. I cannot keep it up. Alyce, that is fantastic news."

Alyce snorted, and his eyes widened when he realized what he had said. "It's okay, Tanyth." She leaned in and lowered her voice conspiratorially, "I won't tell anyone. Your secret's safe with me."

King Tanyth Dal'or laughed, and leaned against the railing of the terrace, looking over the project site. "It's coming together, Alyce. You're doing great things for my kingdom."

Alyce smiled and joined him. "It is indeed. Have you heard anything?"

Tanyth's smile faltered, and he placed a hand on her shoulder. "I haven't. I'm sure your sister is out there. We'll find her. We just need to be careful. My generals say that the war may soon expand."

Alyce sighed.

"I hope we hear something soon. Until then, we will keep pushing forward." Tanyth squeezed her shoulder before pulling back his hand. The two fell into a comfortable silence in the setting sun. Two people from worlds apart stood there, staring longingly at the source of one man's hope of safety for his people, and a woman's of finding her sister.

"Done!" Sloane looked down and smiled. The last rune on her sword was complete. Gisele had asked to have her *Zweihänder* done first, but there was no way the first weapon she enchanted would be that one. *I'd be crushed if I ruined that beautiful thing.*

"May I see, my lady?" Koren asked from where he sat across from her.

She rotated the sword so the smith could see the runes she had finished. They were nearly overflowing with mana, and their blue glow was bright. Koren whistled and put aside the armor he was reassembling for Cristole.

"That is gorgeous. I dare say it looks better than the work you did for Ser Gisele's armor."

Sloane smirked and handed the smith the sword. "I had to make sure my own sword looked the best."

He chuckled, and examined her work. "This has the |Repair|, |Sharpen|, and which else?"

"|Strengthen|, |Lighten|, and an experimental one: |Spell-Piercing|. I am hoping that one will allow me to use the blade against magic similar to Gisele's shield. I can't wait to test it."

The orkun nodded as he handed the sword back to her. "Beautiful. You did great work, my lady. This set will be ready for you probably tomorrow."

"I hope so. We may need it. Cristole is back, and I want him to wear that before he goes out again."

Sloane looked up at Gisele, who wore the first set of armor Sloane had enchanted. The runes on the knight's armor glowed; the ones supplied with mana from the woman herself blushed a soft red. There were only a few of those, but they were mainly the runes that would allow her to strengthen her swings and spells. The remaining runes were the more standard enchants, as Sloane called them, and they glowed a light blue that looked almost white.

It seemed that once they were |Renewed| by surrounding mana, the runes started to lose the blue that she channeled. She would need to test their strength to ensure they did not degrade by mana other than her own.

"I'll start working on pieces Koren is done with. Did Cristole see anything?"

Gisele shook her head. "No, but we're getting close. We need to get eyes on the town. We'll enter the plains tomorrow."

Sloane returned her sword to its sheath on her side and stood, wiping the dirt off her backside as she did. "I have an idea. Let's walk?" She looked over at the smith. "I'll be back, Koren."

The man just waved, as his focus was already back on the armor in his hands.

Gisele nodded and fell into step beside Sloane. They moved away from the smith's wagon and toward the camp, where everyone else was. She looked around. Elodie was speaking with Ismeld and Deryk, while Stefan stood with Rel, who had Kemmy attached to her hip.

I don't think she's over the incident at their shop yet.

The knight next to her snorted softly and Sloane glanced at the woman. "What?"

Gisele jutted her head and Sloane looked over to see Ernald sitting away from the camp, speaking quietly to Adaega. The human woman was leaning against him as they looked at a book together.

"She went through a lot. I'm glad she found someone to talk to. She didn't seem to want to talk to me for some reason," Sloane whispered.

"Give her time."

Sloane agreed. The woman was resilient, but that would get one only so far.

It was good that Ernald was spending so much time with her. Perhaps it would be the start of some healing.

Sloane laughed when they walked around the knights' wagon and saw Maud. Her falcon was perched on Maud's arm as if about to launch into flight. "What are you doing with my bird?"

Maud jumped and Tiberius jerked his head toward her, settling his wings back down. "Nothing! We were just practicing. Tib is upset he couldn't do more in your fight."

Sloane smirked. "*Tib?* Is that right? Well, it just so happens that I have an idea of something Tiberius can do to help."

Gisele looked at them. "What's that?"

"Tiberius? Come here, please."

With a swing of her arm, Maud helped the bird launch into the air, where he flew in a circle before landing on Sloane's bracer, which she had modified for just that purpose.

"Okay. So, buddy. One of the reasons I made you was for scouting. However, the biggest issue we've had so far is communication. I was able to think while working on the runes." She reached over and opened the panel that protected Tiberius's core. She handed the cover to Gisele, who looked confused. Sloane smirked.

"I've been looking over and over at my watch for inspiration. It's the only thing besides my clothes that came with me. This whole time I have been making up reasons as to why that is. My initial thought was silly and made no sense. *Metal?* Come on."

"So what was it?" Gisele asked.

Sloane shrugged. "I still don't know for certain, but I have an idea. I had a major hand in making this watch. I ran the teams who designed it. I made key decisions regarding it and would consider myself one of the main reasons for how it ended up. Now, I have been wracking my head around *mana* and everything about it. Well, I think I have something. It *knows*. It knows that in my heart and at my *core* that I am an Artificer. I love doing this," she said, gesturing to Tiberius.

"I don't know for sure about the why or how, but I think that, somehow, whatever is guiding the mana let me keep my watch because it saw it as a core part of my being. Now, I have been trying to figure out what all the watch could do for as long as I've been here. I . . . think it can do much more than I had first imagined."

She brought the watch up and touched it to Tiberius's core, channeling her mana and intent into the watch and then through it into the sphere itself. She closed her eyes and pushed some more mana until she felt a *click*, almost like a button press on a phone. She opened her eyes and saw Tiberius tilting his head at her. She reached out her hand, and Gisele handed the cover to her.

Slotting it back into place, Sloane gave a little smile while looking over the little guy. She channeled more mana as she focused on him.

Fly. Find what's ahead. Then show me.

"Wryatt wryyyatt!"

Tiberius crouched down and then flew into the air, racing until he was out of sight.

Sloane closed her eyes and—

Tiberius flew.

Below him stretched a small forest of trees of all shapes and colors, a beautiful sea of orange and red leaves, with the occasional flash of yellow or green to break up the monotony. He glided along over the treetops, the breeze flowing against his metal feathers as he tried to see what was beneath the canopy. There was no sign of danger, and he could tell that his maker and her followers were nearly out of the forest, moving on to the vast rolling plains beyond.

Satisfied his maker was safe for the immediate future, he climbed, turning his sensors toward what lay ahead. Clouds and a large fog bank obscured his optical senses of everything east of him. He turned his head toward the south as he flew on. Channeling mana from his core into his optical sensors, his sight sharpened, allowing greater magnification and processing. In the distance was a forest that made the one his maker was in seem small. He could just discern several glowing pillars of light coming from within. His sensors detected a large mass of mana at the locations, enough to be dangerous.

He flapped his wings and flew higher, his optics returning to what lay ahead. As he approached the fog, he strengthened his wings and dove. Fifteen point six seconds later, Tiberius made it through the thickest of it, leveling off as he searched the area. The fog was still present, but even that didn't hinder what he saw.

In the distance, smoke billowed from a fortified town and its castle. Tiberius felt the presence in his head recede, and he calculated it as a cue to return.

LET US BEGIN

C ount Sylvain Kayser stirred from slumber, stretching languidly as consciousness seeped in. Sitting up in his makeshift bed, he scanned the tent,
frowning. His attendant, who should have been on standby, was conspicuously
absent.

It was unfortunate that he'd had to leave his usual servant in Thirdghyll. That
man would have been on hand immediately. Gathering his troops for a quick
escape from the besieged city had hardly left Sylvain with enough time to take in
the full gravity of the situation. News of the monstrous onslaught had reached
him just as the attack on the city commenced. He knew then, with a grim sense
of certainty, that Thirdghyll would fall when news of the West Gate's breach
came to light. His immediate call to arms had granted them just enough time to
organize an emergency departure.

Sylvain knew that the terran had come from Valesbeck and Vilstaf. It was
only logical that she was the cause of the beasts running rampant through his
county and city. He'd had spies shadowing her since her departure from his
estate. Reports of her and her knights brutally slaying those he'd dispatched after
her, including Captain Lars and his troops, who had foolishly tried to ambush
her, only solidified his conviction. It was as that imbecile terran baron had said.
The woman's witchcraft was the cause of all the issues. Clearly, she had used her
dark powers to direct the beasts to attack his forces.

Damn that terran woman.

His seething thoughts clung to the previous night's near escape, and the bit-
terness of it all hit him anew as he stepped out of his tent. The onslaught of
bright morning light made him squint and cover his eyes. That he had narrowly
escaped the city with whom he could infuriated him.

It was *his* city! And that . . . *terran* had ruined everything.

Vilstaf would be his refuge for now, a place to gather strength. He vowed to reclaim his seat and pursue vengeance against the cause of his humiliation.

Then I'll hunt that woman and kill her. I will spend every coin, if I have to. She will . . .

His eyes narrowed as he realized that there was no one around at all. It infuriated him further.

Sleeping in these squalid conditions is one thing, but to not even have my servants around to do their job properly . . .

Striding around the tent to the firepit prepared by his guards, he was met with a sight that left him rooted in place.

The moon elf lounged on his high-backed chair, nonchalantly cleaning a long dagger with what appeared to be one of Sylvain's silk handkerchiefs.

But it wasn't the audacious elf that stole his breath away. It was the horrifying pile of bodies on the other side of the fire, stacked higher than Sylvain himself. The lifeless forms of his guards and servants had been haphazardly thrown together, reduced to a grotesque heap of discarded bodies. Thirty of his men and women, slaughtered silently and dumped like garbage. A chilling realization washed over him—he hadn't heard a thing.

How dare he.

The mysterious man abandoned his blade, placing it to the side before removing his vibrant yellow hat. He fixed his gaze on Sylvain, a touch of bemusement crossing his features. "Ah, Count Sylvain Kayser. Good morning. You slept much longer than I figured you would. Cost me a few small silver in that bet."

Sylvain's eyes narrowed into suspicious slits. "Identify yourself."

"My identity bears no relevance. This is an interrogation, not a discussion. You'll answer my inquiries until I am satisfied, after which we will both depart."

"Where exactly are we going?"

His question was answered not with words but with an unexpected, piercing pain that shot through his kidney. He stumbled, dropping to one knee with a strangled cry. Whipping his head around, he spotted a raithe man, previously unnoticed. Sylvain seethed. "You dare lay your hands on me?"

The raithe's hand came down heavily on Sylvain's shoulder, fingers burrowing into his flesh. A wince contorted his face as he looked back at the moon elf. The man was already on his feet, replacing his hat and adjusting it as he sauntered over.

Bending down to Sylvain's level, the elf reiterated with a steel edge, "Now, now. I informed you. This isn't a conversation." His voice softened somewhat as he continued. "Perhaps an introduction really would set the stage better. My name is Giallo, formerly of the Ghyll Academy. The Crown sends its regards."

A cold dread plummeted through Sylvain, pooling in his stomach. Fear's icy tendrils snaked through him. "Wait," he blurted. "Just hold on. I can provide you with whatever information you require. I am a loyal servant of the—"

His plea was cut short as a sharp "Gah!" escaped him. The yellow-hatted man had slammed a ruthless fist into his stomach, leaving him gasping for breath as he doubled over. Before he could fully process the pain, he felt himself being hoisted up, suspended between consciousness and a world of pain.

The man, Giallo, leaned in, his words a chilling whisper in Sylvain's ear. "We are going to have so much fun, you and I. *Now*, let us begin."

ACKNOWLEDGMENTS

Writing *Reverberations*, both the second book in the Manabound series and the second one I've ever written, was a crazy journey as I bounced around the globe like a ping-pong ball while traveling and moving from one continent to another.

Major props to my wife, Bri, who kept my sanity in check when my world was spinning—literally and figuratively. Bri, your advice and support were the magic antidote to my chaos. Seriously, back-to-back MVP.

I really want to thank the team at Podium and all of the great people there that have worked to make Manabound into this real thing. You've all worked literal magic into this work and transformed me from a hobby writer into an author. Cass, thanks for the patience, all of the help and support, along with putting up with my frustration with Word. Vincenzo will make his literary debut one day!

Thanks to Jodie for making the characters come to life. They don't just live in the words on a page, they speak and breathe them because of you. Shout-out to my amazing beta readers who've stuck around for so long. Your feedback was the secret ingredient that transformed this whirlwind of ideas into a story that somehow continues to make sense. So, cheers to you guys for making *Reverberations* a whole lot better than it was originally.

Also, I want to thank all of the RoyalRoad fam. Both the team that runs it and the readers that make it special. You guys gave a newb author a chance, and look where we are now. Publishing a second book. I wouldn't have made it without all of you.

To everyone who played a part in this wild ride of creating *Reverberations*, your vibes are etched into every word. Couldn't have done it without you all. Thanks a ton!

ABOUT THE AUTHOR

Travis Albrecht spends his days working and traveling the globe for the US Air Force. When he's not doing that, you can usually find him reading fantasy or science fiction stories or playing a plethora of PC games. You can often find him seeking retribution for his consistent losses in *Mario Kart* to his daughter by teaching her resilience through an unyielding reign in *Super Smash Bros.*

Travis lives in California with his wife and daughter. This is his second novel in the Manabound series.

DISCOVER
STORIES UNBOUND

PodiumAudio.com

Milton Keynes UK
Ingram Content Group UK Ltd.
UKHW020756130524
442628UK00001B/143

9 781039 450608